"I WANT TO MAKE LOVE TO YOU, SAMANTHA."

David's words were a whisper in the shadows beneath the diving board. As his lips massaged hers, Sammy's hesitancy changed to fervor. She had never taken the initiative in lovemaking before, but now her hands began to move down his body, and a deep groan escaped him.

Her hand slipped between his thighs as she murmured his name, and her lips moved across his chest. Impatiently she pushed at the resistant fabric of his suit, until it drifted off to join hers in the middle of the pool.

She felt the heat of his need against her abdomen, even in the cool water. She wanted to blend with him and never be alone again. Boldly she touched him, and he shook with desire.

"I want you, Sammy...now!"

WELCOME TO...

SUPERROMANCES

A sensational series of modern love stories
from Worldwide Library.

Written by masters of the genre, these longer,
sensual and dramatic novels are truly in keeping
with today's changing life-styles. Full of intriguing
conflicts, the heartaches and delights of true love,
SUPERROMANCES are absorbing stories—
satisfying and sophisticated reading that lovers
of romance fiction have long been waiting for.

SUPERROMANCES
Contemporary love stories for the woman of today!

SALLY GARRETT
UNTIL
FOREVER

A SUPERROMANCE FROM
WORLDWIDE

TORONTO · NEW YORK · LONDON · PARIS
AMSTERDAM · STOCKHOLM · HAMBURG
ATHENS · MILAN · TOKYO · SYDNEY

To Beverly Schronce,
who read and reread,
challenged and encouraged,
and is still my friend.

Published December 1983

First printing October 1983

ISBN 0-373-70090-3

Printed in Canada

PROLOGUE

I

"Psst!"

Sammy Gardner moved her head, curled her body into a snug ball and tried to ignore the intrusive noise. She listened to the soothing hum of the evaporative cooler and savored the feeling of the gentle breeze drifting across her small thin shoulders.

She smiled, thinking of her recent birthday. She was finally nine years old. Her friend David Caldwell had given her the loveliest present. It made her warm inside just thinking about the pretty cigar box he had covered with blue tissue paper. For her secret things, he had told her.

These pleasant thoughts almost canceled the upsetting images of the war she heard her parents discussing each morning during breakfast. The year was 1945. A horrible bomb had been dropped on a Japanese city on her birthday, they had said. Yesterday she had learned that her girl friend's older brother had been killed.

A frown furrowed her tanned brow as she wondered what it would be like to be dead, then she smiled, knowing that her family and friends would always be with her.

"Psst!" The sound intruded again. "Sam!" a boy's voice whispered. "Wake up, it's important. Please."

Sammy turned toward the window next to the post of the sturdy metal bedstead. She rubbed her eyes, trying to focus on the blurry face through the window screen. "David?" she whispered. "Is that you? It's too early to get up...I'm sleepy...come back later." She reached out her hand and slipped her fingers through the narrow opening at the bottom of the window until she touched the screen. His warm breath blew on her finger tips, and she giggled softly and raised her head again.

Now she could see him more clearly. His suntanned face wore a heavy frown. "What's the matter, David?"

"Meet me at the irrigation ditch. Hurry! Before it's too late," he whispered and was gone.

David had been her best friend for almost three years, ever since he had rescued her from three older boys when she had been only six. She felt safe and secure with him. She liked him as much as she did her two sisters and two brothers. She wished that David could have been her brother, too.

She quietly rolled from the double bed she shared with her older sister, slipped out of her short nightgown and dressed quickly in a halter top and a pair of worn blue shorts. Shoes were unnecessary so early in the morning. The ground would still be cool from the night and wouldn't burn her bare feet.

As Sammy crossed the narrow paved road, she could see David's back glistening. She knew he had taken a dip in the deep pool near the headgate where the irrigation water could be channeled into her father's property. The water was always cloudy with silt, but she liked its cooling effect, especially during the hot August days.

She crept up behind him and playfully poked him in the ribs, but he didn't react.

He would be having his eleventh birthday in just a few days. He was at least a head taller than she was. His auburn hair had been shorn in a practical crew cut for the hot Phoenix summer and was beginning to grow out. She thought it might be curly like her own, but it seldom got long enough for her to find out for sure.

"What is it, David? What's the matter?" she asked.

David lowered his head and hid his face in his arms for a short while, then turned to her. His green eyes sparkled, but she knew it wasn't for joy.

She touched his arm. "What is it? It must be terrible."

"We're moving," he groaned.

"No! You can't do that!"

"We're moving...today," he insisted.

Her blue eyes grew dark and round. "Oh, no, David," she said, shaking her head, determined to cancel the strange tight feeling building inside her chest. "You're my best friend. How can you move away and still be my best friend?"

David turned away. "My mom says we're moving to some place way up north. Oh, Sam, there was a big fight at my house last night. Our landlady called us a bunch of transplanted fruit pickers. No better than cotton-picking Okies, she said. She started shouting and calling us white trash and said we had to be out by noon today because my stepdad hasn't paid the rent."

He turned to her, still frowning. "I'm not even sure what white trash means, but it made my mom real mad.

My stepdad said he didn't want to live in this hot ugly town anyway, but, Sam, I don't think it's hot and ugly here. I like it. Our landlady even said to just look at your family. She said...she said...the Gardners are poor, but not white trash.''

He sniffed and rubbed his forearm over his reddened nose. "Sam, am I different?" he asked and quickly looked away.

He stared down at the swirling water for a few moments, then took a deep breath and turned to her. "Let's take a swim." He jumped into the water. "Come on in, Sam, but stay out of the deep part. Gee, Sam, who's going to save you from drowning when I'm not here? You're going to have to give up swimming altogether, I guess.''

They splashed around and dog-paddled a little, then climbed up the muddy bank and stretched out on the grass to let the early-morning sun dry their skin.

"David, do you think we'll ever see each other again?''

"Sure, Sam. I'll find you.''

"But how?''

"Maybe I'll send out a Morse code message, and you'll perk up your ears and know it's me. Do you think you'd recognize my signal? Maybe you'll just forget me.''

"Oh, no, David, I'll never forget you,'' she assured him. "Could you write me a letter, too?''

"Sure,'' he said. He turned to her. "What do you want to be when you grow up? Maybe we'd better make some plans, Sam. I need to know where to start looking for you.''

She thought carefully. "Well, momma says girls should be teachers, nurses or secretaries, so-o-o...I think I'll be a secretary...in an office! Then, when I'm too old for that, I'll get married and have lots of babies."

"You're silly," he laughed. "How many babies would you have?"

"Well, I think about ten would make a nice family. I like lots of sisters and brothers. Momma's going to have another baby, and that will make six of us. Yes, I think ten would be just right." She studied his fingers lying next to her elbow. "How about you, David? What do you want to be?"

"Mmmm, I think I'll be a rancher...and have my own horse. Last year in fifth grade, I read the best book called *My Friend Flicka*. It was all about a boy just my age who lived on a ranch in Wyoming. Mom says I have an uncle who lives on a ranch, but I don't know him. Yeah, I'll be a rancher. Hey! If I find you when we're grown up, maybe you and your ten babies can live on my ranch. Gee, I'd sure need a big house to fit your ten children into, wouldn't I?" he asked, and they both laughed.

David started to sing softly near her ear.

> Ten l'il babies, riding in a line,
> One rode away and then there were nine.
> Nine l'il babies, fishing with worms for bait,
> One fell in and then there were eight.

Sammy broke into highpitched giggling as David continued to sing.

Eight l'il babies, Sam couldn't catch 'em,
One ran away and then there were seven.

"Hey, that doesn't even rhyme," she challenged.

"Well, that's the best I could do," he replied as he tickled her in the ribs, and she giggled. He began to sing again.

Seven l'il babies, with fences to fix,
One cut his fingers and then there were six.

His green eyes sparkled as he asked, "Is that better?"

"Much," she smiled. "Now it's my turn."

Six l'il babies, glad to be alive,
But one of them died, and then there were five.

Her voice trailed off as she thought of the war, her friend's brother who had been killed and now her best friend moving away from Phoenix forever. "I know the next one," she said.

Five l'il babies, friends forevermore,
One moved away and then there were four.

Her eyes grew misty again.

He patted her shoulder gently and lowered his voice.

Four l'il babies, happy as could be,
But grownups made one leave and then there were three.

His voice had a bitter sound that made her turn to him. She sang,

> Three l'il babies, watching cows go moo,
> One went with David and then there were two.

"That's corny," he smiled and gave her curly wheat-colored hair a gentle tug.

Sammy concluded the parody.

> Two l'il babies, feeling so glum,
> 'Cause one's moving away and then there'll be one.
> One l'il baby, lonesome as could be,
> 'Cause she misses David, and that lonely one is me!

They sat up and dangled their feet in the cool water.

"Remember the kitten you found?" David asked.

"Yeah, he was pretty," she replied.

"Whatever happened to him?" he asked.

"Daddy gave him away when he got big and had four kittens." She sighed. "I wish you didn't have to go."

He looked at her. "If I were older, I'd marry you and then you and your ten babies could live on my ranch, and we'd all be safe and happy together."

She giggled again, in spite of the emptiness in her chest. They heard her mother calling from the kitchen door of the house across the road.

"Sammy, breakfast's ready. Bring David. He can eat, too," Mrs. Gardner called.

Suddenly David's rust-flecked eyes filled with tears, and a deep tremor shook his body. Sammy waved to her mother, then reached for his hand and squeezed it. "We'll find each other again, maybe when we're all grown up. You said we would! I believe you, David,

'cause you're my very best friend and always will be.''
She leaned closer and lightly kissed his cheek.

David rubbed his eyes furiously, trying to clear away
any trace of tears, and turned to her. "Let's eat. One
last meal together. Will you come say goodbye when I
leave at noon?''

"Sure, best friend," she replied as they crossed the
narrow road, leaving their favorite irrigation ditch for
the last time.

The morning passed quickly as Sammy searched for a
solution to her distressing problem. By the time the
scorching August sun was high overhead, she had
worked herself into such a state of indignation that she
decided to go to his mother and insist that he remain
behind to live with her own family. She knew her
mother and father would welcome David into the Gardner family as one of their own. Perhaps they would
adopt him and make him a real brother.

As she cut across the vacant lot to his road, she
looked up and saw his stepfather's car already moving
down the dusty lane.

"David!" she screamed.

She stopped, stricken with unbearable loneliness. She
saw an arm appear out of the rear window of the old
dilapidated automobile. The arm waved frantically to
her.

She heard David's faint voice in the distance as he
called to her, "Bye for now, Sam!" His arm continued
to wave until the smoking automobile turned the corner
and disappeared.

"He's gone," she murmured. "He's gone. Oh,
David."

II

SAMANTHA ROBERTS eased the old automobile into the gravel driveway as the dashboard warning light began to flash. She breathed a sigh of relief as she climbed out, but her fists were clenched tightly as thoughts of the announcement from work rushed in.

She slammed the car door. The unfairness of her predicament had moved her to the brink of retaliatory action, but some deep underlying force welled up and took control, and reason had prevailed as the long day slowly passed.

Her thoughts returned to the present as she heard her youngest son call to her. She waited beside the old Chevy sedan, patting it affectionately and silently thanking it for running one more day.

She smiled as she watched the eight-year-old boy ride his bicycle up the driveway and skid to a dusty stop at the toes of her worn pumps. She could smell the dusty aroma of his young body. Sweat streaks ran down his temples from his damp brown hair. She waited as he handed his baseball glove and cap to her, then jerked off his team T-shirt and used it to wipe his flushed face and neck.

His face beamed as he proudly informed her, "We won! Finally! Ten to seven and I didn't drop the ball when it came to me...except once."

"I'm sorry I missed the game, John. I had to work late again," she explained and thoughts of the unpleasant announcement intruded, but again she banked the flames of anger as her son positioned his bike in front of her and gave her a signal. She pushed the wobbly bike, and he rolled up to the door of the small apartment. She had lived there with her four young children since her divorce three years earlier.

Sammy wiped the perspiration beads from her forehead. It was May, and already hot weather had set in. She checked the mailbox, noted the orange delinquency note showing through the holes of the computer punch card utility bill in the lone envelope's window. She moved through the door, greeted the backs of her two older sons' heads and acknowledged their grunts as they continued to stare at the rerun on the old black-and-white television set.

"Where's Sarah?" Sammy asked. Her second son came into the small kitchen. He tagged along behind her as she began to prepare supper. She started to boil water for spaghetti, then opened the refrigerator and removed a small package of ground beef. A repugnant odor came from the package, and she groaned as she sniffed the meat and confirmed that it was spoiled, mentally noting the cost as she discarded the small package in the garbage can.

"Where's Sarah, David? Do you know?" she asked. She noted his heavy frown. She pulled him to her and gave him a gentle hug. "What's wrong, honey? I can tell something's bothering you. Can I help?"

"I got called into the principal's office today," he said and gave a deep sigh.

"Oh, David! Not you! You're my best...." She stopped as she saw his eyes glisten. "Why, honey?"

"Sarah," he replied.

"Sarah? Why would they call you in if Sarah...?" She rolled her eyes heavenward and sighed, "What has Sarah done now? Why didn't they call me at work?"

"Mr. Black said he tried, but couldn't get through to you." His curly head hung forward. "Sarah was caught smoking in the girls' bathroom with another girl. An eighth grader! Mr. Black said I should tell you in case he wasn't able to tell you himself. Oh, mom! I hate having Sarah for a sister. She's always doing things that...." And the tears overflowed, but he brushed them away. "Mom, can't you do something so she'll act better?" he pleaded.

"I'll talk to her again, David. I can try, but I'm afraid she's the one who must—" She stopped as the front door flew open, and her wayward daughter burst into the living room.

Sarah's arched dark brows frowned furiously over her blue eyes as she glared at her brother. "You told! I knew you would. You're a tattletale, David, and I hate you!" She stomped past him to the bathroom and slammed the door. Several moments passed before she reappeared with a fresh face and combed dark hair. The gentle waves fell to her shoulders and enhanced her emerging beauty.

Sammy sighed as she watched her only daughter. Sarah was developing early and already had signs of budding breasts. It was hard to believe she was just ten years old.

Sarah stared defiantly at her mother, silently challenging her to bring up the matter from school, but Sammy didn't speak.

She finished preparing the meatless spaghetti and set the large serving bowl on the table. She spooned generous servings onto each child's plate, and smiled as her three sons attacked the plates of food.

Sarah looked at her mother. "I want some meatballs."

"I'm sorry, Sarah, but the hamburger was spoiled."

Sarah repeated her request. "I want some meatballs."

"Sarah, please. Just eat."

Sarah stuck her chin out a little farther and insisted, "I want meat in my spaghetti."

"I don't have any meat."

"Go buy some," Sarah said.

"I don't have any money to buy more meat," Sammy replied.

"I want meat . . ." Sarah persisted.

"Well, you can't have any. I'm broke. Be thankful you have something to eat, Miss Priss. That's all there is," she cried. "Take it or leave it." She detested the trembling in her voice and the weakness it implied.

Sarah squinted at her. "I won't eat it," and she pushed her plate away.

Sammy felt her self-control slipping as she stared at her haughty daughter. "Sarah, please, not tonight."

"No, I won't eat this slop," Sarah replied, flipping her hair back over her shoulder.

Blind rage swept away any hope of parental control. Sammy shouted, "Young lady, now you won't have to eat it, will you?" and she picked up the plate full of tomato sauce and soggy pasta and hurled it against the white kitchen wall.

Her heart was pounding and her head throbbing as she blinked several times, trying to focus. As her vision cleared, she saw the tangled mess slowly sliding down the wall. Her three sons sat staring at her.

She heard John whisper to Sarah, "You shouldn't oughta done that, Sarah. Mom's real mad now," and he stared at his mother but stayed firmly in his chair, his small shoulders stiff and his pale blue eyes round with concern.

Sammy ran from the alcove, stumbled over a shoe abandoned in the hallway and locked herself in her bedroom. She threw herself on the bed, and the tears she had tried to suppress all day burst forth as she buried her face in a pillow.

She hated her former husband and her poverty-level existence since the divorce. How could she afford hamburger when she couldn't pay the electric bill? She hated her new supervisor and wanted to quit her clerical job at Mastiff Corporation but knew she couldn't.

"I hate them, I hate them all," she sobbed and pounded her clenched fist into the soft pillow.

Voices were coming from the living room when she awoke. Adult voices. *Mike,* she thought, as she recognized her younger brother's laughter and his girl friend's response. She glanced at the clock on her nightstand. It read ten o'clock.

"Oh, good grief, the spaghetti," she mumbled. She slipped on her robe, checked her face and hair in the mirror and sheepishly entered the quiet living room.

"Hi, Mike. . .Maggie. I didn't mean to fall asleep. How are you? How long have you been. . .here? Where are the children?" She slid a glance toward the kitchen and saw a clean wall and a cleared table. "Oh, I'm so ashamed," she murmured as she dropped in defeat to the old sofa.

Maggie came and sat beside her. "It's all right, Sammy. We all reach our limit sometime. The kids are in bed asleep, the kitchen is clean. . . ." Maggie chuckled and added, "Sarah and John helped me. Mike and I just want to visit. Okay to stay?"

Mike added, "We even brought along a six-pack of beer. Have one. You take things too seriously, sis."

Sammy wiped her eyes again. "Thanks. You two really came along at the right time. You're both very sweet."

She sipped on the cold can of beer and tried to explain the events of the day that had led to the spaghetti-throwing explosion.

The corporation's chairman had announced that the new manager of the systems department in which she had worked for several years was the young systems analyst whose name was Wesley Franklin. He was twenty-eight years old and had worked at Mastiff for less than four months.

"In fact," she explained to Mike and Maggie, "I showed him the department when he first started. I explained to him what we were doing. I even brought him up to date on the projects under development. Darn it all, Mike, I trained him! It's just not fair."

The president had taken her aside and tried to explain that Wes Franklin had his degree in computer sciences, while she had only three years of college, even with the five years of experience. Perhaps someday, if she completed her degree, the president had hinted. Sammy had tuned his words out as the numbness had set in.

"How can I possibly go back to school? I can hardly make ends meet as it is." She choked the tears back. "I'm so tired of being broke. It's not fair. It's never fair!"

"Easy, sis, easy." Her brother moved to her side and clasped her hands. "Hey, where's your spunk?" he challenged. "You're a fighter, so let's fight. We'll help you, won't we, Maggie?" He turned to his girl friend, and Maggie nodded her support.

"I'll tell you what, Sammy. If you can find the time and money, we'll provide you with child care any night of the week. Why don't you ask Mastiff to help pay your tuition?" he suggested. "And if they're too cheap, I will." He smiled. "You can do it, sis, I know you can. You always did before. You helped me through school. It's about time I returned the favor." He gave her hand a squeeze, handed her another beer and said, "Sammy, Maggie and I came over here to tell you that we've finally set a date. We'll be married in June, right after I get my master's degree."

He laughed softly and winked at Maggie. "Since we intend to make you an aunt several times over, we might as well get some on-the-job practice with real kids. Frankly, I can hardly remember what it's like to be a kid. Remember when I graduated? You told me you needed twelve more hours credit to make it yourself. At six hours a semester, you can finish in a year. If Mastiff won't give you a hand, by golly, I will. You can show that Wes guy what you're really made of. Deal?''

Sammy's hands gradually relaxed, and a smile softened her attractive mouth. "Let me think about it, Mike. Maybe I... maybe... I'll let you know. Thanks, little brother. I love you both." Her smile grew, and her pretty features changed to reveal a glowing warm beauty.

CHAPTER ONE

SAMANTHA ROBERTS looked up as giggling came from the office-pool area of the systems-coordination department. She tried to ignore the noise, but louder laughter came from her staff as work stopped and the obligatory coffee break began.

She startled at one man's loud guffaw, snapped her pencil lead and threw the broken pencil down on her desk.

"Darn!" she mumbled and rapidly tapped her fingers on her desk as she struggled to recapture her thoughts. She reached for another pencil and tried to concentrate on the proposal before her. She was attempting to suggest a compromise in a new computerized information system that her own department and the larger corporate-systems department were responsible for implementing in the late summer.

She left her desk and quickly went to close the door of her private office, trying to insulate herself from the distraction. Just as she reached for the knob, her secretary looked up and shrugged her shoulders, but the smile on her normally composed matronly face aroused Samantha's curiosity.

"What's so funny, Dorothy?" she asked.

"Oh, nothing," Dorothy replied, but her smile lingered.

"That's a lot of boisterous noise over nothing," Samantha said, a frown settling on her face. Her soft blue eyes were her best feature, but this morning they contained little warmth. She was forty-three years old, and lately she felt every year of it.

Her newest employee in the department, a young clerk typist, jumped from her word processor and rushed to Samantha.

"Oh, Ms Roberts, it's just so romantic! At least I think so, but the others think it's funny." She giggled again.

"What's so romantic, Debbie?"

"Oh, the article in today's paper. Didn't you see it, Ms Roberts?" Debbie gave a deep sigh and sauntered back to her desk. Her small bottom wiggled just enough to draw the attention of her co-worker, whose desk was covered with programming coding sheets.

"Shake it, babe," the good-looking man murmured, and Debbie turned to him and smiled coyly.

Samantha groaned. "Ladies and gentlemen, what in the world has all of you so stirred up this morning? We have a deadline and it's fast approaching. Much more of this fooling around and giggling and we're in serious trouble." She frowned at Debbie's admirer. "Herb, what *is* the matter?" She leaned her shoulder against the door jamb, interested in hearing his response.

Herb shrugged his broad shoulders. "Oh, some cowboy dude has advertised for a wife. The dumb yokel has been in the boonies too long. Damn, Sammy, all he has to do is go to the Satin Lady singles' bar here in Phoenix, and he can pick up any broad he wants. They're all willing." The programmers and clerks broke into laughter. "They put out," he concluded with confidence as Debbie smiled at him.

"I still think it's romantic," Debbie retorted. "Imagine how lonely it must be out on a giant ranch. I can just picture it—marooned in a blizzard, with nothing but a roaring fire, a bottle of champagne and your favorite handsome cowboy...." Her voice trailed off as her imagination completed the fantasy.

"Debbie, please," Samantha cautioned. "I believe you have the middle portion of our proposal to finish typing. Is it done?"

"Oh, no, Ms Roberts, I've been so...." Debbie hesitated. "But it will be by lunchtime. I promise!" She leaned over her machine and tried desperately to find where she had left off in her assignment. Herb whispered something to her, and she blushed.

"Herb, have you finished making the modifications in the marketing report?" Samantha asked. "Why don't you bring what you have into my office, and we can discuss your approach," she suggested with a coolness that left little option available to him.

Samantha turned away from the door and stared out the window of her sixteenth-floor office at the view to the northeast. Discontentment surged through her as she admired the purple and pink sandstone mountains. She frowned as she noticed the brownish layer of pollution in the cool desert air over Phoenix. She wished for a fleeting moment that she was on the other side of the mountains, heading for some vague unknown destination—somewhere other than this stuffy office with these nonproductive employees and all the burdensome corporate intrigue that Mastiff Corporation excelled in lately. Her long struggle up the corporate ladder had been successful, but even with the financial rewards now hers, she felt an emptiness and wondered if the accomplishments had been worth the struggle.

Her attention was jerked back into the room as Herb entered the office carrying his coding sheets and instructions and a newspaper clipping.

He sat across from her and began to explain his work, but Samantha's eyes wandered to the clipping, and she had difficulty concentrating on his presentation.

Finally she said, "Okay, Herb, it sounds as though you're right on target. Just try to keep the noise down. Some of us find it hard to concentrate when.... Is that the article that you were all so...caught up with?"

"Sure is. Here, you can have it. Poor rube, he should live in Phoenix, where all these good-looking sun babes live." He handed her the crinkled news clipping and left the office.

The department settled into a work routine, with only the soft clicking of the plastic keys on the computer terminals and word processors breaking the silence. Samantha completed the details of the compromise proposal and was about to start on the summary paragraph when her eyes fell on the clipping.

She glanced up through her doorway, saw her staff with their heads bent over their assignments, looked again at the clipping and reached for it.

It was from the Continental News Service, which had recently begun transmitting its news via satellite, and came with a Butte, Montana, dateline.

(CNS) It can get lonely on Montana ranches where neighbors measure the distances between each other in miles. Rancher David McCormack, whose previous marriage dissolved from the isolation, is seeking a new wife in the want ads.

His ad was straightforward: "Lonely rancher on isolated 5000 acres needs wife to enjoy ranch with me, help check out the cattle and keep track of me on cold winter nights. I don't smoke or drink. I like to dance and go out for dinner, help with house-work, and I make the best biscuits in the world."

McCormack, 35, said his former wife was ter-rified of ranch life. "She didn't like being alone and I was gone a lot," he said, but added, "I don't want to live alone any longer. It's awfully lonely coming home at night to a dark empty house."

His present Crest Mountain Ranch is 25 miles southeast of Dillon, and his nearest neighbor is eight miles away.

So far, said McCormack in a recent interview, six women have responded to his ad. Most were "des-perate women," more interested in finding shelter for themselves and their numerous children than in forming a loving relationship with a new husband, he said.

"It's not an easy life," said McCormack. "A rancher is very dependent on his wife and family to get along, especially if he works away from home."

He also noted that if he was injured on the ranch now, "No one in the world would know where to find me." McCormack says the want ad is a last resort.

He has owned his present ranch for nine years.
His cattle herd now numbers 400 head. He works at
the Anaconda Company's copper smelter near
Butte as a chemical engineer to keep it all going,
but hopes to devote full time to the ranch...and a
new family...in two or three years.

"I'm mostly a homebody," he said. "I just want
to stay at home and enjoy the ranch. I saw a doe
and fawn the other day. Damn, they made a beautiful sight, but there was no one around to share it."

Samantha finished the article and reread it twice, then
laid it aside. She found its subject haunting. "At least
that man has enough fortitude to do something," she
murmured to herself, "not just talk and complain about
his predicament as I've started to...I wish his picture
had been...."

She forced herself to forget the article and returned to
the summary paragraph, completed it and delivered it to
her secretary just as lunch break approached. Most of
the staff had left the area. Debbie was still typing.

"Debbie, aren't you through with your assignment?"
Samantha asked.

Debbie reached for a stack of papers at the corner of
her desk and handed them to her manager. "Here." She
smiled.

"What are you typing now?" Samantha asked.

Debbie stammered, "I...I...thought I'd try to write
that poor lonely cowboy a letter of.... I'll never mail it,
but I think it's fun to pretend." She returned her attention to her word processor and clicked away.

Samantha laughed softly and went back into her office, closed the door and reached for her brown lunch sack and a book she had started the previous night.

She had chosen a contemporary romance novel with a Western setting—a ranch in Utah—involving a beautiful, rich, young heroine and a handsome, mature, dynamic rancher, the perfect substitute for the heroine's domineering father, who had recently died a tragic death. Samantha already knew the pantherlike rancher would seduce the grieving daughter and bring love, comfort and security to the rich but helpless beauty. She began to laugh at the predictable story line, then her eyes fell on the article, and she reread it.

Now, that's the way it probably really was, she thought cynically. Desolate, hard work, even holding down two jobs, and how come the rancher in the article hadn't met some beautiful and willing rich, young heroine?

Samantha choked up with startling empathy for the faceless man somewhere in the vast wilderness of the Rocky Mountains. "I understand, Mr. McCormack. I feel the same way sometimes, trapped, alone. Oh, Mr. McCormack, I wish you luck...you'll need it." Laying her head down on her arms, she shed a few tears for the rancher.

She had stayed awake late reading the novel the night before. The short night's rest crept up on her and she quickly fell asleep.

The noise of returning employees awakened her, and she felt embarrassed about her sympathetic response to the rancher's plight. Thank goodness her door was still closed. She slipped the article into her purse and quickly busied herself with the corporate problems at hand.

SATURDAY MORNING was free of commitments. Samantha had left her cool facade at the office and now found herself easing into the dual role of Sammy Roberts, divorced head of the household, mother of four young adults all taller than she was and frighteningly independent in their life-styles. The three older children had already left home. John, the youngest of her three sons, still lived with her in the large family home.

Sammy sat beside the pool, enjoying the warm weather and a hot cup of coffee. This was why the snowbirds came to Phoenix, she thought. It was 9:00 A.M. and seventy-five degrees on a beautiful March day.

Thoughts of her children interfered with her reading of the morning paper. Their interests were so varied, their personalities—especially that of her only daughter, Sarah—so different. Had she given up on Sarah too soon? The guilt of the troubled years of Sarah's teens, the many trips to juvenile court, the bickering and quarrels, the tears and screams and accusations from both Sammy and her daughter had left permanent scars on each. Sammy doubted if the wounds and scars would ever completely heal.

She shoved the memories back into the recesses of her mind and finished the morning paper, then returned to the kitchen for a coffee refill, making a detour by her bedroom to get her book. She had slipped it into her canvas bag the night before as she left the office, late in the evening as usual. In spite of the story's predictability she had found the characters interesting and likable. As she reached for the book, the crumpled news article caught her eye. She tucked it into the book and quickly went back to the patio.

The employees in her department had continued to poke fun at the poor fellow for the rest of the week, and Sammy had found herself growing progressively more defensive of the rancher's actions.

Debbie had decided on Friday that her letter was best forgotten, and she erased it from her word processor's floppy-disk memory. Herb had asked her out, so she didn't need the lonely rancher anymore she had explained to her co-workers.

Sammy sat by the pool, sipped her coffee and began to wonder what her clerk typist had written in the mysterious letter.

CHAPTER TWO

DAVID MCCORMACK finished his dinner in the restaurant with his friend and physician, Dr. Robert Morrison, then hurried to the small town's post office to pick up his mail.

David lived several miles beyond the mail delivery service's boundary and usually stopped in town on his way home from Butte to collect his mail. He had been forced to work late each day the past week and now, on Saturday, he collected a week's worth of correspondence.

He caught the post mistress about to lock the doors for the weekend. He flashed her a smile of apology, and she let him in to open his box. Although she had jet black hair, he knew she was in her early sixties, and he smiled to himself as he felt her eyes follow him. He suspected she was attracted to him in spite of their age difference, and at times he used the fact to entice her to make small concessions when his schedule prevented him from keeping the official hours.

"Sorry, Mrs. Lambert," he said, as he hurried to the door and smiled at her again.

"Oh, David, that's all right...and please call me Bea."

"Bea...I'll try to remember.... Thanks again."

She smiled. "Anytime, anytime for you. I know how busy you must be," she replied, and her fingers brushed his forearm.

David gave her a light kiss on the cheek and heard her sigh. "Bye for now," his low voice murmured, and he hurried to his truck. He knew she would probably tell all her dear friends that he had kissed her.

He scanned his mail. Several pieces of junk mail, three bills, a letter from his son in Missoula and a strange letter in unfamiliar handwriting with a postmark from Phoenix, Arizona. He knew no one in Phoenix, only a good friend and former neighbor who now lived in Scottsdale, a suburb of the capital city.

David laid the mail aside on the front seat of the sky blue pickup, turned the ignition key, pulled out of the parking space in front of the post office and quickly moved through the small town to the southern rural area. He lived twenty-five miles from town, and he was positive he could have driven the route blindfolded. He knew every rut, ranch and family along the way. He wondered if it was possible to have a love affair with the land, for he felt an attachment that grew with each passing year.

After several miles he stretched his long legs and tried to ease the numbness settling in his buttocks. As he left the smaller ranches behind, the paved road changed to gravel. He was forced to slow his speed as the ruts grew deeper, and the road began to wind through the foothills.

He braked quickly as a Hereford cow and newborn calf roamed onto the roadway. Patches of dry stubble showed through the snow at the edges of the gravel road, and the cow ignored the approaching truck as it continued grazing on the sparse grass.

David rolled down the window and slapped the outer side of the door panel. The cow startled, ran a few yards, then turned to stare at him. He noticed it wore the Russell brand. He'd call his neighbor when he arrived home and tell him of the wayward pair.

"Damn," he mumbled as he saw that the mail had slid off the seat and scattered across the floorboard. He glanced at the envelopes, noting the one from Phoenix, and his curiosity was piqued.

As he pulled over to the side of the gravel road, he hit a rut. Melting snow and slush splattered onto the hood and windshield. "Damn," he mumbled again as he frowned at the small envelope.

It was another five miles to his ranch, and he felt compelled to read the mysterious letter. He ripped it open and checked the signature on the last page.

A woman named S. Roberts seemed to have written a rather long-winded letter regarding...oh, no! Another reply to that god-awful article and advertisement. Would he ever live that mistake down? His anger smoldered as it mixed with an ongoing sense of embarrassment over the publicity of the matter. He wanted to regain full control of his private life. This unwarranted publicity often caused a burning desire in him to withdraw once again behind the conservative facade he was noted for in the community and at Anaconda.

Her opening paragraph caught his eye, and his irritation changed to curiosity as he began to read her letter in earnest.

Mr. David McCormack
Crest Mountain Ranch
Dillon, Montana

Dear Mr. McCormack,

Please read this letter to its end before you judge or jump to conclusions. I probably sound as screwball to you as you sounded to those who read about your advertisement.

If the article is correct and you're thirty-five years old, I qualify more as an older sister than as a prospective wife. I'm forty-three. I'm not applying for the position.

I make a good salary, so I'm not desperate for financial security. I have a five-bedroom house with a fifty percent equity and swimming pool, so I'm not looking for shelter. Depending on your definition of "numerous," I do have four children, but they are twenty-one, twenty, nineteen and seventeen, so I'm not looking for shelter and security for them, either. Besides, what's wrong with a lot of kids? I might have had ten or twelve if I'd married the right man.

Since about the age of twelve, when I discovered horses, Zane Grey westerns, livestock shows and 4-H fairs, and having grown up on a small ten-acre farm in east Phoenix, I've had a fantasy about living on a ranch. Would you consider letting me come for a working visit for a week or so to experience what ranch life is really like?

Good luck on your quest for a wife who likes the outdoor life. I don't understand women who insist their husbands live in the big city, make big money, own big houses, pay big taxes and have big heart attacks.

I'd rather have a loving man who wants to share life and events, the excitement and the planning, the disappointments and the accomplishments of growing together and doing things for each other, but I'll probably never meet such a man.

The letter continued for several long paragraphs, and David quickly scanned their contents.

I'm serious about a visit. If you could use a short-term cook and helper for a week or so in the spring or early summer, write me.

I make good biscuits, also, but even better green chili burritos. Tell me something about your ranch and the country and your neighbors. I'd like to know about them.

Sincerely,
S. Roberts
1816 North 57th Place
Phoenix, Arizona

SAMMY FELT EXHAUSTED after the long week at Mastiff. She pulled her green sedan into the driveway, hurriedly collected the mail and the evening newspaper and let herself into the quiet house. Her son was at work busing tables at a nearby Mexican restaurant. Only her aging black-and-white tomcat greeted her.

She dropped the mail on the kitchen table, hurried to

her room and changed into a two-piece swimsuit. Laps before dinner were her penance for gaining ten pounds during the winter.

When a promotion had enabled her to buy her own home with a swimming pool, she had signed up for swimming lessons at the local YWCA and had learned to swim. It had been one of her goals since childhood, when she had played and dog-paddled in irrigation ditches, where she could always touch the bottom.

Her movements broke the surface, causing only slight slapping sounds as she glided through the water. She did twenty laps before stopping.

As she climbed from the pool and dried off, Sammy could hear the faint sound of the buzzer on the oven timer and knew her frozen entrée was ready. A light salad completed her dinner. She sat down at the table to eat the solitary meal and reached for the mail.

She choked when she saw the large white envelope with bold handwriting and the Montana postmark.

"Oh, my goodness...he answered," she whispered aloud. "He wasn't supposed to do that." Why had she written and then impulsively mailed the letter? "Oh, dear..." she groaned.

The meal was forgotten as she studied the unopened envelope. She laid it down, left the room and went back to the pool. The night air had chilled considerably, but she dived into the water and did ten more hard, fast laps.

She shivered as she left the pool. After drying herself off she returned to the kitchen. She would just ignore the letter, she decided as she hurried to her bedroom and changed into a comfortable pink print smock. As she

walked by the kitchen table again she quickly turned the
envelope face down and hurried to the living room. She
brushed a damp curl from her forehead with an irritated
sweep of her hand and flipped the control knob of the
television with more force than was necessary.

A conspiracy was at work, she finally decided. Two of
the channels had Western movies, and a third had a travel
special about the Northern Rockies. Everywhere she was
reminded of the letter from the strange man in Montana.
She could feel his beckoning call. She finally gave in to
the urge to discover the letter's contents. With great apprehension, she opened the envelope and began to read.

Dear Ms Roberts,
    Thanks for the letter, and no, I don't think
you're a screwball. It's strange, but you were the
only person to respond who seemed to understand.
That ad appeared in the Butte paper a few months
ago. I took a lot of flak from my friends.
    I received twenty-eight letters and most were
from nuts. Six were from gays who wanted to keep
me company. Five were from "good" people, who
said I should pray about it and let God take care of
my needs. Three said I was obviously under the
control of the devil, and no good Christian woman
would ever answer such a dangerous advertisement.
Three were from teenage girls who wanted to leave
home. Nine were from women who wanted me to
pay their bills and feed their kids.
    One was from a man in California, named Mc-
Cormack, who thinks we might be relatives. . . and
then there was yours.

It's strange that even with an error in the article you answered. No, I'm not thirty-five years old but actually forty-five. It was a typesetting error, I guess.

I lived in Phoenix when I was a kid, during WW II, but we moved. Write and tell me more about yourself.

Sincerely,
David E. McCormack

DAVID MCCORMACK collected his mail and strolled down the block and around the corner to the restaurant. Some friends and fellow members of the local chapter of the Montana Stockgrowers Association had agreed to meet for dinner to discuss a controversial water-rights issue on the meeting's agenda that evening.

David was early, so he sat at the counter. He smiled as the young waitress approached with the glass carafe.

"Menu, Mr. McCormack?" she asked, leaning over the counter and resting her heavy young breast against the sugar container.

"No, Suzy, just coffee, thanks," he replied and tried to ignore her suggestive maneuver as she filled his cup. "I'm eating with friends later." He smiled slightly as she shrugged her shoulders, dismissing his lack of interest with a mumble that he couldn't make out.

He sifted through the three days' collection of mail and recognized the feminine handwriting on the small green envelope postmarked Phoenix. The lady had replied to his response. The first letter had been rather stilted. Perhaps this one would be a little warmer.

Only one way to find out, he decided, as he slid his long tanned index finger along the back flap of the envelope. For some reason he could imagine her tongue licking the flap. Damn it, he needed a woman. It had been a long time.

He unfolded the sheets of paper and began to read.

Dear Mr. McCormack,

I enjoyed hearing from you. I was most surprised, for I never thought I'd get a reply. I wrote you on impulse. I usually don't do such things. I was feeling sorry for myself—one of those "nobody loves me" stages of life.

I've spent the last thirteen years fighting a financial battle to make ends meet and to raise my children. A few years ago I received a really nice promotion. Now I make a good salary, but I still tend to stew over money. Being broke can be in the mind as well as the purse.

My oldest son is married and will make me a grandmother soon. My second son is a junior at Arizona State University. He's majoring in anthropology and has taken a summer job in Quebec as an assistant to his favorite professor. They have received a grant to research the Hudson's Bay Company and the effects of its early business practices on the Indians of northeast Canada. It all sounds rather complicated, but he's excited, and I'm glad for him, but there goes my David.

My daughter is nineteen and has been mad at me about one thing or another for the past ten years. School, smoking, boyfriends, beer, pot, money, sex, freedom—you name it and we've fought about it. She and her latest boyfriend left Phoenix last month in his van to try living in the Oregon back country. I gave up trying to mold her or change her. She's my thorn, and I doubt if I'll ever be close to her.

That leaves my youngest son, John. He's about to graduate from high school. He leaves in July, shortly after his eighteenth birthday, for four years of navy life.

Watching my children leave, along with receiving your letter, reminds me of a very good friend from my childhood. His name was David, too, but his last name was Caldwell. He lived on Taylor Street in east Phoenix. He was very nice, and I missed him terribly when he moved to some place in Washington state. His parents had jobs picking apples. I wonder whatever happened to him. He wrote twice, then I never heard from him again.

Write and tell me more about yourself. I find a certain security in knowing we'll probably never meet, but I'd like to continue writing.

Sincerely,
Samantha Roberts

ONE MORE NIGHT of returning to an empty house was more than Sammy could bear. She went to a restaurant, then purchased a newspaper and selected a movie. She chose an *R*-rated feature, hoping to see something that would shake her from the boring routine her life had settled into the last year. Except for the letter from Montana, life was dull and predictable.

So was the movie. She left before the conclusion and drove home. She collected the mail, skimmed through it and smiled as she noted her pen pal from Montana had written again. Her heart began to pound as she fumbled with her door key. She hurried through the house to her bedroom, changed into her nightclothes and stretched out on the comfortable bed.

"Now, Mr. McCormack," she murmured aloud as she fluffed the pillows once more and reached for his letter. "What do you have to say this time?" She smiled, yet wondered at the unexplained tremor in her fingers.

She sat bolt upright, her heart racing, as she read his opening sentence.

Dear Samantha,

Was your maiden name Gardner? Is your name really Sam? Did you live on old Route 10 in east Phoenix during WW II?

You won't believe this, but my stepfather's name was Caldwell, and from 1942 until the summer of 1945 I lived on Taylor Street. I remember this skinny, curly-headed little girl with the prettiest soft blue eyes who was my dearest friend. If you're my long-lost Sam, you should know I had an eleven-year-old crush on a cute nine-year-old who had the sweetest smile in the West.

If you're really my old friend Sam, include your phone number next time. I tried to call, but directory assistance in Phoenix said your phone number was unpublished.

Hurry and write me; the mail's slow.

David McC.

DAVID MCCORMACK knew Samantha Roberts would reply right away if she was really his Sam. His mind raced back over the years, skimming past his own marriages, his son, to the happy summers in Phoenix. They had been the joyful years before his own childhood had fallen apart and his mother had vanished, just as his father had earlier.

He began to stop at the post office each day to check his box for her green envelope. It was day five on his desk calendar at Anaconda. When he realized he would have to work late, he called the post mistress and asked if any mail had come.

"Just a small green envelope from Phoenix, Arizona," Bea Lambert replied. "Who do you know in Phoenix, David?"

"Later, Mrs. Lambert. Thanks," he said, and abruptly ended the conversation. Damn it all. A meeting with representatives from the Environmental Protection Agency had caused him to miss the opportunity to read her confirmation or denial. He'd have to wait until the next day.

He had seldom been too ill to report to work, but he called in sick the next morning. He couldn't wait all day and then take a chance of missing the mail again. The representatives from Washington could find plenty to keep them busy without his help.

He dressed and drove into Dillon for an early breakfast. As soon as the post office opened, he collected his mail, hurried to his truck and ripped open the green envelope.

"Thank goodness," he murmured as he reread her letter. A youthful grin warmed his handsome face and

softened his features. "She's my Sam...that's good."
He closed his eyes and sighed in relief.

Dear David,

Yes, I'm Sam, mostly Sammy now, and Samantha on my paychecks. I went looking through an
old photo album, and look what I found.

You weren't the only one with a crush, but then,
nine- and eleven-year-old children can't have
crushes, can they? I'm also enclosing a photo taken
last year at my oldest son's wedding. I was a little
plump. Since then I've lost twenty pounds and have
added some gray hairs.

Some old friend you are. You asked for my
phone number and forgot to include your own.
Mine is 602-555-4431. I'm usually home before
seven and after five. I've noticed how slow the
mail delivery is. I hope to hear from you in a week
or so. Call me! I can hardly wait to hear your
voice.

A long-lost friend,
Sammy

P.S. Send a photo.

David called her number in Phoenix, but there was no
answer. As he glanced at the clock in his kitchen he
laughed at his impatience. It was 11:00 A.M. Of course!
She must be at work, where he should be. He called
again in the early afternoon. A young male voice
answered, said she wasn't there and offered to take a
message, but David declined.

He'd try again that evening. She'd better be home.

THE PHONE HAD RUNG INCESSANTLY since Sammy's arrival home in spite of the lateness of her return. There had been a collect call from Sarah, who wanted to borrow one hundred dollars. Sammy laughed at the thought of her daughter's borrowing money. That implied repayment, and Sarah seldom repaid her debts. Sammy had reluctantly agreed to send her fifty instead.

The irritating phone rang again.

She knew David McCormack had not yet received her response. It was probably a call for John. She had answered two for him in the past fifteen minutes. She took a sip of fresh coffee, hoping it would rejuvenate her enough to keep her awake for several more hours so she could work on the computer conversion application that had stumped her junior programmer.

She frowned as the phone rang again. "Darn phone. . . shut up!" she exclaimed. She was determined to ignore it. She unclipped the removable ends of the plastic lead wires to each phone extension and the ringing stopped. She concentrated on the problems before her and soon found two errors. Fatigue settled on her, and she laid her head down on her crossed forearms.

Suddenly someone was shaking her shoulder. "Mom," John said. "Mom, go to bed. And why did you unplug the phones? I tried to call a few minutes ago."

A look of alarm crossed Sammy's face, but his pale blue eyes twinkled, and he assured her he was fine. "I clipped them all back in," he said. He leaned and kissed her cheek and ambled off to his room, stumbling once as his long legs tangled.

"Good night, John," she called. She felt exhausted. She stretched and slowly moved to her bedroom. She wondered who had tried to call and now regretted disconnecting the phone. Could it have been...? No, not this soon. His letters had always taken at least four days. She smiled as she speculated on what she would say to him if he actually did call her. Would it be the same as when they were children?

Sammy slipped into a new white silk nightgown. She had purchased the gown and a matching peignoir on an impulse—something she seldom did—the day before receiving David McCormack's revealing letter. She normally slept in pajamas, but for some reason lately she had had the desire to feel cool silk against her body at night.

She set the alarm for 6:00 A.M. to allow for a leisurely cup of coffee and a quick swim before work. She crawled into the bed, but her eyelids refused to stay closed. Fourteen years of sleeping alone should have been long enough to condition her to the spaciousness of the queen-size bed. Several times recently she had awakened during the night and found herself hugging a pillow.

She thought of her children, the memories of their early childhood experiences, the joys and pain of raising the children all alone. She thought of Jake, her former husband, and his image brought long-forgotten memories to the room. "Damn you, Jake!" she hissed softly. "I showed you, didn't I? I didn't need you at all!" She wiped away a few uncontrollable tears that spilled down her cheeks. The financial burden had often been heavy, but Sammy had made it and without a dime from Jake.

She hadn't seen him since the divorce. She had received one letter from him explaining why he'd be unable to pay any child support for a while. The letter had been written in a familiar feminine handwriting, and she knew that her young friend, Kali, was still with him. A while had turned into a permanent status, in spite of the divorce decree's stating otherwise, and she had not pressed the matter. The letter had been postmarked New Jersey, and she had written off any hope of child support.

Sammy wiped her eyes and pulling the spare pillow to her bosom, she tried to clear her mind for sleep. The pillow gradually absorbed her warmth and sleep descended.

She was sure she had just closed her eyes when the rude buzzing of the electric alarm filtered through her sleep-fogged senses. She staggered out of bed, slipped on her swimsuit and headed for the kitchen. The drip coffee machine had been set up the night before and was finishing the first pot.

She rubbed the sleep from her eyes as she poured the coffee and carried her cup out to the patio. She then carried the phone to the pool in case it rang, though the likelihood that anyone would call at such an early hour was remote. She dived into the cool water and felt the blood begin to surge through her veins. It was mid-May and the water was brisk.

She did several laps, climbed out to dry and sat by the family picnic table, sipping her coffee.

Her mind brought problems of work into formation, but she suppressed them. Time enough for them later. She thought of Sarah—no, that was beyond her power to handle. Lawrence was absorbed with his approaching fatherhood and advancing career at the bank. David had met a new girl at ASU and had fallen madly in love for the first time. Only John remained to remind her of how her family used to be.

The phone's ring startled her, and she spilled some of the hot coffee. She stared at the spill, then the phone.

It rang again. Only bad news arrived at 6:30 A.M. Sarah? Sarah was in trouble! Sammy didn't want to answer the phone, but with pounding heart and trembling hand, she picked up the receiver on the third ring. "H...hel...hello?"

There was silence for several seconds and then a deep unfamiliar voice asked, "Sam?"

"Oh...oh...oh!" She stared at the receiver. "David?"

"Sammy, is it really you? My old Sam?" the voice asked as a burst of deep rumbling laughter flowed out of the earpiece and fell around her.

"Oh," she whispered.

"Sam? Are you there? It's me, David McCormack!"

His deep voice sent a shiver through her, and she wasn't sure if she could retain her grip on the receiver.

"Oh," she gasped.

"Is that all you can say after all these years? Sammy, it's really me. David!" She could hear his breathing. "Did I wake you? I tried to call last night, but the phone just rang and rang. You must have been out."

"Last night. Oh, David. I'm so sorry. The phone was ringing so many times that I finally just disconnected it. That last call must have been you! But...but...how did you get my letter so fast? Oh, I'm so sorry...." She knew she was about to lose control. "Hold on, David. I'll be right back. Don't go away, now." She carefully put the receiver down on the redwood slats and ran to the house.

She was sobbing by the time she reached the kitchen. She pressed her face against the cool metal refrigerator door. Her hands trembled as she wiped her face with a cool cloth and blew her nose. She should be happy and shouting with joy, not sobbing like a little girl. She poured herself another cup of coffee and carefully carried it back to the picnic table, then picked up the phone.

"Are you still there, David? Goodness, this is long distance and costing you a small fortune, and I put you on hold and go away and cry! I'm sorry."

"Quit apologizing, Sam. I understand. I'm just a little choked up myself. You gave me time to get myself settled. Hey, what are you doing at this time of day?" His throaty baritone swirled around her head and shoulders and settled on her bosom, where it bored right into her pounding heart.

"I...I...actually I was swimming," Sammy explained. "I'm a morning person. I love to swim early in the morning. I leave for work about seven-fifteen, so this is my private quiet time. What about you?"

"I have a ninety-mile drive each morning, but with my heavy foot, once I hit the interstate I can make it in less than an hour and a half. I just returned from checking on some late calves in the cow barn and feeding the dogs...just the normal things on a ranch, but I have to get them done a little faster since I work in Butte. I love to get up at the crack of dawn and have a cup of coffee down by the stable—in the south pasture if the weather isn't too cold. I keep a coffee maker in the barn. I sure love my coffee. I guess I'm a morning person, too."

"How do you manage to do the ranch and work full-time, too?" Sammy asked. "That must be difficult."

"I have this wonderful neighbor who helps a lot," David replied. "I don't think I could get along without him. His name is Russ, and we know we can count on each other. It's sort of an informal partnership."

They chatted about his ranch and her children. He said, "It's getting late, isn't it?" He hesitated. "Sam, can I call you again?"

"David, of course. We certainly can't catch up on everything in just...." She glanced at the outdoor clock and gasped. "Oh, I didn't know we'd been talking for so long. I'll be late for work."

"Do you have to go now? I'm already late, so what's a few more minutes? Can you stay for just a little while longer, Sam?"

"Sure," Sammy agreed. "David," she asked, "what do you look like?"

"A man...middle aged."

She could sense his smile. "Is your hair still reddish?" she asked.

"Some...darker...plus a lot of gray."

"Are your eyes still that strange shade of green?" She thought of how she had teased him when they were young.

"Yes, I suppose so, but they're the only ones I've ever had, and I'm kinda used to them."

"David, you're teasing. Are you tall?"

"Sort of."

"David, you're not really telling me anything. How big are you? Are you fat or thin? You were always so skinny."

"How about five foot six and two hundred fifty pounds?" he suggested and laughed. "Would that stunt our renewed friendship, Sam? Is it only my good looks that interest you?"

"I'm sorry, I didn't mean to pry. Of course, it's not! Are you serious or are you teasing me? I wish I could really see you. You have the advantage. I sent you a picture. I shouldn't have."

"Too late, my dear. You can't have it back unless you come up here and get it. Seriously, Sam, we'll have to figure a way to meet. Maybe this summer. There are lots of three-day weekends ahead. Think on it, okay? It's already eight o'clock, Sammy. If I call you in a few days, say Thursday evening, would you be home? I want to talk to you again. Am I being too pushy for a stranger?"

She laughed, "You're no stranger. I feel as if it was only yesterday that we played as kids. Of course I'll stay home Thursday night and wait for your call. I'll turn down any other offers. David, it's good to hear your voice again. I can hardly believe we've found each other after all these years. Goodbye, David."

"Bye for now, honey," and the line went dead.

SAMMY SPENT Memorial weekend home alone. Her children had scattered to the four winds for the long holiday. She tried to phone David McCormack at his Montana ranch, but there was no answer. He had called almost nightly following their first conversation, but she hadn't heard from him since the middle of the week. Had he grown tired of their long-distance visits? Perhaps her friendship was too expensive. Surely he had women friends closer to home. Was he involved with someone special?

A surge of jealousy swept through her as she flicked at the pool water with her feet. She swam until she was exhausted and could barely drag herself from the pool. Where was he? True, they had no strings on each other, but she had thought...perhaps...no, just a silly fantasy.

She slept restlessly, the large bed reinforcing her sense of aloneness. She hugged the spare pillow and murmured, "David, what are you really like?"

She recalled their phone conversations. How could he possibly stir her when she hadn't even met him? Was she in love with a deep voice? It had been five days since he had called. It was probably all over, and the pain of losing him again left her burning. Just a flash of hope now buried in the ashes of time and distance, too cold ever to flame again.

She closed her eyes and decided that it was a hopeless fantasy but allowed her mind to form images of an encounter with him. He would be tall and thin with an auburn crew cut and a tanned face that showed no sign of a beard. His ribs would be visible and his chest devoid of hair.

She laughed and hugged the pillow tighter, finding a serenity that lulled her to sleep.

Sammy was awake at the phone's first ring, her senses keen with anticipation as she grabbed the receiver. "David," she said breathlessly.

"Yes, how did you know?" he chuckled, and the deep vibrations sent a tremor through her.

"I was afraid something had happened...to you... hurt or...sick or...something. Are you all right?"

"Sure, but I did receive my phone bill and am considering declaring bankruptcy." He laughed again.

"Oh, no!"

"No, I'm kidding, Sam. Actually, I went to Bozeman for an E.P.A. workshop, then came home by way of Yellowstone. I needed to get away from...people and phones and think about...things. This is my favorite time of year at the park, before the tourists, and it's beautiful. My friend watched the ranch. How about you? Did you have an exciting weekend?"

"Not really. I was all by myself. I just swam and read three books...and worried...about you. Isn't that silly? Sounds boring, doesn't it?"

"What do you have planned for the Fourth of July?" he asked.

"We usually have a picnic at my house. I hope some of the children will be here. Why?" Sammy asked.

"I thought maybe we could meet somewhere. Las Vegas or Salt Lake City or even here."

"Oh, dear, I don't think I could afford it, but why don't you come here? Oh, my, with that phone bill, maybe you're a little strapped, too. I didn't mean to pry into your finances. I'm just a little money conscious. Could you come? Really!"

"Sure, why not? I'm not wealthy, but I have a little saved for just such an emergency." He laughed softly.

"You shouldn't consider our meeting an emergency," she said.

"Ah, but it is, my love, it is. You'll see. Yes, I'll definitely try to be there. I'll call you for sure. I'm working late the next several nights, so I probably won't be calling." He whispered a phrase she couldn't hear clearly. "Just think, Sammy, five weeks and I'll see you in person. I can hardly wait. Sleep tight, honey."

"Good night, David." She thought she heard a strange sound, a kissing sound, but knew it was only wishful imagination. He was surely more restrained and mature than that.

She smiled again and recalled his parting words. "Sleep tight, honey," he had said. She closed her eyes and was soon asleep.

CHAPTER THREE

SAMMY PACED BACK AND FORTH, stopped to read the television monitor showing the arrival times of Western Airlines flights, then glanced at her watch. What if the flight number was wrong? John had taken the call from David McCormack while she had been shopping for the holiday weekend. Perhaps David had missed the flight. Maybe he'd changed his mind about coming.

The voice from the overhead public-address system began, "Western flight 38 from Missoula, Salt Lake City and Las Vegas has landed. Passengers will be entering through Gate 14 in ten minutes."

What if I can't recognize him, she worried. *What if he looks disappointed when he sees me? I should have colored my hair to hide the gray! Am I too fat? What if...? Don't be silly,* she scolded herself.

Was he really as nice as he sounded on the phone? He sounded so confident...about their liking each other again...about his career...about...everything, while she remained filled with doubt and apprehension. She was Cynical Sam to his Dauntless David, and she smiled slightly as she thought of their many phone calls since the initial exchange of letters.

She watched nervously as the passengers came through the gate. Dozens of people filled the area, and she had to stand on tiptoe to see the entrance. Her apprehension increased to near panic as the milling crowd grew. Passengers and waiting family members and friends reunited with waving arms, shouts and cries of affection. More travelers came through the door, followed by an attractive flight attendant carrying her luggage. Sammy's heart sank as she realized he had not been on the plane. She turned away to leave, then glanced over her shoulder to make sure there were no other passengers. A handsome gray-haired man in a pilot's uniform appeared, and then... there he was. Her recognition was emotional rather than physical, for he bore little similarity to her fantasies.

"Oh, my goodness," she murmured as she studied him. Her hands covered her mouth in a futile effort to maintain her poise. He was taller than she had imagined. Her former husband was five feet nine inches. This man was at least four inches taller and almost husky. No, she quickly changed her mind. The broad shoulders of his buckskin jacket appeared well filled, with no sign of a slouch to diminish his confident stance, and this made him appear larger than those men around him.

He wore a clean but seasoned rust-colored Stetson. Its color matched the wavy hair that brushed the fold of his jacket collar. Sammy watched as he moved a large hand and pushed the hat brim back a few inches. A scattering of gray appeared at each temple. The gray seemed premature against his tanned face. He was smooth-shaven, with deepening sun wrinkles etched around his mouth and eyes. His angular chin hinted at stubbornness.

Even at a distance Sammy could see his eyes were the

same strange, rust-flecked green she had found so fascinating as a child. She had often teased him by saying his eyes matched the old tamarisk trees they played under during the hot Phoenix summers.

Goodness, he's handsome, Sammy thought. The tightness in her stomach worsened, and she felt light-headed as she watched him begin to look across the heads of the crowd, trying to find her. She felt like a girl of nine again, and she wanted to run away and hide. Her eyes misted, blurring her vision. She ducked her curly brown head as she groped for a tissue and clumsily wiped her tears away.

She sensed rather than saw a form step from the crowd around her. The pathway opened, and she caught sight of the brown stitching on the tips of his leather boots. Her eyes swept up the long pant legs of his denim jeans; her face burned as her glance took in his silver belt buckle. She caught the image of a molded oil derrick and the words Montana Crude. Impulsively she laughed aloud at the motto, which was in sharp contrast to the crisp clean-cut stranger standing in front of her. She knew he'd never be crude. Her laughter died abruptly as he stepped a pace closer and cleared his throat.

Slowly she raised her head and stared at his shirt, her mouth forming a small silent oval. His tanned chest, lightly matted with dark hair, showed in the open V of his olive green shirt. More tamarisk memories. She looked up and met his broad smile and sparkling eyes.

"Sammy?" His hands touched her shoulders.

"Oh, yes, David," she replied, and the years fell away.

In one hand he carried a large package, held loosely by twine binding. Carefully he set the box down beside his leg.

She had intended to shake his hand, but her carefully laid plans evaporated when he tipped her chin up toward his face.

"You're the missing piece to my puzzle," his voice rumbled, and he opened his arms.

"Sammy!"

She was engulfed in the warmest, strongest set of arms, different from any she had ever encountered before. She felt as though she'd come home at last.

The crowd had thinned when David eased her slightly away. "Let me," he suggested as he took a fresh tissue and wiped her eyes. He laid a light kiss on her cheek, then gave her shoulders a squeeze. "Let's get my luggage."

"I didn't mean to be so emotional," she said with a nervous laugh. "Come, it's downstairs. Should I get my car? How many pieces do you have?"

"That's not necessary. I have just one. I'd rather walk and see this airport of my old home town." He turned and smiled at her. "Feeling better?"

She nodded as she took his hand, and they moved to the escalator. The package he had brought from the plane bumped against the side of the escalator, and he jerked it away as though the contents were fragile. At the same moment a man behind him dropped a heavy briefcase, which fell to the steps and bounced against the back of David's knees. His legs buckled, and he lost his balance. Sammy dropped his hand and grabbed his upper arm to break his fall, but the package sailed away and landed several steps below. A sickening sound of breaking china filled the air.

"Oh, no," David groaned. By the time he regained his balance, the package had reached the lower level and was being retrieved by a security guard. As David and Sammy stepped off the escalator onto the main floor, the man behind them grabbed the dropped briefcase, exhaled a slurred, whiskey-scented apology and rushed off with an older woman.

"Damn drunk," David mumbled as he watched the receding figure disappear in the crowd.

"Sounds broken," the security guard commented, shaking the package gently. "Sorry, sir," he said, and handed the damaged package to David.

"What is it?" Sammy asked.

"Something special for you from the ranch," he replied.

"Is it ruined?"

"I'm sure part is, but some of it should be all right. Damn." He glanced at her and then shrugged off his disappointment when he saw how solemn she looked. He caught and held her gaze. "It's okay...really...let's get out of here." He smiled.

They hurried to the baggage claim area, retrieved his lone piece of luggage and left the building. The first blast of hot desert air hit them.

"Wow! Did we really play in this heat as kids?" he asked as they made their way to the parking garage.

Sammy laughed. "Sure, don't you remember how we would run barefoot from one cottonwood shade spot to the next?"

"Oh, yes. I actually got a blister once," he recalled.

"Remember that old irrigation ditch?"

"Ah, yes. Our own private swimming hole. The trees grew by the ditch, didn't they," he said, "and those salt cedar tamarisk trees were on your side of the road. Remember how salty the needles were? We used to chew on them."

"Yes. . . I remember one time when I knew I couldn't possibly make it to the next patch of shade and my feet hurt so much that I jumped into the water to cool them off."

"Yes, and you almost drowned. The water was deeper than you thought, and I had to haul you out. You looked like a drowning kitten."

"You laughed at me!" she retorted.

"You were so mad that you cried and tried to kick me."

"You dragged me to my house. My mother was mad at us both, and she chased you home and made me stay inside the rest of the day."

They were laughing as she opened the automobile trunk and he lifted the suitcase into the compartment, then carefully placed the broken package beside the luggage.

"Nice car. New?" he asked, as she unlocked the passenger door.

"Yes, about a year ago. I especially liked the color."

"Tamarisk green?" he asked.

"I guess it is." The darkness hid her blushing cheeks.

"I have a pickup truck that's sky blue," he said. "I bought it last fall. Do you think that's prophetic?"

She didn't answer as she handed him the car keys.

"I'll navigate if you'll drive," she said, and gave him little choice as she slid into the passenger side.

Thirty minutes later they pulled into her driveway.

"It's nice," he said, turning off the headlights.

"You haven't seen it yet."

"But you told me all about it, remember? Five bedrooms, fifty percent equity and a swimming pool. Sounds great in weather like this," he said, wiping his damp brow.

"We can swim tomorrow. Did you bring a suit?" she asked.

"Sure did. I had a two-hour layover in Las Vegas. I found one in a gift shop at the airport. A little skimpier than I'm used to wearing. I'll try to hold my gut in." He laughed.

Sammy felt his presence behind her as she fumbled with the door lock. The key didn't fit. The opening was too small. She couldn't concentrate on the simple task at hand.

"Let me," he murmured by her ear as he brushed her hand gently aside and finished the maneuver. He opened the door and exclaimed, "Beautiful!"

To the left, a large living room in shades of cream and rust was accented with colorful Mexican paper flowers and Indian accessories. Through the graceful Spanish arch spanning the width of the room, he could see a glass-enclosed sun-room. The reflection of the swimming pool rippled on the ceiling. Sammy flipped a switch, and subdued lighting came on in the sun-room.

She turned to the right and moved through a smaller archway into a central kitchen and on into a hallway leading to the sleeping area of the spacious home.

"Come on," she called. "I've put you in Lawrence's old room. Bring your luggage. There's a bath off the bedroom. Would you like to freshen up and change into something cooler and more comfortable? I'll make some coffee. Or would you rather have a beer or iced tea?"

"Iced tea sounds great," he replied. "I think the heat is getting to me. I feel exhausted. Maybe a shower will help." He laid the suitcase on the bed and turned. "Sam?" He reached out and held her face in his hands as he stared down into her blue eyes. He lowered his face and kissed her cheek, brushed her lips and suddenly embraced her again.

"Oh, Sam," he whispered softly as his lips caressed her forehead. She tensed, and he released her. "Sorry, honey, I couldn't help it." Her expression was puzzling and dark as she frowned up at him. "See you in about thirty minutes." He smiled and turned his attention to his luggage.

Sammy stared at his broad shoulders and tried to regain her composure. She carefully closed his door and hurried to her own room, locked the door and threw herself on the bed. She had never felt such turmoil in all her life. Images of a thin red-headed boy conflicted with this dark-haired, ruggedly handsome middle-aged man now in her house. Was she crazy to have invited him here? She lay without moving for several minutes, her thoughts jumbled, then she heard the muffled vibrations of the shower stop and knew he would be looking for her soon.

The color began to subside from her flushed complexion as she applied a cold wet washcloth. She changed into a pink print smock and tied the sash in a quick bow. She ran her fingers through her short curly hair and pulled a few curls down over her high forehead. Ready or not, it was time to start the meeting. She tried to relax, then unlocked the door and quickly went to the kitchen to prepare two tall glasses of iced tea.

THE SHOWER had revitalized David's tired body, even as his mind recalled the events of the long day. There had been last-minute chores at the ranch, a quick stop at Russ's place to leave final instructions, the long drive to Missoula, where he had lunch with his son. Lunch had included a bit of lighthearted teasing by his son, caution about his behavior, with neither father nor son willing to delve into details on the subject. Each gibe had heightened David's anxiety over the trip. Finally, a heavy frown troubling his features, he had said, "Ease off, D.A. I've been with women before, and I hope I know more about it than you do." His son had laughed and agreed that that might be true, but to be careful. They had parted at the airport. As the plane left Missoula, David's apprehension increased. He had stayed on the plane in Salt Lake City and began to regain his self-confidence during the long layover in Las Vegas. Now that he had actually met Sammy, touched her and found her the way he had imagined her to be, he was in control again.

He dried quickly and stretched. He glimpsed his reflection in the bedroom closet mirror and looked away. For forty-five he was well preserved, he decided, a slight smile of approval on his lips. He had added several pounds these past few years, but mostly in the shoulders and chest and only a muscled inch or two filling out his waist. His body was still rock hard and his stomach flat. He'd better watch it, he warned himself, thinking of some of his co-workers at Anaconda. Those middle-aged bellies had a way of sneaking up on a fellow. He laughed aloud.

Suddenly he felt a stirring in his loins and chuckled softly at his reaction to finding his long-lost childhood friend.

"Control thy lustful nature, my good man. She's just a pretty lady who happens to be an old friend." Exhilaration quickened his pulse.

"Hey, that's enough self-admiration." He laughed softly as he slipped into a comfortable pair of tan denim jeans. He had lived alone for so long that he had picked up the habit of talking aloud to himself just to hear a voice. He'd better watch that, too.

A short-sleeved shirt of white batiste made his skin appear darker. He quickly buttoned the shirt but left it loose and casual. Vanity, thy name is man, he thought as he ran a comb through his thick damp hair, ducking slightly to see his head in the dresser mirror. He knew he had been blessed with grayness rather than baldness.

David thought of Sammy again. He found her beautiful and poised, but . . . stiff? He wasn't sure of the right interpretation of the messages she was sending. He shrugged off the feeling. She just needed time to get to know him. Would she find him acceptable? He felt like a teenager on a first date.

The thick velvety carpet felt soft and lush under his feet, and he decided to stay barefoot. If this was to be a nostalgic visit, he might as well be as comfortable as possible. He thought of his Phoenix days and the pain of new shoes when school started each fall. He opened the bedroom door, retraced his earlier steps and found her in the sun-room.

Sammy was on the sofa studying the dark liquid in her tea glass, her bare feet tucked under her smock. David paused, reaching for the slump blocks of the archway overhead.

Suddenly a large black-and-white cat rubbed against the inside of his pant leg as he stood watching her, his legs slightly apart. The cat mewed, sauntered to the sofa and jumped onto Sammy's lap. She looked up, startled at the sound of the cat's voice.

She saw David in the archway and smiled. "Come and sit," she said. She held out a sweating glass of tea as he sank into the comfortable cushions.

Duke eased the tension as he rose from Sammy's lap, began a long feline walking stretch and moved onto David's legs. The cat turned a few times, mewing, then settled down for a short nap. David began stroking the cat and casually glanced at Sammy.

"Well, what shall we talk about?" he asked.

Her words came tumbling out. "Do you know how many years it's been? My goodness, David, thirty-four years! I always hoped we'd meet again someday, but it seemed so.... You said you'd send a signal. Remember?"

David nodded. "I try to keep my word. I'm glad you received the message. I promised you a signal, but I didn't know that Morse code would be replaced by satellites."

Her eyes clouded a little. "It's like a miracle, isn't it?"

He nodded and continued to admire her.

"I remember when you left," Sammy said. "I can close my eyes and still see that dusty old road and you waving to me. I had just had my birthday. You gave me a cigar box covered with blue tissue paper. Our birthdays are just ten days apart, aren't they? I had been working on a gift for you, too, and was so upset at your leaving that I ran home to my room and stomped on it and broke it all to pieces."

"What was it?" he asked.

"A Quaker Oats box, giant size, covered in green and brown crepe paper—for you to keep your own secret things in. It even had a good lid. I had saved it from Easter time when we made baskets. Mom had picked out the strongest box for me to use. I think she understood...about us."

"Is your mother still...?"

"No, she died a few years ago. So did my father."

"I'm sorry." David continued to pet the sleeping cat.

Sammy found his stroking hand hypnotic. "When I dated boys in high school, I often thought of you and wondered what you looked like, what you were doing, who you were with."

"Do I match your expectations?" he asked, smiling slightly.

"No."

"Oh?"

"Oh, that's not bad!"

She saw that he was staring at her mouth. She tried to choose words to explain but wondered how his lips would feel on hers if he kissed her.

She smiled. "You're bigger, taller...more handsome. I think I just imagined you as an older boy, but you're definitely not a boy.''

He laughed and dropped his dark head against the high back of the sofa. ''I must have done a better job of imagining,'' he said. ''I could have found you in a crowd. I did. Your eyes are the same, even though your hair is darker. You're not just pretty—'' he lightly brushed her cheek with his fingers ''—you're lovely.'' Her smile was replaced with a solemn frown as he held her gaze. Then he smiled. ''Go on.''

''I answered both of your letters,'' she said, ''but the last one I wrote to you came back marked, 'Moved, no forward.' ''

''Let's see, I wrote the first that same year, right after Christmas,'' David replied, staring at the pool reflections dancing on the ceiling. ''I wrote the second the next summer, but by then my mom and stepdad were having problems again. I was just twelve and didn't understand what was going on. Apparently my mother had written to my real father's older brother about me. My uncle Jeff had a ranch near Forsyth, Montana. He had five sons and told her that one more boy would be no trouble. I mailed my second letter to you at the Greyhound bus depot in Spokane.''

He groaned slightly. ''I don't know about my mother. She always had a way of waiting until the last minute to tell me things and then not explaining. That morning she told me that she and my stepdad were going to Portland and that I would go live with my uncle. She said I needed to get there before school started. To this day I don't know if my mother is alive or dead. I hated her for years, but I guess I've mellowed. I still don't understand why she didn't...." He sighed. "Uncle Jeff used to say she was scatterbrained. Once he got mad and accused her of being crazy. She was never a very good mother. Some women aren't, but...." The lines around his mouth deepened into hard grooves of hatred as he leaned his head on the sofa back and closed his eyes. "I've supposedly mellowed, haven't I? I always tried to tell my son why I did things. Do kids ever understand their parents?"

Sammy reached out in concern. He opened his eyes at the warm touch and grabbed her hand before she could retrieve it, preventing her return to the safety of her end of the sofa. He held her hand in his, studied her a moment, then took a deep breath. "Sorry, Sam, for getting so serious. Actually, moving to my uncle's ranch was a good thing for me. Uncle Jeff was a terrific man. Still is. Do you know he's seventy-three years old and still runs his place? It's doubled in size. He raises cattle and grows wheat...and is still fighting off the oil and coal companies. Two of his sons help him, but he's a tough, proud old man. Maybe you'll meet him someday." He tugged at her hand. "Come sit closer."

She sat up straight and stiff and tried to pull her hand away.

"Hey, honey, relax." His rust-flecked green eyes penetrated her mind. "I won't hurt you. I've waited too long to see you again to spoil this reunion like that. I wouldn't do anything you wouldn't want me to do." He stopped, for she had gasped.

Had he read her thoughts, she wondered?

"I just wanted you a little closer, that's all," he

assured her as he released her hand and moved his arm to the back of the sofa.

Duke mewed and jumped to the floor. "He wants out," Sammy said, relieved at the distraction. She hurried to the door leading to the pool area and let the big cat out for the night. She turned as she closed the door and saw David watching her. His presence had thoroughly unsettled her, but she wasn't ready to evaluate the implications of her pounding pulse. She returned to stand in front of him. If he stood up and towered over her, she would probably swoon. "Do you want some more...."

He lifted his hand and tugged on the bow of her sash. She had intended to sit near him in some discreet manner, but she found herself moving into the circle of his open arms as the sash loosened and fell to the floor.

"Oh, David," she cried as he pulled her to him. She luxuriated in the feel of his strong, protective arms surrounding her. He gently stroked her hair and shoulders, then her bare arms.

"It's okay, it's okay, honey. Go ahead and cry." He kept repeating the phrases as he kissed the top of her head, and she felt his arms tighten slightly. She cried for several minutes, then he handed her a fistful of tissues, and she wiped her eyes and nose. As her tearful outburst subsided, she became aware of the wetness of his shirt front.

She lifted her face and sobbed, "Look what I've done to your shirt. I'm so sorry. Oh, David, I don't understand this at all!"

He brushed the dampened hair strands from her temple. "I do. You're my Sam and I've found you again...

and we're not kids anymore.'' His face came closer. He hesitated, his mouth inches from hers. "Sam," he whispered huskily as his lips descended to hers. No light brush this time, but a sensuous massaging of warm flesh on flesh.

Her senses reeled as her lips parted slightly, and she began to respond to his caressive pressure.

He eased away from her mouth, kissed her cheek, her hair, then pressed her head against his chest and whispered, "Be still, just be still, sweetheart."

Several minutes passed as she savored his embrace. She could hear his baritone begin to softly sing a lullabye that she remembered from their childhood. It was a Scottish song, taught to him long ago by his natural father, and he had taught it to her one afternoon as they had sat near their favorite ditch.

She looked up and murmured, "That's beautiful. . . I remember. . . oh, David."

"I'm sorry, Sam. I didn't mean to upset you. I wanted to calm you. . . I. . . just be still," he whispered, and again hummed the lilting melody as she regained her composure.

She kept her head nestled on his chest as she began talking again. "I was married for nine years, and when things began to press in during the bad times, thoughts of you would help me get through the long days and lonely nights. I even insisted on naming my second son David. My ex-husband would have just killed me if he had known the reason."

He chuckled at her revelation.

He kissed her forehead and whispered softly, "Go on.''

"You were my fantasy friend all those years. After my divorce I used to stand in the shower and cry. I guess it was the hurt and frustration of trying to deal with it all. I felt so victimized! I'd talk to God and then to you and then to God. Between the two of you, I made it through those really rough years."

She was quiet again and could hear the steady beat of his heart. The front of his shirt was thoroughly wrinkled, with only two buttons still fastened. Impulsively she slipped her hand under the soft fabric and felt his heart pounding. "You make me feel like I've been in a holding pattern all these years and now I can move again," she murmured. Embarrassment for her action swept over her, and she eased back and smiled broadly at him. Her eyes were sparkling and her lashes dark and wet from the tears. She quickly kissed him on his lips, withdrew to a safer distance and said, "Now, tell me about yourself. I'll get more tea. We have lots of time."

Before David could begin, the living room door was thrown open and a young man burst through the door.

"Oh, my goodness," she exclaimed, "it's my son John. I forgot about him."

"Hey, hey, who's this?" John began to tease, as he entered the sun-room. He pretended to ignore his mother's tear-streaked flushed face.

Introductions were made, and after several minutes of polite conversation, excuses were given by all three to retire for the night.

CHAPTER FOUR

WHAT A PERFECT FOURTH OF JULY HOLIDAY, Sammy thought. It was Friday, the beginning of a three-day weekend. Lawrence and his wife were there. David had called from Quebec. Even Sarah had called collect from Oregon. John was making a sincere effort to control his teasing streak.

A young man who had identified himself as David Alan McCormack had called from Missoula asking to speak to "David, Senior." Sammy didn't know David had a son. Did he have other children? She faintly remembered he had said something about talking to his son, but she had been so tense the previous night, she wasn't sure.

She was glad to be secluded in the house, where she could observe them all without their knowledge as she worked at the kitchen sink. She could see through the sun-room windows to the pool area. She heard splashes and shouts and glanced up in time to see John perform his version of a belly flop. David stood on the diving platform, readying himself for a more orthodox dive.

He stood tall and straight, muscular arms poised for the dive. He broke up with laughter, doubling over and pointing down to the rippling surface of the pool just out of her view. She knew it had to be John again. David straightened and tried once again to be serious.

Sammy studied him from head to toe, and a shiver passed through her. The Las Vegas swimsuit was suggestively brief. She blushed. At her age she certainly knew what a man looked like and could judge for herself what was hidden in such a skimpy suit, yet her strict upbringing told her not to look so boldly.

Her mind's voice began to tease...it had been such a long time. She had never been one to fool around during marriage, although she had discovered too late that Jake had had a double standard. She knew her coworkers considered her out of touch with society. She wondered if she was perhaps more of a prude than she cared to admit. She'd done very little dating since her divorce. Maybe her high moral standards were the result of not making opportunities occur to test the waters of temptation.

John would leave Saturday morning for his four-year navy enlistment. David and she would be alone until his return flight to Missoula on Sunday afternoon. She felt perplexed at her responsiveness to his presence. Hadn't she read recently that a woman in her forties was...? What about men? Was he as virile as he looked?

Sammy studied him again. His long sinewy legs were pale, but above that scant swimsuit he was quite tanned. Maybe there was more sunshine in Montana than she had thought. She looked down at her own two-piece suit. She had always thought her legs were too fat and her breasts too small. A tan improved her legs, and having four children had added a few welcome inches to her bust line. At least her breasts didn't sag. Perhaps her penance laps had fringe benefits. She could still go without a bra and did at times. Daily situps for the past several years had kept her slightly rounded belly as firm as nature and age would allow.

Her wandering thoughts came to an abrupt halt as Lawrence called to her from the patio door.

"Hey, mom! Bring the salad. The meat is ready and we're all starved!"

She carried the large salad bowl of greens and several bottles of dressing out to the picnic table. She glanced at David as he climbed out of the pool, then avoided his gaze, too embarrassed by her secret thoughts of him in the kitchen.

David came to her, gave her a wet hug from behind, and planted a damp cool kiss on her neck. He slipped his long arms around her waist, smiled and whispered a low, "Hi, Sam," in her ear. She returned his smile as he quickly released his hold on her.

The afternoon was spent in a leisurely fashion— swimming, snacking and light discussion. Career pressures and corporate intrigue seemed miles away as they lingered by the pool.

Lawrence and his wife, Eve, left at sunset. John announced, "I have a last chance at a hot date, folks," and tactfully departed. Sammy and David were alone again. As they lounged by the pool, enjoying the silence and privacy, he turned to her.

"I've known you again for only a day, and yet I feel like I've known you all my life." He reached out and took her hand. "I think I'd like to kidnap you and carry you off to my ranch. Would you resist?"

She was about to answer when a flash of color burst above the eastern skyline.

"What's that?" he asked as he sat up.

"It looks like fireworks from the university stadium in Tempe," she replied.

He stood and stretched. "Remember how all of us kids used to climb up on your roof and watch the fireworks over the old fairgrounds? That was always fun. I'd forgotten."

She stood beside him. Barefoot, she came just to his chin. His closeness was disturbing, and she needed to get away. She noticed the ladder propped against the storage shed and said, "Why don't we climb up and see them better? I'll get a quilt and some pillows. We might as well be comfortable." She pointed to the ladder and went quickly inside to get the pillows.

David held the ladder as she climbed onto the patio roof. He tossed the quilt to her, then the pillows one by one and climbed up quickly to join her. The panoramic view from the roof enabled them to see displays from several locations around the flat valley.

David lay back on the pillow. He watched her silhouette as she pointed to various bursts of color in the darkening sky. He reached out and touched the curve of her bare waist, but she didn't respond. He compared the few visible stars in the softly lighted sky to his Montana nights on the ranch, where the heavens were dark and filled with thousands of brilliant twinkling lights. He tried to ignore her.

Damn! He wanted to grab her in his arms and make slow, lingering love to her, but knew he could be dreaming a fantasy that she might not share. She seemed to be in tight control, while he was willing to make a fool of himself. He closed his eyes and tried to block her image. He should have stayed on his ranch where he belonged. He was too old for this courtship game.

Sammy turned to him. His eyes were closed. Did he find her so boring that he'd fallen asleep? She stretched out beside him, then propped herself up on one elbow to look at him in the moonlight. The July night air was warm, and there was a gentle breeze moving across the roof, but the shiver that passed through her wasn't from the weather. She lay down beside him, inhaled the mixture of chlorine and male scent of his arm and closed her eyes. She would rest for just a little while. As a wave of drowsiness settled over her, she reached for his hand. She thought she felt a slight tightening of his fingers as she drifted to sleep.

She awakened as something brushed her lips and words were spoken, and she realized that David had kissed her.

"What did you say?" she asked as she moved closer.

"You didn't answer my question before the fireworks. Would you resist me if I carried you off to my mountain hideaway?"

"You're teasing, David. I almost wish you weren't."

"Maybe I'm not," he hinted. "Would you come?"

She shook her head in disagreement. "I have a mortgage, a car payment, my career and a few dozen other responsibilities here in Phoenix. I couldn't even consider it, but...sometimes...David, I'm being silly just having this conversation with you." She reached up and touched his mouth lightly with her fingertips. "No more questions," she whispered, and slid her hands across his smooth-shaven cheek to his neck. "Not now...I don't know how to answer you," she murmured.

The crisp curls behind his ears felt alive to her sensitive fingers. Her hands moved down his chest and around his waist as she inhaled the essence of his nearness.

He gathered her in his arms and brushed his lips over her face, working his way slowly to her mouth. "Sammy, I...I..." he murmured and lowered his lips to hers. His long sensual kiss brought a response from her, and her mouth opened and he probed exploringly. His hand slipped beneath the fabric of her swim top and cupped the underside of her breast, pushing gently upward, as his lips traveled down her throat to the valley between her breasts. His thumb began to work a slow circle around her nipple, and it responded to his touch.

The pleasure Sammy felt grew to an intolerable pitch. She felt his maleness, restrained by the thin swim trunks, pressing against her thigh. The shock of what might happen next brought her crashing to reality.

She jerked his hand from her breast and shoved him violently away. She rolled over and raised herself on her knees, her arms folded protectively across her chest.

David fell back in surprise as she hissed, "No, stay away. Don't touch me! You must think I'm just a... a...a woman who's done without...some divorcée who'll give in to any man who shows an interest. Well, I may have done without, but I won't give in!"

Tears spilled down her cheeks. She didn't know if she was raging at him or herself. "You can't love me!" she cried. "You...you just want to.... We just met yesterday, and I almost gave in to you! Oh, David, what's the matter with me?"

He stared at her through the moonlight. "Damn," he growled. "There's nothing wrong with you. You're a normal woman whom I happen to find both beautiful and very appealing." He paused, running his fingers through his thick dark hair. "I'm sorry, Sam. I lost control. Calm down and be still. Some neighbor of yours will hear us up here, think we're prowlers and call the police. Then you will have something to be embarrassed about."

She continued to frown, and he started to chuckle. "Come on. Let's go for a swim and cool off." He hastily threw the pillows and quilt to the grass below, then helped her down the ladder.

She busied herself at the control panel and switched the pool lights off, leaving only the full moon to light the night.

She watched him dive into the pool and swim several laps. He rested on the submerged ledge under the diving board as she dived from the board and swam to the shallow end, turned and swam to him in the shadow of the board.

The cool water was refreshing, and she began to feel foolish about her conduct on the roof. She touched his chest. "I'm sorry," she whispered. "I overreacted. I don't want you to think I don't like you...I mean I do like you...a lot...I mean...oh, goodness, what do I mean? You make me feel all mixed up inside."

He smiled and his green eyes sparkled. "Good." He stared at her through the moonlight. "Hold on to me," he said, as he reached for her hands and placed them around his neck. He playfully pulled her onto his chest and began to do a slow backstroke around the pool, speaking nonsensical statements that made her start to giggle, and she relaxed.

He made a sharp turn under the board, and her hold slipped. She lost her balance and grabbed at his arm, but missed and went under. David reached for her, clutching the first thing his fingers touched. He heard a snap. His hand surfaced holding the top half of her swimsuit, the hook dangling from a loose thread.

Sammy came up choking and gasping for air. The swirling mass of bubbles began to subside as she brushed the wet, soggy hair from her face and tried to focus her blurred vision on him. He steadied her in front of him until she regained her breath.

"Sam?" He placed a hand on each side of her waist and slowly lifted her out of the water, exposing her round breasts. She buried her hands in his thick hair, clutching his head, but she didn't push him away.

Sammy felt his sharp intake of breath as he drew her to him. He kissed her right breast lightly, then her left, then slowly eased her body into the water against him.

He frowned slightly as he stared into her upturned face. "I think I love you again, Sam."

She buried her face in the curve of his throat, her heart racing. Abruptly auto headlights appeared, and she clutched his shoulders, almost losing her balance on the ledge. The lights disappeared in the garage, a car door banged, and the living room door opened.

"Hold still, Sam. Don't move. It's just John. He can't see us, but I can see him. He'll think we're asleep like good grown-ups."

Sammy was satisfied to stay in the circle of his arms, even without her swim top, but as she nestled closer, she became aware of his rekindled arousal. A feeling of euphoria swept through her as she felt his arms begin to move, and the hypnotic slowness of his touch mixed with the relaxing buoyancy of the water brought a delayed reaction to her senses. Before she could respond to his lips on her throat, his hand and mouth moved on to a new spot that drew his attention.

She wanted to cry out, *go back, touch me again. I need to think about what I feel. Touch me, touch me again. . .slowly.* But the words stayed in her mind.

"Your skin is soft. . ." he breathed near her ear as his hands caressed her back. The kitchen light went on, the refrigerator door slammed, and the light went off. All was dark and quiet again.

"Oh, Sam," he groaned as he held her face in his hands and seared her mouth with his. "I want to make love to you," he whispered in the shadows beneath the diving board, and this time she offered no resistance.

His hands slid along her body, easing the bottom half of her suit down to float away. She buried her head against his throat again and heard his pounding heart and raspy breathing. His lips massaged hers, uneven and hard, and her hesitancy changed to fervor as her wet hands began to stroke his ribs and stomach.

She had never taken the initiative in lovemaking before, but now her hands began to move lower, brushing his suit, and a deep groan escaped him and floated by her ear. Her hand slipped between his thighs as she murmured his name, and her lips moved across the soft hair on his chest.

Her eagerness surprised him. Her hands were on his hips, pushing impatiently at the resistant fabric. His larger, stronger hands covered hers as he helped her.

All reason and restraint left her as her mouth clung to his, and his bikini briefs drifted away to join hers in the middle of the pool. She felt the heat of his need against her abdomen, even in the cool water. She wanted to blend with him and never be alone again. Boldly she touched him, and he shook slightly with desire. She explored him until finally he eased her hand away.

"Enough, or it'll be too late," he murmured. "I want you, Sammy," he whispered. "I want to love you. . . now!"

"Yes. . . yes. . ." she pleaded.

He claimed her mouth again, and she clung to him as his hands roamed and caressed her. She was drowning in desire, until now a dormant emotion for her.

"Hold on to me," he whispered, and she wrapped herself around his body. As he filled her, she knew the sweet impalement was the answer to a lifetime of waiting.

Their movements seemed part of a predestined union, and the litany of a single word began to move from her lips and float past his pounding ears as he became aware of her voice.

"Oh, David. . . David. . . David. . . David. . ." That sound continued like musical notes, reminding him fleetingly of the fast-flowing creek that ran through his ranch, always filled from its source high in the Rockies, always racing down the hillsides in a hurry to reach the Missouri, the Mississippi and the sea, but never running dry; always refilled from the winter snows and spring rains; replenished to be enjoyed again and again.

He leaned against the rough wall and took her to oblivion.

As time began to move again, they held each other, motionless and quiet in the water. He was confident their desire would be renewed, and he held her until his strength returned.

He withdrew, and the unsheathing made him incomplete. He lowered her gently to stand against him. "Oh, Sammy, Sammy!" She clung to him, and he thought he felt warm tears against his chest, but the lapping water diluted them. He held her tightly, reluctant to break the spell cast by their union.

"Come," he finally said, as he released and guided her to the ladder. He helped her out of the pool, and they stood facing each other, water dripping from their bodies.

The moon moved behind a cloud, and in the darkness she swayed, and her hand reached out. He quickly lifted her in his arms and carried her to the picnic bench where they had left their towels earlier in the day. He dried her body with gentle strokes, concerned about her faintness.

As he fluffed her damp curls and dried a few remaining drops of moisture from her forehead, her eyelids fluttered, her eyes opened, and their gazes locked. A slight smile crossed her lips, then she dropped her eyes in embarrassment as she whispered, "I'm all right . . . I think."

He kissed her lightly and admired the gentle heaving sigh of her breasts as he dried himself.

"I don't think I can move," she murmured. He tossed the damp towel down and scooped her up in his arms, crossed the yard and carried her through the house to her bedroom.

David gently set her on the bed, covered her and kissed her again, but as he began to leave, she reached out and caught his hand. "Don't go—not yet," she pleaded.

He sat down on the bed, and as her hand fell on his cool bare thigh, he felt a resurgence of desire. "If I stay here, I'll climb into bed with you, my lovely blue eyes, and that wouldn't look too good to your son tomorrow morning, now would it?"

"I know," she replied listlessly. "Just stay until I fall asleep. David. . .?" Her voice trailed away as she tried to focus on his face in the filtered moonlight.

He brushed a stray curl from her forehead. "I'll stay, love. How about forever?" And he kissed her.

Her eyelids grew heavy, but she forced them open again. "I can't keep my eyes open. I've never felt so relaxed before."

"Yes, my love, I know. It was good. It was right," he assured her.

"But, David, I've never. . . I usually don't. . . not even before my divorce. . . I couldn't. . . ."

"Sleep, sweetheart. It was right." He reaffirmed his statement as he kissed each eyelid shut and held her hand until her clasp relaxed, and her hand fell away in slumber.

He stopped at her door and looked back at her, a firm set to his angular jaw. He turned and hurried to his room, dropped exhausted to the bed, pulled the sheet up to cover his nakedness, and slept.

CHAPTER FIVE

SAMMY WATCHED HER YOUNGEST CHILD enter the building with David alongside him. The two were almost the same height. When had John changed from her sweet small son to this full-grown young man? John and David had convinced her to say her goodbyes in the car, and she had reluctantly agreed to do so.

She could see them through the glass door of the recruitment center. They were shaking hands and talking. David's left hand reached out to grip John's shoulder. They spoke again and parted.

David came quickly through the entrance and out to the waiting automobile. He slid behind the wheel, then turned to her.

"He'll be okay," he smiled. "He's a fine young man. You did a good job raising him."

Her chin trembled and a single tear trickled down her cheek. He drew her to him and handed her a tissue.

"I think I'll see my broker and buy stock in a tissue company," he said, laughing softly as he comforted her.

She wiped her nose and punched him playfully in the ribs. "I'll be all right. It's not every day you see your family disappear before your very eyes."

"Maybe you should start a new one," he replied.

"What?" She had heard only a few words.

He changed the subject. "Let's go for a drive, Sam. I don't think that empty five-bedroom house is the place for you today. Which way to the high country? I miss the mountains."

They filled the gas tank and headed north on the interstate highway. Soft music coming from the car's cassette player was the only sound for miles as they each became lost in private thoughts. They were forty miles from Flagstaff when she realized she had been fingering the soft material of his shirt over his shoulder. He turned off onto a secondary road with less traffic.

He glanced at her as he eased the vehicle onto the loose gravel shoulder and parked under a large overhanging limb of a huge ponderosa pine. He turned off the ignition and reached for her hand. "Let's spend the night in Flagstaff," he suggested. "I leave tomorrow, remember?"

"Of course I remember, but I couldn't. I have responsibilities at church. They need me."

"Call in sick. I need you more."

"I don't have a toothbrush."

"I'll buy you one."

"I didn't even bring a nightgown."

"You won't need one," he assured her, and his wide mouth broke into a smile that reached his eyes.

She was wasting her time making up excuses. She wanted the night together as much as he did. She searched his face for reassurance and understanding. "I'm not used to spending nights in motels with strange men," she said, "but I want to with you."

He smiled. "I'm not a stranger, I'm an old, old

friend.'' His eyes narrowed slightly. "Haven't you ever met a man you could trust?''

She reached up and stroked the mixture of gray and reddish brown at his temple. "I don't know.''

He took her hand and kissed its palm, then laid it against his cheek. "You have now, Sammy.'' He gathered her in his arms. "I love you. I know it seems quick, but this is right. I feel it as I've never felt anything before. Damn it, Sam! I know now that it was you I've been looking for all these years. I'm not putting the make on you. I love you! I'd never do anything to hurt you. Maybe we've both had our share of hard knocks and disappointments in our separate lives, but, Sam, I sent you a signal over the years and you heard me.'' He brushed her lips with his. "Now that I've found you again, I want to tell you all about me and I want to learn all about you, but I know there's not enough time in the next twenty-four hours, so just let me love you.'' Again his intensity overwhelmed her as his light breath moved across her cheek, and his mouth sought hers.

"The next long weekend is Labor Day,'' he said. "I know I can't get away before then, but I'll come and we'll work out the details and somehow solve this problem. Somehow....'' His voice cracked. He held her for several minutes, his long fingers occasionally playing with the curls near her temple. She reached for another tissue, and he said, "I think I could use one myself. Oh, damn, Sam!''

They found a motel on the outskirts of town. David registered, found the room and opened the door for her. She entered and watched him place the room key and the receipt on the dresser. He looked at her, grabbed her car keys, said, "I'll be back," and was gone.

Sammy felt abandoned, and the old nagging doubts began to surface. Then she noticed the receipt for the room.

"Mr. and Mrs. David E. McCormack, Dillon, Montana."

Twenty minutes later David returned carrying a small sack. He handed it to her. "First gift to my newfound love," he said, and bowed. "I couldn't find a gown."

She opened the package and peeked inside. "You silly...." She saw his expression. "No, you're not silly at all...you're...oh, David." Her blue eyes sparkled with love as she pulled a small tube of toothpaste and two brushes from the sack.

He reached for her, pulled her down on the bed and held her against him. As he explored her face and traced a tiny wrinkle from her dark lashes to her temple, he said, "You're very lovely, do you know that? Even the gray in your curly hair is beautiful...it's silver." He kissed her lightly several times and murmured, "We'd better go eat before this gets out of hand." Gently he eased her off the bed.

They showered and went to dinner at a small Italian restaurant. He bought a bottle of Chianti in a basket and she was slightly tipsy as they left the restaurant, the empty bottle clutched in her hand. The cool mountain air helped clear her head. She must be crazy to be here with him. So reckless!

When they returned to the motel room, she disappeared into the bathroom. David finally knocked softly and called her name.

She opened the door and stood there, silhouetted by the light streaming through the opening. "I think I've made a mistake," she mumbled.

"Sammy?" He held out his hand, and she came to stand before him. She looked uncertain and he reassured her. "I know, love. This is different from last night. Last night in the pool just happened. It was beautiful and unexpected. But we've planned for this night, and it'll be even better. Trust me."

He held her very still for a few minutes. She was about to pull away and suggest that they leave when she felt his fingers slowly unbutton the back of her blouse, then unhook her bra. As his fingertips brushed her skin, a tremor passed through her, and she was lost. She was still covered, but his hands moved to her shoulders, brushing the obstructive garments from her. Instinctively she crossed her arms in shyness.

"You described your body as pear-shaped in one of your letters. I want to see for myself." His eyes were dark and smoky as he unbuttoned her waistband and slowly lowered the zipper of her slacks. He kissed her body as the clothing fell away. His mouth left a hot trail down her belly, and her fingers clutched at his head.

"No, David, no...yes," she whispered. She moaned and tugged at him and began to open his shirt. His silver belt buckle was stiff, and he had to help her. His jeans were snug and again he had to help. The pile of garments was forgotten as he led her to the large bed.

His voice was hoarse with need as he coaxed her and brought forth the response he wanted from her. His fingers roamed and explored her body at will until she cried out, "David, no more," and shifted her limbs to ease his way.

His fingers quivered as he touched her face.

"I love you, David," she murmured. "I think I always did." She gazed at his face inches from hers, and her lips parted as he lowered his mouth. He began to move, and it was like the night before in the pool as passion and desire erased reason and control.

They surfaced still clinging to each other, and later, after he fell into a satisfied sleep, she lay against his warm body and wondered at the naturalness of being here in a motel bed, next to this man whom she had known for forty-eight hours.

She awoke during the night, unable to orient herself. She sat up quickly and the warm blanket fell away. She heard David stir, and the memories returned as his warm hand touched the small of her back.

"Are you okay?" his deep drowsy voice asked.

She remained upright, her torso shimmering in the pale moonlight filtering through the window curtain.

"David, are we...?" Her soft voice was filled with doubt.

"Are we what?" His hand caressed her bare back.

She turned to him and his hand moved forward, tracing a pattern around her breast until it reached the dark center. His thumb brushed back and forth across the sensitive core, and in spite of herself she responded.

"I don't know if this is...right...or wrong. David, what's worse, I don't know if I care!"

He smiled at her through the darkness, then reached both hands up to her shoulders and began to pull her down, shaking her slightly. He murmured, "How could this be wrong, Sammy, when we both feel...when we've both been waiting...so long! Sam, don't try to bring morality into this...or guilt...or anything else that inhibits our being together. This time with you is precious. That's not a very masculine word, is it? It's the only word I can think of that fits...and it's because I'm here with you, sweetheart. I love you, and I want you, and I need you...." He began to kiss her again.

"Sammy, do you really love me?" he asked, forcing her to look at him.

"Yes," she declared.

"Do you want me?" he asked as his hand moved across her belly.

"Yes, yes, David. You satisfy me like no man has ever...." Her words changed into an unintelligible sound.

"Do you need me?" he demanded, a harshness in his voice, as he drew her to him and pushed the blankets away.

"Oh, yes," she replied, "until forever." His mouth met hers as he took her again.

SHE WAS QUIET on the return trip to Phoenix. David told her about his ranch and his friend Russ. He was hesitant to speak of his past and told her only current facts about his son. She told him a little about her job at the Mastiff Corporation when he tried to question her.

Thoughts of returning to work on Monday painfully reminded her that he would be gone, back to his world of engineering and ranching, one thousand fifty miles to the north.

Would he remember her for long? She glanced up and

saw that he had moved the rearview mirror so that he saw her face as well as the road behind. He pulled her closer, and she felt his body heat against her arm. They were silent again, lost in their private thoughts.

They arrived at her house with enough time for him to pack his suitcase.

"I'll fix a quick snack. We don't have much time, do we?" she said, and stared at his back as he began to fill his single case.

As they ate by the pool, he frowned, then his face brightened. "Your birthday is one month from today. Want a present?"

"If you still remember me," she replied.

A pained expression flashed across his face and was gone. "Of course I will. Will you give me one if I do?"

"Sure," she answered. "August sixteenth, right?"

"Yes, only thirty-four years overdue." There was a note of bitterness in his voice. He rose abruptly, gathered the plates and disappeared into the house. He helped her wash the few dishes in the sink. As they finished, she turned to him in anguish.

"It's time, love," he said.

"I know. I just . . . ."

"He held her tightly and whispered, "It's only two months until I'll be here again. You can't keep me away, you'll see," he assured her. "I'll call you when I get back to the ranch, no matter how late it is. Okay?"

He kissed her lightly. "God, I love you. I had no idea when I placed that ad that it would lead to this." He held her silently for several seconds.

As they drove to the airport, a self-protective numbness gradually covered her, shielding her from the pain of his leaving, but as she watched his tall figure disappear into the plane, the protective cocoon disintegrated, and she choked with grief. She couldn't bear to stay and see his plane take off, but as she drove down the access road to the expressway, she heard the plane's engines overhead and had to stop the car.

She saw the plane with its jet trail streaming behind like dust from an unpaved road. She gripped the steering wheel, buried her head in her arms and wept.

He called late that night, but the connection was very poor, and she could hardly hear his voice or understand his words.

Time and distance had come between them again.

CHAPTER SIX

THOUGHTS OF THE FOURTH OF JULY WEEKEND and David McCormack were vividly alive as Sammy delayed her departure for work on Monday until the last possible moment, but the telephone was silent. She'd hoped he would call. Was he beginning to forget already?

She was immediately trapped in the pressures and demands of her position within moments of entering her department at Mastiff Corporation. As systems liaison between the marketing and accounting departments and the systems development personnel, she now found herself caught in the middle of a major difference of opinion in the objectives of a new computerized management information-retrieval system.

Lunch with Wes Franklin, manager of the systems department, was followed by a special meeting with the vice-president of marketing, who had been brought into the dispute by his two assistants. The day gradually deteriorated into an ever-widening division between warring camps that appeared irreparable by day's end. She knew the new system had to be implemented by the first of August, but she found the role of peacemaker frustrating and uncomfortable.

The late drive home was a refreshing relief from the stress of the day. The house was a tomb of emptiness when she opened the door. Duke greeted her, mewing for his dinner. As she fed him, she thought of David and wondered what he was doing. Feeding his cows, perhaps. Would he call tonight?

She passed through the hallway to her bedroom and glanced into the main bathroom. A tight knot gripped her stomach when she saw David's swimsuit hanging from the shower rod next to her top. How had they gotten there? She hadn't thought of them since they had been abandoned in the pool. She knew neither David nor herself had used the pool since that night. Suddenly she remembered that John had prepared breakfast for them last Saturday before he'd left. He'd had to knock loudly on their doors to awaken them. Could he have found the suits in the pool? His hair had been damp, but she'd assumed it was from showering. Now she realized that he had gone for an early morning dip in the pool, found the suits and tactfully collected them and hung them to dry, never saying a word to her. She was mortified. What must her youngest son think of her now? Skinny-dipping with a man! She smiled in spite of her embarrassment. Of all her children, John would be the one most likely to understand and not judge her.

She took the dry suits and gently folded them together and placed them in her dresser drawer, next to her nightgowns.

She fixed herself a light snack and moved to the patio. She was about to sit down when a falling leaf drifted onto the diving board. She was overcome with memories of tender love in the moonlight with a man from her past.

Her appetite was gone, and she returned to the kitchen. The food went down the garbage disposal, and the grinding sounds coming from the drain matched her frayed nerves. She desperately wanted to hear his voice again. Should she call him? No, that would be much too forward of her. What if a woman answered the phone? She'd wait for his call.

She wandered into Lawrence's room. Perhaps a little therapeutic housekeeping would help boost her sagging spirits. She scanned the room, and her eyes fell on the damaged package still on the dresser. She had forgotten all about his gift.

She moved the package to the bed. As she did, a note fell from a small tear in the covering. David had apparently stuck it in the hole without telling her. For a moment she was unable to see the letters. She blinked a few times. His handwriting was bold and confident, and she could see his tamarisk eyes smiling as she read the note.

To Sammy, my love,
     My days with you were beautiful beyond anything I could have imagined. You belong with me, darling.

David

She carefully opened the box. Inside, surrounded by mounds of tissue paper, lay several pieces of broken Indian pottery. On a piece of sky blue velvet rested a bouquet of dried wild flowers from the foothills of his country. Pastel blues, corals and pale pinks, soft yellows, white and creams. The leaves and stems were green and rust. She lifted the fragile flowers and hurried to her bedroom, where the empty Chianti bottle had been stored. She smiled. Now she had an excuse to call him and thank him.

She had just finished giving a final gentle touch to the arrangement on her dresser when the phone on the nightstand rang.

"Hello?" she answered breathlessly. "David?"

"Who's David?" It was her sister-in-law calling from the west side of town.

"Oh, Maggie, how are you?" She tried to suppress her disappointment.

"I'm okay, but I'm really worried about Mike and little Danny. That's why I called. Do you think you could come and stay with the twins? We all had summer colds over the holiday. The twins and I recovered, but Mike and Danny are much worse. Dr. Gallen wants us to meet him at the hospital. With their high fevers and congestion, he's afraid it's turning into pneumonia. Sammy, I'm so worried! I can't take the twins with us, and I can't leave them alone. Can you come? I don't know when we'll be back...late, probably."

Sammy thought about David as she looked at the phone. Perhaps she could call him from her brother's house. "Sure, Mag. I'm on my way."

Thirty minutes later she rang the doorbell, and one of the twins greeted her.

"Hi, Aunt Sammy." Christopher, with his blond curls, sky blue eyes and cherub mouth, was her favorite nephew, although she tried not to play favorites. Chris and Amanda were four years old, energetic and very affectionate. He held out his arms to her, and she scooped him up and planted a big kiss on his pink cheek.

"Smooch?" he asked, and kissed her on the mouth. Then he looked sadly at her and said, "Danny and daddy are sick. Momma was crying. Are they gonna get well, Aunt Sammy?"

She gave him a squeeze and returned him to the floor. "I think so, Chris. Let's go see if we can help. Where's Amanda?"

"She's helping momma pack Danny's diaper bag," he replied solemnly. He turned to find his mother and father approaching the door, his sick baby brother in his mother's arms. Sammy held the door as they left.

She diverted the crying twins' attention from their parents' departure, and after several stories, games and tickling episodes, the children settled down and soon fell asleep.

During the next two hours she placed four long-distance calls to the ranch in Montana, but without results. Where was David? He had said he always spent his evenings at home.

At midnight, Maggie called from the hospital to report that both Mike and Danny had been admitted with pneumonia. "Sammy, could you spend the night there? I'm afraid to leave them. I'm so worried. Danny is only eight months old. What if he—"

Sammy interrupted gently and said, "Maggie, now stop that kind of talk. Of course I'll stay with the twins. I'll call Mrs. Green and see if she can relieve me in the morning. I really can't miss work tomorrow, but I'll come back right after five."

After making emergency arrangements with a very sleepy Mrs. Green, she tried once again to call David. Still no answer.

Tuesday was another hellish day of corporate games. Her temper flared several times as she tried to juggle the pressures of work with her concern for her brother and her nephew and puzzlement over David's silence.

Maggie called Tuesday evening from the hospital. Mike had responded to the medication and would be released on Wednesday morning, but the baby had made no change. "He just lies there with his little chest heaving. Oh, Sammy, I don't know what to do. Can you stay again tonight?"

Sammy spent another night at her brother's home with the twins. Each time she phoned David's ranch, a heart-stopping silence ensued. A dark cloud of depression descended over her spirit, bringing fearful storm warnings. She felt as though David had disappeared from her world.

Her brother was released from the hospital and came home to recuperate. Wednesday evening, Sammy went with Maggie to the hospital to see Danny. He was in an oxygen tent, lying in a small pediatric crib.

After consoling Maggie, she went to the small hospital chapel and sat alone in the quiet room, gazing at the altar and stained-glass cross. She thought of the people who were so important to her. David. She loved him very much, but had their weekend been an act of blessed love or just lustful human desires? Her children, now grown. Her brother and his young family. Little Danny, possibly dying only a short distance down the hall. She remained in troubled meditation for more than an hour, then forced herself to leave the sanctuary and returned to Danny's room.

She pushed the door open and stopped, stunned at the

sight of Maggie, Dr. Gallen, a staff resident and two nurses, all crowded around the small tent.

"Oh, my God, he's dead," she gasped. She ran to Maggie, who turned to her with a smile on her haggard young face.

"No, Sammy, he's better. Something wonderful has happened. He's finally responded to the treatment. Dr. Gallen says if he continues to improve, he can be moved to a regular crib tomorrow."

The family physician looked at both women and kindly suggested, then insisted, that they both go home and get some much-needed rest.

Sammy forgot to call David.

Thursday was a pivotal day at work. The two vice-presidents of Mastiff Corporation decided to cooperate. Sammy Roberts and Wes Franklin each breathed a sigh of relief, went to lunch together, then returned to begin planning for the August implementation of the system.

The evening spent with her brother and the twins was a joyful time. If Danny continued to improve, he could be brought home Friday afternoon. Maggie was nearing a state of physical collapse from lack of sleep, so Sammy stayed another night. Her attempts to call David were without success.

The working hours of Friday flew by with hardly a problem. She spent one last evening at her brother's home. She prepared dinner, helped Maggie with some housework and laundry, then read to the twins. After a few hours of quiet conversation and coffee with Mike and Maggie, she was finally able to go home and rest.

David's continued absence became an obsession as she drove through the deserted streets. She had tried to call twice from Mike's house, and again the stomach-twisting tightness returned as she listened to the unanswered ringing at the Montana end of the line.

By the time she arrived home she was nauseated. She was unable to make it to the bathroom and vomited in the kitchen sink. She had never done such a thing before. Thank goodness she was alone.

She quickly cleaned the sink, gargled several times and collapsed on her bed from exhaustion.

DAVID MCCORMACK slammed the telephone receiver down in frustration. "Damn woman! Where is she?" he mumbled as he stared at the phone. He ran his long fingers through his thick dark hair and tried to fathom the possible reasons for being unable to reach her five nights in a row. He frowned heavily as he speculated on her social life in Phoenix and wondered if she dated frequently. If she did, perhaps her response to him was no different than to her other dates. After all, she had been single for several years. She was normal; he'd proved that, hadn't he? No, he decided, she wouldn't lie to him. But she worked in a large corporation with lots of opportunities to meet other career-oriented men and women. He knew how that could be. No, he didn't think she would be the type of woman to use her femininity to get ahead in the corporate world. Of course, a man could never tell, he thought, as he recalled a woman engineer he'd met several years earlier at a west-coast convention.

No, not his Sam. She didn't look or act the type to be

promiscuous, but looks could be deceiving. Of course, she had given him no commitment, and he'd asked for none. He shouldn't assume their involvement with each other to be serious unless he was willing to be straightforward and open with her.

He dropped into a chair and frowned at the silent image on the television screen. He had turned the volume off in order to hear her voice, but that sound had not greeted his repeated effort to contact her.

Since his return to work on Monday, David had been requested by his division vice-president to remain in Butte at the company hotel. Pollution problems at the smelter were proving more difficult to resolve than anticipated, and continuing pressure from representatives of the Environmental Protection Agency to commit the company to build an all-new smelter in the years ahead had added to the morale problem within the engineering department.

Each evening after he finished a late dinner with the other engineers he had hurried to his room and placed a call, received no response and asked the operator to try again later. Maybe she had tried to call the ranch. Other than his two Australian shepherds, the horses and other livestock, the place had been deserted for almost a week. His neighbor, Edwin Russell, was attending to necessary chores for him.

David pushed himself out of the comfortable chair and began to rummage through the hotel-room desk but was unable to locate the usual supply of stationery with the hotel logo. Finally he grabbed his yellow legal pad, clicked his ball-point pen, dropped back into the chair and began to write.

My sweet Sammy,

How does a man explain the impossible? I recently spent seventy-two hours in paradise. Now I find myself sentenced to sixty days in hell.

When I accepted your invitation, I expected a weekend of nostalgia—recounting depression years and World War II stories, recalling childhood memories of two adults who couldn't possibly have anything in common except those memories.

Yet the moment I saw you at the Phoenix airport, I knew there was something special between us that transcended time and distance. I knew that what had begun in our innocent childhood was destined to be fulfilled these many years later.

Why was I so positive when I had just laid eyes on you again? I honestly don't know.

Sammy, I love you and want to have you with me. It's been five days, and already I can hardly stand the loneliness. You, my dear woman, are the delayed fulfillment of all my dreams. Coming from a normally levelheaded, scientifically trained engineer, this sounds very illogical, I suppose, but why do we need to be logical at times such as these?

I was logical when I married my first wife, Mary Anne. We were students at the University of Montana in Missoula when we met. We had a brief affair, then I received a promising offer from Anaconda Company. It meant a move to Butte, and she didn't want to go with me.

A month after moving, I received a phone call from her informing me that I was going to be a father. Being the good guy that I was I married her, and six months later my son, David Alan, was born. Hindsight permits me to see that there was little love involved, just sexual attraction.

We lived together for six years, each year a little worse than the previous. One night, when Davy was six years old, Mary Anne and I had a violent argument. As usual, it was about living in Butte, which she hated, our house, which was not big enough for her, and money...never enough. Before I could stop her she grabbed Davy, both sets of car keys, and drove off in one of our cars, screaming that she was never coming back.

Several hours later, I received a call from the Montana State Highway Patrol. Apparently she had gone to visit some old friends in Missoula, drank quite a bit of alcohol and then decided to drive back to Butte. I suppose it was to have it out with me. About fifteen miles northwest of Butte, she hit a bridge abutment. She died instantly.

It was worse for my young son. He was thrown through the windshield. His left hand had to be amputated, his right arm was broken in three places, and he received a severe concussion. He was in the hospital for three months and had several operations on both arms. The medical bills were staggering, but the company insurance helped, and I sold the house. With the insurance money from her death, I made a down payment on a small ranch just outside of Butte.

Davy was a very resilient little boy and soon bounced back, especially after the casts came off his arms. Like your John, my David is a fine young man. Sometimes I think he's adjusted to his handicap better than his father has, for I still have regrets, but I try not to dwell on what can't be undone. He's now a graduate assistant in agriculture and chemistry at the University of Montana. He thinks he can show his dad how to run a profitable cattle ranch. Some day I'll let him prove it. I love him, too.

Another of my logical decisions involved my second wife. In the sixties, you'll recall, fathers weren't expected to raise their children alone. Davy and I did fine for a year, then some of my friends began to pressure me into marrying again. "To give Davy a mother," they said. "A little boy needs a mother." I met Joyce at a company party, and we began dating. I was thirty-two, and I was beginning to wonder if the years ahead were really as bright as I'd expected.

Joyce acted quite motherly to Davy for a while. Then after we married, I began to notice that she wouldn't touch him. Strange that the very things about him I was most proud of repulsed Joyce. He was nine and loved to play soccer and was quite good at it. His cosmetic hand was a nuisance in soccer. The harness and socket would move during the fast action, and of course the short terminal hook device he preferred to wear in normal activities was a danger to himself and the other players during the physical activities.

I agreed that he could play without the hand during the Saturday games. Joyce thought the sight of a handless arm was disgusting, and she said I shouldn't allow him to play in public. He was the team's star forward, but she refused to go to his games with me. She wanted her stepson to look "attractive." Well, he was to the rest of us...he just happened to be missing a hand.

One afternoon, when he was ten, I came home from work and found him all alone. She had split. She filed for divorce, and I gladly paid the bill. Davy and I discussed the pros and cons of having a woman around the house, and we agreed we would rather do without.

Where were you, love, when we needed you? Sammy, you and your four children could have lived on my ranch, just as we'd planned when we were kids. We were both alone at the same time, weren't we?

The city of Butte had grown by then, and the ranch was prime land for development. I sold to a contractor and used the proceeds to put a fifty-percent down payment on Crest Mountain Ranch. We have matching equities.

My son and I lived alone for the next eight years until he went away to college. I miss him, but if I had to choose between him or you for company, you definitely get my vote.

Which brings me back to you, Sam. I love you very much and would never do anything to hurt you. I've been the victim of mistrust and lying several times, and I know the devastating pain and damage it can cause. I made a resolution a few years ago that if I couldn't be open and honest in a relationship I'd rather not have one. I haven't until I met you.

I want to tell you why I placed that ad in the newspaper. My best friends are Edwin and Julie Russell. He's known as Russ around here. Their ranch is next to mine, but their house is eight miles away. They've been married more than twenty years, have six kids, and I guess the Russells are the family I always wanted. I couldn't do without Russ.

One night I was having dinner with them, and I happened to mention that it gets lonesome out at the ranch. Julie asked me why I didn't just remarry. They know about my past encounters with matrimony. Russ suggested I run an ad. We discussed the possible results of a man advertising for a wife and had lots of laughs. Then Russ dared me to really do it. Who was the bigger fool, Sammy? Russ for daring or me for accepting the dare? Russ knows all about you and is looking forward to meeting you.

He has implied that we need to get to know each other a little better before we do anything rash and he's right, so we will. He says you should have been born a Montanan, but he's wrong there. Sammy, will you make plans to come spend at least a week with me here at the ranch, maybe in early October? I'll buy your plane ticket in Missoula and bring it with me in September.

I know we can have many good years together if

we just don't waste too much time being reasonable and logical. Be rash with me, sweetheart!

> Love me and trust me,
> David

P.S. Don't you ever stay home? I've called each night, and there's no answer. Where have you been?

David mailed the letter in the hotel lobby, then returned to his room. He reached for the receiver again. It was minutes before midnight, but he quickly discounted the lateness of the night. He knew he couldn't sleep unless he tried once more.

FROM THE DEPTHS OF SLEEP, Sammy heard bells. No, they weren't exactly bells, more like a shrill ringing. The phone! David. . .it must be David. She reached for the receiver and shouted, "Hello?"

"Sammy?"

"Oh, yes." Her hand began to shake in relief.

"Sammy!"

In her excitement, she dropped the receiver. It bounced off the nightstand and the side of the bed, then fell to the floor. She retrieved it and placed it securely between her ear and the pillow and said softly, "David."

"What was all that noise?" he asked.

"I was so excited, I turned into a real klutz. Oh, David, I've missed you so much. I've had the most distressful week." Her voice began to quaver.

He chuckled and asked, "Do you want me to wait while you get a box of tissues. You're the cryingest woman I've ever met." He laughed softly.

For several minutes she listened quietly as he whispered sweet love words over the long-distance phone lines. He told her of his week in Butte, and she shared her terrifying experience of fearing for Danny's life. She told him of finding the flowers and what she had done with them. More love words were shared. He told her of the letter already in the mail, and they agreed to write. They exchanged business phone numbers to prevent any recurrence like that of the past week. Sammy agreed on the second week of October for her visit to his home.

"Sammy," he said, "one week ago this night, at about this hour, I made love to you under the diving board."

"Yes," she murmured.

"I wish I could be there with you right now," he said. "I'd do it again."

"David, I love you. I worry a little you'll forget me."

"Sammy, didn't I tell you to trust me?"

"Yes."

"I know, sweetheart, we just need more time together."

"Yes, David."

"And we'll have it, too."

"Yes, my darling."

They were silent as each savored the other's presence, so near and yet so far apart.

"Sammy, it's very late. Are you as tired and relieved as I am?" he asked.

"Yes to both," she said, yawning.

"Goodnight, my sweet Sammy." She heard a kissing sound in her ear.

"Goodnight, David."

The steady hum of the dial tone sounded. She pulled the spare pillow to her bosom and slept.

SAMMY ROBERTS'S monthly period was a week late, but at her age and with the trauma of Danny's illness, she wasn't concerned.

A week later she noticed her breasts were a little tender, which usually indicated to her that menstruation was about to begin. No cause for concern. She would start in a few days. Perhaps menopause was finally arriving. She made a mental note to call Dr. Gallen's office for her annual examination.

Another week passed. Each of the last three mornings she had been slightly sick to her stomach. Between the tensions of Mastiff's systems conversion the past weekend and a flu bug going around in the department, she knew there was nothing to be overly concerned about. The nausea would pass. She needed more rest. She was so tired.

David called on her birthday. "Did you like the gift I sent you?"

"Oh, yes. It was very beautiful," she replied. "How did you know I liked necklaces?" Her head ached, and she could think of nothing more to say.

"Are you all right, Sam?" he asked. "You sound strange."

"I picked up a flu bug at work. Can't seem to shake it. I think I'll call in sick tomorrow and just stay in bed."

"How do you feel?" he asked.

"A little sick to my stomach, a little achy...all over."

"Go see a doctor if you don't feel better in a few days. I want you well for Labor Day," he reminded her.

"I need some rest. I'm so tired after work, I just want to sleep," she said. "I snap at people."

"Take care, love."

"I'll be okay in a few days," she laughed. "I'm never sick for long."

CHAPTER SEVEN

THE MONTANA NIGHTS were cool and beautiful in contrast to the warm dry days of mid-August.

David McCormack knocked on the door of the Russell ranch house. Julie opened the massive oak door and smiled.

"Happy Thursday evening. Come on in, David. Ed and the children are starving and blaming you for their impending demise. I wouldn't let them begin until you arrived."

She took his hat and jacket and hung them in the hall closet. Noisy laughter came from the large kitchen at the end of the hallway. He heard Russ scolding one of the older boys for teasing Mary, one of the younger children.

"Hi, David." They all began to speak at once, voices rising, and his attention was constantly moving from one eager young face to another.

"Okay, kids, now leave David alone for a while," Russ commanded. "The food's on the table. I don't know about you lazy young'uns, but this old dad is hungry after a hard day's work." He served himself from the large platter of meat, then passed it to David, who in turn passed it on. Round and round the serving dishes went as the eight members of the

Russell family performed the nightly ritual of eating together.

David had been coming to Thursday night dinners for the past ten years, and he still felt the same contentment when he was fortunate enough to participate in this event. The Russells were his adopted second family.

After dinner the adults moved into the den, while the children went to their various bedrooms for homework. Next to the family kitchen, this was David's favorite room in the Russell home. The walls were hand-finished knotty pine, and along one wall was a flagstone fireplace. There were two huge windows with a southern exposure on either side of the fireplace. Running completely across the front of the focus wall was a wide platform just right for cats and kids to sit on and keep warm during the cold Montana evenings.

"You were late. Trouble at the smelter or just the ranch?" Russ asked.

David accepted a refill in his coffee cup from Julie. "A little of both. The government paperwork is just unbelievable, and you know about the problems we've been having with that one particular smokestack. I'll be glad when I finally quit next year. I have so many things I want to do at the ranch, and it's frustrating to never have the time."

The conversation turned to families and the two ranches. David's thoughts drifted to Sammy Roberts as he watched Julie and Russ. He wished he had known her at age twenty or thirty or even forty. Why did there have to be so many wasted years? And why this woman, so far away? Would the pain of separation enhance the sweetness of their second reunion? Just two more weeks and he would be joining her again in Phoenix.

His friend's voice brought him back to the Russell den.

"You can't go home until you give us a progress report. What do you plan to do about your Phoenix problem?" Russ asked.

"Russ, it's like this. The second day after I found her again, I considered kidnapping her and bringing her to my mountain retreat, but the lovely lady thinks she has responsibilities in Phoenix. I guess she's right. Now I get a second chance to convince her that maybe those duties aren't quite as significant as she thinks. I've never been a very good salesman. I'll just have to bone up on my Scottish highland charm and bribe her with a plane ticket. Do you think it'll work?"

David's voice didn't sound as casual as his words indicated. Russ studied the tenseness in David's face and his constant fingering of the coffee cup as he spoke. Russ had known David for a decade, and this was the first time he had seen him smitten by a woman. Russ was anxious to meet this person from David's past, but he had his doubts. Was she the right woman for his friend? She came from an alien world, probably unsuited for the rugged ranching life his friend was determined to make his primary vocation in the near future. She was undoubtedly soft...pampered...used to all the conveniences of big-city living. Russ didn't think David could handle another unsuccessful love affair. "I hope so," Russ said. "Keep us informed. If it's right, it'll all work out, but if it's wrong, well...don't push it."

"I want you to bring her to dinner, David. I'm so anxious to meet her," said Julie.

"I accept for both of us. Thanks for the thoughtfulness, folks. Now, quit worrying about me. I'm old enough to take care of myself."

Russ laughed. "I was just thinking about that young woman in town a few years ago who wanted to take care of you in the worst way. She decided you were going to be hers one way or another, remember? What was her name?"

David thought for a moment and said, rather awkwardly, "You must mean that silly waitress, Suzy McCary. She was young enough to be my daughter. She tried to convince me that we had so much in common, that our ancestors were surely from the same part of Scotland. Ha!" he laughed. "I'd rather take a chance with Sammy. She's my age and just right. I hope I can convince her of that. I think my first strategy is to get her up here, then figure out a way to prevent her from getting back to Phoenix. If you think of something that might work, let me know." He stood and stretched his long frame. "Hey, folks, it's mighty late, and I'd better head for home."

Russ walked him to the door. "Take care, my friend. If this Roberts woman is the right one, that's great, but, David, it takes a special woman for this life, so don't be too hasty in choosing someone you might be stuck with for a long time. Good night, David. See you soon."

THE NEW COMPUTER INFORMATION SYSTEM at Mastiff had been accepted by the departments and to celebrate the successful conversion, Wes Franklin had asked Sammy out to dinner. She assumed it would be for all the members of the conversion team, but when she arrived at the restaurant of a new resort northeast of the city, only Wes was present.

"Wes, where are the others?" she asked, puzzled.

"Ah . . . well." Wes stumbled as he tried to explain, then shrugged his shoulders and smiled. "Sorry, Samantha, it's just us. Oh, come on, baby, you owe me this one. It's our victory dinner. We were the brains behind this project."

"But the others . . . they should . . . they had . . . ." She struggled to cover her nervousness.

"Very little to do with it. Just the grunt work . . . besides, baby, you turned on the charm and those vice-presidents swooned at your pretty feet." Wes's smile broadened.

He was six years younger than Sammy. His sandy hair was razor cut, his suits always stylish, and he was vain about his muscular physique. He made quite a production out of his daily trips to the nearest health spa, usually taking two hours for lunch instead of the approved one. Tonight her three-inch heels brought her face to face with his handsome smiling features.

He had been asking Sammy for dates for several years, and she had always refused. Once she had actually slapped him when he had responded to one of her rebuffs with a rather suggestive comment. She recalled his words, "What you need is a good piece of . . . ." He had never finished the statement, for she had stormed out of his office and slammed the door in his face.

Now she paused in thought. There were still two

more weeks before David's visit, and she was tired of being alone. "Since I'm here," she said, "I might as well stay. . . but no funny stuff, Wes!"

The restaurant was known for its prime rib, and she was hungry. The meal was delicious, but as the dessert dishes were cleared and a final coffee refill served, Wes eased his hand across the table.

"Samantha, there's a good film showing at the theater down the road. Would you go with me? I promise to behave." Wes smiled and winked.

"Oh, Wes, I don't think so." She didn't want to hurt his feelings, but he frightened her a little.

He seemed to accept her rejection and escorted her to her car. She had been forced to park at the south end of the resort parking lot, near the seventeenth hole of the golf course. It was dark except for the overhead light near the rear entrance to the restaurant's kitchen.

She had expected an argument or at least an attempt to sway her. He put a polite arm around her shoulder as they rounded the car to unlock her door.

"Key?" he asked, offering to be helpful.

"Yes, thank you, Wes. Here they are," she said, handing the ring of keys to him.

He busied himself at the keyhole, then turned to her. "Sure you don't want to go somewhere with me? We could have a good time. How about just a drink? We could go back to the bar."

"No, Wes. I don't care to drink," she replied, apprehension tightening her stomach.

"Samantha, what's your problem, anyway? Don't you like men?" He stopped his attempt to unlock the door. "Is it girls that turn you on? I've got more than any girl could offer you," he sneered, grabbing her shoulders.

She tried to loosen his hands, but his fingers were made of steel.

"Let go, Wes! This isn't funny!"

"Come on, Samantha, loosen up, baby. It's okay to fool around...have a little fun. I know I can satisfy you." He attempted to embrace her, but she broke away.

"Stop, Wes, please...stop!" Her heart was pounding as he reached for her again. She turned and started to run across the golf green, but she slipped on the wet grass and stumbled as she saw a dark figure approaching. She rolled onto her back and sat up, gingerly touching her knee. It burned, and she felt dampness but couldn't tell if it was blood or moisture from the grass. She must move, fast, or....

Wes was directly in front of her, blocking her view of the car and safety.

"Hey, baby, I like a little preliminary action before the main event. You know, older women really turn me on. You're just a bitch like all the rest. I watch you in some of our meetings, looking at the men. Don't deny it!" He kneeled by her side. "How many years have you been divorced? You must be getting yours on the side from some dude. Every woman needs a man." He laughed. "This'll be good for both of us. We just won't tell anyone at the office. It'll be our little secret. They think you and I are already making it. Now it'll be true."

She tried to rise, but he fell on top of her, pinning her

arms. His wet mouth was on hers, forcing her lips to open. She thought she would gag...she couldn't breathe...the liquor odor...his...hands were everywhere.

One of her arms slipped free. She reached for his face and scratched his cheek, but her short fingernails inflicted minimal damage. He forced his knee between her legs and pushed her skirt up past her thighs as he tugged at her panty hose.

"No, Wes, no..." she cried as his fingers touched her bare abdomen. She struggled, twisting and turning and freed her hand again. She tried to reach his eyes.

"Damn you, bitch," he hissed. His hand had been on her throat, and as he turned his head to avoid her clawing fingers, she felt the burning of deep scratches down the side of her neck from his strong nails.

His wet lips grazed her mouth again, and she was repulsed by his hot breath as he panted from the exertion. "Hold still," he demanded, as he freed her hand and reached for his belt buckle.

David McCormack's face materialized, and she found reserve strength. Her knee! She brought it up as fast as she could, and he recoiled from the sudden pain. It was all she needed.

"Wes!" she pleaded.

"Samantha?" He lay still for several seconds, panting, then slowly stood and murmured in a detached voice, "I'm sorry." He walked stiffly away as though she was not there.

Her sense of panic was rapidly replaced by puzzlement. She stood and tried to rearrange her clothing. Her knees were trembling as she made her way slowly to the car. She found the keys in the gravel by the front tire. She had to use both hands to fit the slender key into the cylinder, and the trembling didn't subside until she drove into her driveway.

A hot shower helped calm her frayed nerves, and as she crawled between the cool sheets, thoughts of David returned. "David, oh, David," she moaned. "Help me. . . I need you."

The next morning Sammy lingered in bed and tried to forget the previous night's encounter with Wes.

Men. They could be such animals! Sammy took several slow sips of hot coffee, then sat the cup down on the nightstand by her bed. As she turned from twisting and reaching, the bouquet of wild flowers came into view. Not all men. David certainly wasn't an animal. Her lips pursed, then she smiled. Maybe there were different kinds of male animals.

Wes Franklin had tried to take her by force, the beast. David, ah, David. . . he had taken her by force, but it had been the passionate force of love, tempered with memories from their common pasts. She had offered little resistance as the weekend had unfolded. It had seemed so right. She touched the gold locket suspended from her throat, her birthday gift from David. The oval case fell just to the swell of her breasts and hung from a fine gold chain. The initials SM had been engraved on its face.

She smiled. When David had called her a few days after her birthday, she had asked him about the initials.

"Well," he had responded, "I had a choice. Samantha Gardner, as I first knew you; Samantha Roberts, as

I found you again; or Samantha McCormack, as I intend to make you and keep you. I just settled on the one I knew you would be carrying for the longest time. Simple, my lovely blue eyes.''

Thank goodness she hadn't worn it last night with Wes. She was sure it would have been damaged or lost. She gingerly touched the three swollen scratches on her neck.

She caressed the locket again, then pushed the thin clasp. The case opened to reveal a small photo and an inscription. The photo was of David and herself. He was kissing her cheek and he looked wet from swimming. The photo had been closely cropped and inserted in the small compartment. Lawrence had taken pictures during the swim party in July, but Sammy had paid little attention. Had David been in contact with Lawrence? She wondered if David had also written to John.

The inscription read: "My Sweet Sammy August 6."

David McCormack. The sound of his name conjured images of strength and character mixed with tenderness, but did she really know him? They had been together for two and a half days, and yet David was so confident, so sure that it was right between them. Why? Was it partly because his two earlier marriages had failed. Had he really told her the truth? She had been upset when she learned that he had been married a second time. It took two to wreck a marriage, she felt, and he'd done it twice. In her own marriage, Jake had been the heavy and she the victim, at least on the surface. She later had to come to grips with the unsettling truth that she was partly to blame for making outside interests more attractive for him than the marriage bed at home.

"Ah, David..." she sighed aloud, and rolling over on the bed, she hugged a pillow and buried her head in its softness.

SHE WAS CAUGHT in a whirlpool. She screamed for help and stretched out her arm. She heard David laughing. A dead infant lay twisted at the water's edge. She screamed again and tried to reach the riverbank. David was laughing—laughing a deep rumbling evil laugh! She called to him, pleading for help, but he ignored her cries. He slowly uncoiled his long body, pointed an accusing finger at her and laughed again, then turned away. She could still hear his deep laughter as he disappeared into the dark forest. She knew he wouldn't return.

She struggled to reach the river's edge, gasping for breath. Her hand touched the infant, and the baby turned to her. Its eyes were tamarisk green and glowing, and it started to cry. She picked up the baby and threw it into the water. She could still hear it crying, crying, crying...why didn't it stop crying? It wasn't her fault it was dead.

Suddenly she sat bolt upright in bed. Her tomcat sat beside her, mewing softly. She slowly realized it had been only a dream, a terrible dream of babies and David. She dropped back onto the bed, trying to regain her composure. Why should a dream upset her so? Her heart was pounding so hard she reached for it with her hand. She felt her left breast unconsciously and wondered at its slight fullness. Her hand slowly moved down across her waist and settled on her abdomen. She knew the reason, even as she denied the obvious.

Her monthly period was five weeks late, but the nausea had gone away. In the quietness of her mind, she thought the unthinkable. A child had been conceived. Oh, dear God! Two nights with David after thirteen years of abstinence. She had never thought of the possibility of pregnancy the two nights David had made love to her. How stupid. Two nights!

Her pulse pounded in her temples as she tried to clear her thoughts. Oh, dear Lord in heaven. What would David say? She wouldn't tell him. He might hate her and she would lose him. She would never see him again. He might still love her and want to marry her right away, but no couple started a family at their age. David Alan was twenty-two and her John was eighteen. No one would understand, but everyone would know what they had done. She could have an abortion. But the baby was David's. He had a right to know. No, he must never know.

Her head was splitting from the pressure, and she closed her eyes tight, trying to shut out all thoughts from her reeling mind. She pressed her fingers to her throbbing temples. Duke mewed again. She sat up and pulled the cat to her, stroking his soft fur. "Oh, Duke, what can I do?"

She closed her eyes and tears of anguish slipped down her cheeks. She would be two months pregnant when David arrived for the Labor Day weekend visit. She was sure that she could keep him from knowing. She usually didn't start showing until well into her fourth month. But it had been eighteen years.

It just wasn't fair. Soon her family would know; her friends would know; her co-workers would know. Some of them had teased her about her righteous behavior. They would surely have the last laugh now.

CHAPTER EIGHT

His big bay gelding nibbled at the drying grass near the outcropping of boulders as David McCormack paused in his return to the rolling foothills. He was still a few miles from the ranch house, but there was no rush. This had been one of the few days he could ride to the high country and enjoy the serenity. Tomorrow he'd be immersed in the problems in Butte, then next weekend he'd take a fast flight to Phoenix.

He had known when he purchased the ranch ten years before that most of the land was good for grazing livestock only. There were some sections of land closer to the house that could be farmed if he had the time and help, but he couldn't afford to hire anyone yet. He had recently started irrigating two meadows, but he was still having problems with that project. He just didn't have enough time to devote to the ranch.

His neighbor, Russ, had turned a comfortable profit at his place when for financial reasons he had made the decision to stop playing full-time cowboy and try a little farming. The cowboy syndrome was hard to break and David agreed with most of the men in the county that nothing could match the freedom of riding and working the open range. Practical wives and family obligations made the compromises necessary.

David threw his leg over the creaking leather of the saddle and eased himself to the rocky ground. He loosened Bay's cinch. Bay snorted and shook his large head. David gave him a few affectionate pats and chuckled. His choice of names for his animals didn't show much imagination. What easier name for a bay gelding than Bay? Even the two Australian shepherds had been tagged Dog One and Dog Two, and then just shortened to One and Two. The rest of the horses were nameless, except for his favorite gray mare, who was registered as McCormack's Gray Melody.

He smiled and sighed deeply. Cold water danced over the rocks in the creek bed as David watched the gelding drink his fill. Two came over, licked his hand and lay down beside him as he rested against a huge boulder. He closed his eyes and listened to the music of the creek. His mind flowed along with the water, and he was thankful to be here—except that one person was missing.

Buying the ranch had been the first step in his master plan toward freedom and independence. When he had negotiated the bank loan he had insisted on a ten-year repayment plan, knowing the financial burden would prevent many additional improvements to the property. But he knew now that the sacrifice had been worth the effort.

His solar generating inventions had made the ranch almost free from outside utility sources, and he was especially pleased about that.

The McCormacks had been in Montana for several generations. They arrived during the middle 1860s by way of Texas and the cattle trails north. David knew the ancestral stories had been embellished in the retelling, but he still found satisfaction and fascination in knowing the origin of some of his traits. The McCormack men had a reputation for following through on their ideas and were willing to work for what they wanted—it wasn't just bullheadedness, as his own mother had often accused him when he was a young child. It helped to know such things, and he was glad. David's love for the land was in his genes, but his appreciation of its bounty had been instilled in him by his uncle.

His rather stubborn determination to accomplish goals had been misread as confidence and sometimes arrogance. He recalled the short period of his childhood he had spent as a Caldwell. That name had never fitted comfortably on his shoulders. He was a McCormack. Sammy's family had given him his first taste of stable family life. Living with his uncle for six years had exposed him to the give and take of several strong-willed boys growing to manhood. His friendship with the Russell family convinced him that large families were special. He liked children, and one of his few regrets in life was having to raise his son without brothers and sisters.

Enough. Regrets over what might have been were time wasters. His future with Sammy was of prime importance now. He had been in control of his life's agenda until their reunion. Would this lovely woman from far away share his priorities?

He rose and stretched. "Come on, Two," he called to his dog. "Let's go home, fella." He tightened the girth, mounted and cantered back to the house, contemplating dinner. He smiled, for his choices were limited. After currying and feeding the horse, he closed the stable for the night and returned to the house. He warmed and ate the canned stew left from the day before, washed the dishes and retired to the living room. He pulled his boots off and wiggled his toes, then wrapped himself in a crocheted afghan, a birthday gift from Sammy, and began to read the latest issue of his favorite magazine, *Simmental Shield*. Someday he was going to have a prizewinning herd of the sharpest-looking, fastest-growing, purebred beef cattle. Someday.

SAMMY HAD TAKEN THE DAY OFF to clean the house. Now that she lived alone, there wasn't much to do, but she knew the hustle and bustle of Mastiff would be intolerable today. David's flight would arrive at 7:14 that evening.

She had just slipped a robe over her damp body after stepping out of the shower when she heard the doorbell ring. She heard tire and engine sounds and glanced out her bedroom window in time to see a yellow cab drive away. She brushed a stray curl from her forehead and hurried to the door, jerking it open. Irritation showed on her face as she impatiently said, "Yes, what is...? David!"

"I couldn't wait." His voice rumbled as he moved his luggage into the living room. "Sam," he whispered. They stood apart, staring and motionless. Her hands started to tremble, and she clutched them to her waist. He slowly raised his hand to remove the same rust Stetson he had worn two months before. He twirled it across the room to a chair, removed his sunglasses and murmured, "Sammy?"

"Oh, yes, David."

She rushed into his arms. He smothered her face with warm kisses, hard then gentle kisses, his lips demanding and inquiring, but always persistent in their return to her responsive mouth.

"You're here, you're actually here," she sobbed. "You're finally here...oh, David! David, do you love me? Really?"

He picked her up in his arms and carried her through the house to her room. There, in the privacy of her bedroom, in a large and empty house, in the middle of the day, he settled her doubts.

She watched as he undressed and turned to her. "Come to me, you lovely woman," he commanded. "I've waited too long for you as it is." He smiled as he eased her closer. She wore a pale yellow, soft terry-cloth robe that darkened her hair and deepened the blue of her eyes. The color gradually returned to her cheeks as she smiled at him, then the smile disappeared. She was hypnotized by his presence as his fingers slowly untied the belt and lightly caressed her soft skin hidden in the shadows of the bulky material. "This has to go," he said, and brushed the robe from her shoulders.

He eased her onto the bed, burying his face in her throat, then returned to her mouth to whisper the words she needed to hear. Her hands moved up and down his ribs as she explored and caressed him, eager to know each sensitive inch of him.

She fondled the soft curls of his dark head as he kissed each rib, lingered momentarily on her slightly rounded belly, then moved on to the soft skin of her inner thigh. "Oh, no, you shouldn't," she cried, but she eased her thighs apart at his subtle nudging and surrendered.

When she could endure no more, she tugged at his head with trembling hands and raised his face to hers. As she listened to his rasping breath near her ear, her body responded to his driving demands, and once again she joined him in a whirlpool of passion. No terror in this swirling sea of movement—only safety, pleasure, satisfaction and David.

SHE AWOKE BEFORE HE DID and waited impatiently for him to rouse. Giving in to the urge to touch him, she propped herself on an elbow and twirled a finger in the dark mat of hair on his chest. He awakened.

She was close beside him, where she wanted to stay. He silently mouthed, "I love you," as she gazed at him, her eyes roaming over his face like a soft mountain breeze.

"This is the first time I've shared your bed," he said. "It was nice. Thanks." His deep laughter rang with joy as he lightly stroked her cheek.

She touched the smile creases near his mouth and fingered the frown wrinkles on his brow, then asked, "How can you be so sure?"

"I just know, Sam. I knew it when I saw you again at the airport after all those years; I knew it when I first made love to you in the pool; I especially knew it when I returned to the ranch and found it empty. I'm complete when I'm with you, Sammy. You're the love I've been looking for all my life."

His green eyes narrowed as he looked at her. "In October, when you come to visit me, I'm going to ask you to marry me. It wouldn't be fair for me to ask you now." A smile tugged at the corners of his handsome mouth. "I want you to see how I live, hear my plans for our lives and our home, meet my friends and know that I intend to leave my job at Anaconda and concentrate on the ranch. I want freedom, Sammy. I want to be free to do and be whatever I choose. I think the price for freedom is risk, honey, but I want you to take that risk with me and share my freedom."

She hesitantly began to nod her head in disbelief as he continued. "Two things have made me complete. One was seeing my son for the first time, the other is you. I only regret that you aren't his mother. That way we could have shared all these years together instead of just a few days, but it's too late for that."

She closed her eyes and returned her head to his chest. How would he react, she wondered, if she told him she was the mother of his child, an unborn, unplanned child. Could this child be part of his plans for freedom? She doubted it.

"Sammy?"

She raised her head and quickly kissed his lips. He held her face in his hands, not allowing her to look away. "Why do you still have doubts? I'd never do anything to hurt you—you must know that by now. Do you love me enough to take chances with me?"

"David, until you came into my life, no one ever loved me just for myself. My husband wanted sex, a cook and maid service; the few men I dated wanted payment after dessert; my children wanted mothering. But you? My mind's all twisted, my brain can't make reason out of what you say. I've always had to do everything myself, and yet now you. . . ."

He laughed. "Try me, just try me. Sixty-day offer at home. Satisfaction guaranteed or I'll return you to Phoenix." He smiled as he stroked her jaw with his closed fist.

"Don't tease," she said.

"Then take me seriously and believe what I say."

"David, I do love you, very much, but I don't see how...."

"We'll work it out. You'll see," he assured her. They rested again.

In the late afternoon, after a leisurely swim, David grew restless. "This is a bonus evening," he declared. "Let's do something different. Any suggestions?"

"Yes. How would you like to meet some other members of my family?" she asked.

"Fine. Who?"

"My youngest brother, Mike, and his family. I think mom was pregnant with him when you moved away. They live on the west side of town. It was Danny who almost died. Mike's wife has been bugging me about who David is. I hope you like kids. They have four-year-old twins. I'll call, and we can take over a pizza. It'll be fun."

As they traveled through the city streets, she glanced at the dashboard clock. It read 7:10.

"David!" she exclaimed.

"What?" he frowned with concern. "What's wrong?"

"Why are you here?"

"You invited me back, remember?"

"Oh," she laughed, "I mean how did you get to Phoenix? This morning. There's only one flight down from Montana each day, and it hasn't landed yet."

"Oh, that." He smiled at her and explained. "I heard a few days ago that Anaconda's corporate jet was due to stop in Phoenix this morning on its way to Dallas. I've taken it before, so I just asked if I could hitch a ride. I know the pilot. I wanted to surprise you."

"What if I had gone to work?"

"I called your office from the airport. I knew you were at home," he assured her.

They arrived at her brother's house and parked on the street to avoid a driveway cluttered with tricycles. David held two aromatic pizzas as Sammy rang the door bell.

The door opened wide. Maggie stood in the entrance, flanked by wide-eyed blond twins. She smiled. "So. This is David. . . . Do come in."

The pizza was gone in no time. Danny was put to bed by his father as Maggie served coffee in the family room.

The twins gradually warmed to the strange man with their favorite aunt and accepted his presence. David sat on the love seat, holding an inquisitive Christopher on his lap.

"What's your name, son?" David asked.

"Christopher Adrian Gardner, or just Chris. What's yours?" he asked.

"David Edward McCormack, or just David," he replied, smiling at the boy. "How old are you?"

"Four." Chris held up the appropriate number of fingers. "How old are you?"

"Just past forty-six."

"Wow, that's old," Chris declared. He examined David, then touched his shirt front, looked down at his own small T-shirt and frowned. His lips pursed, then spread wide as he exclaimed, "Wow! You're big. Are you a cowboy?"

"I'm too big and old for a cowboy. I guess I'm a rancher."

"What's that?" Chris asked.

"That's the fellow who owns the ranch and cows and tells the cowboys what to do."

"Wow," Chris said again. "Do you ride a horse?"

"Sure do, young man. A big brown one. His name is Bay," David told him, glancing at Sammy as she held Amanda on her own lap. Amanda had her blond head nestled on Sammy's bosom, her small thumb in her mouth, as she listened to her brother and the man talk.

Chris's eyes roamed over David, then he lightly touched David's biceps through the sleeve of his yellow-and-lime-green Western-style shirt. "Are you strong?" he asked.

"I think so. You have to be strong to live on a ranch."

"Are you Aunt Sammy's boyfriend?" he asked, and Sammy laughed.

David replied, "I'm too old for a boyfriend. How about a future husband?" Sammy gasped.

"What does a husband do?" Chris asked.

"Well," David began carefully, glancing at Mike and Maggie, then at Sammy, who raised a slender brow in question. "Husbands are men who marry women they love, so they can live together and share things." Sammy's hand slipped over to rest on his pant leg as he continued. "So he can protect the woman and take care of her and give her nice things, all because he loves her.

Like your mother and dad, I imagine.'' He lowered his eyes and smiled at Chris.

Maggie sighed. ''That was beautiful. Sammy, I'm so happy for you. When? Where?''

''We. . .we have lots of things to resolve, Maggie,'' Sammy replied. ''We need time. . . .''

''You see,'' David added, ''we have this problem. We live a thousand miles apart. But we'll work it out, won't we, love?'' he asked as he leaned over and kissed her.

Chris tugged David's shirtsleeve and regained his attention. ''Do you have a little boy?''

''I used to, but he's taller than I am now. He's all grown up,'' David explained.

''Will you and Aunt Sammy have a baby like Danny?'' Chris asked.

''Chris, you ask too many questions!'' Maggie cried, concerned over Sammy's sudden loss of color.

David laughed. ''That's okay, Maggie. Sure, Chris. We could, but we're a little old for that. I'm sure we won't. It doesn't matter. I just want to have her as my wife, because I love her.'' He gave the little boy a gentle squeeze.

''We do, too,'' Chris assured him. Chris studied David for a few minutes, then declared, ''I think we like you, David.''

''Thanks, son. I feel better knowing that I have your stamp of approval.''

SATURDAY, DAVID AND SAMMY played tennis, went paddle-boating, walked the paths of a city park and talked. That evening he took her to an elegant dinner at the Compass Room, overlooking the city's nighttime brilliance.

Sunday, they slept late, enjoyed coffee and lunch by the poolside, then swam and played in the water until the sun began to sink behind the house in the pink western sky.

David was stretched out asleep on a blanket near the picnic table, but Sammy felt restless and her turbulent mind brought doubts again. Would they really get married? He had said he didn't expect them to have any children. Did that mean he didn't want one?

She placed her hand on his broad muscular back and absorbed the steadiness of his deep breathing. His skin was cool from the swimming, and she laid her cheek lightly against him. He had said that her back was smooth as satin. She thought his was more like rough velvet, tough and strong, yet gentle and soft when stroked the right way.

Her thoughts were interrupted as he moved. He turned onto his back, looked up at her and smiled a sleepy grin.

"Did I bother you?" she asked.

"You always bother me," he murmured.

"Oh, I'm sorry, I . . . ."

"You bother me because your nearness arouses me—" his voice hoarsened "—and I want to strip you . . . and admire your beautiful body. It's a woman's body, full and mature and responsive . . . and I can't get enough of it, Sammy. I don't think I ever will."

He reached behind her and untied her string top. It fell away. She collapsed beside him, hiding herself, and he laughed as he rolled her over.

"David, it's still daylight," she protested. "Someone might see." But she began to smile as he kissed her collarbone.

"You're wrong, love. The fence is high, we're surrounded by trees and shrubs, and it's almost dark. No one can see, but if they want to peek, we'll give them a show. Do you care, sweetheart?" His mouth had worked its way down her arm and was nibbling at the crease of the inside of her elbow.

She trembled as he kissed her navel. "No, not really...it's none of their business, is it?" She let him loosen the side tie on her bikini bottom.

"Mmmm, you smell good...fresh...sweet," he said as his mouth lingered on a pale blemish marring the skin just below her rib cage. "How'd you get this scar?" he asked.

"I don't remember. I think I was a teenager and went tubing on the river," she replied.

"I wish I'd been with you. I'd have saved you from injury." His lips moved on to a pale brown mole just under her left breast.

"Stop," she said, pushing on his chest. "Lie down," she whispered, and he fell back. She sat up beside him as he lay still, staring at him and trying to understand her own mood.

"David, I find myself doing things with you I'd never dream of doing with anyone else. You bring out a side of me that I didn't know existed."

She frowned. "I want to undress you and touch you and...even make love to you. David, is this right?" Her hand remained motionless on the snap at the waistband of his new swim trunks.

He reached for her hand. "It's right, Sammy. Whatever we do, willingly and together, is right." He released her hand and pulled her down beside him. As he gazed at her, he said, "If you're not sure, we can wait." His dark brows furrowed. "Do you want to wait?"

"No, David, no. I couldn't bear the thought of not having you. It's just that you arouse me so and bring out.... What happened to Miss Prim and Proper me?" she pleaded.

"Since I've never met her," he said, kissing her throat and feeling her racing pulse, "I hope she's gone forever." He nibbled his way to her shoulder and glanced at her. "She sounds like a real drag. I want the woman I have now." His mouth lowered to hers in passionate union, and her hands unsnapped the elasticized trunks surrounding his hips.

Later he murmured against her ear, "This is even more erotic than making love to you in the pool... and a hell of a lot easier." His deep laughter surrounded her in a blanket of warmth.

"Yes," she agreed, letting the essence of him calm her into slumber.

They spent the night out under the stars in the privacy of her enclosed backyard, near the pool where they had first known each other.

Once during the night she awoke to find his arm and hand draped across her abdomen, its slight roundness impossible to conceal. She thought of the infant conceived two months earlier, and her predicament weighed heavily on her again. Perhaps he would reject her if he discovered the pregnancy. She knew this was not the time or place to tell him, and she carefully turned onto

her side. His arm slid to the curve at her waist, and the
pressure was removed.

Somehow, she'd work it out and decide later what to
do.

Monday they parted again, her secret safe and un-
shared.

SAMMY HAD POSTPONED the appointment several times
and finally kept it only because of the impending visit to
Montana.

"Sammy, why didn't you come to me earlier?" her
doctor asked, a fatherly disapproval sounding in his
voice as he helped her sit up. She tucked the paper gown
around her body.

"I know I'm eleven weeks pregnant. I have no doubt
when conception occurred," she assured him cynically.

"Sammy, there are certain risks for both a mother
and her unborn child for a woman your age," Dr.
Gallen said. "Fortunately, your medical records are
still in my files. Your previous pregnancies were rather
uneventful, as I recall. It's been a few years, hasn't
it?"

She nodded quietly.

He snapped the disposable gloves off his hands and
she jumped, her nerves frayed. "Easy, now," he said,
frowning at her. He tossed the gloves into the trash can.
"I'll be right back. You can get dressed." He patted her
shoulder and left the examination room.

She hurriedly dressed, wishing she were far away. Dr.
Gallen was a long-time family physician for the Gardners and the Roberts. Would he understand? Would he
keep her secret? His return interrupted her thoughts. He

was carrying a small book and several sheets of printed material.

"I want you to take these and read them before your next visit. Write down your questions so you don't forget them. Because of your age, Sammy, I want to see you every three weeks. Since you aren't having any problems, just continue your current life-style. Avoid heavy lifting or strenuous exercise." He paused. "Sammy, does the father know?"

"No."

"Are you going to tell him?" he asked.

"Yes."

"When?" he persisted.

"Soon, when the time is right."

"Do you love him?"

"Very much," she answered.

"Will he marry you?"

"He wants to, but will he if he knows about the baby? He has so many plans for us and I'm afraid—" Her voice broke. "Dr. Gallen, please don't tell anyone what's happened. I'd just die if anyone found out...."

"Sammy, you know I don't gossip. I leave that to my patients. What happens in my office is confidential. I'd fire any nurse or other employee who violated that confidentiality. I feel very strongly about that."

She dropped her head and nodded her understanding. "I'm sorry I asked. I knew you wouldn't...I just... I...I just don't know what I'm going to do...he might not...he...."

"Sammy, I've known you for a long time. I can't believe you'd fall for just any bum passing through. He must be special if you love him. Take care now, and I'll see you in three weeks.''

"Better make it four and a half," she smiled. "I'm going to visit him out of state the second week of October. I'll be gone for a week."

"Well, tell him before he finds out for himself," he reminded her.

"I will," she said.

"Time's running out, Sammy," he said, as he escorted her from the room. Putting his arm around her shoulders, he walked her down the hallway and gave her a reassuring squeeze. "Goodbye now, and have a nice trip."

CHAPTER NINE

As THE JET BEGAN ITS DESCENT into Missoula, Sammy tried to absorb the vast breathtaking view.

David had told her that the snow never melted on the high peaks. A light blanket of white lay on the middle ranges. She saw patches of yellows and reds but couldn't tell if the leaves were still on the trees or not. David had said the first snow of the season had already fallen at the ranch but had melted within a few days. He had also assured her not to worry about warm clothing.

"We'll go shopping in Missoula for a mountain wardrobe for my little desert rat from the sun country."

The plane's wheels screeched as they made contact with the runway. The patches of white flashed by the window as she pressed her forehead against the insulated glass. She felt intoxicated with the excitement of actually being in his world. Except for the impending announcement of the child, she was deliriously happy.

She heard the pilot announce, "The temperature in Missoula is a warm forty degrees with a low of twenty-one predicted for tonight. No snow expected for a few days. Enjoy your stay in the Big Sky Country."

She was so anxious to see David that she rushed down the aisle and was the first person to leave the plane. He must have known, for he was at the front of the crowd.

He wore a gigantic smile when he saw her, and she had the same feeling of coming home again as he embraced her.

He smiled and picked up her small suitcase. As they moved through the airport lobby he gave her shoulders a squeeze. "First we're going to have lunch with my son, then we'll shop for your winter wardrobe. I have some definite ideas about what you need. You're in my care up here. In Phoenix you can always shed clothing when it gets too warm. Up here if you don't dress right it can kill you. Then we'll drive to the ranch. It's about two hundred miles." He stopped abruptly. A frown settled over his face, and his eyes riveted onto hers as though he could read her mind. Did he suspect her secret?

He whispered in her ear, "I don't know if I can stand four hours on the road with you without stopping and making love to you along the way." He kissed her ear.

"David, hush...you embarrass me. Someone will hear." But she was overjoyed. She took his offered arm and, holding tightly to him, felt the first blast of frigid air on her face as they left the warm lobby and headed for his truck.

They met his son outside a restaurant near the university.

"Dad, Sammy's as pretty as you said she was." His son shook her offered hand, then leaned forward and kissed her cheek. He was slightly taller than David, slimmer, the way she imagined David had been when still a young man. He had his father's facial structure and rust-flecked green eyes, but his hair was blond. It was curly and hung just past his shirt collar. He wore wire-rimmed glasses and looked quite academic. Under the bulky knit green sweater he wore, she could sense the muscles and strength he had inherited from his father. He seemed quite at ease, even when her eyes moved to his left hand.

"That's okay. Dad said you knew, but I wore my hand, just in case it might bother you. Let's eat."

He escorted them inside the rustic building. It looked like a weatherworn ancient barn transplanted from a mountain ranch to the bustling city, slightly out of place nestled between a modern bank branch and a savings-and-loan association's chrome-and-glass structure.

The restaurant was noted for its cowboy steaks, and it lived up to its reputation. As the waitress served the dessert and refilled their coffee cups, Sammy looked from David to his son.

A grin was tugging at his son's wide mouth. "Is it true that you're going to be my new mom?"

David smiled broadly as Sammy turned to him in surprise. Her blue eyes were huge as she silently pleaded for him to speak up.

His son broke into light laughter. "I'm sorry," he halfheartedly apologized. "I couldn't resist. It wasn't very tactful, I suppose, but I see such a change in my father since he found you again. He was beginning to act like an old man, and now he's received a new lease on life. Do I embarrass you, dad? It's true, you know. You have changed." He touched David's hand, excused himself and headed for the men's room.

David kissed her lips and said, "Don't be upset. He doesn't know as much as you think he does. He just knows I love you very much and plan to marry you. Is that right?"

"Yes, your persistence has worn me down," she smiled, her soft blue eyes sparkling with excitement. "What is our agenda for the week, darling?" she asked.

"Tonight we're going to be all alone at the ranch. Tomorrow we have a dinner date with the Russells. The third day I plan to show you the ranch...and then the special plans. We're going up to an old rider's line shack that I use sometimes for trips into the high country. I've fixed it up a lot, and it's quite comfortable. There's a stone fireplace, and I've cut a winter's worth of firewood. I drove up last weekend and stocked it with some special provisions. There's not even a telephone to disturb us. Do you think you can stand being marooned with this ravished timber wolf for a few days?" he asked, kissing her again. It was a slow, suggestive, warm, lingering kiss, just as his son returned.

"Um, excuse me, folks. Maybe I should go away again."

Sammy pulled away and said, "Please, David, sit down. Goodness, there are too many Davids. How can I distinguish between you."

"I'm the one who kisses you like this," David said, and he attempted to give her another example of his technique.

"Why not call me D.A.," his son suggested. "That's what my friends call me."

They chatted about his position at the university for several minutes. David glanced at his watch and said, "We really must go, son. I want to buy Sammy some warm clothes before we start home.'' He began to move from the comfortable booth.

They stood in the parking lot saying their goodbyes. Sammy smiled as she watched the open display of affection between David and his son. D.A. gave Sammy a hug and kiss and said lightly, ''Bye, mom.''

He laughed again, then said more seriously, ''When you two finish playing around in the woods, come back to Missoula and visit for a day or two.''

Farewells were exchanged again as they climbed into the truck. She turned to David and said, ''I like him.''

''I thought you would,'' he replied with a hint of parental pride. ''Let's go shopping.''

She was amazed at the length of his shopping list as he guided her through the departments of the store he had chosen. He purchased a fleece-lined long leather jacket that matched his own, a sky-blue hooded parka, two pairs of boots for cold or wet weather, several pairs of thermal underwear and woolen socks. She tried to stop him, but he insisted on adding three sets of slacks and sweaters to the growing assortment of items.

''David, you're overdoing a good thing. Please stop.'' She laughed.

''We're almost finished,'' he assured her as they headed for the exit. Suddenly he changed directions and routed her to the ladies' apparel, where he insisted, over her embarrassed objections, on buying her a beautiful white fleece robe, matching slippers and a nightgown of the sheerest material in the palest shade of blue she had ever seen.

''It's so revealing, why bother?'' she whispered, pleased.

"I want the privilege of removing it," he answered, kissing her again as the sales clerk returned with his change and receipt.

The long drive home took them through the back country, down the Bitterroot Valley. They drove for miles by a river that meandered from one side of the roadway to the other.

"The rivers," she tried to explain, "they run so fast . . . and they all have water in them!"

"Good grief, Sammy, that's what rivers are for," he laughed.

"Not in Arizona, my dear," she replied. "Our rivers, creeks and washes are usually bone dry. These are nicer." She stared in admiration out the window at the racing stream of water.

They stopped for a snack at a roadside rest area, and David talked about several historical points of interest, including Lewis and Clark's trek over the area on their way to the Pacific shortly after the turn of the nineteenth century. He pointed out Chief Joseph Pass, named after the great chieftain of the Nez Percé Indian tribe, and later showed her the area known as Big Hole Battlefield and told her all about the battle between the cavalry and Indians that had taken place there many years earlier.

"I didn't know you were a history buff," she said.

"There's a lot of things you don't know about me, Sam. I just hope you'll think they're mostly good as you discover them. Do I know all about you?" Before she could answer, he continued, "Of course not! We've spent a total of seven days together since childhood. Now we can have a lifetime."

The time was tender. This was his country. Phoenix seemed in another world, and she wasn't sure if she ever wanted to return. The last thing she remembered was a road sign showing a highway number and a mileage sign.

She awoke as they bounced over the drainage ditch culvert leading to the ranch yard and was startled as she saw two large Australian shepherds lunge at David and bark noisily.

"Down, One! Down, Two!" he commanded. "Now shut up, you hounds. Come and meet your new mistress."

DAVID MOVED QUICKLY into his kitchen, catching the outside door with his boot heel before it collided with the wood frame. He had been to the stable and broken the thin layer of ice on the horse trough, fed the dogs and surveyed the breaking dawn. Brilliant fuchsia rays streamed through the clouds, trying to bring light to the new day. He had inhaled the frigid air and felt its invigorating effect rush through his veins.

He shed his jacket, then stomped and removed his boots. His wool socks made a soft sound on the seasoned wood floor. He had left Sammy curled like a kitten in the warm space their bodies had made in the bed.

He began to prepare breakfast, and soon the smells of coffee perking and bacon sizzling filled the air. He wondered if she liked biscuits. With one hand he pushed the coffeepot to the back of the stove, with the other he gathered the bacon strips into a stack and dumped some chopped potatoes into the bacon drippings for hash browns. Scramble the eggs, stir the hash browns, check the biscuits, get jam from the refrigerator. Does a woman have three hands when she cooks? His meals were usually simple affairs, but this was special.

As he passed the small mirror near the sink, he saw a darkly stubbled face looking back at him. He noticed the white mixed in the reddish beard. Was he getting old, he wondered? His face was still lean and tanned, but the sun was leaving its mark in the squint wrinkles around his eyes. He supposed it was from the long white winters. The gray at his temples, no longer just a touch, was gradually winning the battle to replace the auburn of his youth.

He pushed the skillets of eggs and potatoes to the rear of the old stove, humming softly as he worked. He'd better plan on replacing the stove if Sammy agreed to live with him. Part of his plan to keep her. The smells from the kitchen were probably drifting throughout the house.

The biscuits looked golden brown and mouth-watering as he placed them on the table. Everything was ready, everything except his face and the sleeping woman in his bedroom down the hall. Hard to believe, but she was the first woman to sleep in this bed. For some unknown reason, he'd never brought a woman to this ranch. When he had become aroused by a woman and things had worked out to a mutually agreeable arrangement, they had gone to her place, or simplified everything with a neutral motel room. Other than a woman during his son's high-school basketball career, there had been very few since he'd moved to this town. Of course, there had been Nelda, but just a few times. Damn, Nelda was fun, but just a little kinky. He laughed aloud. He knew he had the right woman now!

As he steamed his beard for shaving, his mind was full of jumbled thoughts. Images tarried, then were swept from his brain to be replaced by new and different ones. Here in his bed was a woman out of his childhood who had given herself to him last night with such passionate feeling that the fervent force of their union had left them visibly shaken when reality brought them back to the room. She had tried to explain, but his kiss had stopped her. "Hush, love, I understand. I feel it, too, you know."

He smiled as he thought of the sheer blue gown. It had remained on her beautifully mature body for just about sixty seconds before being discarded and forgotten.

A thought flashed through his mind. Had she put on a few extra pounds since he had first seen her? Her breasts had filled his hands more than he remembered, and her waist felt a little thicker. Maybe she'd gained weight; he didn't care—just more to love. He smiled. "Ouch!" he hissed, as he nicked his cleft chin.

He finished his shaving, splashed on a few drops of after-shave, and pulled the sink plug. *Food's going to be cold if I don't hurry,* he thought as he flipped off the light and walked quickly to the bedroom.

He opened the door softly and looked across the room. She was still sleeping. Easing his body to sit alongside her, he gently kissed her slightly parted lips and said, "It's ready, love."

For a few seconds she was frightened, not knowing where she was. She must be still dreaming, because there he was, David McCormack from her past, leaning over and kissing her.

"Oh, my David, my childhood friend, my love. After all this time, am I really here?" Her arms moved with a will of their own and encircled his neck. The goosedown quilt was a barrier of insulation, preventing his burning touch from reaching her warm body.

"To hell with breakfast," he mumbled as he raised the blanket. "It can wait."

An hour later, Sammy stretched contentedly and tried to cover a yawn. "Breakfast is ready, did you say?" she asked.

"It's cold. Are you warm enough?" he asked.

"With you next to me, I'll always be warm." She crowded closer to him.

His hand moved under the covers, stopped at various spots to caress and linger awhile, then moved on. Suddenly his hand passed over her abdomen, moved on, then returned. She stopped breathing as his palm and fingers grew hotter, burning into her secret. She closed her eyes and turned her head away.

He was about to tease her that she was getting her own belly when the truth of her condition seared through his wandering thought patterns. His hand moved to her rounder breasts and returned to the gently swollen mound, where he now realized his own child lay.

He was speechless with disbelief. As the full realization soaked in, he gathered her closer and held her tightly. "Oh, Sam," he whispered, nuzzling her curly head. He closed his eyes, trying to sort out his emotions.

His heart had been pounding, and as it settled down he propped himself on his elbow.

"Look at me, Sammy," he insisted.

She refused. He turned her face to him and saw the tears sliding from her closed eyes.

He kissed her moist cheeks and asked, "The first weekend?"

"Yes."

"Why didn't you tell me?"

"I was afraid. I didn't believe it at first, then I was afraid you wouldn't return." She broke into sobs and clung to him. His strong, protective arms held her, and he stroked her hair, her shaking shoulders, her bare arms.

"It's okay, it's okay, honey. Go ahead and cry," he said.

She told him of the terrible dream about the dead baby and David laughing and leaving her. She told him of her fears of discovery by her family and co-workers, the unbearable gossip and taunting she knew would follow. She shared the irony of the long abstinence after her divorce and then said how right she had been all along, since the first and only time since the end of her marriage she had succumbed to sexual intercourse had been with him, and just look what had happened. She looked up at him through her tears and saw him smiling.

"You just picked the right fertile cowboy to mess around with, didn't you?" He laughed and kissed her long and hard, then eased the pressure to a massaging gentle caress. He looked down at her again and said, "I think it's fine."

She frowned. "But what of your plans—us, the ranch, your plans about quitting Anaconda? I'm sure you didn't count on this. What will our children think?'' She burst forth with an abundance of obstacles until he finally stilled her mouth with his.

''I said it was fine, Sam. Better than that, it's great.'' Suddenly he groaned.

''What?'' Fear that he had thought of an objection struck her and the doubts swelled again.

''The breakfast—I forgot all about it.'' He eased the comforter away and reached for their robes. He dressed quickly, then held the white robe for her as she slipped her arms into the sleeves. He tied the sash around her waist, patted her abdomen affectionately and said, ''I think we'll have to warm everything up a bit. It's been two hours since I cooked it. Do you like biscuits?''

''Don't you have a microwave oven?'' she asked as they strolled to the kitchen.

He stopped abruptly and frowned at her. ''You're in the rugged wilderness, woman. Don't you know that we get our electricity from the nearest currant bush?''

He broke into lighthearted laughter at her puzzled expression. ''I'm teasing, Sam. I suppose we could get a microwave, maybe a new range, too. Would you like that?''

They reheated the meal and ate quickly. She helped with the dishes, then they lingered over a final cup of coffee. He wouldn't take his eyes off her.

''You look very lusty, David, in spite of that dignified gray.'' She smiled.

''Now that you've proved it, I must confess. . . it's true,'' he replied.

''Do you really think it's going to be all right?'' she asked. ''It's been a long, long time for both of us. Maybe we won't know what to do.''

"Sam, if this is the biggest problem we ever face in our marriage, life together will be a breeze," he assured her.

"But we're not married. You haven't even officially asked me," she reminded him.

He reached across the table, took her hand and looked intensely into her eyes. "Miz Samantha, now that ya'll are goin to have ma baby, would you do me the honah of marrying me?" he asked teasingly.

She tried to pull away, and he knew he had said the wrong thing. He held her hands tightly. "Sammy, I'm sorry, I didn't mean to tease. I just feel so damn good about the whole situation, I could do handsprings like a kid. Let me try again, please." He paused and started over very seriously. "Sammy, I love you very much. Would you do me the honor of becoming my loving wife, having my child and living with me for the rest of our lives?"

She frowned and asked, "Really?"

His exasperation slipped through as he sighed and said, "Yes, damn it, I mean really. Now will you?"

She still hesitated. "Ye. . . yes. . . I will."

"Good."

He studied her for a moment and suddenly pulled her from her chair. "Let's go riding; I'll show you the ranch."

"David, I haven't been on a horse in years."

"Let's go riding."

"David, I don't think I could sit on a . . . ."

"Let's go, Sam."

"Oh, David, do you. . . ?"

"Let's go." He gave her a gentle push toward the

bedroom. They hurriedly dressed and raced each other back to the kitchen. He grabbed her arm, and she fell against him as he reached for the jackets. "It's cold outside. Bundle up! Wear the gloves and your new scarf and cap, too...wear the boots." He shoved a battered tan Stetson on his head and soon had her warmly dressed against the icy morning air.

Outside he held her face in his gloved hands and brushed her lips with his. Their breath made small clouds between them, and they laughed together, filled with exuberance. He put his arm around her shoulders, gave a squeeze and pointed to the stable.

"There's a beautiful little gray mare in there, just right for an old lady like you, sweetheart."

Sammy looked up into his green eyes. Was he joking? Did he think she was old? They were about the same age, but didn't men in their forties prefer young girls in their twenties? After all, hadn't Jake?"

David stopped. "Sam, what is it?"

She unconsciously brushed the patch of gray at her temples. "Nothing," she sighed.

"Sam?"

"I guess I'm just embarrassed about the baby, being here and all. You'd think at my age I'd know better than to get myself into such a predicament."

He stepped off the path, the icy grass crunching under his boots. She jumped, and he grabbed her shoulders, forcing her to face him.

He peered down at her. "You're beautiful, do you know that?"

She shook her head in disagreement.

"Sammy, I love you. I loved you when we were kids,

and I love you now that we're in our forties. I want to love you when we're in our eighties, and can't even make it to the barn. Do you understand?'' He touched her cheek and drew her to him. "I love you, honey, that's all there is to it.''

He reluctantly released her, and she took his gloved hand in hers. "I'm sorry, David. I keep looking for trouble. Now, where's that old gray mare you think I can stay on?''

The dappled gray mare was a beautiful half Arabian. David made the introductions. "She's eight years old and has foaled three of the sharpest colts you'd ever want. Her sire was an Arabian stallion from Scottsdale, Arizona, and her dam was a quarter horse I owned. My friend, Jonathan Ryan, owned the stallion and was visiting here on his way to a horse show at Missoula. They spent three days at the ranch. I guess that stallion took to the mare the way I took to you, Sammy. During the second might he broke into the south pasture where the mare was, and this beautiful piece of horseflesh is the result. Come to think of it, it was their first time together, also. Her name is Melody. That's short for the longer official name of McCormack's Gray Melody. She's yours, love.''

As he saddled the mare and his gelding, he turned to her. "The riding won't hurt you, will it?''

"No, the doctor said regular activity was fine. I'm more concerned about soreness. Let's just take it slow and easy the first few times.''

They rode to the foothills and stopped by a creek. He showed her the major points of interest near the ranch and helped her get a feeling of directions. The sky was rather overcast, but the temperature had warmed to the low forties. She missed the sun and found she needed it to get her bearings.

"Where's the cabin we're going to visit?" she asked.

He pointed in the direction that she thought was southwest. "Those mountains are the Blacktails. They can get pretty nasty later in winter, but it's early yet for the heavy snows. We'll probably get a few inches, just enough to make it beautiful and cozy in the cabin." He paused to allow her time to enjoy her new surroundings. "I'll take my ham radio in case we have any problems. Russ has a radio, too, if we have to call for help. We'll probably never use it."

He looked at his watch. "It's almost two. We have dinner at six with the Russells. We'd better head back and get cleaned up."

He turned to help her remount. "Are you okay, Sam? You don't look like your usual self," he asked with a frown.

"I'm okay. I have a touch of indigestion, I think. That big breakfast, then this riding that I'm not used to. I'll be fine," she assured him.

"Maybe it's those biscuits. They weren't the lightest," he said.

The mood brightened as they rode back to the house, and Sammy began to feel more comfortable in the saddle and accustomed to the gaits of the mare. She knew the discomfort would go away once she returned to level ground and a solid footing.

THE RUSSELL CHILDREN were on horseback, riding double, waiting for the dinner guests at the entrance to their ranch. The house could be seen in the distance, about two miles farther down the tire-worn roadway.

David waved to the children and applied the brakes, gradually pulling the truck to the side of the dirt lane. Sammy watched his face as he acknowledged the greetings from waving hands and arms and the shouts of laughter.

"Lisa, why don't you, Tim and Mary climb into the back of my truck, and I'll give you a ride to the house," David suggested with a smile wide enough to split his face.

The three younger children yelled in agreement, slid down from the broad rumps of their older brothers' horses, and climbed into the truck bed.

"We're ready," they shouted in unison.

David called to the older boys, "I'll race you to the house."

"You're on," the youngest of the teenage boys shouted, as the three reined their horses around and raced off, their mounts kicking up small clumps of mud splatter and gravel.

David squeezed Sammy's hand and said, "You'll love them. They're like my second family." He pressed the accelerator, and they moved down the rut-filled lane, just fast enough to give the youngsters a pleasant bounce, but slow enough to let the horses stay in the lead.

Sammy turned once to look at the children, saw Lisa point to Sammy and watched from within the cab as silent lips formed unheard words. Three heads turned to stare at her; Mary's enormous brown eyes held a questioning look under her raised slender brows, Tim frowned, and Lisa had a look of apprehension and uncertainty on her fair features. They continued to stare at Sammy until she smiled. Three young faces slowly smiled in return, and the mouths began to move silently again. Had she passed their test, she wondered?

Confusion reigned as they pulled into the circular drive in front of the rambling porch. The three older boys were waiting with their horses tethered to the porch rail.

A stocky, ruddy-faced man waited on the porch steps. His boots and lower pant legs were mud splattered. His eyes were hidden beneath the wide brim of a worn black felt hat, but Sammy had an uncomfortable feeling that he was staring at her side of the truck's cab. The woman beside him wiped her hands on a flour-soiled apron. She looked a few years younger than Sammy and about the same height, but Sammy found her appearance a picture of contradictions. Her slight plumpness added a roundness to her pretty face, giving her a youthfulness that belied the fact that she was the mother of six children, the oldest already a young man. Her caramel brown hair was long and pulled back into a matronly chignon, but curly tentacles had worked their way loose to frame her warm hazel eyes and rosy cheeks. Sammy quickly decided that this woman was warm and friendly, feminine and maternal and devoted to her husband and family.

If this was David's friend, Julie Russell, Sammy felt sure she'd like her, but the hidden eyes of the man on the porch concerned her. He was still frowning while the woman now smiled.

As the truck stopped, David jumped from the cab and quickly lifted the three children from the truck, then moved to Sammy's door and helped her down the steep step. The family's blue heeler barked, a tabby and three kittens were soon underfoot, and a large gray goose honked and nipped at Sammy's pant leg.

"He's Abner," Lisa volunteered, tossing her pigtails out of her way as she skipped around Sammy and the goose. She had her mother's caramel brown hair and sapphire blue eyes, which sparkled when she laughed at the goose's antics.

"He's very pretty," Sammy replied, and bent to stroke Abner's head and long neck.

Lisa giggled as the goose lost interest in Sammy's leg and waddled off. "I'm Lisa. You have blue eyes like me, don't you? My daddy says he doesn't know where my blue eyes come from. Momma says they came from the blue sky. Did yours come from the sky, too?" She waited expectantly for Sammy's answer.

"I think your mother is probably right. Are you Lisa?" she asked. "David says you're the youngest."

Lisa smiled and said, "Daddy says I'm his baby, but I'm not. I'm already nine. Are you David's new... friend?"

"Yes," Sammy replied. "My name is Sammy Roberts. Can you help me meet everyone?"

"Sure, they're just my brothers and my sister, but they're all older than I am." Lisa took Sammy's hand and led her to the three young men and made the introductions.

"That's Paul. He's the oldest and meanest. He's always mad. He's nineteen. This is Russ, Junior. His name is really Edwin...isn't that a funny name? He's seventeen and sometimes he helps me. This is Steven and he's fifteen and I hate him. He's always teasing me.''

Lisa pointed to the two remaining children. ''That's Mary. She's thirteen and my only sister. Steven says she's ugly and skinny and a runt, but I don't think so. I like her. And this is my brother Tim. He's eleven and I like him, too. And that's all! Hey, everyone, this is Sammy. She's David's new friend.''

A round of greetings was exchanged and Sammy looked around for David. He had moved to the porch to join Russ and Julie. She heard laughter and words being exchanged in the shadows of the house. She looked at Lisa and asked, ''Who are those two grownups?''

''They're my mom and my daddy. Do you want to meet them, too?''

''I think so,'' Sammy answered. As she was escorted to the porch, she felt a premonition that the testing had resumed at a more significant level.

She climbed the few steps to the porch platform as David turned to her, smiled and held out his hand. Confidence returned as his warm strong fingers encircled hers. He drew her close and pressed a kiss to her temple. He whispered softly, ''Relax, sweetheart. You're doing fine. They're probably just as nervous as you are. I love you, you know.'' In a louder voice he said, ''Julie, I want you to meet my dear friend from Phoenix, Samantha Roberts. Just call her Sammy.''

Julie smiled and took both of Sammy's hands in hers, gave her cold fingers a gentle squeeze of reassurance and said, ''Welcome to Montana, Sammy. David has told us so much about you. I've been dying to meet you. I'm glad to see the kids and animals didn't bother you.''

"Not at all. I've four children of my own, although they're all grown. We always had a few pets around. My brother has three preschoolers." She looked around. "I think you must have a perfect place here to raise a family."

Sammy and Julie chatted a few minutes. Julie's face glowed as she discussed her children, and Sammy confirmed her first impression of the younger woman. As she listened to Julie, she sensed a pair of eyes burning into her. She turned slowly and found the source of her concern as she met a piercing pair of deep brown eyes staring at her from under a dark and heavy set of brows. For an instant she felt threatened, then David spoke. She heard no words of the greeting as Russ continued to glare at her.

Russ listened to David while glancing down Sammy's body, taking in her tailored slacks and bulky-knit pale pink sweater. She was definitely city, he concluded from his quick appraisal. Soft, in spite of her tan; probably used to having things done for her. Yes, definitely soft.

David shifted his attention from Russ to Sammy and back to Russ. "Hey, aren't you two going to speak? Sammy, are you...?"

Sammy brushed the concern from her mind and offered her hand.

Russ hesitated, then reluctantly shook it, discounted its firmness and quickly released it. "Welcome to the Russell ranch, Mrs. Roberts. Shall we go inside?" He held the door as they entered, a frown still on his dark ruddy face, his husky shoulders rigid and unyielding.

In a matter of minutes, David and Sammy found

themselves alone in the den as Julie returned to the
kitchen, the children went to their rooms for predinner
cleanup, and Russ hurried to complete a forgotten chore
at the barn.

"David, he frightens me. I know he doesn't like me. I
don't think he approves of us." She touched his arm.

"Now, Sam, that's not true."

"He called me Mrs. Roberts," she said. "He said it as
though I'm an adulteress for being here with you. I
don't think I like him, either."

David turned her to him and held her chin, shaking
his head in disagreement. "Russ is just not as outgoing
as Julie. He's my closest friend. He's six years younger
than I am, but sometimes he tries to give me fatherly advice. He thinks we haven't known each other long
enough, but I know he's wrong on this one. He'll
change his mind when he gets to know you. I think he's
probably already trying to figure out how the man-
stealing woman from Phoenix could like children and
animals. He's stubborn, but when he finally changes his
mind, you'll find that he's the most loyal friend a person could ever want."

"I do hope you're right. I don't want your best friend
as my enemy." She moved from the sofa and he joined
her, embracing her with reassurance. She attempted a
smile, but it quickly faded. "I think I should go help
Julie in the kitchen. I feel better about her. Can you
show me the way?"

"Good idea. It's this way." He led her to the large,
pleasant kitchen. The aroma of baked ham and warm
mince pie filled the air.

Sammy's mouth watered, but the lingering burning

in her stomach had returned. Just indigestion and tension over meeting David's best friends, she assured herself.

The meal went more smoothly than Sammy had anticipated. Russ had little to say and always directed his comments to David, but Julie went out of her way to make Sammy feel part of the group.

The children bombarded her with questions about Phoenix and her own four children, and finally Lisa, in her nine-year-old innocence, came forth with the question she and Mary had discussed in their room during their cleanup. "How much do you like David?"

"I love him, Lisa," Sammy replied. She had spoken without hesitation but now wanted to withdraw the response as she glanced quickly at Russ and saw his intimidating frown.

The younger children giggled, and the older boys snickered. She reached out under the table to David, and her hand came into contact with his hard thigh.

He patted her hand, leaned his head to hers and kissed her cheek. She heard the two young girls sigh in unison.

Spoons and forks were suspended in midair as David tapped his water glass and paused to capture the attention of all at the table. A cup clinked as it was hastily returned to its saucer. Feeling the suspense growing, Sammy turned to him as he cleared his throat.

"Russells, pay attention now. You're my very favorite family in all of Beaverhead County, and I want you to be the first to know. Not only do I love Sammy very much, but this morning I asked her to become my wife...and...she said, yes." All eight pairs of eyes were on the couple as he continued. "I was going to save this until later tonight, but I might as well do it in front of witnesses."

He reached into the inside pocket of his leather vest and removed a small case. He slowly opened it, knowing they were all staring. He took a ring of white gold containing an oval-cut solitaire diamond from the case, held it up for all to admire and said, "Thank goodness for royalty payments."

The facets sparkled as he brought the ring down and turned to Sammy, reached for her hand and asked, "May I?" Without waiting for a response, he slipped it onto her finger and whispered, "This ring is only half the bargain. Let's complete the other half of the transaction as soon as possible." In a public voice, he asked the group, "Approve, folks?"

The Russell family broke into applause, and even Russ, Senior had a slight smile on his previously somber face.

CHAPTER TEN

"WHAT'S THAT?" Sammy asked, pointing to the unusual structure a few hundred feet from where David had parked the blue truck, the first stop on his promised tour of his ranch property the following day.

"That, my dear, is the source of my ever-increasing financial independence. That strange little building houses one of my inventions that I've been meaning to tell you about. You're going to marry a multitalented man, do you know that? The royalty payments enabled me to finance our two rendezvous in Phoenix, buy most of your new clothes and purchase that little piece of glass on your left hand." He looked very pleased with himself as he turned in the cab and faced her. He eased his right arm along the back of the seat and lightly stroked the back of her neck with his long fingers.

Sammy touched the unfamiliar ring on her finger, wondering momentarily what all the people in Phoenix would think. What did it matter if they approved or not? This decision was for David and her to make, wasn't it? Besides, with the pregnancy no longer a secret, his proposal was definitely the best solution.

Her hand brushed against her slightly rounding abdomen as she thought of the unborn child. She was now well past three months and had added a few inches in her waist. Her increasing size had been a concern for her each day as she had dressed for work at Mastiff. She glanced at David as he reached across the space separating them and placed his large palm on her belly.

"I hope it's either a girl or a boy," he said, a grin tugging at the corners of his mouth.

"Oh, David." She laughed. The burning sensations had gone away during the night. It had been indigestion, just as she had thought.

David opened the cab door and helped her down. "Let's walk." He steered her away from the cab. "I'll tell you about my invention." They walked to the small building, which was located next to a small turning windmill and a full livestock-watering tank. David removed the padlock on a narrow door.

"It sounds more complicated than it really is. I got the idea shortly after I bought the ranch, when an old generator that was my primary source of electrical power was on its last leg. It's sort of a combination of wind and solar power. It also provides just enough heat to keep the water thawed when the weather is below freezing. Like most of my inventions, it makes me wonder why I took so long to think of it. There are solar collection panels near the top of the windmill, and a series of solar rods bring the heat and energy into the storage cells inside the housing unit. I figured out a way to store the unused energy from both the solar heat on sunny days and the wind energy on windy days, so it can be held in reserve and used on cloudy and still days. The unit's very versatile and can be built in many different sizes. This is a small one, since its purpose is to pump water to keep this stock tank filled. There are deer and other wildlife around here, too, and they benefit from the consistent water supply.''

He paused a moment, like a teacher waiting for questions from a student. ''I built a much larger unit that serves the house and barn. I still keep the old generator in running condition, but it's more for security than for actual use. When I first bought the ranch, Montana Power service wasn't available. Although it's this far out in the country now, and I'm wired for it, I prefer to stay as independent from public utilities as I possibly can. I'd rather sell to them,'' he said.

He looked at Sammy questioningly, and she nodded her understanding. ''I plan to install one at the line shack soon,'' he continued. ''Russ has a unit serving his house and is adding two smaller ones next summer out on the range. I sold the use of the designs to a manufacturing firm in Billings and a public utility in Wyoming. That's where the royalty checks come from. I have a patent attorney in Missoula who is negotiating with another firm in Utah. He's a friend from my university days, and I trust him.''

He was silent for a while, deep in thought, and Sammy felt excluded. She reached out to touch his arm, wanting to be a part of his thoughts.

He smiled. ''Damn, that's too serious. If I hadn't majored in engineering, I probably wouldn't have been able to think of it. Let's see some more of the country.''

Sammy surveyed the land around the water hole. The rolling hills were covered with straw-colored grass, which appeared lifeless after the nightly freezes. Small patches of snow abounded. She knew that next spring, when she brought forth a new life, this country would be bursting with fresh sweet green grass and an abundance of rainbow-hued wild flowers.

In every direction from the yellow rangeland she saw small herds of Herefords in the distance, their white faces like mime masks. Above the rolling foothills the mountains rose in deceptive ease and simplicity, but as she tried to put the tall pine trees in perspective with their background, the mountains became awesome in magnitude. The greens darkened as she studied the higher elevations. David had named the trees, but the words of lodgepole, larch and ponderosa were mixed in her mind. The dark greens changed to hazy blues, darkening to deep purples and patches of naked gray rock, then softening to white as her vision moved to the snowcapped peaks.

"These mountains could kill you," David had said. She shuddered, torn between appreciating their breathtaking beauty and being frightened by their potential danger. David had lived in this country most of his life. She would be safe with him.

Soon they were driving down the winding road on their return to the house. The truck bounced over a deep rut, and she clung to the door handle, trying to suppress the burning pain that raced through her then vanished, leaving her gasping for breath.

David frowned but didn't turn to her. "What's wrong?"

"Nothing," she assured him, and in an attempt to divert his concern, added, "God bless slow cookers." David looked puzzled. "Remember the one Julie gave you last Christmas?"

"How did you know?" he asked.

"She told me about it last night, so while you were at the barn this morning, I looked for it. Shame on you for not using it before. I found it and filled it with chunks of your own beef, potatoes, carrots and a can of green beans. When we get home, my lustful fertile husband-to-be, you'll have a delicious homemade beef stew with a pan of slightly lighter biscuits than you served me yesterday. Then you can decide if you really want to keep me around on a permanent basis."

During the meal they discussed the ranch, the cattle herds, the business records and David's plans for making the operation a financial success. He confirmed that he saw no reason to change any of their plans because of the baby. Hadn't she told Julie last night that this area was a perfect place to raise children?

As he served himself a second helping of the thick, aromatic beef stew, he looked at her and announced with a smile, "I'll keep you. You and that pot make a good pair."

SAMMY TIED THE BELT of the soft white fleece robe snugly around her waist as she left the steamy bathroom and reentered their bedroom. Her hair was damp from the shower and lay in soft ringlets against her head.

She looked at David stretched out on the bed. His blue robe was loosely tied, his long legs showing below the hem. His feet came almost to the end of the quilted spread. He lay with one arm behind his head on the pillow, the other arm draped across his waist. He looked like a satisfied lion after a full dinner, his rusty brown mane contrasting with the white pillowcase.

Would his desire for her slacken as time passed, she

wondered? Would the newness wear off? Had he been this way with other women? Thoughts and images of David and his past life rushed through her mind as she stared across the room. She couldn't ask him about the other women he had known. As virile as he was with her, she was sure he hadn't lived a celibate life, but the thought of another woman in his bed sent pangs of jealousy through her, and she frowned.

He remained motionless and silent, watching her, seemingly waiting for her to take the initiative and come to him. What did he really want of her? She walked to the large bed and sat beside him, carefully tucking her feet beneath her.

His hand slid through the opening of her robe and came to rest on the inside of her knee. Her blue eyes now had a look of intensity, and her damp dark hair contrasted sharply with the white robe.

His green eyes were the color of wet tamarisk needles. His hair was still damp from his shower and reminded her of rusty bark as she studied him.

"We must talk," he said.

She tensed. "What about?" She frowned, for she had expected his lovemaking, not his questions.

"Us." He didn't smile.

"Do you want the ring back?" she offered, her confidence evaporating.

"No, of course not, Sammy. I just want to talk. I want to know you better. Can I tell you a story?" he asked, his voice warm and soft.

"Of course," she said. The last thing she had expected was a story hour. She could feel her cynical side taking control.

"About one hundred twenty miles northeast of here is a place called Three Forks. It's the headwaters of the Missouri River, but it doesn't begin with a spring as so many mountain rivers do. It's really the merging of three smaller rivers. Do you remember the creek we rested beside yesterday? That was the Blacktail. It empties into the Beaverhead near Dillon. The Beaverhead joins the Big Hole and then becomes the Jefferson."

She frowned and expressed her puzzlement. "David, I didn't expect a geography lesson. What are you trying to tell me?"

"The three rivers, Jefferson, Madison and Gallatin, coming together and forming a new river is like our lives. I think we have three levels of existence, Sammy. Our rational selves, our sensual selves and our emotional selves. These three parts of our personalities merge and make us what we are."

He moved his hand on her soft inner thigh but didn't seem to be aware of the effect it was having on her senses. She tried to concentrate on his words and ignore his fingers.

"I know you're an emotional woman. Didn't I tell you once you were the cryingest woman I'd ever met. It's true and I love it, but I think you still have doubts and try to hide them. Sometimes I think you still expect me to be playing a game. I'm not."

His eyes roamed her face. "I guess for us so far we've been the most successful on the sensual level, Sammy." He moved his hand to her cheek and brushed away a single tear as it moved down her cheek. "Don't cry, sweet blue eyes, this is the good part," he said as he wiped her eyes with a dry tissue.

"Sammy, I want to know what pleases you; I want to know what you don't like. I want to tell you what I like and dislike. Why should we endure years of displeasure just because we can't share our feelings with each other? Do you understand what I'm trying to say, Sam?"

She knew her voice would fail. She moved to him and lay quietly beside him for several minutes, her hands and arms around his neck and her face buried under his chin, trying to organize her thoughts. She felt his warm breath against her face as he kissed her forehead and the top of her drying curls. His arm tightened around her shoulders as his free hand massaged the small of her back. She withdrew from his embrace and sat upright alongside his supine body. His eyes narrowed slightly as he watched her.

She sighed. "May I speak?"

"Of course, that's what this is all about, sweetheart."

"David, no man has ever asked me to tell what I really thought or felt before. There was one man who came close, but nothing like you. This is very hard for me. I've kept most of my feelings hidden. I learned over the years that it was much safer that way. So let me try to tell you how I feel, but be patient. I'll probably cry."

He propped himself in a more upright position on the bed and took her hands in his, then released them when she pulled away.

"Since we're here on the bed and I thought you were going to make love to me..." she began. David's lips silently formed the word *soon*, "...I'll start with S-E-X. My first sexual encounter was such a disaster I couldn't even tell when it was finished. I was eighteen. It was in the front seat of the boy's car, parked out on the desert. I believe he convinced me to go all the way by using the 'You wouldn't buy a pair of shoes without trying them on' sales pitch. Obviously, the shoes didn't fit properly. All I felt was pressure and pain. All he did was press, poke and pant.''

David began to laugh, and she continued, ''It does sound rather comical, doesn't it? So much for the wonderful world of sex for a while. We broke up right after that, and I dated a lot but never seriously. Then I met a young man at college. Our relationship rapidly developed into an affair and lasted two years. He opened a new world of intimacy for me and taught me what giving and receiving were all about.'' She stopped and stared at her tightly clasped hands.

''Next there was my husband. I think I married Jake for protection. The breakup of the two-year affair was devastating because it was so unexpected. When I met Jake shortly after the breakup, I needed a hiding place. I thought I found it in marriage. Jake thought he was very macho, and I didn't care. Do you know that in nine years of marriage I never had a satisfying sexual experience? I soon grew to hate it. It was nine years of hell, David.'' She tried to smile, but the memories were still framed in pain, hurt and disappointment.

''It wasn't all hell, really. I did have four sweet children, although they were a little too close together, but the pregnancies gave me an excuse to not have sex with Jake. Oh, David, I must sound terrible.'' She looked at him and found his face unreadable.

''Go on, Sammy,'' he prompted.

''The marriage broke up because he was fooling around with a young friend of mine. I threw him out, and he was glad to go. He thought the kids were a drag on our freedom. There was a long period when I avoided men. One day I read that article in the newspaper. People at work were talking about it and making fun of it. I don't know why I decided to write. I never expected to hear from you. Then you answered my letter, and you know the rest.'' She paused, frowning. ''I was really shocked that night in the pool to find that after all those years, I could respond to you as I did. I assumed that I'd dried up like a prune.''

''Even a prune becomes sweet and delicious when someone gives it tender loving attention and care, Sammy.''

She touched his face and gave him a light kiss. When he tried to embrace her, she stopped him. ''I'm not quite through.'' She patted his chest. ''Patience, my lion.''

A trembling sigh shook her. ''You asked me to tell you what I like. Goodness, David, everything you do to me makes me want more. You bring out responses in me that I didn't know I was capable of! There's just one thing. I'm ticklish, especially...afterward...you know. Oh, David, you embarrass me,'' she exclaimed, collapsing against him.

Before he could react, she sat up again and said, ''Okay, mister, now it's your turn. You started this discussion.''

He laughed a deep, rumbling roll and his eyes twinkled. ''Okay, here goes.'' His hand slid through the front of her robe and rested on her thigh again. ''I tend to be ticklish, too, but I guess I'm a toucher, and I like to be touched...all over. The feel of your cool fingers excites me beyond belief. Remember that first night in your living room, when you cried and made my shirt all wet? I remember your hand was on my chest, and your fingers were caressing my skin. I was about to try to make love to you on the spot if you didn't stop touching me. I knew there was something special between us then and confirmed it the next night in the pool. Sammy, neither of us tried to resist each other that first weekend, did we?'' He searched her face. ''Don't ever be ashamed or embarrassed when we're together, Sam.''

He smiled and her heart lurched. ''You know, I expect to make love to you for the next forty or fifty years, and I think I'll start now!'' He grabbed her and threw her on her back across the bed and kissed her. She wriggled and squirmed beneath him and their robes opened to allow roaming hands to enter. She moaned with pleasure and returned his movements with caresses of her own.

The fires were out of control, stoked to an explosion point. He murmured strange words to her, but she understood. She repeated them to him, and a new language was born. Each plateau of excitement and delight was replaced by another higher plane, until neither could continue, and they let their passions burn to cinders.

CHAPTER ELEVEN

THE PICKUP WAS LOADED with extra firewood, a box of food, extra clothing and an emergency first-aid kit. David had called Russ early in the morning to remind him of their trip to the high country. Sammy had tugged at his elbow and whispered, "Julie knows, Julie knows," but he had brushed her aside with a kiss.

The sky was overcast. Three inches of snow had fallen during the night, but the sky was predicted to clear in the afternoon and remain clear until the weekend. They would be home by then. They planned a day in Missoula with David's son, then Sammy's return flight to Phoenix at the end of the week would conclude her visit.

They had had a disagreement during breakfast over her return. David wanted her to stay longer, but Sammy tried to explain her obligations. "I can't just walk away from them, David. I don't have a job, I have a career. I worked very hard to get where I am at Mastiff. I'm the only one who can wrap up some of the loose ends and train a replacement. David, it's important to me. And my house, there's the mortgage, and—"

David had interrupted her. "Sam, I'm only asking for another week. If you were sick, they'd do without you."

"No, David, I can't," she'd replied firmly, and he had worn a scowl while loading the truck.

They hadn't set a definite date for the wedding. Perhaps Christmas. She would be five and a half months by then and conspicuously showing.

As he finished packing the truck, she tried to make amends. "David, sometimes this all weighs very heavily on me." He kissed her, but the silent concerns remained strong in her mind as thoughts of her career and financial responsibilities fought with the pregnancy and her love for David.

The temperature outside that morning had been a crisp twenty degrees and would be warming to thirty-eight, the weather report had stated. The coldness settled on her, filtering through her parka to chill her heart and soul, numbing the slow burning in her body.

David had told her the weather could change suddenly in the Northern Rockies. He had made two calls to his meteorologist friend in Helena. "Only fools and strangers predict the weather in Montana, love," he said. His friend had forecast definite clearing. The blue patches of sky enlarged as the day passed into midafternoon, then receded slightly as the afternoon wore on.

They traveled through a wonderland of powdery white snow and stopped often to admire the scenery. The trees on the mountainsides were like small furry green toothpicks erupting through a lopsided white frosted cake. They arrived at the cabin as the shadows lengthened and the mountains to the west grew dark. As they finished unloading the truck, the sun sank behind the western snowcapped peaks, and darkness arrived with an alarming abruptness.

Julie had packed a large basket of fried chicken, homemade bread and a freshly baked apple pie and delivered it to Sammy the evening before. As David prepared the fireplace, Sammy laid out the dinner in front of the stone hearth. They ate by firelight and talked into the early fall night.

They decided to remain by the fireplace in down-filled sleeping bags rather than warm and use the bedroom of the remodeled shack. They zipped the bags together, and as Sammy lay enjoying the tranquility and stillness of the moment, she began to accept the possibility that David had been right when he had tried to explain to her that sex was secondary to love in their relationship. It had been after the previous afternoon's lovemaking, and she had reminded him that he definitely wasn't practicing what he was preaching.

"I just wanted to show you the difference, my love," he had said.

Tonight she understood. His steady breathing and his close warmth were bringing serenity rather than excitement to her troubled soul.

THE MORNING was clear and frigid. The outdoor thermometer registered eight degrees. The wind had blown the powdery snow into intricate patterns of lacy filigree during the night. The snow felt dry when Sammy touched it. She and David stood on the porch and watched a small herd of deer foraging for food in a nearby meadow, but the air was painfully cold to breathe and they returned to the warmth of the cabin.

"Look what Julie loaned me," she said, surprising him with a fireplace popper and some popcorn. "If you'll make the hot chocolate, I'll pop the corn." He agreed and disappeared into the small kitchen. As she leaned near the crackling flames, she suddenly felt a resurgence of burning pain in her lower abdomen, and she was forced to admit that it wasn't indigestion. When the cramp subsided, she prayed for continued relief. She didn't want to spoil David's plans with sickness.

They snacked and talked of many things. David smiled and said, "Last night I was thinking of our own little boy or girl toddling through our lives. It's even more than I'd hoped for, Sam. I know I'm selfish, but I wish you didn't have to go back to Phoenix at all."

She shook her head. "But I must. You know I can't stay." The painful cramp shot through her again, and she paled.

"What's the matter, Sam?" he asked. "You've lost all your color."

"It's nothing. I'm fine." She smiled. "Have some more popcorn? Let me refill your mug. Your hot chocolate is delicious."

The discoveries they were making about each other were limitless. Thirty-four years of missing lives and experiences couldn't be covered in a day or a week, perhaps not in a lifetime, he reminded her. She detected a hint of bitterness in his voice.

As the afternoon changed into evening, she made more frequent trips to the small bathroom. She returned from the third trip, and David asked, "Sam, what's the matter. You look like you've lost all your color, but your cheeks are rosy."

"I...I'm not sure," she stammered. "I feel almost crampy, as if I'm trying to start a period. I'm spotting a little, just a little. Maybe if I stay off my feet, it'll go away."

He scrambled up to help her. He made a comfortable place for her on the old sofa. She felt warm to his touch. He called Russ on the radio and asked for an updated weather report. He had been concerned since early afternoon when he noticed a gray, solid cloud mass moving in from the northwest.

"It doesn't look too good, David," Russ said. "They've issued a blizzard warning for livestock for tonight and tomorrow with up to six inches of snow."

"Where the hell did that come from?" David barked.

"Hey, hey, friend, take it easy. The weather boys in Helena predicted it would hit here during the weekend, but it looks as if it moved in much faster than anticipated. Is everything cozy up there? Having fun, hey, buddy?" Russ asked.

"Sam's a little sick, but she says it's nothing serious. I just don't know. I'll call you tomorrow for another update. Damn, I hope it clears soon," he said and signed off.

Sammy lay dozing on the sofa. David went to the window and peered into the darkness of the evening, then returned to her and shifted a chair beside her. Perhaps he should wake her and head for home. Thoughts of driving the winding mountain trail in a blizzard as well as darkness made him rule out the idea.

He turned quickly when he heard her moan softly in her sleep. She turned onto her side and drew her knees up. Was she in pain? Had she understated her problem for his benefit? What did he really know of pregnancies? Damn little, he admitted. What if her problem grew more serious? What could he do to help?

He moved from the chair and began to stalk through the small cabin, trying to shake out the tension in his body and relieve the burning in the pit of his stomach.

The cabin definitely wasn't equipped for long-term visits by people who expected comforts and modern conveniences. He had remodeled the former line shack slightly the first two years on the ranch, then gradually added the bedroom, along with the bathroom and chemical john, and moved in enough furniture to make it livable for times when he or his son had felt the need for privacy and mind-clearing meditation. They had named it their Therapy Shack one afternoon when D.A. had returned from a visit to it after a heated disagreement with his father over marijuana smoking.

He returned to the chair and found her awake. He kissed her lightly as she said, "I didn't mean to sleep all evening. What time is it? Nine o'clock? Oh, you must be hungry. I'll fix something." She made an attempt to move, then stopped, collapsing onto the pillow.

"Sam, what's the matter?" David grabbed her hand.

"Nothing...I just felt...lightheaded," she assured him. Something was wrong, but she wasn't sure just what. The pain had lessened. She had to distract him from the room. "Could you get me some hot tea, darling?" she asked.

As he left the room, she slipped on the white robe and hurried to the small bathroom, not knowing what to expect, but fearing the worst. She heard him return to the room and called to him, "Could you bring my luggage, please?"

A hand materialized through the small door opening,

and a tense voice asked again, "Are you sure you're okay?"

When she returned to the room, David had placed two steaming mugs of cinnamon tea on the low table near the fireplace. He looked up as she joined him. She smiled softly as she noticed he was wearing the bulky sweater that she had purchased in Missoula during the few minutes he had left her alone.

"A thank-you for all the nice clothes you gave me," she had said. It was ecru and knitted in an Aran design. The soft cream color contrasted sharply with the rusty brown and gray of his dark head as the firelight and shadows flickered across his face. He looked older, with lines of concern showing on his ruggedly handsome features.

"I feel better," she answered his unasked question. "How's the weather?" She sipped the tea, inhaling the pleasant aroma. "This tastes delicious."

He studied her and saw the soft blue eyes of the little girl from his childhood in the face of a mature woman whose personality continued to puzzle him. The years had seasoned her beautifully. The chubby cheeks of childhood, gradually evolving through the lean and taut structure of young adulthood that he had been deprived of knowing, were being softened and gentled once again, as though the Master Sculptor had not finished the design.

"Your face is almost as white as your robe," he said, but she gave no response and continued to sip the tea. "Sammy, I feel. . . at a disadvantage. Level with me, please. I want to know what's happening to you. If it's minor, fine. We'll just enjoy the privacy and let the storm blow itself out. We have plenty of firewood and food, but if you get worse, I've got to know what to do. It's you and me and our child, Sammy, and it frightens me.''

She had never heard him speak with such concern. His physical size had always given her a reassuring sense of strength, power and security. She accepted his offered embrace and tried to explain what had happened. When she finished, she said, ''Just hold me, David. I need you.''

HER SCREAM jerked him out of a heavy, troubled sleep. He scrambled from the sleeping bag and moved to the fireplace, where he had made her a bed using the mattress from the bedroom and extra blankets. He threw the covers aside and drew back.

''Oh, my God.''

The beautiful white robe was heavily stained with blood. He reached for her, but she screamed again. ''Don't touch me. It hurts!'' She moaned, rolling slowly from side to side, and pulled her knees up, seeking relief. She cried out, ''David, I hurt. Make it stop.'' Her eyes pleaded with him. ''Am I going to die?''

David tried to remain in control. ''Be still, love. I'll help you as best I can. Be still now. I know it hurts. Let me clean up a little. You'll be more comfortable.''

She lay motionless, her eyes following him. He had no idea how serious her condition was as he worked quickly to help her. She was warm to his touch and slightly flushed.

''I'm going to call Russ,'' he said when he had finished.

JULIE RUSSELL slid the tray of chocolate-chip cookies into the hot oven just as the ham receiver came to life. It was probably David asking about the weather again. She smiled, thinking how nice it would be to be marooned with Russ, all alone for a few days in the mountains, without six children. Lucky Sammy and David.

"Russell ranch," she said into the microphone.

"Julie, it's David." His voice came over the receiver as a shout, and its loudness alarmed her.

"David, wait." She stepped to the kitchen door and shouted down the hallway, "Russ, come quickly. It's David and something's wrong." She quickly returned to the radio set. "I'm back," she said.

"Julie, it's Sammy. I think she's having a miscarriage. My God, Julie, she needs a doctor. She's resting now, but I don't think it's going to get any better. Get me help, Julie," he pleaded.

"The weather is terrible, David, and now the bureau says the blizzard is going to continue for two more days. Wait, Russ is here. Talk to him. We'll help you somehow."

She listened to Russ's conversation as he attempted to get facts about the situation in the mountains as well as relay weather information to David.

"David, getting a doctor to the cabin is impossible until the weather breaks. We'll call Dr. Morrison in town. Hold on while I have Julie use the phone. Calm down and get control."

As the answering service patched her through, Julie removed the cookies from the oven and said a silent prayer for David and Sammy. She had become quite fond of Sammy. Her thoughts wandered to David's trips to Phoenix, and she found a new understanding for him.

Dr. Morrison was on the line, and a three-way conversation about medical information followed.

David's voice came through the speaker, crackling with disappointment and sadness as he signed off.

"That's rough. I hope he can handle this," Russ said to Julie, shaking his head. He joined Julie at the kitchen table and accepted a cup of coffee. "Damn it all, Julie babe, why didn't that woman stay in Phoenix where she belonged? I certainly don't want anything to happen to her because of David, but I knew she wasn't the type to ever adjust to this country. She belongs in the city."

"Russ, don't say those things," Julie replied, laying a cautioning hand on his dark muscular forearm. "He loves her."

"Shit, that doesn't matter, Julie. She's soft, just as I suspected. You know I think the world of David, but I feel sorry for him if he insists on staying involved with that Roberts woman. He's going to regret it. She's just a damn bit of cotton candy fluff."

"OUR BABY IS DYING," Sammy said. The finality of her blunt words twisted like a sharp knife in David's chest.

"Yes."

"Why?"

He was numb. She continued to search his face for an answer.

"Sammy, I don't know why. If I did, don't you think I'd turn back the clock and change everything? Maybe there's something wrong with the baby. Maybe the horseback riding I insisted you do caused it, or maybe the bouncing in the truck. Maybe I loved you too much.'' His voice broke, and he lowered his face. His shoulders shook with grief. His face was hidden in his hands as she reached out from the bed and touched him.

"It's not your fault, David.'' She paused, pain reflected in her pale features as another contraction worked its path to completion.

"It's mine,'' she said, closing her eyes and breathing heavily from the burning pain in her body.

"Sammy, no.''

"Yes, David. Even though I love you, what we did was wrong and I know it now.'' She closed her eyes. "I enjoyed it, I encouraged you, but it was wrong. My dream told me the baby would die, and I refused to admit it. Yes, I loved you too much, and I'm being punished and the baby is going to die. Maybe I'll die, too.''

The listlessness of her words frightened him, then filled him with anger. "Sam, you're wrong. I can't believe God would punish a man and a woman for loving each other. God wouldn't kill a baby created from that love. You're wrong, Sammy, you're wrong.'' His words were interrupted by her cry of pain.

The contractions began again, stronger, closer. She knew she would die if the pain didn't stop. "David, help me,'' she pleaded. She clung to him, terrified.

"Sammy, it's about over. I love you, honey. Baby, don't leave me—I need you. Oh, my God, Sammy,'' he cried. He watched helplessly as her face contorted with pain, and she convulsed with a final contraction.

SAMMY'S BREATHING WAS SHALLOW but steady as David maintained his vigil. He had lost track of time. As he looked at her ashen face, framed by dark curls against the stark white pillow, he thought of the short time they had actually spent together. In those thirteen days he had brought her from a healthy, vibrant woman to this unmoving, critically ill person who might even die before he could get her to a medical facility. He had assured her several times that he would never do anything to hurt her, and now he had killed his own child and possibly the woman he loved as well. If he hadn't made love to her so fiercely that afternoon only a few days ago; if he hadn't insisted she go riding; if he had stayed off the back roads with the truck and been more considerate of her condition; if he had only controlled himself that first weekend.

He couldn't remember cleaning her up. He did faintly recall talking to Russ and Dr. Morrison on the radio but couldn't remember the words they had spoken.

She wore his Aran sweater. He remembered her complaining of the cold but didn't recall removing the bulky sweater or putting it on her. He looked at his watch. It was early evening. Where had the hours gone? Perhaps he had dozed. Damn it, how could he have slept, knowing what he had done to her?

He moved to the window and felt the coldness of the pane as he pressed his forehead against the frigid glass. He cupped his hands around his eyes and tried to focus on the storm outside the warm cabin. Snow was swirling, and the wind was howling around the corner of the building. The blizzard was due to continue until tomorrow. Is that what Russ had said? Why couldn't he remember? His mind was confused, his thoughts scrambled.

He returned to the fireplace and put two more logs on the fire. He placed his sleeping bag near her makeshift bed, sat down and rested his head on his forearms...for a few...moments...damn, he was tired. He would close his eyes, just for a moment.

The fire was reduced to glowing embers and a chill had settled in the cabin when he awoke. He felt a warm hand on his shoulder and raised his head to see her soft blue eyes watching him. He sat up, ran his fingers through his rumpled hair and reached for her hand. He held it gently, massaging the soft skin. It felt toasty warm in spite of the chill in the room.

"Be still, love, while I build up the fire." He moved away, reluctant to leave her. He quickly rekindled the fire and disappeared into the kitchen.

He returned carrying two mugs of soup. After propping her up with several pillows, he handed the mug to her and watched her sip the hot broth.

"It's good," she said.

"Yes."

She abruptly stopped, sat the mug on the low table and looked at him. "It doesn't hurt anymore," she whispered.

"I know."

"David, what went wrong?" she pleaded.

"Sam, I just don't know," he said, but she wasn't satisfied.

"David, was it a boy or a...?" The tears began to move silently down her cheeks.

"Oh, Sammy, don't ask me that question. I don't

know what...damn...what good does it...?'' His voice broke under the burden of her questions.

Never in his life had he felt so inadequate. Even when his young son had been critically injured and his wife killed, he hadn't felt like this. They were isolated in the cabin, without assistance of any kind. If she continued to hemorrhage...if she developed a fever...if she died....

He forced himself to think of the worst and then found it so painful that he lost all control and began to sob, crying as he hadn't cried since his son's mutilating accident.

Sammy found the strength to gather him to her. His shoulders felt broad and powerful as she gently stroked his back. His head lay on the wool sweater against her breast. She smoothed the wavy hair from his brow and gently touched the white of his temple. Her hand began to move down his face, and she felt the stubble on his lower cheek and chin. She smiled slightly as she felt the sharp yet soft bristles. He had always been so clean-shaven.

"You need a shave, my darling," she said as she kissed his hair. She sensed his embarrassment as he raised his head. He adjusted their positions and gathered her in his arms.

"I'll get you out of here, Sammy. I promise."

THE DAYS AND NIGHTS in the cabin became blurred as Sammy lost track of time. The sun peeked through the thick cloud cover, stayed for a few minutes, then disappeared again. David was on the radio talking to Julie Russell. She heard his troubled deep voice say, "I'll hold," and a silence came from the kitchen.

The miscarriage was no longer a secret. What had started three months before as private love between a man and a woman was now public information. Sammy wished desperately that she had never written the letter, never gone to the airport, never learned to swim, never met a thin red-headed boy who was easy to talk to.

She slowly left the bed, pulling his blue robe snugly around her. The floor was cold, but it felt soothing to her warm feet. Her strength was returning, just as David's physician friend had said it would.

She made her way to the window and brushed back the curtain. The snow piled on the outer ledge reminded her of the artificial canned snow her friends used on their windows every Christmas in Phoenix to make the warm desert winters appear New England authentic— until one looked outside and saw colorful African daisies in bloom, freshly mowed winter ryegrass and children playing in shorts and T-shirts.

Christmas. She thought of her children, Mike's family, her childhood holidays with large family gatherings, and a wave of depression settled. Where would she be right now if she hadn't written that impulsive letter in response to the newspaper article? Where should she be spending this Christmas, with David or at home in Phoenix with her family? How did she feel about him now? Did she really know him, or was he still a stranger? Did he still feel the same toward her, especially now that the reason for marrying her no longer existed?

She glanced down at her hand lying motionless on the cold windowsill and looked at the diamond ring. She hadn't worn it long enough to become accustomed to its strange feel. It was a lovely ring, but she no longer was

sure it belonged there. She still loved David, but they
hadn't had enough time together to get to know and
understand each other.

These past few days had been a nightmare. She felt
empty, as though she had never been pregnant. She heard
voices coming from the kitchen again. David and Julie
were discussing D.A., who had apparently called the
Russell ranch. Oh, dear Lord, now his son would know,
too. She felt so ashamed.

She gathered a change of clothing and proceeded to
the small bathroom. Perhaps a sponge bath would boost
her sagging spirits. As she undressed and poured cold
water into the small basin from a nearby pitcher, all she
could think about were the differences between them.
She knew computer systems while he raised beef cattle.
She was accustomed to the hustle and bustle of the
metropolis, while he complained if three cars were
stopped at once at the town's only traffic light. She
worked for a major multinational corporation with
thousands of employees, yet he wanted to give up the
security of his profession and start over all alone and
build a new career from scratch. She was surrounded
with choices of hospitals, shopping centers, cultural
events and self-service gas stations, while he had to drive
twenty-five miles to reach what few businesses the small
town had to offer. As she touched her arms with the
frigid washcloth, she thought of the joy of summer
warmth in Phoenix. Would she ever again feel warm
enough? David had grown cold toward her, she was sure
of that. He was like the wilderness that surrounded the
cabin. His insistence on taking care of her and making
the decisions for them both was as unmovable as the

snow and ice outside. He was frozen in his plans to move ahead without wanting to know if she agreed. She had run her own life in Phoenix, and she was sure he didn't know the meaning of the word partnership. He was a loner and she loved her family, yet he expected her to give up everything while he kept his world intact.

She hurriedly dried herself and dressed, shivering uncontrollably as she finished. She heard David reenter the living room, and she thought of D.A.

"What did you tell your son?" she asked from the bathroom door.

She had shed his robe and now wore a shirt of green-and-blue plaid, a wraparound blue denim skirt and a pair of blue fuzzy slipper socks.

"Sammy, do you think you should be..." he began, but his frown was quickly replaced with a relieved smile. "Sammy, you look so good."

She started to walk casually toward him, but halfway across the room the walls began to wave just as the floor tipped, and she felt herself falling. The last thing she saw was his look of alarm as he lunged for her from across the spinning room.

She opened her eyes and quickly discovered that as long as her head remained motionless, his face was in focus. "What happened?" she asked weakly, trying to make the walls stop undulating. "Goodness, did I faint? I've never fainted in my life." She was again lying on the pallet he'd made for her.

"You overdid it, Sam. You've lost a lot of blood. You're weak...you're...." The anger in his voice slipped out as he comforted her.

"Blood? I don't know...what?" Her mind cleared,

and she remembered her earlier concern. "Was D.A. on the radio?" she asked.

"Yes. Well, not really. He called the Russell ranch while I was talking to Julie, so I just held on and we had a confusing three-way conversation."

"Does he know?" she asked.

"He knows you're sick, but not the cause, and he knows we're snowed in. Sammy, you've got to be careful because we can't get out of here for a few more days. When the snow stops falling, Russ and his two oldest sons will come for us on their snowmobiles. There's no way I can get the truck out even with chains until the snow packs or melts a lot. It's just too deep.

"This was a foolhardy decision I made to bring you up here. I was stupid and careless, and I sincerely regret—" He stopped. "Are you hungry?" he asked. "Neither of us has had a decent meal for days. I'll fix something."

He left the room, and she felt relieved to be alone again.

When he returned, their time together was spent in subdued politeness as though the killing cold had seeped into the warm interior of the cabin. She drew a protective veil around her pain.

During the afternoon, Sammy stopped moving from room to room and was content to lie quietly on the pallet. By late evening her pallor was alarming. She lay dozing and soon fell into a deeper sleep. David watched as her paleness was slowly replaced by a flush. Reacting to a groan from her while she slept, he touched her cheek and found it burning.

His hands shook as he examined her. He followed Dr.

Morrison's emergency instructions and confirmed she was hemorrhaging again. The fever alarmed him with its implications. He covered her again, then tried to rouse her from sleep. She opened her eyes partially and stared with dilated pupils, unseeing dull blue eyes that did not know him.

"Sam, Sam, wake up." David spoke harshly to her, but there was no response. He slapped her cheek with a sharp crack and pleaded, "Sammy, for God's sake, wake up!" He shook her again.

She moaned and settled deeper into a blissful state of painless unconsciousness. He rubbed the sweat from the palms of his trembling hands as he worked. It was his carelessness that had reduced her to this condition, he thought. He had to save her.

He applied cold compresses to her head, but she gave no response. He bathed her with soothing alcohol from the first-aid kit, and she moaned when he touched her. The heat left her for a while but returned. He resumed the alcohol baths, continuing them throughout the evening.

Near midnight he placed an emergency radio call to the Russells and pleaded with them to get help. As dawn broke, the radio came alive. It was Russ.

"Just as soon as the weather breaks, the rescue helicopter from town will be airborne. They're on standby right now. Hold on, friend, help's coming."

"When?" David demanded. "Goddammit, when?"

"Soon, just as soon as they can safely take off. Do you want them to crash and die, too?"

There was a silent pause as David mulled over Russ's sharp comment. He heard mumbling at Russ's end of the radio.

"Sorry, man. I didn't mean that. She'll make it. Help's coming just as soon as they can take off with some degree of safety. We're coming."

David continued attending to Sammy's needs as the morning light grew stronger. Once she recognized him, called his name and reached for him with a shaking hand. His voice soothed her feverish movements, and he spoke of all the experiences they had shared, not knowing if she understood him or heard his words after the first few sentences. He continued speaking long after he knew she had slipped back into unconsciousness.

He lost track of time. Suddenly he heard a whirling sound. The wind had stopped. He rushed to the door, threw it wide open and squinted into the blinding whiteness of the day. A helicopter was approaching from the northwest, over the tall pinetops.

"Oh, thank God," he mumbled as he rubbed his weary eyes and refocused his attention on the hovering craft. He watched it circle as the pilot looked for a safe landing spot.

The helicopter gradually descended and landed on the flat area near his truck. Three men climbed from the craft, each strapping on a pair of snowshoes just before he jumped into the soft powdery snow.

David recognized the pilot as Mike Adler. He was carrying a portable stretcher. His friend and physician, Bob Morrison, carried a dark medical satchel. The last to leave the helicopter was Ed Russell, with an extra pair of snowshoes tucked under his arm and a worn Stetson jammed down on his head.

The next several minutes were a flurry of activity in

the cabin as the pilot and Dr. Morrison prepared Sammy for transportation to Missoula.

Russ listened as David struggled to express his appreciation, then gave up as his eyes reddened with tears. "I'm sorry, Russ."

"It's going to be okay now, David," Russ reassured him. "Didn't I tell you? Hey, friend, you look terrible...and you sure need a shave. Come on now, old buddy. They're ready with your woman. Let's go to town." He placed his arm around David's shoulders and led him out of the cabin. Soon they were airborne.

As they skimmed the treetops, David slumped against the interior wall of the helicopter cabin.

SAMMY WAS CAUGHT in a white-and-gray whirlpool of noisy vibration. She felt weightless, except for her hand. Something had trapped it and held her prisoner. She tried to free herself from the entrapment and felt the vice tighten. As she turned her head to find the source of the pressure, her gaze fell on a sleeping face, lovingly familiar in spite of the week's growth of reddish beard. David held a death grip on her hand, and she stopped trying to free herself.

She moved her head to see more of her environment and stopped, her eyes frozen on Ed Russell sitting opposite David in the shaking and cramped box. She wondered what he was doing with them.

She heard a strange man's voice. "Hold on, everyone, we're going down. Steady the little lady now, Russ. We're almost there."

Russ shifted his seat and placed a hand on either side of the stretcher. As he met her troubled gaze, he tried to reassure her. "You're in a chopper. You're safe and almost to the hospital in Missoula."

She reached out with her free hand and touched his arm. Russ held her hand and patted it.

"It's going to be all right, really all right, and David's with you and he's okay, too."

She listened and could tell the rotary blades were slowing. She tried to open her eyes again to see who had spoken, but the white and gray changed to a swirl of crimson pain, and she gave in to the urge to sink into another black void.

CHAPTER TWELVE

SAMMY SAT PROPPED UP in the hospital bed with several pillows behind her back.

She wore a new blue robe made of soft velour, trimmed in white satin braid. Beneath the robe was a matching blue gown of lighter weight velour. It was designed with a prim high neckline and long sleeves gathered at the wrist with white lace and satin braid. The fabric felt cool to the touch, yet warm to her skin.

Her hair had been freshly shampooed and dried for the first time since the nightmarish week in the mountain cabin. Six days had passed since her arrival at the hospital.

David had stayed with her the first day, but she had been so drowsy from the anesthetic that she could hardly do more than hold his hand as he talked to her. The second day she had been in intense pain, and he had comforted her. She slept the third day and could remember his deep velvet voice but nothing else. Yesterday he had visited her twice, encouraged by her improvement. Last evening he had brought her the gift package containing the gown, robe and matching slippers.

Dr. Morrison had already explained to her about the life-threatening infection and resulting emergency surgery. He had advised her what to expect during the recovery weeks ahead, with the assurance that she'd feel as good as new before long. This morning David was to join her for a meeting with Dr. Morrison to clear up any questions they might have and to tell her when she could leave.

David had extended his vacation with Anaconda for two more weeks. He was staying with D.A. at his apartment near the university campus so he could be close to her and available to take her home to rest and recover at the ranch.

She heard a soft knock on the door and looked up as David entered. He was smiling broadly, and his green eyes sparkled with delight as he quickly crossed to her bedside and laid a gift-wrapped package on the nightstand.

He sat on the edge of the high bed and placed his palms on either side of her cheeks. Tipping her face up, he lowered his mouth to hers and pressed a long, warm kiss on her lips.

She slid her arms around his neck and hid her face in his jacket front. She felt him nibble at her ear and move his lips to the pulse point in her temple and wait for it to react. When it throbbed to his satisfaction, he returned to her lips.

"Sammy, you look wonderful," he said, as he let her get a badly needed breath of air. "Your eyes are back to their beautiful Phoenix summer sky blue, and your lovely cheeks have color in them again, and your beautiful frosted curls are bouncy and bright again, and your lips...ah, your lips." He kissed her again.

"David, you embarrass me with all this flattery." She

blushed but continued to look into his rust-flecked green eyes. "You look quite nice yourself, Mr. McCormack. You looked rather haggard a few days ago. I can faintly remember seeing you on the helicopter, and you had a reddish growth on your face. What happened to it? I rather liked it."

"I shaved it off. It had too much white in it," he laughed.

She smiled and asked, "What did you bring me this time?"

"I think you need some fattening up, my sweet. So until I get you home, I brought you this. Open it and see if they're any good."

She tore the wrapping from the box and discovered a container of delectable-looking cream-filled milk chocolates. She tried one and licked her fingertips. Then, catching him leering at her, she said, "Open wide," and inserted a tasty morsel into his mouth.

"Mmmm, very good. Whoever chose those chocolates sure has good taste in sweet things," he said, smiling broadly, a devilish twinkle in his eyes. Suddenly the smile left his face, and he stared at her and whispered hoarsely, "Good taste in women, too." His mouth swooped down to recapture hers.

She was almost overwhelmed by his nearness, then she heard a voice behind David's broad shoulders and stiffened guiltily.

"Hmmm, excuse me if I'm interrupting a reunion, but I believe we had an appointment?" Dr. Morrison stood in the doorway, chuckling to relieve the awkwardness of the moment. He entered and moved to the chair near the bed. "I'll just wait here until you two finish.

Don't mind me," he said, as he took his pipe from his tweed jacket and pretended to ignore their embracing.

David started to leave the bed, but Sammy grabbed his arm and restrained him. "Stay with me, please?" she whispered.

After a few moments of casual conversation about the weather and how Sammy was feeling, Dr. Morrison asked, "Do you still plan to marry?"

Sammy turned to David for the answer to the question that had been troubling her for the past few days.

David scanned her face for a sign, then said confidently, "Definitely."

"Do you know when?" Dr. Morrison asked. "I don't mean to pry or pressure you. I just wondered if it would be soon. Would you rather not answer right now?"

"I don't mind," David said. "If Sammy is willing, I think we should be married in Missoula. We could have the ceremony at my son's apartment, as soon as Sam is released from this hospital. Bob, couldn't you pull a string or two and help us get our blood tests done here? We could get the license as soon as she's out of here. That's what I want, Sammy." He paused, but before she could reply, he continued. "I think we should return home married. It would solve a lot of problems and settle some questions before they get asked. You know how some small-town people are. I personally don't give a damn, but I don't want Sammy subjected to any gossip. Sammy, will you marry me right away?"

"Yes, I suppose..." she answered, not knowing what else she could say.

Dr. Morrison regained their attention. "You both know what caused the miscarriage—I've explained it in some detail—and why the hysterectomy was necessary, but there are a few facts I omitted. Sammy, you were still too sick.''

The color drained from Sammy's face.

Dr. Morrison patted her hand. ''It wasn't your fault,'' he reminded her. ''You couldn't have stopped it.'' He waited for her nod of agreement. ''The baby was normal.''

She began to tremble.

''It was a girl,'' Dr. Morrison said gently.

She stared at him, pleading for escape from her torment.

''I thought you'd want to know,'' he said.

''No, no, I don't want to know,'' she cried. ''Don't either of you understand?'' She turned to David. ''I want to forget.'' A grim tightness altered her features as she confronted him. She had a tight grip on his hand, but he turned away and stared out the window of the third floor room at the mountain range in the distance.

''Did you want this child?'' Dr. Morrison asked him.

''Very much,'' he whispered.

''Really?'' There was a challenge in Sammy's voice.

''Yes, damn it.'' He closed his burning eyes and tried to ease the anger and frustration he'd kept under control since their rescue.

Dr. Morrison rose from his chair. ''I think we need a break. I'll get us some coffee.'' He turned and quickly left the room.

Sammy eased herself off the bed and disappeared into the private bathroom. When she returned, David had moved to the small love seat near the window. She came to stand beside him, feeling a silent barrier between them.

"I'm sorry," she said.

He raised his arms and offered her the comfort of his embrace. She accepted, and the barrier crumbled.

"David, what are we going to do?" she cried.

"We're going to get through this, Sam—together."

Dr. Morrison returned with a coffee flask and three cups. As they sipped the coffee he spoke to them about possible problems they might encounter. Finally he said, "I want you to both be aware that it might be difficult for you the first few times you make love, so go slow.

"Sammy," he said, "how would you like to check out tomorrow? If you promise to take it very easy and get lots of rest, I'll sign your release. Send me an invitation to your wedding. I like you both, and I hope to see you in the café more than in my office. Bye now." He smiled and left the room.

THE WEDDING TOOK PLACE in D.A.'s apartment four days after Sammy's release, just as David had planned. A telephone invitation was extended to the Russells and the Morrisons and accepted.

David wore a trim-fitting suit of gray wool, a white silk shirt and tamarisk-green tweed tie. His eyes sparkled and his temples seemed stark white in contrast to the dark rusty bark of his head.

Sammy had never seen him in a business suit before. "You look very, very handsome," she said, as he took her hand for the ceremony.

Sammy had gone on a brief shopping trip to a small dress shop near D.A.'s apartment with D.A.'s girl friend, who lived in the apartment above him. Betsy was twenty-two and thrilled to be involved in the romantic wedding.

Sammy had selected a lavender wool two-piece suit. "Something practical for afterward," she had insisted. The suit jacket and the matching chiffon blouse had plunging V necklines.

David smiled approvingly when he saw her. She wore the gold locket he had given her for her birthday, and it hung just to the swell of her breasts. He touched it lightly and his fingers lingered over her bare skin in the V as he whispered, "Beautiful."

She carried a small bouquet of blue flowers that matched her eyes. They were a gift from David. The ceremony was brief. Julie Russell stood beside Sammy and impulsively hugged her, kissed her cheek and gave her hand a reassuring squeeze as the ceremony began. Ed Russell, on the far side of David, acted as his best man. David's tall form blocked Russ from Sammy's view, so she leaned forward and caught his glance. His intimidating scowl frightened her, and she drew back. The ceremony was nearing its end when the minister paused, waiting for her response, and Sammy realized that her preoccupation with Russ's surliness had overshadowed her attentiveness to the words of the wedding ceremony. David lifted a dark brow in question, and she hastily responded, "Yes, I do—I mean I will...of course I do."

The minister cleared his throat in embarrassment and said, "Just repeat after me, my dear...I, Samantha, take thee, David...."

Sammy blushed and whispered the words in short

jerky phrases, relieved that the minister carefully enunciated each word.

The rest of the ceremony passed without error. The white gold wedding band was slipped on her finger, the register was signed and witnessed, and the minister hastily left for another wedding.

D.A. and Betsy surprised the group with a bucket of chicken and a bottle of champagne. The bubbles tickled Sammy's nose as David toasted his bride, and hugs and kisses were freely exchanged. Dr. Morrison and D.A. kissed the bride, but Russ sidestepped her when his turn came. Sammy shuddered with relief.

She clung to David as he drew her closely against his side, and the security of his love insulated her from all her fears and doubts.

Telegrams were sent to her children and brother and to David's uncle. "Married today, details later. Love, David and Sammy McCormack."

The wedding party soon dispersed. David and Sammy made their way to his blue truck after thanking Russ for recovering it from the cabin. Russ brushed off David's comment and ignored Sammy. For a few brief moments, Sammy felt as though she were being swept out to sea, far away from all the places and things and people who were dear to her, swept by a tidal wave of new emotion that filled her with the discomforting knowledge that she'd lost all control of her own destiny. Now she was a pawn in David's plans for them both. Yet when she turned to him as they drove out of his son's apartment parking lot, she knew she loved him with all the intensity of her being, loved him as she'd never loved any man before. The painful thought of life without him took her breath away, and she audibly gasped.

"What?" he asked.

"Nothing," she murmured and kissed him.

The miles slipped past as they drove in silence. The ice along the highway glistened in the sunlight, but a blue haze still hung over the distant forest as she gazed out the window. She felt physically weak, but happy and contented.

"It's beautiful," she remarked, as David pulled into the rest area where just a few weeks before they had stopped for bread and cheese on her initial arrival to his country. He had been right; it was a killer country. Her happiness wavered.

"Do you want to get out and stretch?" he asked.

"I think so." He helped her fasten the hooded parka. The stinging frigid air burned her cheeks. The weather report had predicted a high of twenty-eight degrees. "It's so cold," she murmured.

"Just wait until it hits zero degrees and the winds bring the chill factor to sixty below," David teased. "Then it's cold. This is just a cool spell."

She shook her head in disagreement. Her desert-acclimated blood told her differently.

As he lifted her from the cab seat to the ground, her foot slipped on an icy patch, and she fell against him. He grabbed her in his arms and steadied her, a dark frown on his face.

"Are you all right, love?" he asked, refusing to let her go.

"I'm fine," she assured him. "Do you know that I've been in a blizzard and rescued in that helicopter, but this is the first time I've tried to walk on normal ice and snow? I think I've done my orientation in reverse.''

She felt on the verge of tears as the memory of the blizzard came sweeping through her mind again.

''I've got to stop this crying,'' she apologized. ''I have so much to be happy about, why do I have to cry?''

She turned in his arms. ''David, I don't understand it, but sometimes I feel so empty, almost as though I was never pregnant. Then suddenly I'll feel so pregnant that I can actually feel our baby in my arms. She always has your green eyes. That's crazy, isn't it? Sometimes I just want to cry and cry, and I dream that I'm drowning in my own tears and you're not there to save me. Am I crazy?''

She seemed to be insisting that he answer, but he couldn't help her with words, so he held her until the moment passed.

''Let's walk to the guardrail. It's not far. Can you make it?'' he asked, offering his arm, and she nodded. They looked off through the silver blue haze. The world was silent and at peace, and she tried to accept her new position in it.

''The mist is starting to burn off. It'll be gone by noon if the sun continues to shine,'' he said. This was his home, his country, and he loved it, but now he wondered if she would ever accept it as her home, too. Perhaps her ties in Phoenix were too strong. She was his wife, but he suspected she had entered the marriage with unvoiced apprehensions. His plan had appeared so simple when he had first decided to entice her to his ranch, but this was all beyond his realm of expectation, and the shared tragedy was still painfully raw. Fate had dealt them a cruel and unexpected hand.

The next several weeks would be a difficult time for them as her recovery continued. He thought of the subjects that Dr. Morrison had discussed with them and felt inadequate to handle such heavy responsibilities. She stirred in his arms, and he released her.

"It's breathtaking, but this land is a trifle frightening," she said. "It's always so cold." She shivered. The color drained from her face as weakness crept through her, and she reached for his arm again. "David," she said in a shaking voice, "I don't think I can make it back to the truck . . . my legs. . . ."

He smiled and said in a teasing tone, "Shall I just leave you here?"

"David, no! I'll die!" A look of terror crossed her features, and he quickly picked her light body up in his arms and stood motionless, holding her, but his eyes continued to stare off into the distance. At last he looked down at her pale face. "I'd never leave you, Sammy. I want you with me always." Swiftly he turned and carried her to the waiting truck.

SEVERAL DAYS LATER David returned to work. Concerned that she wasn't well enough to be alone, he arranged for Sammy to stay at the Russell ranch the first week. Twice Dr. Morrison's wife invited her to spend the day in town.

As November began, Sammy insisted on staying at the ranch, assuring him that she was fine and that the Russells were only a phone call away. She didn't tell him that she didn't want to be around Ed Russell. Julie was rapidly becoming a very good friend, but she was puzzled about Russ. He had made it obvious to her that he didn't like her or approve of her, and the marriage seemed to have worsened his opinion. She felt it was best to avoid him whenever possible.

Sammy had looked forward to the recovery time with David, never stopping to think of his necessary return to work in Butte. The drive took more than two hours when the weather was bad, which seemed to be most of the time. Eight hours of stress-filled work, three to five hours of commuting time and several hours of sleep for him left little time for strengthening their relationship. Why had he bothered to marry her if that was all the time they would have together, she began to ask herself.

During the quiet days without David, the loneliness of the ranch pressed in on her, and her mind wandered to Phoenix. She had called Mastiff Corporation once from the hospital in Missoula to report her illness and extend her stay. Now she called the company again and made arrangements for the corporation's medical-insurance department to pay the hospital bills. She certainly didn't want to burden David with that problem.

As she hung up the receiver, she realized she'd neglected to report her change in marital status to Mastiff.

David was upset when she told him about the bills, and he reminded her that she was his responsibility now. The company reclassified her employment status to a two-months' medical leave. She had until the middle of December to make a decision about cutting her career ties with Phoenix. She didn't tell David that she was still officially an employee. She would deal with that problem privately. She didn't want another argument.

Her sons, Lawrence and David, had each phoned her and expressed delight at her remarriage. Her son David had never met her husband, David, but he assured her that with a name like that he had to be the best. She wrote him a long letter and explained the namesake relationship between the two men. She was sure her son would be surprised.

The phone calls were exciting but so short-lived. Letters could be read and reread many times. As the days without David grew longer and the homesickness grew stronger, the letters from her children and relatives became more precious.

One evening, David returned from Butte with two letters from the Dillon post office. They were from John and Sarah.

The letter from her youngest son was a delight. She had seen him for a few days in late August after his completion of boot camp. He had been assigned to a destroyer, with a home port in San Diego, and was now on a six-months west Pacific cruise. She had written him a letter, and this was his reply.

It was long, affectionate and funny. It brought tears mixed with smiles, especially when he reminded her that he and only he had been the one, that early July morning, who had fished three pieces of swimwear from the pool and saved his mother and her guest a great deal of embarrassment. He wrote, "I'm glad for you, mom. You deserve the best, and I think David is. I liked him very much."

The letter from Sarah was a different matter. Sarah

and her boyfriend were having problems, and she was thinking about returning home. She expressed her shock and disapproval at learning that her middle-aged mother had actually married again, and to a total stranger at that. "What could you two possibly have in common? You're too old for sex and that sort of thing. Is it companionship? Is that why you married him? Maybe I'll get to meet him someday. Is it okay if I decide to move back to Phoenix to stay in our house? You do still have it, don't you?"

She sounds like a little bitch, Sammy thought as she reread the letter. Then she felt ashamed for thinking such thoughts of her only daughter. Dear Sarah. Sammy doubted they'd ever have anything in common other than quarrels.

DAVID COULD HARDLY WAIT to share his excitement with Sammy. There had been bad news and good news at Anaconda. It was a perfect solution to his problem. He was sorry it would be so rough on some of the other men and their families, but for him it was the answer to his dreams.

The Anaconda vice-president of environmental controls had called him into his office early that cold November morning.

"I have something to tell you, David," said Joseph Steiner. "It's still highly confidential, and under no circumstances are you to divulge this information to outsiders or even the men below you. Only selected key personnel can know at this time."

"I understand, Joe. I know how to keep silent," David replied, wondering what he was about to learn.

"I hate to have to tell anyone such distressing news. You know when we shut down the Anaconda smelter in September, we really had plans to reopen it. I knew you were skeptical, but I felt somehow we could do it. Well, you were right. The EPA has made the requirements for reopening the smelter so stringent that it is just not financially feasible. I really feel bad about it. Just think of the families affected by this closure."

"When did you get their requirements, Joe? I knew they were expected while I was in Missoula," David said.

"They came several days ago. We've had meetings of the board, and there's just no other solution. Even our legislators have been trying to find a compromise, but it's hopeless. We've also begun negotiations with a Japanese consortium, and would you believe it? It's cheaper to ship the ore concentrate to Seattle and all the way to Japan for refining than it is to build a new smelter here.

"We're still working out the details, but we plan to move the ore concentrates from here at Butte to Ana-conda for drying and then on to the west coast for export. This'll mean a lot of changes around here. The people we kept around while we anticipated reopening will have to be terminated. Some of the men and women will be retrained for new jobs, others will just have to find different employment. We'll help all we can. We might relocate some of the professionals and middle managers if they're interested in a transfer.

"We'll be sending official notification to the senator next month, and it'll all be out in the open. But until then, we've work to do—paperwork, David, and that's where you come in. We'll be letting two of our engineers go. Stan Bernstein's wife has been after him to move to southern California, so I chose him. Marguerite Sanchez was next under consideration. She's a very sharp young woman, and I'm sure she could find work anywhere. Yesterday, my secretary reminded me that you had requested early retirement, effective next June. Is that right?''

David nodded silently, his face a blank mask.

"I guess I've been so preoccupied with this problem plus your absence that it slipped my mind," the vice-president explained. "You just may have saved Ms Sanchez her job, David. So, my good man, as they say on television, let's make a deal. I know you haven't been very happy working as the liaison with those government bureaucrats, but I knew if anyone could pull it off, you could. I know now that it was an impossible task. You certainly warned me enough. I should have listened to what you were trying to say, but it's too late for that now.''

As the discourse continued, David gradually slipped into a more comfortable position in the soft chair, his long legs stretched before him, his hands jammed deep into the pockets of his gray wool slacks. They were the trousers to the suit he had worn the morning of his wedding. He had never been very sentimental about clothing before, but somehow these slacks held memories . . . silly for a grown man to have such a feeling . . . he certainly wouldn't want anyone to know . . . but Sammy. . . . Damn it, would Joe ever get to the point? As the words began to sink into his spinning thoughts, his legs began to react to the wool. It was suddenly too warm in the room and he felt itchy.

He straightened in the chair, rubbed his chin, tapped his mouth with his index finger and felt the tension growing. His stomach had been giving him trouble lately...worse than before. He'd better see Dr. Morrison one of these days.... *Relax. It's good news, remember?* His tie was choking him, but he resisted the urge to loosen it. Instead he laced his restless fingers across his flat waist, forcing his hands to remain steady. A frown wrinkled his forehead as his eyes narrowed. A muscle twitched near his clenched jaw.

"Here's the deal, David," Joe Steiner said. "If you stay around until June, you have eight months of frustration to endure. If I lay you off, you can receive severence pay, and it counts toward your service record. If you'll stay until the end of January and help me process some of this awful government paper, you can leave here with the same benefits you had planned on and go to that isolated ranch of yours and be free. What do you think of that, my good fellow?"

David sat silently trying to absorb the offer just presented to him. Images of the ranch and Sammy flashed through his mind; all the plans he had in reserve, work to do.... He had reconciled himself to another eight months of work, and yet now a period of less than three months suddenly seemed unbearable. A broad smile spread across his face.

"What do you think the answer is, Joe?" He stood up and impulsively gave a loud shout of joy, crossed over to where the vice-president stood and pumped his arm with unrestrained enthusiasm. The executive's door flew open, and a startled secretary stared at the two laughing men.

"Are you two all right?" she asked, looking at her boss.

"Come in, Mrs. Nobel," he said. She entered and closed the door. "David is just expressing his feelings about leaving the company. It's okay, David. She knows about my plans. After all, she's the one who reminded me you wanted out of the rat race."

David turned to her and gave her an unexpected embrace and planted a kiss on her surprised mouth. He lifted her off her feet and swung her around twice, then returned her to the floor and said with a grin and a sparkle in his green eyes, "Thank you, thank you, Genevieve. I love you and Sammy loves you. You've solved all my problems. Thank God for your good memory." He kissed her again.

Joe laughed as he moved to his private liquor cabinet and offered a round of drinks to celebrate. As they joined him in a short toast of brandy, the vice-president looked seriously at David and with a note of sadness said, "David, I envy you. Sometimes I think I'd like a change, too, but my wife would never hear of it, so I don't even suggest it. Invite me out to the ranch some time, you lucky guy, you. Why don't you go home and tell your new bride your good news. We'll make it through the rest of the day without you."

TWENTY MILES OUT OF BUTTE, David met a traffic jam on the interstate, the result of an accident involving a semitruck and trailer and a station wagon. The truck had jackknifed off the overpass, and all traffic was stopped until the wrecking crews righted the dangling cab. Three other vehicles had been involved in subsequent collisions when they slowed to gawk at the mangled vehicles. Two ambulances transported the victims back to Butte, but it was another hour before the state highway department's cleanup crews had the debris cleared and traffic was allowed to pass.

The highway was snowpacked, and David had to reduce his speed. It had been three hours since he'd left the company offices.

As he drove through Dillon, he glanced at the clock on the county courthouse spire, then noticed the sheriff in his official car pull in behind him in traffic. This was no time or place to be stopped for speeding, he decided, and tried to keep his foot off the accelerator. He drummed his fingers on the steering wheel as the slow line of traffic worked its way to the southern edge of town.

The road south of town was much worse than the interstate. Several times he had to stop and shift into four-wheel drive in order to get through some abnormally deep ruts filled with slush and mud. "Damn it," he hissed as he made the gears grind for the fourth time.

He reached home in the late afternoon. After parking the truck he ran up the steps two at a time and into the kitchen.

"Sammy, Sammy! I've got great news. Sammy?" The house was silent. Where was she? The Russell ranch, visiting Julie. No, she would have left a note. He called Julie, only to learn that she had not spoken to Sammy at all that day. Julie told him she had tried to call about an hour earlier, but there had been no answer.

Perhaps she had gone for a walk, he decided, realizing that the two dogs hadn't greeted him on his arrival. He pulled on his overshoes, left the house and hurried to the barn. His thoughts were heavy with concern for the periods of depression Sammy had been struggling with the past week. Maybe it was time for a joint visit to Dr. Morrison. Her checkup appointment was for the next week. Perhaps. . . he looked up and saw one of the large dogs at the opening of the stable door.

"Here One, come girl," he called and the dog came bounding toward him, barking loudly. David stroked the animal's thick coat and endured a few licks of affection, then stood up and asked, "Where's your mistress, One? Where's Sammy? Show me, girl." The dog turned and trotted into the barn and David followed.

He found Sammy sitting on a bale of hay near Melody's stall, her head resting against the wood partition, and the gray mare nuzzling her curls. She looked up when she heard his footsteps.

He thought his heart would break when he saw her face. He had never seen her look so forlorn. He hurried to her and took her outstretched hands. "Sammy, oh, honey. What's the matter?"

"David," she cried, and a tremor shook her. "Lawrence and Eve had their baby. I'm a grandmother."

"Sam, that's wonderful. That should make you happy. What's all this sadness? What was it? A boy or a. . . ?"

He saw the tears begin as she choked, "It was a girl." She collapsed against him, immersed in grief, and he held her.

"I couldn't even congratulate him," she sobbed. "All I could think about was our little. . . girl." She shook his shirt front, clutching at the material. "I don't remember what they named her. She's my first grandchild, and I hate her! I think sometimes that I'm going crazy, David. All I think about is what happened in the cabin, and it makes me hurt so much. I can't stand the pain much more." She looked up at him through her burning eyes. "David, sometimes I want to run back to Phoenix and hide in my house and never think about you or our baby or this place or *anything*! What's the matter with me?" She began to shake with the hard force of her crying.

He held her tightly and waited for her pain to ease. They sat together on the bale of hay, rocking gently as her tears washed away some of her torment.

The interior of the stable was already dark from the shadows of dusk when he moved her. "It's too cold to stay here, Sam. Come with me to the house. You're not crazy. You've got a broken heart, and I want to help mend it. Let me try."

He helped her up and they made their way back through the slush and mud to the house.

CHAPTER THIRTEEN

THE EPISODE IN THE BARN had brought a change for both of them. Laughter and joy had reentered their lives. Sammy had visibly brightened at the prospect of David's early retirement. Five weeks had passed since her rescue, and during a recent office visit, Dr. Morrison had announced her recovery complete, but he had wagged a finger in caution at David.

"Physical activity won't hurt you at all, Sammy," Dr. Morrison had said. "But, I'd watch out for that drooling big fellow there." He laughed and pointed to David as the couple left his office. "All things in moderation, my friend."

Dr. Morrison drew David aside. "Physically she's fine, David," he cautioned in a lower voice, "but sometimes invisible scars take longer to heal. Be gentle... and patient."

Each February, David received a substantial year-end settlement payment as part of his patent-royalty contracts. The previous year, in a moment of winter madness, he had purchased a snowmobile, but he seldom had the occasion to enjoy it or even use it except for a few times to travel to the high country on a ranch emergency.

The Russell family had several machines, and David

invited them to go on a winter outing into the Beaverhead recreational area with Sammy and him.

Sammy helped him load the snowmobile. He had
built a ramp and taught her how to operate the machine.
He laughed as she drove the noisy vehicle up the ramp
into the bed of the pickup, the tracks making a dreadful
clattering racket when they touched the truck bed. As he
lifted her down she smiled with satisfaction and he re-
joiced in her delight.

David and Sammy left the ranch early Saturday
morning as the sun peaked over the southeastern mountains. The weather was perfect. Several inches of snow
had fallen during the past few days, but the highways
were plowed and the sky was a brilliant blue with only
an occasional high cloud.

The Russell Wagoneer had a trailer hitched to the rear
and two snowmobiles were loaded for the pleasure trip.
David and Sammy brought fried chicken and sliced
ham. The Russells were providing the rest of the meal
plus snacks and table service. Some of the Russell children wanted to travel with the McCormacks, and David
felt apprehensive when Sammy chose Lisa and Mary to
join them in the truck cab.

Lisa chattered constantly and kept them laughing
most of the way. Mary was a petite rather shy teenager,
but David noticed that several times Sammy and Mary
whispered to each other and Sammy smiled. Once he
thought he heard them speak of his son.

He looked past the two young heads and caught Sammy's attention. "You okay?" he asked softly.

"Fine," she replied, smiling in return.

They snacked on Julie's oatmeal cookies and a thermos of hot chocolate. David hit a bump just as he attempted to take a sip from his cup, and his passengers laughed gleefully and teased him when he dribbled the chocolate down his jacket. Sammy took out a napkin and changed places with Mary, then Lisa. Sliding in next to David, she playfully wiped his chin and the front of his jacket.

Her eyes sparkled, and he held her gaze for a moment. She motioned for him to lower his head, and as he did she kissed his tanned cheek and whispered, "I love you."

They rode the rest of the way with her hand resting on his thigh. She seemed unaware of the effect her warm hand had on him, and for several miles he wished the girls had been traveling in the other vehicle. Six weeks was a long time.

They found a perfect spot for the picnic away from other families out for winter fun. Julie and Sammy chose an area level enough to set up the portable picnic table and soon had the food ready, but Julie cautioned, "Not until the proper time."

The snowmobiles were given to the three older boys, who reluctantly agreed to give the younger children rides, then proceeded to hold several short races. Russ challenged David to a race, and off the two men went on the noisy machines, snow flying, the children cheering when their father won the heat.

As the men returned to the family group, David demanded a rematch, this time with the wives as partners. Sammy was skeptical, but Julie quickly challenged her and the rematch was on.

Sammy carefully climbed on behind David. "Hold

tight," he instructed, and gunned the engine. The
course was approximately a mile through the trees and
back to the table. Russ hit a hidden boulder, and Julie
was bucked off into the snow. David slowed their
machine slightly, but when he saw the other couple was
uninjured, he continued to stay just far enough in the
lead to win the second heat.

"I demand a runoff, but after lunch," Russ said.

"You're on," David replied. They all laughed and
began to serve themselves at the heavily laden table.

A quietness fell over the group after lunch. The older
Russell sons left to explore some animal tracks. Hunting
season was upon them, and they wanted to reaffirm
their tracking skills. The three younger children were
stretched out in the bed of David's pickup, Lisa and
Tim asleep while Mary read a book. The friction
between Russ and Sammy had been set aside for the
day.

David rose and stretched. "I want to take Sammy for
a ride in the snow, all alone, and show her what a Montana winter landscape looks like. Don't come looking
for us unless we're not back in two hours. No rescue
teams this time, please. Coming, Sam?"

He held out his hand, and she accepted. She joined
him on his machine, and her arms encircled his waist in
a caressing embrace as he slowly moved out into the
countryside. He headed in the opposite direction from
where the boys had gone for their tracking.

They traveled through the snow and trees and only
the soft hum of the engine disturbed the winter wonderland. Sammy tightened her embrace and rested her head
against his broad back.

Their relationship had been a succession of traumatic experiences. She wanted a peaceful period with herself well enough to return his love and affection. She knew he had used great restraint and consideration in his own physical need for her. She loved him and wanted him, but uncertainties plagued her, especially when she thought of her Phoenix ties and responsibilities.

They were isolated, far from the sounds and sights of other visitors to the area. He stopped the engine and parked the machine. He helped her off, and they paused to absorb the beauty of the rugged countryside.

She stepped away, reached down for a handful of snow and playfully threw a large, misshapen snowball at him. She laughed, for she had caught him completely off guard. He grabbed for her, but she ran away, her lighthearted laughter filling the air. He chased her into a small thicket where the snow wasn't so deep. She tripped and fell, and he threw himself on top of her to prevent her escape.

He rolled her over onto her back. "This is for being a temptress," he panted. Taking a small handful of snow, he poked it down the front of her parka. She screamed as the icy snow touched the warmth of her skin. A small piece slipped down the inside of her sweater to settle between her breasts as she attempted to sit upright.

"Get it out, get it out, please," she pleaded as she tried to open the parka. She fell on her back in the snow with him astride her, a knee on either side of her.

He smiled wickedly and asked, "May I help?"

As she lay panting from the wrestling, he slowly be-

gan to loosen her outer clothing. The parka was un-
zipped, then the sweater unbuttoned. He removed his
gloves to undo the small buttons of her blouse. She was
breathing heavily, and as she inhaled he became aware
that only the thin material of her blouse separated his
sensitive fingers from her warm skin. Her habit of going
braless had almost been his undoing several times in the
past week.

She was mesmerized as he unbuttoned and slowly
opened the blouse, exposing her breasts to the cold air.
He was like a moth drawn to a flame. His fingers moved
over the twin mounds, circling the outside swell, moving
under and around to the valley between. He could feel
her heart pounding against his fingertips. His thumb
moved from her pale soft skin and passed over the
darker rose area to brush across the peak. It hardened as
he dropped beside her in the snow.

His attention moved to her face, but his hand continued to trace patterns over her breasts. "I don't see
any snow," he whispered softly. He spread light warm
kisses on her breasts, and her pulse raced as he worked
his way leisurely up her neck to her face. Her eyes
darkened as her eyelids fluttered closed, and her lips
parted as she waited to receive his mouth.

She whispered a single word, "David," and tried to
move her hands under his heavy jacket in order to feel
his warmth.

A guttural sound came from his throat as he explored
her willing mouth.

Suddenly they both tensed. Voices off in the distance called out, "David," then, "Sammy. Where are
you?"

He lifted his head and looked into her questioning eyes. "Damn kids," he muttered.

Off in the distance they heard the call again, recognizing Lisa's young voice. "Are you lost again?" There was a pause, then "David, where are you?"

Sammy sat in the snow, and he kneeled in front of her.

"Sit still, love," he said and quickly fastened her clothing and zipped the parka. They stood and brushed the snow from each other, then watched two small children work their way through the snow, carefully following the snowmobile tracks in their search for the missing couple.

"Let's go," he said, kissing her again. "We'll resume this later, my dear."

When they got home that night Sammy began to run a slight fever, and David called Dr. Morrison. The next day was Sunday, but the doctor insisted David bring her to his office.

"Your resistance is low," Dr. Morrison said, as he gave her an injection.

She was ill for the next few days, and David's promise of resumption was tabled.

THANKSGIVING DAY was bright but cold. Dinner at the Russells was scheduled for 5:00 P.M. The morning passed rapidly as David attended to a minor repair at the stable, and Sammy attempted to recapture the lost art of making a mincemeat pie from scratch.

By midafternoon, they were on the road to the Russell ranch. The kitchen was bustling with last-minute food preparation as David and Sammy arrived. Russ greeted them at the door, shaking David's hand and scowling at Sammy. He had an open can of beer in his hand.

Sammy handed her pie to Julie and helped the girls with final table preparations. Julie was quieter than usual.

"Try to stay away from Russ," Julie warned.

"Why?" Sammy asked. She had no great desire to associate with him, but she was curious.

"We had words. It was silly, but. . .he's been drinking." Julie pleaded silently with Sammy for understanding.

"What did you quarrel about?" she persisted. "Oh, Julie, surely not about David and me? How could he? It's none of his business," she protested. She stopped when she realized her friend was close to tears. "I'm so sorry, Julie."

"Me, too," Julie replied. "Try to forget I said anything, but, please, I don't want anything to spoil this special day."

"Of course," Sammy assured her.

Julie paused in her preparation. "Sammy, I love him. I know he can be very unpleasant and even nasty at times, but I'm married to him. He's very jealous at times and not just about me. We actually separated once because of his temper and jealousy. Please try to understand. I love you and David, and sometimes Russ can't understand that kind of love." She smiled and wiped her eyes. "Let's call everyone to dinner," she said. "It's all ready. Happy Thanksgiving, Sammy."

It was the usual Thanksgiving dinner menu. Anything different would have been a disappointment. The muffled sounds of eating were all that could be heard for several minutes. The turkey and dressing quickly disappeared, the baked potatoes and mixed vegetables were consumed. There was a big bowl of sweet-potato salad, a new taste experience for Sammy. She asked Julie for the recipe and caught Russ's surly frown. The hot fresh bread was buttered and eaten with mounds of homemade strawberry preserves.

Russ snapped at Lisa and Mary, who tearfully restricted their chatter to requests for serving dishes. As dessert and coffee were served, Russ asked for another can of beer and Julie cautioned him. He ignored her and went to the refrigerator and helped himself, giving her a harsh look on his return trip to the table.

Sammy finished serving the coffee and returned to her seat beside David. She served herself a piece of her mince pie and stole a glance toward Russ.

"Russ, apple or mince?" Julie asked.

"Mince with ice cream, babe," he replied, reaching out to give her a friendly suggestive pat on her behind. Julie blushed, but smiled a little.

Sammy took a small bite of the pie and stopped short in her chewing. Its taste was bitter, and she realized she'd forgotten to add sugar to the mincemeat mixture. How could she have made such a stupid mistake?

"Julie, I made a..." she cried, but Russ interrupted with a snarl as he took two large bites of the pie and made a face.

"Who the hell made this pie?" he asked boisterously.

Julie looked across the table to Sammy and motioned her to remain silent. Russ persisted. "This pie tastes like sh...garbage!" He stalked over to the kitchen trash container and spat the pieces of crust and filling out.

The festive mood evaporated. Russ returned to the table, but glanced at Sammy as he reached for Julie's apple pie, served himself a large wedge and proceeded to finish it with gusto. "Now that's made by a real Montana country girl," he said. Abruptly he left the table. On the way out of the room, he stopped at the refrigerator and took another can of beer.

Julie tried to make amends for Russ's behavior, then stopped and busied herself clearing the table. She assigned the older boys the job of washing the dishes.

She sent the girls to their room and told Tim to feed the pets. "Please, go to the den. David, maybe you can help him. He's...he's...so rude," she cried. She turned her back to them as she wiped her eyes again. "I'll be right there."

The more Sammy thought about Russ's insulting remarks, the more convinced she became that he had baited her deliberately.

As the two couples settled in the den, Julie and David tried to make pleasant conversation, but Russ and Sammy eyed each other like sparring fighting cocks. Russ's thick dark brows and hooded lids gave his features a sinister look of aggression.

David tried to bring Sammy into the conversation, but her blue eyes were smoldering as she gave a mumbled response to his question.

"Russ?" Sammy asked, her heart pounding as he looked at her. "I knew what was wrong. You didn't have to be so rude and uncouth."

"Some women can cook and some can't," Russ replied with a smirk on his face.

"What do you mean by that?" Sammy demanded.

"I've been cooking for most of my life." She felt David's hand on her forearm and brushed it away.

"It hasn't done much good, then, has it? Is that why your first old man left you?" Russ sneered.

"Why, you...." She couldn't think of an appropriate reply.

Julie and David sat in disbelief as the conversation deteriorated.

"Lady, if that pie was any indication of your cooking talents, I feel sorry for David. He's going to have to stop here to eat every night before he goes home," Russ laughed. "Montana women are all good cooks. Maybe Phoenix broads are just good with their...." Russ leered suggestively at Sammy. "Maybe you know big-city tricks in the bedroom. That right, David?" Russ saluted his friend with his beer can.

David rose from his seat, but Sammy responded before he could react.

"What's your problem, Russ? You sound like you want him for yourself. Is that why you two are so close? Maybe you're gay, and David has never realized it before."

Immediately Sammy regretted her words, but she was too angry to retract them. In her rage she continued. "Keep your insulting comments to yourself. What happens in our home is none of your business." She began to sob. "I...I'm leaving! I'm sorry, Julie, but I don't see how you can stand to live with that... that...." With tears welling up in her blue eyes, Sammy stumbled across the room. Suddenly she turned and hurled her empty cup and saucer at Russ's sinister face. In the split seconds between the china pieces leaving her hand and hurtling toward her target, she wanted desperately to recall them. She watched with relief as the cup bounced into his lap, but relief changed to horror when the saucer flew like a discus and clipped his forehead.

Russ's face flushed with raw hatred as he charged out of his chair. Sammy searched the room for David's protective presence, and was alarmed to find his head turned toward Julie. She jerked her attention back to Russ and knew she was in danger. Obviously, David had refused to come to her rescue. She had to save herself. Without looking back she bolted for the door.

As she rushed through the doorway, Russ shouted after her, "Some women just aren't made for this country. You're soft. You couldn't begin to pull your weight. He needs a woman who can help, not some city bitch who clings. Go back where you belong. He'd be better off without you!"

"Sammy!" David shouted, but she had already slammed the heavy front door. He turned to Russ, grabbing the material of Russ's shirtsleeve with one hand, making a tight fist with the other.

Russ whirled back to his friend. "She's a dangerous bitch, David, can't you see that? Let her go . . . good riddance." He seemed to puff with pride that he'd chased her out.

"Shut up, Russ. She's my wife," he said. "Leave her alone."

Russ turned away, dismissing his guest, then suddenly turned to David again, a sneering, drunken smirk on his face, and David no longer saw his longtime friend standing before him.

He took one swing at Russ, connecting with his jaw, and Russ staggered off balance. Without waiting to see the damage, David charged out the doorway after Sammy. He found her sitting in the truck cab, her lips in a straight, grim line, tears streaming down her flushed cheeks.

"Don't say a word to me, you coward, just take me home," she hissed. She was livid with rage. She couldn't understand why he hadn't come to her defense.

The drive to the McCormack ranch was made in silence. Sammy stared at the white patches of snow on the side of the road. The snow reflected the moonlight, sending icy beams back to the scattered night clouds. She flinched as some of the slivers of moonbeams came toward her, then bounced off her window just before piercing her heart. The cold seeped through her parka and into her body. Maybe she was too soft. Maybe she did belong in Phoenix, where life was warm and friendly.

She was out of the truck as soon as it stopped near the kitchen of David's home. She stood impatiently as he fumbled with the key. She shivered in the frigid night air and finally said sharply, "Hurry up." David frowned as he unlocked the door.

She hurried to the bedroom and quickly undressed. She had just slipped the blue velour gown over her shoulders when she heard him enter.

"Sammy, what got into you back there?" he asked.

She whirled around. "Into me? What about that fat cowboy friend of yours? Ask him!" she cried.

"Sammy, he didn't mean any...." He tried to calm her.

"You're wrong. He meant everything he said. He's hated me from the first time we met, and now he's turned you against me at last."

"No, Sam—" He tried to explain, but she interrupted.

"He insulted me and you did nothing! David, does his friendship mean more to you than our marriage? Is that why you didn't come to my defense?" she demanded.

"Of course not, Sam, but—"

"Is he right?" she shouted. "*Am* I an outside here? *Am* I a clinging hindrance to you? Maybe he's right, and I should go back to Phoenix where I belong." Her face was red and tear streaked as he came to her.

"Don't you dare touch me," she cried. She jerked her arm away, her face flushing again with anger.

He smiled. "You look like a little—" He didn't get a chance to finish his statement as a small fist hit him in the fleshy part of his cheek with minimal force.

"Don't you laugh at me, you big brute." As she drew back her other arm he grabbed her by the shoulders, trying to restrain her, but she continued twisting and turning hysterically.

"Is he right? Is that the only reason you married me? For my...well, you sure got cheated that way, didn't you? Even that's no good anymore, is it? I probably can't even...do...that...right." She stopped trying to speak as the sobs took control. Suddenly she broke free and whirled out of his reach. Her toe collided with the wooden leg of the bed, and she lost her balance.

"Sam, watch out!" he shouted as he grabbed for her

gown, but the force of her falling body ripped the material from his hand.

She reached for the ornate bedpost of the old-fashioned Early American bed, but her vision was blurred, and her hands found only air. Before her furious thoughts could cope with her predicament, the thick wood post was inches from her face. The painful impact painted stars of crimson throughout her brain. She fell back onto the bed, cowering from him. Her head rang from the blow, but she fought to make sense out of her conclusion that David had either shoved her or hit her.

"Oh, my God," he groaned as her forehead turned white, then red from the harsh impact of the heavy wood bedpost.

"You're cruel, David, cruel. You take my baby, now you...we're all alone, so are you going to beat me, too?" she demanded as she gingerly touched her bruised face.

He had to stop her words. They were lies. He hadn't hit her; he'd tried to save her. He loved her and hadn't meant to see her hurt, but he'd failed once again to save her from harm. He dropped to the bed and pinned her arms to the mattress.

As he looked at her flushed face his anger and concern changed to a surge of desire, and he tried to kiss her. He would show her that he loved her. He had been patient long enough.

She turned her head to avoid his lips, and his mouth found her arched neck. He moved his mouth to her ear and whispered, "Sammy, love me, love me."

She turned back to him, trying to force his mouth and

the words from her ear and encountered his face inches from hers.

Memories of summer love cascaded over them as his mouth met hers. Her struggles changed to caresses as he assaulted her mouth, bruising her lips. He had no time for patience or preliminaries as he shoved her clothing aside.

Through his passion-drugged senses, he heard her cry out, "David! You're hurting me."

He had completely forgotten her condition in his desire for her. He buried his face in her hair, knowing that he had been willing to force himself upon her just to have her again.

He heard her soft sobs of anguish as they lay together motionless.

She called to him, a soft and pleading tone to her voice. "David, please look at me."

"No!" He tried to get up, but she had her arms around his waist and refused to release her hold on his body.

He buried his face again in her hair for several moments, then raised his head and looked at her. "God forgive me for what I almost did to you," he said, his voice choked.

She touched his cheek with her trembling hand. "I'm sorry, too, my darling." She laid her fingers against his lips to silence his apology and softly whispered, "I know you didn't mean to hurt me. David, love me, but love me gently like you always did before. Make love to me. I want you to. Maybe I can still.... Oh, I'm so afraid, David. Help me!"

She began to caress him and as she made the initial

moves of love, she brought his hands to her and guided his hesitant movements in the gentle ways of their past.

A blanket of healing tenderness covered the painful memories as they became husband and wife.

CHAPTER FOURTEEN

DAVID RELEASED THE HORSES to exercise in their pasture south of the stable. He started toward the house, but stopped and smiled as he watched the two dogs play a game of tag with the frisky horses. Sammy's gray mare kicked her heels with vigor after the night in her stall. The sun had not yet decided to appear over the snow-capped peaks, but he knew the day was going to be beautiful.

If Sammy was still asleep, he would rejoin her and try to make amends for the previous night. Although it had ended in love and satisfaction for both, he still felt remorse about their fight and her injury. He had been alarmed to learn she had thought he had shoved or hurt her. He hated the cruel words and the painful actions. They had been said and done in the heat of anger, but could never be withdrawn from sensitive memories. They would lie in wait to fester and grow if not weeded from their relationship. Their lives had become infinitely more complicated than he had planned.

She was still asleep, so he stripped off his clothes and rejoined her in the warm bed. As he moved closer, she turned to him in her sleep, and he saw her bruised forehead. A vertical purple bar marred her smooth skin where she'd collided with the bedpost. It had been his fault, for she had been trying to escape from him. Never again, he swore. He touched the marks, and she flinched in pain. Her eyes opened slowly, and he thought he read fear.

She smiled slightly and moved into his embrace to lie quietly against his shoulder, her arm sliding around his waist and her leg tangling between his long limbs.

"You've been out," she said.

"Yes, how did you know?" he asked.

"I awoke earlier, and you were gone," she murmured. "Besides, your feet are cold."

He chuckled. "If we stayed in bed every morning till noon, my love, the ranch would soon go to seed." He kissed her hair, relieved at her change in mood from the previous night.

"I must learn to be a rancher's wife. I really don't know what to do."

"Let me teach you, Sammy." He gently kissed her forehead.

She raised her head to look at him. "Do you really think I could learn? Russ said I'm an outsider."

"Russ doesn't decide what's right for you and me. We do. Russ is wrong. You don't belong in Phoenix anymore. You belong here with me," he insisted.

He gingerly touched her discolored face. "I'm so sorry, Sam. I never meant to hurt you. . . ." He stopped. "It was my fault. I frightened you."

"No, it was my carelessness and anger. I tried to hit you. I was so furious I couldn't see."

She lay quietly in his arms, listening to his deep breathing and the pounding of his heart.

"I remember a time," he began to reminisce, laughing softly, "when you took out after three boys with a stick. It was the first time I ever saw you, remember?"

She smiled. "Yes, by our irrigation ditch, and you rescued me. I was so mad at those mean boys." She frowned.

"You always were a fighter, and I loved you for it, Sam, but never again like last night. It tears me up to think what could happen." He pulled her closer and they lay quietly.

"David?"

"Yes."

"Why did Russ act as he did yesterday?"

"I wish I knew. I've never seen him like that. Maybe it was the beer. Maybe he was bothered by something. I just don't know."

"He doesn't like me. He keeps saying how soft I am. I try to be tough, but I cry so easily. I try." Her words were choked.

"Don't, Sam. You don't have to try to please Russ," he reassured her. "Besides, I like you a little soft and round and womanly," he whispered. "Just be your sweet self."

"I wasn't very sweet last night, here or at the Russell place, was I? I owe Julie an explanation."

His lips brushed her cheek.

"We'd better stay away from them for a while and let things cool off. Maybe you two can figure out what the clash is between you and Russ. Until then, just be with me, Sammy. I want to make up for those lost weeks. I need you, honey. You were afraid last night, but it turned out fine, didn't it?"

She nodded, but frowned. "At least that once."

"Bob Morrison said we should practice getting used to each other again. Why don't we take his advice?" He smiled and playfully nibbled at her ear, then kissed her lightly several times on her lips.

"Doctor's orders?" She smiled as she warmed to his overtures and returned his caresses.

"Dr. Morrison himself," he assured her.

"I think you set him up to give this advice," she murmured, "but I'm glad."

Later that morning, the ringing of the phone brought Sammy from the depths of sleep. She hurriedly slipped her robe around her shoulders and ran to the kitchen. She caught it on the sixth ring and breathlessly said, "Hello," panted a few times and added, "McCormack ranch."

An extremely deep voice said in a rather loud tone, "Hello, little lady, could you be my nephew's new wife?"

"Who is...is this Uncle Jeff?" she asked with a smile.

David came through the door of the kitchen and stopped, listening to her conversation. He moved to her side and motioned for the receiver.

"Uncle Jeff, is that you?" David asked, a look of fond affection on his features. Sammy admired him as he talked with his uncle.

"Yes...yes...yes." He kept pausing and repeating the single word. Finally he said, "Why don't you ask her yourself," and handed the receiver to Sammy again.

Sammy and the older man chatted for several minutes. She laughed as he told her a few stories about David as a youngster. She fell silent again as she listened. "Wait just a moment, Uncle Jeff, and I'll see. David, he wants us to. . .?"

David nodded. "I know. Do you want to go?"

"Very much," she said, and gave him a kiss of gratitude. She spoke into the mouthpiece and said, "We'd love to come. We'll be there on Christmas Eve, weather permitting. I can hardly wait to meet you. David has told me so much about you and your lovely family." There was silence as she listened, smiling and laughing as he enlightened her about David's teen years.

She listened and exclaimed, "Oh, no! Did he really?"

David reached for the phone and said, "I think I'd better put a stop to this true-confessions hour before I'm ruined." He spoke affectionately to his uncle, then said goodbye.

"Well?" he asked, turning to her.

"Oh, David, I feel like part of your family," she said as she embraced his waist.

"Sammy, sweetheart, you are. Hey, that old gray mare of yours needs some exercising. Let's go for a ride. I'll show you some more of the ranch."

As they walked to the barn, he looked down at her. "It's going to be a fine day, Sam." She nodded in agreement.

Later in the day, D.A. called from Missoula to see if a visit to the ranch the following weekend would be satisfactory. He would be bringing Betsy, and he had some early Christmas presents for the newlyweds.

That same evening, Sammy accepted a collect call

from Portland, Oregon. Sarah and her boyfriend, Paul, were returning to Phoenix for the winter, having decided that Oregon was too wet and cold for them. Could they stop at the ranch the next weekend on their way home, provided they could find Dillon?

David talked to Sarah and repeated the directions four times before he convinced her to write down what he had said. He wondered if she was intoxicated or high, but said nothing to Sammy.

Sammy awoke during the night as David returned to the bedroom from the bathroom. She noticed he looked wan.

"Are you okay?" she asked.

"Fine," he replied. "I just have a bit of indigestion. Bob Morrison gave me something." He adjusted the bed covers. "Are you warm enough?" he asked.

"As warm as a summer day in Phoenix," she said as she slipped back into his embrace.

SAMMY WAS HESITANT to explore the house, feeling she might be invading David's privacy.

"Good Lord, no, Sam. It's been a bachelor's abode for too long. I don't want you to become my cleaning slave, but if you want to tidy the place up a bit, do whatever you want. Maybe you can make some order out of this chaos. If you need or want anything, just ask. I can afford it," he assured her.

Still she asked for little. One morning after David had left for Butte, she sat at the kitchen table making out her mortgage-payment check to be mailed to Phoenix. She mentally calculated the number of future payments on her home and car before she ran out of money. She couldn't ask him to assume her financial obligations, yet she couldn't put them up for sale while she was at his ranch and the house and car sat idle in Phoenix. She had struggled hard for her house; it was one of her major accomplishments since her divorce from Jake. She knew she had to keep it, yet without her position at Mastiff it was impossible.

David's ranch mortgage was on the verge of being paid off. Hadn't he bragged to her about his financial expertise? She knew he wouldn't understand her dilemma.

Impulsively she placed a call to her sister-in-law, Maggie, in Phoenix, and asked the operator to charge the call to her home phone, rather than to David's. She mentally made a note to repay him for the collect call from Sarah.

As she hung up after chatting with Maggie for more than an hour, she regretted making the call. She was a fool. She was on the verge of running out of money, yet she had squandered funds on the call. She thought of Maggie's family, and a wave of homesickness swept over her. She wondered if the twins had changed and recalled Maggie's comment that Danny had learned to walk. Thoughts of Danny brought memories of the cabin. She tried to imagine what a daughter would have looked like. Would she have had David's eyes or her blue ones? A pain pierced her as she acknowledged that she could never have his child, never fulfill his desire to have more children, never be a complete woman for him.

Grief tore at her, and she ran into the bedroom. Sprawled across the bed, she stopped trying to control herself and gave in to the torment that buried her in misery.

At last she sat up and looked at the clock on the nightstand. Two hours had passed, yet she couldn't remember the time spent on his bed or what she had done. Her hand touched the damp pillow, and she recalled the telephone call to Maggie but refused to give in again to the depression. She scolded herself and promised to take David's advice. Housekeeping had always been therapeutic for her; perhaps it could be again. She pushed herself from the bed.

As she explored his house, she discovered more about him. She found the stack of responses to his advertisement and couldn't resist the urge to read some of them. She reread her own letter and was so embarrassed by the stilted and lengthy piece of correspondence that she wondered why he had had the desire to reply. She put the letters in a special place for safekeeping.

He seemed to be a collector of magazines. She began to sort and classify the several stacks she found in the living room and in the bedroom closet. She flipped through a copy of a small issue of *Rural Montana* and found an article on solar energy written by David. My goodness, she thought, he's a writer as well as an inventor. By the time he returned home, her spirits were high, the damp bed linens washed and dried and her checks sealed in envelopes ready for mailing.

When he returned from chores at the barn, she asked him about the magazine *Simmental Shield* and learned that he had always wanted to raise purebred cattle, but didn't have the time or money to devote to it. He made a point of staying up to date on the latest information, though.

"Someday, maybe soon, now that you're my soft wife, and Anaconda is about to fade from my life, I'll have the chance," he said as he pulled her to him. "Come here, softie," he murmured, nibbling at her ear as she tried to tear some lettuce for a salad. "Russ is right, you are soft. . .and luscious. . .and I think I want you now." With those words the dinner she was preparing was forgotten.

The next morning, she plunged into the sorting job started the previous day. She asked David to buy shelving for bookcases, and he promised to stop and get some on his way home. She found books and current general magazines, but all in boxes, and she had an exhausting but satisfying two days creating a usable and orderly library at one end of the living room.

Each afternoon she saddled Melody and took a short ride. One and Two were always close at her heels. She met David at the ranch entrance and cantered beside him as he slowly drove the last mile home. She was becoming quite a horsewoman and was pleased to see David's face beam each time he spotted her waiting at the gate.

Suddenly the week was nearing its end. Friday evening David gave her a letter from Mastiff, frowning as he watched her disappear into the bathroom with it unopened.

She locked the door, tore the envelope open and read the letter. It was a reminder to her that her medical leave would expire the middle of December, along with proof of payment for her hospital stay in Missoula. She tore the letter into tiny bits and flushed it down the toilet. When she returned to the kitchen, David was still waiting.

"What was it?" he asked.

"Just confirmation of their payment of my hospital bill," she said.

He left the room without a comment, but she knew he was angry over her continued refusal to submit to his care.

She regretted telling a lie but couldn't think how to undo the misdeed, once committed. She finished preparing dinner and went to the stable to announce the meal.

She sensed his dissatisfaction, but knew he'd be even more irate if he knew the real reasons for her concern.

"I'm sorry, David. I'm just not used to being taken care of. Try to understand, please," she said as they slowly walked back to the house.

"Try being my full-time wife," he replied. "I'm sorry, too, Sam. Let's just forget it." Quickly he changed the subject. "D.A. and Betsy will be here soon, won't they?" He held the door for her. She brushed against him as she entered the warm kitchen, and he grabbed her arm. He turned her toward him and slid his hands up her arms and held her face. "Sam, I do try to understand, but it's hard. I love you. If you love me, you'll be my wife, my full-time wife and share everything I have. Why is that so hard to accept?"

Before she could reply, he covered her mouth with his warm lips, massaging the tension from her, and she pressed against him, seeking the shelter of his security, wanting to accept the comfort and warmth of his promise.

During dinner, she expressed her concern over sleeping arrangements. D.A.'s room was available, but would it be used by the two men or two women or one couple? She wasn't sure of D.A. and Betsy's intimacy and was reluctant to ask. She knew Sarah and Paul were living together, but still felt like a prudish mother when faced with her daughter's life-style.

D.A. and Betsy arrived very late and the sleeping problem solved itself as they each opened separate sleeping bags and bedded down on the floor in the living room.

Sammy was forced to examine her own hypocrisy as she undressed for bed. Was the October experience proof of her own double standard? She felt a twinge of depression as her mind wandered to the mountain cabin, and she tried to shake the feeling off.

"David?" she asked, as he drew her close and tucked the quilt around her shoulder when they settled in for the night.

"What's wrong, love? You've been quiet. I told you to not worry about us."

"No, it's not us, it's...."

He raised himself to look at her. Her bare shoulder reappeared, and he covered it with a slowly moving caress, his warm mouth sliding to the hollow below her collarbone. He traced the bone to her throat, where he concentrated.

A shudder of excitement shot through her. "Goodness, David, you make me forget what I was worried about," she sighed, returning his kiss.

"Mmmm, good. That's what I had in mind," he assured her.

"Darling, please pay attention," she admonished, but his hand began to play explorative games beneath the blankets. "Please," she begged, but tickled his ribs playfully. His fingers walked up her thigh as he attempted to untie the tiny ribbons on her gown. "Stop," she pleaded, laughing softly, but all was lost as she gave in to his persistent lovemaking. "You have the slowest hands in the Rockies, and I love them," she murmured. His mouth prevented her from saying more.

Later, she listened to his breathing return to normal.

"You're a witch," he whispered.

"Thank you," she giggled, as his fingers traced her ribs. "I'm not *too* soft, am I?" she asked as she followed the line of his beard from his sideburn down to the faint cleft in his stubborn chin.

"Just enough, my love, just enough," and he rolled onto his back.

She remembered her concern before his distractive seduction and tapped his cheek slightly to get him to listen. Her concern was overlaid by a new revelation. "Do you know that this is the first time we have made love with someone else in the house?" she asked.

"Mmm, not so," David disagreed.

"What do you mean? How could I be mistaken about something like that?"

"John was home when we were in the pool," he said, and a wicked smile moved across his face.

"That doesn't count. He was inside and we were outside."

"Merely a technicality, sweetheart. Do you realize the

risk you took when you let me carry you naked through the house? Imagine the possibility of John's hearing us and opening his door and discovering us.''

"Oh, my. I never even thought of that! You must have seduced me to the point where my good sense was numb.''

"I don't recall that you acted very numb. In fact, for a self-professed old-fashioned prude, you were rather... responsive?''

She interrupted him with a kiss, trying to cover the turmoil she felt. "Don't tease me. I'm still a prude at times. David, do you think the weekend will be okay? I get an uneasy feeling when I think about all these people being here. Sometimes my daughter can be, well, a troublemaker. I'm not sure how to explain it, but I'm more than a little worried.''

"It'll be fine, love. After all, she's your child, isn't she? If she's half as sweet as her mother, there's nothing to worry your pretty head about.'' He pulled her into a more comfortable position against him and whispered softly, "Be still, love. Now sleep. Tomorrow will be a busy day for both of us.'' He kissed her temple, slipped one hand around her waist to tug her a little closer and whispered in her ear, "Love you, honey.''

She was aware of his steady deep breathing as she continued to lie awake, thinking of the visitors. She wondered when Sarah would arrive. Sarah had never been known for her tactfulness. If Sarah caused problems or did anything to hurt or embarrass D.A., Sammy would never forgive herself for allowing the visit. Dealing with Sarah usually made her feel inadequate. If the roaming couple decided to bypass the ranch, Sammy would be greatly relieved.

She listened to the wind rustling the limbs of the cottonwood tree near their bedroom window. Each time a limb would scratch against the window pane, she visualized the naked limb, stripped bare by the change in the fall temperature. Winter hadn't officially arrived, yet the temperature outside was well below freezing. She still had to continually fight her fear of the cold. No matter how warmly she dressed, its killing effect filtered through her clothing into her body, reminding her of the mountain cabin.

She sighed and adjusted her position in the bed. David's arm tightened slightly around her waist in his sleep. She moved her head against his chest and listened to the steady beat of his heart, but it was well into the night before her mind could find the peace needed to permit sleep. Perhaps she could draw some needed strength from her husband. He seemed to have a reserve supply.

CHAPTER FIFTEEN

SARAH ROBERTS crawled from the old van, stretched her long limbs and surveyed the ranch yard. In the distance, the sunlight reflected off a shiny object in the hand of a tall blond man wearing a plaid Pendleton jacket. She wondered who he was; probably a ranch hand. She would investigate later.

First, she had to satisfy her curiosity regarding her mother's new husband. Remarriage was the last thing Sarah had ever expected of her straitlaced, narrow-minded, middle-aged mother. What in the world would this David McCormack look like?

"Oh, my, my, my," she murmured to herself, as a tall muscular man dressed in Western clothes appeared in the doorway. She pegged him as old from the gray in his hair, then had second thoughts as she whispered, "But, you're gorgeous." So this was her stepdaddy. How had her mother managed to snag him?

David stood on the porch and watched the young woman approach him. She was tall, probably five feet nine at least, he estimated, and slender, judging from her long legs. But busty, he concluded, as he took in the drape of her ski sweater. It was royal blue and matched her eyes. Her eyes were a brilliant dark blue rather than the soft blue of her mother's, and he saw her long sooty lashes swoop down as she scanned him from his head to the tip of his boot. Her hair was long, dark like her mother's, and gently wavy. It glistened in the bright winter sunlight. So this was Sarah, his new stepdaughter. The thought of having her as a daughter struck him as funny, and he laughed aloud.

She pranced up the steps and stopped directly in front of him. "Hi!" she smiled. "You must be David." She reached up and kissed his mouth, threw her arms around his neck and hugged him, confirming his estimation of her bosom.

David stepped back, startled by her boldness, and said, "Yes, but... I'll... I'll get your mother. She must be around here somewhere." He untangled himself from her embrace and hastily retreated inside the house. "Good Lord," he exclaimed, as he shut the door behind him. He found Sammy in their bedroom. "Sam, your daughter is here," he announced, then began to laugh.

"Sarah's here? Where?" she cried.

"Outside." He laughed again.

"What's so funny?" she asked.

"She kissed me."

"She... kissed you? Why?"

"Oh," he said, "just because she wanted to, I guess." He laughed again, then sobered as he read her worried expression. "You'd better go greet her, Sam. She's too much for me."

When Sammy stepped onto the front porch, Sarah had disappeared.

SAMMY SLIPPED the chicken casserole into the oven, burning her hand as she carelessly touched the hot rack. She concentrated on preparing a tossed salad and tried to forget the guests. They were all outside, including

David, who'd left the house still smiling about the kiss from Sarah.

Flashes of motion and color caught her attention, and she strained to see out the window, across the yard to an old tree where a broken swing hung, and five people stood motioning wildly to one another.

David and Sarah appeared to be the central figures in an argument. Was D.A. trying to bring peace to the group? Sammy wasn't sure. She knew it was Sarah's fault; wasn't it always Sarah?

The group spun apart. David went quickly to the stable, his movements angry and hostile. What had happened? D.A. had put his arm around Sarah's shoulders and appeared to be talking to her. Reasoning, more likely, Sammy surmised. Paul and Betsy followed them to the house in animated conversation. The four stopped just below the porch steps and out of Sammy's view. She heard their voices but not their words.

They entered the warm cozy kitchen and looked at her, then all but D.A. went into the living room.

"D.A., what happened out there between your father and Sarah? Did they...?" Her voice broke, as a premonition of trouble brewing settled over her.

"I'm afraid middle-aged conservatism met head on with liberated youth over the subject of pot," he explained. He smiled slightly. "It was a draw."

"Oh, no! I've told her again and again to never... what did your father do? He must be furious. He hates that kind of thing," she said, but D.A. turned and left the room, refusing to elaborate.

David returned just as lunch was ready. He had little to say during the meal, but his attention strayed to

Sarah several times, and Sammy's questions were ignored more than once. What was going on between them? She couldn't decide whether she sensed hostility or attraction.

Her appetite diminished, and she left the table before the meal was over. She remained in the kitchen, concentrating on the hot soapy dishwater in the sink, her thoughts dark with turmoil.

David entered, came to her and kissed her neck. She jumped at his touch, emitting a startled cry.

"What's the matter, Sam?" he asked as he kissed her cheek. "Here, let me help." Before she could decline the offer, he began to dry the dishes she had stacked in the drain rack.

"What do you think of our guests?" she asked.

He paused in his wiping. "Betsy is her usual good-natured self. I'd almost hoped she might become my daughter-in-law, but I hear she's marrying Jason, a friend of D.A.'s. I've met him. Now talk about a straight guy." David laughed. "Paul is jealous of anyone who notices your very attractive daughter. I think D.A. has done just that and is a little overwhelmed by her. D.A. and Sarah do make a striking couple, don't they? He's good-looking and she's beautiful, and they're both so tall. I think there's something between them. Maybe it runs in the two families—attraction, you know? It's probably a good thing she's leaving tomorrow for Phoenix."

"What about Sarah?" Sammy persisted.

"Sarah? I'm just not sure of her. She's quite beautiful, like her mom," he said. He kissed her lips, his mouth lingering as his hand slipped under her sweater to touch her bare skin. He moved his hand to her breast, then quickly withdrew it as Sarah and Betsy slowly pushed the kitchen door open, arms loaded with dishes. ''Damn houseguests,'' he muttered, and left the room to join the younger men in front of the television set.

The sun advanced across the afternoon sky and the atmosphere in the house warmed considerably. As Sammy returned from a trip to the kitchen, she noticed her daughter had moved to the arm of David's large overstuffed chair.

Sarah draped her arm around the back of the chair and leaned against David's shoulder. Sammy tensed and held her breath. What was she up to now? Sammy felt ashamed of her suspicions. Why couldn't she just accept her as an affectionate daughter getting to know her new stepfather? Her attempted rationale vanished abruptly as she watched Sarah lean her face toward David, her long wavy hair blocking Sammy's view for an instant. As Sarah's hand reached up to brush her hair out of the way, Sammy saw David raise his face to Sarah. Sarah gave him a light kiss on his lips before David could pull away.

Fear and jealousy gripped Sammy, and a blind fury took hold. The little tramp...how dared she! David frowned and said something to Sarah as he glanced toward Sammy standing in the doorway. Sarah shrugged her shoulders, then slithered away from his chair and joined Paul on the floor. Sammy considered David's reactions and was unable to decide if he had liked the attention from Sarah.

She steeled herself against the emotions building inside her. ''It doesn't matter,'' she said aloud, and retreated to the kitchen, her mind full of memories of Jake and her young friend Kali.

MARY RUSSELL called later that afternoon and reminded David and Sammy of their promise to attend a community Christmas program that evening. The outing had been planned long before the families' fight. David answered the phone and assured her they would be in the audience. When he reminded Sammy she seemed hesitant at first, and her mood grew somber as they prepared to leave for the performance.

The presentation was to be held in the junior-high auditorium in town. The traveling took almost as long as the performance, but they kept their promise and sat in the fourth row.

David saw the look of pleasure in the young girl's brown eyes when she located them in the audience. Mary had her father's dark eyes, and David was reminded of his rift with his friend. When he and Sammy met the Russells at the school auditorium exit they were forced to acknowledge each other's presence. The two men shook hands formally and moved apart. Sammy returned Russ's glare with one of her own. Julie and David exchanged smiles, then Julie shook her head in a silent message, and David lifted his brows in frustration over the continuing division between the two couples.

"I'm glad we went," David remarked as he helped Sammy into the high cab of the truck.

"Yes," was all she said.

Damn it all, what's the matter with her, he wondered. Was it just Russ or the events of the day? Tension over their families coming together for the first time?

Sammy noticed his heavy frown as he drove silently down the dark winding road to the ranch. Why was he mad at her? She hadn't done anything to anger him. He was the one who had made a fool of himself over Sarah. Couldn't he keep his hands to himself? He had told her he liked to touch her. Maybe he enjoyed caressing her daughter as well.

As she looked at him through the darkness of the enclosed cab, she was torn between her love for him and a new feeling of dislike and uncertainty about the future. She was trapped against her will, and her mind began to search for solutions.

The truck turned into the ranch yard and the headlights fell on the two couples sitting on the porch. As David and Sammy walked to the house, the heavy odor of marijuana smoke permeated the cold air. D.A. rose quickly and disappeared inside.

David rushed into the living room and slammed the door, leaving a shocked Sammy outside with the other three guests.

"It's my new stepdaddy," Sarah volunteered, giggling. "He disapproves of pot and thinks his goody-goody son should, too, but he doesn't!" Her musical laughter filled the pungent night air.

"Oh, Sarah, how could you!" Sammy cried. She jerked her head away from her daughter as angry voices came from the house. She ran inside, just in time to hear David's voice raised as he described Sarah's conduct. Sammy could hear D.A. defend her daughter. She closed the door and sagged against it in defeat.

"At least we did it outside and didn't pollute your damn house," D.A. shouted at his father.

"My house? It's your house, too. Doesn't it mean anything to you?" David raged. "That bitch of a girl reeks of drugs and God knows what else!"

Sammy stood motionless, sick to her stomach with grief.

D.A.'s voice had a tremor in it as he replied, "Damn it all, dad, don't be so old-fashioned. You're a hypocrite. You and Sammy and her pregnancy prove that!"

Sammy closed her eyes in shame and opened them just in time to see D.A. rubbing his jaw and David stomping to their bedroom, his face livid with color.

D.A. continued to rub his bruised jaw. "I'm sorry, Sammy," he said as he left the room. The door slammed, and he disappeared into the cold night.

She was frightened as she looked down the hallway to the closed bedroom door. As she entered the room, David mumbled, "I'm glad they're all leaving tomorrow." He sat on the side of the bed gripping his stomach, but Sammy was too upset to notice. He calmed considerably as he undressed, and some of the fear left her.

He slid under the quilt and bed linens and gave her a slight smile, but the insulting words he had spoken about her daughter churned in her mind. She had raised her daughter the best she could. Was he really saying that it was her fault? Her sons had turned out fine, why not Sarah? Sarah had made a mistake by encouraging the others to participate in the smoking episode, but David had no right to insult her as well as her daughter. Her thoughts were interrupted by his touch.

"David, why did you call...?" The question was

halted by his mouth as he kissed her and tried to initiate lovemaking.

She tensed as he moved his hand up past her breast to her neck and tried to arouse her. She neither warmed to nor rejected his overtures. After a few attempts to draw a response from her, he gave it up as a wasted effort and took her selfishly, angrily. For the first time in their lovemaking, there was no satisfaction for her.

He turned his back to her, in rejection of her silence and passivity.

Was he painfully telling her that the honeymoon was over? She lay awake long after he had fallen asleep. Was he more like Jake than she had thought? Was this the existence for which she was sacrificing her home and career in Phoenix? He had apparently put on quite a show of affection to persuade her into being his helpmate, but bedmate and servant were more like it. This was not her willing submission: this was his domination.

She stared through the darkness and listened to the cottonwood limb scratch against the windowpane. The more her mind dwelled on being marooned in this frigid wilderness, the more she longed for the warm desert climate, the security and independence of her own making and under her own control. Here she was at his mercy. She had thought she loved him, but now she wasn't so sure.

Maybe she was trying to recapture her dreams of romance when she was young and innocent. Maybe she was just fooling herself that such a loving relationship could ever exist between herself and a man like David. Wasn't he really just a stranger whom she had known for a few years long, long ago? She was a fool!

Her sick leave would expire in just nine days. She had to show up for work or she would be terminated. How could she make the mortgage payments on her home if she didn't have a job? She certainly couldn't expect David to cover that expense. She would never ask him for money.

Her family would all be coming to her house for Christmas, just as they had each year since Lawrence's birth. It had become a tradition—Mike's family joining hers for a rousing and sentimental Christmas dinner followed by phone calls to the other Gardner sisters and brothers now scattered to the four winds.

She had to get back to Phoenix. So many matters were at stake.

David had his family in Forsyth; and she only rationalized that they would accept her, the way the Russells had pretended to accept her for a while.

The soft outsider had to find a way home. There were too many differences in their life-styles to ever make it work. Montana cold was a long way from Arizona warmth. Determination settled over her and she lay awake, chilled, until the small hours of the morning.

DAVID WAS GONE when Sammy awoke, but she heard voices coming from the kitchen. She quickly dressed in a bulky sweater and wool pants and tried to relax her tense body in order to face the group down the hall. She was surprised when she entered the warm kitchen to find David, Sarah and Paul talking quietly over steaming mugs of coffee. It was as though last night had never happened.

"Where's D.A. and Betsy?" Sammy asked.

"They left about an hour ago. They said to tell you goodbye, and D.A. said he'd call us for Christmas," David replied as though all was well.

What had happened while she slept? Had they made up or left still angry? Was it her fault they had fought? Had David ever hit his son before? She began to suspect that David was really a more violent man than she had ever imagined. He put on a good show of pacifism, but she was convinced that underneath there was a cruel streak, dangerous and evil. Would she be safe alone with him? Her fears grew as she observed his apparently carefree chatter with her sparkling daughter.

David rose and came to give her a kiss. She would play his game for a while. Dutifully she raised her face to accept his show of affection, but couldn't bring herself to smile.

"Don't forget our luncheon with the Morrisons today. I've told Sarah and Paul, and they understand. They're planning to leave late this afternoon. The weather bureau predicts snow tomorrow, and they should get as far south on the interstate as possible before the bad weather hits," he said, seeming to take for granted her agreement.

"Fine," she replied.

The luncheon with the Morrisons was tense but tolerable. David was convinced that he and Sammy were acting the parts of newlyweds and even played his role by displaying affection several times.

Sammy reluctantly accepted his overplaying in their charade, but he knew it was a game for her when he felt her cold hands and stiff shoulders as he stood with his arm around her while they said their goodbyes at the door.

The drive home was made in silence until they turned into the main gate of the ranch.

"Sammy, we must talk," he said.

"What's there to talk about?"

"Sammy, last night you...."

"That's strange, I thought it was you who...."

"Damn it, Sammy!" he growled and then stopped trying to explain.

They were both sullen and silent as they entered the house. The living room was dark with the draperies drawn. The odor of marijuana drifted through the room. Muffled laughter came from David and Sammy's bedroom, and David charged through the hallway and threw the bedroom door open wide.

"Damn you all to hell!" he shouted. "Get out of my house and don't ever come back!"

Sammy rushed to the bedroom door in time to see a partially clad Paul run to the bathroom. Sarah sat up in her mother's bed, defiantly displaying her naked bosom.

Sarah held up her hand in greeting. "Hi, dad." She smiled flirtatiously.

"You little bitch, didn't you have any upbringing at all?" he thundered, heading for the bed.

Sammy ran to him and grabbed his jacket sleeve. "No! Don't, David. Don't hit her," she screamed.

David turned to her as she jerked at his sleeve, and he switched his attack to her, anger mixed with frustration on his weary face. "Sammy, don't you care, either? This bitch of a daughter of yours has defiled our bed.

Don't you care anymore?'' A note of pleading entered his voice, but Sammy was too upset and frightened to notice.

"Leave her alone, I'll take care of her. Just don't you touch her, David,'' Sammy threatened.

David's anger was replaced with disgust for her defiance of him and support of her daughter's conduct. He whirled away, and as he left the room he said, "To hell with it all. It's not worth it.''

Sammy heard the living-room door slam, then the muffled sound of an engine as the truck left the yard with tires screeching and flying gravel hitting the porch.

"I'm sorry, mom,'' Sarah apologized as she quickly dressed. She looked at her distraught mother. "Want to come with us? We'll be back home by Wednesday. You might be... safer there. Do you really want to stay here with such a violent man after what he's done and said to you?'' She turned then and left the room.

Thoughts of her waiting career, the security of her own home and the warmth of her family and friends in Phoenix suddenly jelled in Sammy's mind and buried any hope of a future with David McCormack. The decision was made. She quickly packed the clothes she had brought from Phoenix and stood hesitantly by the bed.

"We're ready, mom,'' Sarah called from the door. "We'll be waiting in the van. You'd better hurry.''

Sammy looked around the bedroom trying to avoid the memories that began to creep in to her thoughts. She found a small piece of paper and wrote a short note. He deserved at least that consideration.

She laid the note on the dresser next to a piece of jewelry, unable to see clearly through her tears. She ran from the room, the house and the memories. She stumbled to the van with her one suitcase, and the vehicle was soon moving down the narrow road.

She was sitting in the second seat of the van, staring at her clutched hands, and didn't notice that as they turned onto the access road to the interstate highway, a pale blue pickup truck passed them. Its driver wore a sullen frown as he slowed and turned onto the same narrow gravel roadway they had just left.

A small smile tugged at the corners of Sarah's beautiful mouth as she watched the receding truck in the van's rearview mirror.

CHAPTER SIXTEEN

WHEN DAVID FOUND HER NOTE, he read it over and over, unable to accept the finality it brought.

> Dear David,
>   It was a mistake. I really thought it would work, but I was wrong. It was a big mistake.
>
> Love, Sammy

On Monday he slipped the note into his shirt pocket, hidden by his suit jacket, and somehow made it through the day in Butte. His return to the quiet house in the evening brought the memories of her brutally alive again. He opened the bedroom door and dropped onto the bed. Tenderly he fingered the gold locket she had left behind, opening the clasp to stare vacantly at the tiny picture of a smiling woman and a wet man, both in swimsuits.

How had things gone so astray when they had seemed so right? Was it the sudden collision of family members? Was it that bitch of a daughter, who had flaunted her youth and bosomy sexuality at him? Lord, was she endowed! He started to smile, but the seriousness of the problem sobered his thoughts. Sammy had hinted more than once that he was attracted to her daughter, but how wrong she was. There was only one woman he loved and desired. He thought he had made that perfectly clear; apparently he had failed and failed miserably.

David's thoughts turned to his son. He had never hit D.A. before, even when he was young and possibly needed a spanking. The two of them had always reasoned the problems out, but suddenly he had spoiled it all with violence.

Just when he thought he had his life under control, Sammy had come along and caused an upheaval. How could they have gone from a beautiful Friday filled with warmth and love through a weekend of fighting and violence to a Sunday of hell?

Stubborn woman! She was gone, but he was surrounded by her presence. Her blue gown lay on the foot of their bed. His fingers touched the soft material, bringing memories of her soft skin and her willing responsiveness. Now she was gone. . . for good. He tried to throw the gown across the room. Its light weight resisted his effort, and it fluttered to the floor near his feet. He retrieved it and held it close, choked with feelings of frustration and futility. His thoughts were too jumbled to make decisions. Maybe tomorrow he'd know what to do.

When he returned to the silent and lonely house on Tuesday, the phone was ringing. Sammy. Of course he'd go get her wherever she might be. He fumbled with the key and lock, listening to the ringing of the phone inside. Finally the door opened, and he lunged into the kitchen and grabbed the receiver. "Hello?"

It was D.A. calling from Missoula. He apologized for the part he had played in the terrible weekend.

"I made a fool of myself over Sarah, dad. She played us against one another. I can see that now. Dad, I don't want to ever come between you and Sammy. You shouldn't let Sarah cause problems, either. What you and Sammy have is special, so keep it that way. Can I talk to her?" he asked.

There was silence, then David said, "She's gone."

"What do you mean, gone? Dad!"

"Gone is gone. We had another argument about Sarah. I left in anger. . .in the truck. When I returned, she was gone. She left with Sarah and Paul and has returned to Phoenix. I guess she's on the road somewhere in Arizona by now. I don't know if it was her idea or Sarah's, but she's gone."

David listened disinterestedly as D.A. tried to offer advice and alternatives. Finally he interrupted his son. "It's over. She's gone."

D.A. disagreed. "You shouldn't give up. Go after her."

"It was her decision. She's too stubborn. If she and that daughter of hers agree about me, then. . . ."

"Dad," D.A. pleaded, "you're wrong. Don't let your pride come between you two. I know she loves you. She's upset just as you are. Call her when she gets there and talk her into coming back."

"No, I won't go running after her."

JULIE RUSSELL called the McCormack ranch and asked for Sammy. She glanced at the calendar on the wall. It was Thursday, almost a week since she'd heard from her friend. She was alarmed when David answered her abruptly and said, "She's not here, Julie."

"When will she be back, David? I need to talk to her."

"She's gone, damn it. She's gone and won't be back. She's in Phoenix, where everyone thinks she belongs," his deep voice stated flatly, and then the connection was broken.

Julie turned to her husband, but before she could tell him what had happened, he snarled, "I told you not to call them."

"Oh, shut up, Ed!" Julie cried. "She's not there. David says she's returned to Phoenix. They've separated!"

WES FRANKLIN stood in Sammy McCormack's office door, looking confident and well-groomed. "Hello-o-o, doll! I see the one and only Ms Samantha Roberts is back at the mighty Mastiff Corporation. Are you going to solve all the computer-systems problems that have been bugging us while you were away?"

She rose from her chair, adjusting her white knit sweater over the flared rust Ultrasuede skirt. She felt self-conscious at his use of her name.

"Hey, doll, you're looking great. You've lost weight. You were getting a little chunky just before you left on that extended vacation of yours. I heard you were ill. What was wrong? All we heard was that you were rushed to a hospital. What the hell were you doing in Montana anyway? That's cowboy country." He bombarded her with questions and then sauntered to one of the chairs near the window and waited for her explanation. His confidence in his right to know irritated her.

The intercom on her phone buzzed and she picked up the receiver. "Yes, Dorothy?"

"Do you want to be rescued?" her secretary asked from the outer room. "I can fake a call if you want to get rid of him. You know, Sammy, while you were gone he hinted that the two of you had something going."

Sammy frowned at Wes as she listened to her secretary. The arrogance of him; he wouldn't dare! Yes, she decided, he probably would. She knew some of the programmers had thought she had received her promotion a few years ago by sleeping with her boss. If they only knew how she really felt about the debonair Mr. Franklin. "No thanks, I can handle it," Sammy replied.

"Have a seat, Wes. Make yourself at home." She looked at him, feeling she had a slight advantage. She sat in her chair and dropped her hands into her lap beneath the desk top. Her nervous fingers toyed with the rings, causing a swell of memories to surface. Why hadn't she removed the rings? The marriage was over, wasn't it? Still, there was a rightness about their placement. Maybe...no, it was finished. David hadn't bothered to call. He was apparently satisfied and had accepted the separation.

"Hey, doll, the company Christmas party is Saturday evening at the Biltmore. How about you and me...?" Wes winked at her. "Besides, I want to apologize for last summer. Your charm and beauty just overwhelmed me, and I lost my cool. I wouldn't want that little episode to come between us now that we'll be working together...late hours...private meetings...you know."

Sammy groaned. "Wes, some people around here

have the mistaken idea that we.... Wes, I think I'd better clear the air about us." She tried to explain, but the words didn't seem right.

He ignored her attempt and continued. "What was wrong with you anyway? You were gone for more than two months. It must have been serious, but you sure look beautiful now. Why, Samantha, my little doll, you look even younger than when you left, and you know how good-looking older women turn me on. It's almost noon. Can I take you to lunch as a welcome home treat? It's on me."

Perhaps away from the office would be the best place to enlighten her overzealous suitor. "Okay, Wes, I suppose lunch would be safe enough. Meet me here in an hour. Now, please, I have work to do. Would you close the door as you go out. Thanks," she murmured, ducking her head to hide the gleam of tears in her eyes. Wes's gray suit had triggered memories of her wedding ceremony with David. She hadn't noticed the suit until Wes turned to leave and suddenly his wide muscular shoulders brought vivid images of David as he had waited with her, holding her hand, while the minister found his place in his Bible. That scene disappeared, and the memory of her first sight of him at the airport took its place. The Ultrasuede skirt she was wearing matched his hair as well as the Stetson he had had on that memorable night last summer when love came to her. She touched the skirt and sobbed.

"Oh, God, give me strength," she prayed. "Help me to forget."

She was in firm control by the time Wes returned for lunch. They left the department area together. Wes put his arm casually around Sammy's shoulders. Dorothy frowned, and Debbie stared wide-eyed as Herb whispered something to her.

During lunch, Wes brought her up to date on all the latest items on the corporate grapevine. When he hinted that the president and two vice-presidents had been involved in a running dispute with the board chairman and three other senior-level executives, she groaned, "Not again. Oh, I hate to hear that."

"You know how that dictatorial chairman of ours is," Wes said. "Anyone who disagrees had better either come around and see the light his way, or start looking for alternative employment. Samantha, doll, I sure hope you know which side your bread is buttered on, because I think old man Pike is going to clean house again."

Jonas Pike was known for his strong leadership as board chairman. In the fifteen years that Sammy had worked at Mastiff he had gone through a number of presidents. In her position as liaison between the computer-systems groups and the user groups in the company, she had had occasion to work with the last three presidents and had found them all to be quite capable, but two had left after only a few years, and now Stan Birdseye was probably on the way out as well. She liked him. He cared about employee problems and had supported Sammy several times when management disputes had caused friction and she had recommended compromises.

It felt invigorating to be back in the excitement of the systems environment, but the underlying corporate intrigue had a very different effect on Sammy. She had almost forgotten the stress and pressures of the business world during the two-month hiatus on the ranch with its blue skies, horses and cattle, white snow...and David.

She heard Wes call to her through her rambling thoughts.

"Samantha, are you all right, doll?"

She recovered her composure. "Wes, there are a few things I think we need to clear up, especially between us. Please listen and don't interrupt." She looked at his familiar, rather handsome face, but saw David's rust-flecked green eyes and easy smile. Tears quickly formed to blur her vision.

Wes handed her a napkin from the table. "Samantha, you aren't okay, are you? What the hell happened up north?"

She knew she had his undivided attention. "Wes, my name is no longer Roberts. It's McCor—"

Wes interrupted, "I know that. I saw the rings this morning when everyone was making a big fuss over your return. I listen to the grapevine. I've even fed it a few times." He smiled.

"Please, Wes. My name is McCormack. My husband is a dear friend from long ago, and his first name is David. He's an engineer but plans to retire to his ranch next spring and...." Her voice broke with a sob.

Wes sat silently studying her, waiting for an explanation. When it didn't come, he asked, "Doll, then why are you here in Phoenix again?"

She fought for the composure necessary to continue. "We had some differences of opinion...personal matters...and I have obligations here. I have my career at

Mastiff to consider... I can't just give that up. Maybe I'm just... I don't know." She frowned at him.

"Anyway, here I am, back in Phoenix, for what it's worth. I just don't know what's going to happen. I haven't heard.... I need time to think things out. I just don't know." She sighed, burdened by the uncertainty.

He moved his hand to her arm. When she didn't withdraw, he began to massage her soft skin suggestively and whispered, "Let me help you, Samantha. I can make you forget him. He's hurt you—I can tell that. I like you, baby, I always have. I can even make it worth your while here at Mastiff. Jonas Pike is my friend. I'll put in a good word for you if he decides to clean house as I think he will. When you divorce that McDermitt guy you'll need your job here, and I can help."

She sat glaring at him as his words began to make sense.

Wes interpreted her silence as acceptance. As they prepared to leave the restaurant, he assisted her with her jacket and his hand brushed against her breast. He smiled at her.

She was furious at his misunderstanding and jerked away. "No, Wes," she tried to explain, and once again David's face filled her thoughts. "You don't understand at all!"

"Sure I do. I can help with what you need most. I can make you forget him."

"No, I don't want to forget him. I love him! Wes," she seethed, "you're the last person who could make up for him. He's twice the man you'll ever hope to be." She clenched her fists tightly, trying to control her emotions, but the tears flowed down her cheeks and she ran from the restaurant, leaving a startled Wes Franklin behind to pay the bill.

Gradually she regained her composure as she walked around the business complex several times, trying vainly to sort out her feelings. She avoided the noisy crowd of employees waiting at the bank of elevators and shielded her privacy by walking up sixteen flights of stairs, slipping quietly into her office and catching her breath before calling her secretary on the intercom. "Dorothy, take all my calls this afternoon. I can't talk to anyone...thanks." She quickly buried herself in the work before her.

As she left the Mastiff office building that evening, she tried to shut out thoughts of David as well as the unpleasant luncheon with Wes. Her head throbbed, and her body ached with tension. She'd been home a week, and already she knew she was crumbling.

In her initial numbed emotional state after returning to Phoenix, she had agreed to let Sarah and Paul stay in her home until they could make other plans. Now Sammy knew it had been a mistake. She knew that Sarah had made only a halfhearted attempt to find employment. She resented Paul's presence in her home. Something had to be done.

In the past few days, she had had several heated discussions with Sarah. David was never discussed. However, Sarah was willing to bring up D.A.'s name often in the conversations, especially when Paul was present.

Sammy pulled into the driveway and rested her head on the steering wheel of her car, wanting to avoid any unpleasant confrontation with Sarah and Paul. She forced herself to leave the car and approached the house. As she entered the quiet living room, she knew something was amiss. Usually Sarah played the stereo at decibels painful to Sammy's ears, but tonight there was only silence. She was greeted by a hungry Duke, mewing for his dinner. Sarah should have fed him. The silence led her directly to Sarah's room. It was bare.

She quickly went to John's room, where Paul had pretended to stay. It was cleaned out of all signs of occupancy. Sarah had been the reason Sammy had used to convince herself that David was a dangerous man. Had she let this irresponsible daughter push her to a decision that might be sickeningly wrong?

She ran back to Sarah's room. She could see no reason for the absence of clothing and belongings. She walked in a daze to the kitchen. As she turned to the refrigerator, she saw a note from Sarah scrawled on the message board attached to the refrigerator door.

Mom, we left for San Diego. Paul has a brother there. We want to spend Christmas on the beaches. Sorry.

                                   Love, Sarah
P.S. We took John's portable stereo. I'll give it to him the next time I see him.

The telephone rang, jarring her out of her trance. She reached for it and said, "Hello?"

"It's David," a male voice said. She was stunned, until the recognition registered through her fog of thoughts about Sarah and David.

"Your number-two son, mom. David. Remember me?" he laughed. "How are you? The reason I'm call-

ing is that I won't be able to be home for Christmas.
You remember Cathy Carter, the girl I brought home
last September, just before you left for Montana? Well,
things are getting pretty serious. Her folks live in New
Mexico, and they've invited me to spend the holiday
with them. I knew all the other kids would be there with
you, so I accepted. You understand, right? Mom, are
you still there?" he asked.

"Sure, David, I understand. Thanks for warning me
in advance. I won't have to cook quite as much food.
Have a good time. I love you. Say hello to Cathy for
me. Goodbye, darling."

She hung up the phone and mentally ticked off the
family members who would be missing from the tradi-
tional Christmas dinner at her home. John was on
board ship somewhere in the south Pacific; Sarah was
frolicking on the southern California beaches; David
would be visiting a prospective fiancée in New Mexico.
That left only Lawrence's family and Mike's family.

The phone rang again. It was Lawrence to give her
advance warning that they would be there in about an
hour. Would she be home?

"Of course. I'd love to have you." She had seen her
new granddaughter once since returning to Phoenix.
Loretta Evelyn was her name, and the proud mother
and father called her Lorrie. Sammy knew she should
love and enjoy the baby, but the painful memory of her
own lost daughter hindered her effort.

Lorrie was almost six weeks old. She had her
mother's auburn hair, which only served to remind
Sammy of David's rusty brown waves of thickness...
she could almost feel the texture. She had been able to

hold the baby for only a few moments before the emotional reaction had forced her to return the infant to Eve. Lawrence had looked puzzled at her actions, but Sammy had volunteered no explanation. Her children knew of her surgery but not of the pregnancy, and she intended to keep it that way. D.A. knew, but he was in Montana. Montana...David...what was he doing... did he ever think of her?

She had no pictures of him, and the thought disturbed her. The locket had been overlooked as she had hastily packed at the ranch. She had been halfway to Phoenix when she had reached up to touch the treasured gift and found it missing from her throat. She remembered removing it that last night, the night of the unsatisfactory lovemaking, the night he had turned away from her in rejection, the night she had decided to leave.

That night was in the past. Their relationship had been so tied to the past that it had blinded them to the present and future. What on earth could two people actually have in common when thirty years of separate experiences divided them. Love? That was romantic foolishness. Would she be able to forget what he looked like, his smile, his gentle touch, his patient way of arousing a passion she hadn't known she was capable of? She shook the memories away.

She would concentrate on her future at Mastiff, her growing family, her home—all the things she could depend on and control. There had to be more to the rest of her life than that one impossible dream of a life with David.

The doorbell interrupted her reverie and spared her more upsetting thoughts. She was determined to make

an effort. She opened the door and greeted her oldest
son, who was laden with Christmas packages, and Eve,
holding a beautiful tiny baby girl.

"Mom, the tree lights aren't turned on. Shame,
where's your Christmas spirit?" Lawrence scolded as
he switched on the colorful twinkling lights on the tree
that Sarah and Paul had decorated. He arranged the
packages around the tall tree and admired his handi-
work.

Sammy pushed herself and tried to enjoy her grandchild. Lorrie smiled at her and made all the right cooing
noises to impress a first-time grandmother while her
proud parents beamed.

After a half hour of casual family chatter, Lawrence
grew serious and said, "Mom, the real reason we
came over tonight was to tell you that we won't be here
for Christmas like most years. I knew all the others
would be here, so when Eve's parents invited us to
spend the holidays in San Francisco, we accepted.
They've never seen Lorrie, and this is a perfect time
to go. I have a week off from the bank, and we're leaving Saturday morning. We'll be back the next weekend.
You don't mind, do you? We've spent all the other
Christmases together so this one won't make a lot of
difference."

Sammy looked down at Lorrie, regained control of
her emotions and said in a reassuring voice, "Of course
it's okay. George and Emily have a right to see their
granddaughter. I'm lucky you two live right here in
Phoenix. Of course you should go. Have a lovely time.
We'll miss you all, but sooner or later our family has to
divide."

On Thursday Sammy received a call from a nervous Maggie. Maggie seldom called Sammy at work.

"Maggie, what's wrong?"

"Sammy, I meant to call you last night, but we were so busy with our packing that Mike and I both just forgot."

"Packing?" a puzzled Sammy asked.

"Oh, yes. I'm so excited. You remember my dad was transferred to Fort Bliss last summer? Well, mom has sent us some plane tickets as a Christmas gift, and we're flying to El Paso for Christmas. Mike and I knew your children would be there with you, so it's not as though we're leaving you all alone. I've always enjoyed the Christmases with your family, but I miss my own family, too. With mom helping with expenses—well, how could we refuse? You do understand, don't you?"

"When do you leave?" Sammy forced an interest that she didn't feel at all.

"Tonight at 8:30. Oh, Sammy, I'm so excited I can hardly wait. We'll spend Christmas with mom and dad, then we're going to Juarez for a day and then up to Carlsbad Caverns. Doesn't it sound great? We'll be back here in time for Mike to be ready for work on the Monday after the holidays."

Sammy's secretary came to the door and indicated she had a call waiting. "I've got to go, Maggie. I'm very pleased for you. Have a great time. Say goodbye to Mike and the children."

The call was from Stan Birdseye, Mastiff's president. "Sammy, welcome back. Can you come to my office, please?"

"Sure, Stan. Right now?" she asked. Stan had been

out of town when Sammy returned, and this was the first time she had spoken to him.

"No, no, after lunch will be fine. How about 1:00 P.M.? I need to do some things before I see you."

"I'll be there. Should I bring anything?"

"No, no, young lady, just yourself, please."

Sammy laughed softly as she returned to her work. Stan Birdseye was fifty years old, but he always called her young lady. She preferred that to Wes Franklin's girl and doll phrases. For Wes there were only men and girls in the business world. She hadn't seen Wes since their unpleasant luncheon. She wondered if he was avoiding her. Office rumors were flying again, with some proving to be true. Two middle managers had been pressured into resigning. One had been a close friend.

The presidential suite was tastefully decorated, but Sammy felt a sense of foreboding as the secretary led her into the office. Stan Birdseye sat behind a beautifully carved but slightly outdated desk and was fingering several sheets of paper and an envelope as she entered.

"Sit down, young lady. I have some good news and some bad news." She watched him nervously shuffle the papers and wondered how bad the bad news might be. Had the corporate housecleaning finally taken place? Who had been affected? She knew she was far enough down the corporate ladder to be spared from the politics that went with the executive level of management at Mastiff.

"Our illustrious but dictatorial chairman of the board has finally carried out his threats, Sammy. He gave me my official notice this morning," Stan said with a hint of cynicism in his voice. "I knew it was coming, but I didn't think he'd do it so soon, and just before Christmas, too! Three presidents, all chosen by him, and terminated within the last five years. I suppose I should feel flattered that I lasted longer than my two predecessors. Since he chose us himself, I wonder if he stops to think of what that may say about his ability to choose chief executives. One of these days he'll wake up dead and find the company going on without him." He laughed at his illogical statement, then returned to the sobering matter at hand.

Why was he telling her all this, she wondered?

"Old Jonas offered to announce the people leaving," Stan continued, "including myself, and notify those affected, but I felt it was best to do it myself before the gossip mill picked it up. Two vice-presidents have resigned." He leaned back in his executive chair and chuckled. "We seldom fire people here at Mastiff, do we? We just make life miserable enough for them that they either get angry and quit or slink away by resigning. Old Pike's tactics with his people always did disgust me. Why didn't I speak up before this?" He shrugged. "Oh, well, too late now. The VPs were Lee from finance and Ronan from sales. I'm sure you knew them both. There's also going to be a major reorganization, and this is the part that sticks in my craw." He paused, a troubled frown settling on his face. "Sammy, Wes Franklin is being promoted to a new position of assistant vice-president of systems and will be in charge of.... You'd better sit down for this bombshell, Sammy."

She had started to walk restlessly around the suite

when he had begun to name the casualties. The mention of Wes's name stuck a spear into her chest, and she knew it was being slowly turned by Wes Franklin himself.

"Wes has convinced old Jonas that his department and yours should be merged," Stan continued as she returned to her chair. "I think it's a big mistake, but why should I care? I won't be here to know whether it works or not. Anyway, Wes has made his case convincing by arguing that since your department operated without you the two months you were gone, you really aren't needed. Sammy, you and six others in your department are being terminated, effective today. I'm sorry about the short notice, but then I didn't get much myself."

The color drained from her face as the crushing significance of his announcement smothered her. Stan paused to let the bad news register through the thick cloud of depression that had settled in the office.

"If that's the bad news, what in the world is the good news?" she asked, trying to suppress the trembling tone in her voice.

"The company isn't all heartless. We're being paid off quite generously with severance pay. The good-hearted board voted to give us two weeks' pay for each year of service, plus two months' full pay. For me that's just four weeks plus two months. But Sammy, for a longtimer like yourself, that's thirty weeks plus two months. That's enough to get you through the winter and spring and maybe into the summer if you want to take a breather before starting to job hunt again. I know how most of you ladies would like to stay home once in a while. Now you can."

He handed her an envelope containing two checks, shook her hand and made closing remarks of sympathy, but she paid little attention to his words. Wesley Franklin had taken his revenge.

Sammy spent the rest of the day calling her staff into her office and telling each the bad news of the department's dissolution. Some of the workers had been with her for several years, and a team spirit had held them together to such an extent that they knew what she would say even before she began. Only one person blamed her for not cooperating with Wes and giving him what he wanted.

Herb's corporate friendship had paid off. He had received a promotion to systems coordinator, the same title that Sammy had formerly carried, but he would be reporting directly to Wes Franklin. He had selected Debbie as his new secretary.

Sammy's secretary and another assistant turned in their resignations in support of those who had been fired.

Sammy packed her personal belongings, gave Dorothy an affectionate hug and reassured her that she would give her a letter of recommendation if she wanted one. She left the building feeling as though fifteen years of her life had been wasted.

When she arrived home, she fed Duke and went directly to bed, seeking escape in sleep. She didn't know how long she had been asleep when the ringing of the phone on her nightstand awakened her.

"Hello?" she said in a sleepy voice.

All she heard was breathing for several seconds. Thinking it might be an obscene phone call, she started to return the receiver to its cradle when she heard a low masculine voice say angrily, "Nothing!" and the line went silent.

"David!" she shouted into the dead receiver. "David, are you there?" She choked back the sob that tried to slip out. Had she been mistaken? It was probably a wrong number. Or was it David? Her eyes filled with tears. Why hadn't he said more? It had to be him! Maybe they had been disconnected. Should she call him back? Her anguish changed to anger. No! If he wanted to talk to her, he was perfectly capable of redialing a simple phone number. She finally convinced herself that it wasn't him at all, but still she lay awake long into the night, her thoughts filled with memories of the brief time they had shared.

Perhaps if he didn't call again by Christmas, she would try to call him. Maybe they could still be civil to each other and work something out. Love had never been so painful for her; life without him was unbearable and without purpose or direction.

The next several days passed in a fog of inactivity as she spent the time staring at the television set or napping on the sofa. The lights on the tree remained off.

She left the presents untouched under the tree on Christmas morning, but tried twice to call the ranch. There was no answer. David had apparently found something to do for Christmas. His uncle? D.A. in Missoula? Maybe he had renewed his friendship with the Russell family now that she wasn't around to cause trouble.

David's face was vividly before her as she brushed a tear away and fell asleep once again on the sofa with Duke curled beside her for company.

CHAPTER SEVENTEEN

DAVID MCCORMACK displayed little curiosity when he returned to the ranch from Butte several days after Sammy's departure and found his son waiting on the porch for him.

D.A. unfolded his six-foot-two form and smiled. "I was hungry, so I thought I'd just stop by. What's for dinner?"

David grunted something unintelligible and unlocked the door. Bypassing the kitchen, he headed straight for the living room and dropped listlessly into his favorite chair. He sat there staring at the blank television screen.

"Dad, what's for dinner?" D.A. asked again.

"I hadn't planned on anything," David replied, making no effort to rise.

"Stay put and I'll fix something," D.A. said, laying his hand on his father's forearm. He removed his rust suede sheepherder coat, rolled up the sleeves of his cream dress shirt, and loosened and removed a rust-and-cream tweed tie.

David smiled and asked, "Did you dress for dinner, son?"

D.A. glanced down at his wool slacks and dress shirt. "Oh, I was in a hurry and didn't change after my last class. This is what I wear to impress all those pretty freshman girls in my biology class. Sometimes I think they come to class to flirt with the male students more than to learn about me and life sciences and earn a credit toward graduation.'' He laughed good-naturedly and disappeared into the kitchen.

David heard pots and pans banging in the kitchen. He tried to ignore the sound and succeeded for several moments as he gave in to his dark thoughts about his dilemma with Sammy. Finally curiosity brought him to his feet. He entered the kitchen just as his son was scooping out two large servings of spaghetti and meat sauce onto two plates.

D.A. returned to the stove, removed a tray of garlic toast from the broiler, expertly stacked the toast on a plate and slid the plate onto the table. ''Dinner is served,'' he said with a flourish of his serving spoon, his green eyes sparkling behind the wire-rimmed glasses.

A tiny crack of a smile touched David's mouth as he sat down and began to eat. When he had finished the last bite, he said, ''Not bad. I'd forgotten you could cook, D.A.''

''You taught me, don't you remember? I was twelve when we first moved here. You said I had to cook at least one night a week. You were my guinea pig. A lot has happened since then, hasn't it?'' D.A. brushed a few unruly blond curls away from his lean handsome face.

David frowned and his shoulders drooped a little. ''Too much.'' He pushed his chair away from the table and stomped out of the kitchen.

He turned the television knob, paying little attention

to the program he selected by chance, then sat staring at the set for more than an hour.

Each time D.A. asked a question, David frowned and mumbled. Finally in desperation, D.A. jumped up and snapped the TV set off. David continued to stare at the blank screen.

"Dad!"

"What . . . what's the matter?" David looked up with a puzzled expression on his face.

"Dad, what's the matter with you? You have dark circles under your eyes," D.A. asked. "Are you sick?"

"No . . . it's nothing . . . I was just thinking."

"What about?"

"Nothing," David mumbled.

"Sammy?"

"Who? No, of course not," he replied defensively.

"Dad, do you still love her?" D.A. persisted.

David frowned but said nothing.

"Well," D.A. asked, "don't you know?"

"Of course, but what difference does that make?" he asked. "It's over . . . all over."

"How do you know? Maybe she's as unhappy as you are."

"Couldn't be," David replied. "She would have called."

"Have you tried to call her?"

"Of course not."

"Why not? Dad, if you still love her and are too proud to call her, why couldn't she still love you and be just as stubborn and proud as you? Did you ever think of that?" D.A. laughed. "I can just see the two of you, both too obstinate to admit you might be wrong, each determined to suffer in silence a thousand miles apart rather than be the first one to say he's sorry or that she still loves and cares for you.''

David didn't particularly like what he was hearing. No, she was his wife, and she'd been the one to initiate the separation. His brows almost met in the center of his forehead as he scowled at his son.

"She's the one who left, D.A. I didn't throw her out."

"Didn't you tell me that you left in the truck first and that she was gone when you returned?"

"Yes, I did say something like that," David muttered.

"Dad, did she leave a message to explain why she left?" D.A. asked.

"She left a note. . . ."

"Can I read it? Do you still have it?"

David fished in the pocket of his shirt and pulled out a very dog-eared, folded piece of paper and handed it to his son without a comment.

D.A. read it several times. He returned it to David and stared at him for several minutes.

David began to feel uncomfortable under his son's scrutiny. "Stop staring at me. What am I, anyway—a freak or something?"

"No, dad, just a fool."

The sharpness of the cutting remark made David bristle. He glared at D.A. and said, "You'd better have a good explanation or an apology for that!"

"Dad, read the note again," D.A. insisted. "Aloud."

"Dear David—"

"Why would she call you 'dear' if she hated you?"

interrupted D.A. "My dear father, it's a term of affection. Continue, please." He placed his hand over his mouth, shielding his response to his father's fidgeting actions.

"Dear David," he read. "It was a mistake. I really thought it would work, but I was wrong. It was a big mistake. Love, Sammy." David frowned at his insolent son and suspected a smile lurked behind the hand covering the lower portion of his face. "So?" he demanded.

"If she hates you, why sign the note 'Love, Sammy'? Isn't it a little strange for a woman to do unless she really loved the man she was leaving. She must have been terribly upset that day. She was torn between the new husband she loved and her only daughter. Even at my tender age, I'm smart enough to know that a woman can turn into a ferociously protective mother hen when she thinks her children are in danger. Dad, did you threaten Sarah or call her insulting names?"

"I'm afraid I called her a bitch and accused her of having no upbringing," David confessed.

"Oh, is that all?" D.A. said, lowering his hand. A smile spread across his face in spite of the seriousness of the moment.

"I was angry, damn it. I didn't realize until now what an insult that was to Sammy. It wasn't her fault at all. Oh, Lord, how can I be so stupid?" He pleaded for help to deal with his predicament.

"Dad, it's just that you're too close to the problem. Sammy's the woman you loved enough to marry. You avoided women for several years, at least as far as bringing them home. Now Sammy is your wife, and if you love her as much as I think you do, you'd better get down the interstate and bring her home where she belongs.''

D.A. rose from his chair and moved to his sulking father. He gave David's broad shoulder a squeeze. "Well, I'd better head back to Missoula. I've got a long drive, and I have to teach an early class tomorrow. So long, dad. Take my advice...go get her.'' He picked up his jacket and tie and walked out the door.

DAVID TOOK until the following Thursday afternoon to finally overcome his pride and give Sammy a call. The phone rang several times, and with each ring David felt anger, fear and anxiety build. She probably wasn't home...probably out somewhere enjoying her freedom...maybe on a date with that Wes Franklin fellow she'd told him about. She would probably just reject his attempt at a reconciliation. Finally the phone was answered at the other end by a sleepy voice, but by then he was so upset that he had decided it was all a mistake, anyway. "Nothing!" he'd snarled angrily, and slammed down the receiver.

He was furious with himself for being so indecisive. Maybe tomorrow he'd stop at the Russells. He missed them. No, why wait another day? It was just 5:00 in the afternoon, too early to go to bed. Maybe Julie could help him figure out the female mind.

He suddenly realized how hungry he was. Perhaps some of Julie's Thursday-night cooking would be the therapy he needed to work out the solution to his problem.

It was 7:00 when he knocked on the Russell kitchen door. He found Julie alone in the large cozy room, cutting out pieces for a patchwork quilt. The younger children were doing homework in their various rooms, Paul was on a date, and Russ was at a Montana Stockgrowers Association meeting in town.

"Sit down, David," Julie said, clearing away the stacks of purple and lavender print fabric she'd cut into various shapes. "It's good to see you. It's been too long. You look as if you could use a friend about now."

"Does it show that much?" he asked.

"I'm afraid so, dear, at least to me." She collected several sandpaper templates, scissors, straight pins and two long rulers, then wiped the table.

David spotted a diamond cut from fabric with tiny pink-and-white flowers on a field of deep purple. He picked it up off the floor and felt the soft cotton material. "Pretty," he commented. "Who is it for?"

"Mary," Julie said with a pleased smile. "It's called a blazing-star pattern. Now that Mary is getting to be a young lady she wants...oh, David! When I see her changing from my little girl into a young woman, I don't know if it pleases me or frightens me. I love my children so very much, but sometimes love can be very painful, can't it?" Julie's hazel eyes grew large with concern. "David, I'm so sorry—I didn't stop to think. Sammy's been gone for two weeks, hasn't she?"

"Is that all? It seems longer," David replied.

Julie busied herself at the kitchen counter and brought a platter of roast beef and home-baked bread to the table. "Eat something," she suggested. "You've lost weight." She filled a mug with her home-ground coffee and pushed a half-filled plate of brownies closer to him. "I suppose I always try to solve problems with food, don't I?" Julie laughed. "But sometimes it does help."

She watched him eat half of the sandwich he'd made, take one bite of a brownie and drain his cup, but his interest in the meal lacked his usual gusto. She shook her head in sympathy. "For adults, you two have had the most turbulent relationship I think I've ever known. I've never quite understood the strong love bonds between the two of you, but they were so obvious that I didn't question them."

She sipped her coffee and waited for him to speak. When he didn't, she continued. "Russ and I began to notice each other when we were still in high school, right here in town. I had another boyfriend, but Russ began his pursuit and won. We fell in love, married and settled down to produce kids and cows. We've had problems along the way, but we've worked them out. Sometimes it's been exciting, and sometimes it's quite dull, frankly, but it's what I want.

"With you and Sammy, I don't know. Maybe it's like education. Russ and I started in kindergarten and are working our way through school. I think with you two, you skipped from preschool to the college-graduate level. Maybe you need to go back to school and take a review course on how to get along with each other, because it does take some time, no matter how much you love each other." She looked at him and, seeing the look of amusement on his face, laughed.

David smiled in return. "Julie, what's this homespun philosophy? You surprise me."

"I can do more than just bake and cook and sew, David," she replied. "I still know how to think. Sometimes you men underestimate us women who stay in the background.'' Impulsively she kissed his cheek and went to the stove for a refill of fresh coffee.

Returning to the table, she touched his hand reassuringly. ''Tell me about Sammy and yourself. Go way back and tell me all about the two of you. I won't tell anyone, not even Russ, but maybe it will help. Trust me, David. I want to see you two happy again if it's at all possible. Besides, I need a friend and neighbor, and I happen to think Sammy's the one. She belongs here.

''Russ feels partly responsible for your breakup, and I think that's one reason he's avoided you these past few weeks. He desperately wants to be your friend again but is too ashamed to face you. I think he thought you and he were inseparable. He was jealous because the private boys' club had been invaded by a girl—and not just any girl. Sammy was attractive, self-sufficient, had a career and had made it financially without a man. Maybe if she had been a protesting, noisy women's libber, he could have handled the opposition. But she didn't play fair, David. She was a lady. Maybe he thought some of her liberation would rub off on me. He forgot I'm liberated right here, because I'm doing what I want to do.''

She reached over and touched his arm. ''David, he likes the hunting and fishing you do together. He likes the ranch talk, the plans, the construction projects—all those jobs that only men who are close can share.'' She started to laugh and threw her head back in pure delight.

''What?'' he asked, starting to smile without knowing her secret.

She tried to stop, but succeeded only in reducing her laughter to a giggle. "Remember when Sammy called Russ gay? That really wiped him out. She intimidated him so badly that he began to question his own manhood, fearing that others might think the same thing about his friendship with you. She emasculated him with that one, right down to his you-know-what."

She wiped the tears away as he broke into laughter again. "I shouldn't laugh at my husband, but he's recovered now. I helped him. What he forgot and I had to remind him of was that he had me, a wife, along with six children, for companionship. You had no one...but him. Sammy came along and absorbed your time, your interests, and I really think it was mostly plain jealousy along with concern for you as a dear friend who might get hurt. The last thing he expected to do was to be the cause of that hurt, and he knows he's guilty. That's his problem. He'll come around.

"Now tell me about Sammy and yourself. I want to help if I can."

David went back to the early days of his childhood: the sudden death of his father when he was only five; his mother's remarriage at six; their move to Phoenix the summer he turned seven. It was the middle of World War II, and his new stepfather had thought he could earn high wages at any one of several military bases opening in the area. Since Jim Caldwell had no skills or education, he ended up with a job picking cotton, then worked at a cottonseed-processing plant near their east Phoenix home. The family lived on an unpaved street just a few blocks from where the Gardners lived.

"Julie, I can remember the very first day I met

Sammy. It was the summer of 1942. School was about to start, and in Phoenix it stays very hot until October. I was coming home from the small grocery store down on the main street through town, when I heard this little girl screaming and crying over by the irrigation ditch, near a large cottonwood tree. There were three older boys playing in the water, and they had something in their hands.

"The girl was furious. She was stomping her foot and finally picked up a long stick and hit one of the boys over the head. He screamed in pain, grabbed his bleeding head and ran down the road. I was beginning to wonder who needed rescuing the most—the little girl or the boys. As I got closer, she picked up a handful of dirt and threw it in one boy's face, and he ran away. That left one defenseless boy of about nine, and I guess he knew when he was outclassed. He dropped the thing they had been playing with and I heard him say, 'Here, you brat, we didn't want it anyway,' and then he ran off.

"What they had been abusing turned out to be a small kitten the boys had found. They were throwing it into the irrigation water to see if it could swim. Sammy's house was across the road. She had just turned six, and she had gone to find out what was going on. In those days, Phoenix was a small town. Her street was a two-lane road with seldom a car passing by. Now it's a six-lane expressway that's an access to an interstate. I remember I picked up this soggy gray kitten and tried to dry it off a little on a patch of grass growing near the ditch. She was still sobbing and had dirt streaks down each cheek where she had wiped at the tears.

"I calmed her down, and we sat on the ditch bank and petted the kitten and talked. Can you imagine a six-year-old girl and an eight-year-old boy having a conversation about being kind to animals, birthdays, school starting, brothers and sisters and things like that? We sat there for quite a while with our feet in the cool water, just talking.

"Julie, you should have seen her. She had curly wheat-blond hair, the biggest blue eyes and the darkest lashes and rosy tanned cheeks, and skinny tanned arms and legs. She was wearing a kind of sunsuit young girls wore in those days. Before long I had her laughing. She had the prettiest smile I had ever noticed on a girl.

"We played with the kitten, then I remember her looking at me so seriously and saying, 'You have funny eyes.' I wasn't sure if she had insulted or complimented me. She said, 'See those trees? Your eyes look like those trees in my yard.' She was pointing to some very old tamarisk trees that have long, green, salty-tasting needles and a rough, rust-colored bark. The old-timers called them salt cedar trees. I think they're a desert variety of pine, but I'm not sure. My hair was redder then, and it was growing out from its summer crew cut. She always said when I laughed my eyes sparkled like the wet needles of that tree. Isn't that a strange thing to say?" His voice quavered, and he stopped and closed his eyes.

Julie touched his hand gently and waited. "It's okay, David. Please go on," she encouraged him.

"I'm sorry. It brings back some painful memories and makes me realize how much I miss her.... Well, she was afraid of the three boys who had pestered her, so when school started the next week, we agreed to meet at the corner of my road, and I walked her to school and home each day. I was always tall for my age so the guys thought I was older than I actually was. Some of my friends teased me, but I made up a story that her mother was paying me to be her bodyguard. They bought the story and left us alone.

"That's how it all started, and we became the best of friends. I had a rather unstable home life, and I gradually became part of the Gardner family activities. I think Mr. and Mrs. Gardner knew how my mother was, and they just included me when they did things with their own five children. That was my first contact with big families.

"We were very close until one summer when I was about to turn eleven. My mother informed me that we were moving to Chelan, Washington. Have you ever heard of Chelan?"

"No," Julie replied and smiled.

"It's right in the middle of the apple country of Washington state. Beautiful place, but I hated it. I received just about four hours of advance warning that we were leaving. It tore me up. I had roots—the Gardner family, my friends from school and especially Sammy. What can you really say about a three-year relationship like that? I never tried to understand it, but I made myself a promise that I'd find her again.

"We wrote twice, then I was sent to my uncle in Forsyth. We lost contact, but I never forgot her. You know the rest until that night when Russ dared me to place that fool ad. Russ was so encouraging about following up on that particular letter and visiting Sam in Phoenix that I could never understand why he did such an about-face when he met her here. It was as though he hated and resented her from the start.''

Julie refilled his mug. "Russ will come around. Tell me about the first trip to Phoenix. I suspect something happened that changed your lives.''

David hesitated, then began. "The minute I saw her in that airport lounge I just knew she was the person I'd been looking for all my life. I'd had it for three years in my childhood, and here she was again, and I had to keep her this time. Sounds possessive? True, but that's how it was.

"I've had my share of women, but this was different. I wanted her with me. I had these wild ideas flash through my head. If I had been a Neanderthal man I would have dragged her to my cave. If I had been a primitive savage I would have bought her for some goats and skins. If I had been an outlaw or a pirate I would have kidnapped her. Anything to keep her! I had this compulsive desire to make a complete fool of myself in order to make her all mine. I found myself resenting the years apart and the experiences she had had without me. I knew when I saw her house that she didn't need my financial security. She has a gorgeous five-bedroom home with swimming pool, and she's paid for it herself. She has a successful career, and I found myself resenting her co-workers, especially the men I knew she worked with. Julie, this was all the first night.''

Julie laughed. "Cupid really hit you between the eyes, didn't he?''

"Does this all sound silly to you, acting like a lovesick

kid at my age?'' David left his chair and stretched his long body, his fingers touching the ceiling. He began to pace around the room, moving restlessly, then turned to her. ''Julie, within twenty-four hours I made love to her and felt a fulfillment I'd never known before. The next day, her youngest son left for the navy, and we went to the mountains and spent the night in Flagstaff. I made love to her again, and it was even better. God, Julie, every time I make love to her, it's better! Imagine what it'll be like in—'' He stopped abruptly and frowned at her. He dropped his gaze quickly, embarrassed at his outburst. Moving to the stove, he busied himself refilling his coffee mug.

Julie smiled. ''I promised not to tell a soul what you've told me, David. It's private. Please go on.''

''One of those two nights she conceived, and life began to get complicated. The last thing either of us thought about that first visit was pregnancy. It never entered my mind, and that's terribly irresponsible on my part. She went through hell down there alone when she realized what had happened. She thought I might pull a disappearing act. She didn't tell me until she arrived at the ranch, and by then the miscarriage was beginning. It's been either heaven or hell for us ever since.''

He studied his coffee with an intensity it didn't deserve. Julie listened as he painfully shared his feelings during his wife's unconsciousness in the mountain cabin when he thought she was dying.

Julie wiped her tear-filled eyes. ''David, maybe Sammy is going through similar problems adjusting to this experience. I think she needs you just as much as you need her. I think you should go to her, talk this over and bring her home. If you hurry, you can have her back here for Christmas!''

Several minutes passed in silence.

"Thanks, Julie—maybe you're right. At least it's helped to talk about it. Don't tell anyone.... I...I know you won't." David reached across and gave her a brotherly kiss on her cheek.

The kitchen door opened, and Russ entered. He stopped abruptly when he saw David leaning over Julie.

"What the hell's going on?" Russ demanded.

"Oh, Russ, David came to see you and then stayed to talk," Julie explained, trying to cover her embarrassment.

"Hello, David. How are you?" Russ asked awkwardly.

"Fine, Russ... and you?" David asked politely.

"Okay. Will we see you at Christmas?" This was obviously Russ's way of issuing a reconciliatory invitation.

David hesitated. "I think I'm going to take a trip." He glanced at Julie, who smiled.

"Where?" Russ asked, surprised.

"To Phoenix, to get my wife and bring her home." Grabbing up his coat and hat he turned and quickly disappeared into the soft snowy night.

DAVID McCORMACK was running out of time. If he intended to drive to Phoenix and arrive by Christmas, he would have to leave on Saturday in order to allow for bad weather along the way. That would give him five days. If he made good time, he would bring her back and...too many ifs, he decided. He'd better take the days as they came. He told his company that an emergency had come up, and he'd have to be gone for a week or two; he'd let them know when the situation was under control.

He left the ranch early Saturday morning, his adrenaline flowing. He vowed to show patience when he confronted her in Phoenix. Rather than chance a rejection, he hadn't phoned her again. She had just better be there. Damn, how short his fuse seemed to be.

As he drove from the access road onto the interstate, he scanned the sky. He had set his goal for the first night's layover at Ogden, Utah, but knew he would be lucky to make it to Pocatello if the weather prediction was accurate.

It was more than accurate. Snow was falling heavily as he crossed into Idaho. The interstate was closed in the late morning, and he spent the night alone and angry in Idaho Falls. The next day the snowfall continued, but the interstate was reopened for a while and he traveled fifty miles to Pocatello before the highway was once again closed because of dangerous road conditions. Cynicism replaced anger, and he concluded that at the rate of fifty miles per day, he might make Phoenix by spring. He skipped the evening meal and went to bed.

He awoke with his heart pounding from a nightmarish encounter with Sammy. In the dream he had walked into her house on Christmas day and found her with four young men, all laughing and frolicking and having a dandy time. He berated her for her unwifely conduct, and she then introduced him to her four sons.

"You don't have four sons," he had shouted.

"One of them is yours," she'd sneered back at him.

In the dream he had turned and had seen a small toddling girl child with soft blue eyes and rusty curls who
smiled at him.

"You've been fooling around. Whose child is that?"
he had demanded.

"She's yours, you hardheaded fool," Sammy had
screamed, then she had turned and marched out the
door, slamming it.

The girl had cried and held up her hands to David,
pleading to be comforted. Then she had changed into
ten crying children, and one by one they'd begun to
drown in the swift-running creek on his ranch. They had
all been crying, "Save me, save me," but he had been
stuck in a snowbank, unable to move.

Sammy had materialized. "You said you'd take care
of me," she accused him. "You can't even take care of
your own children."

The babies had cried louder and louder and the snowbank had grown in depth and covered his head.

He awoke in a cold sweat, the white motel bedsheet
wrapped around his head, and he felt a split second of
sheer panic before he was fully aware of his surroundings.

He showered. Perhaps a meal would help. The motel
had an all-night restaurant, and he spent the next hour
eating a late dinner served by a pretty young waitress
who hinted several times that she finished her shift at
6:00 A.M. He smiled once, realized she mistook the smile
as encouragement, then ignored her and returned to his
room for a short night of restless sleep.

Each time he closed his eyes he saw the blue eyes and
rusty curls of his little girl, and he realized that on some

level he had still not come to terms with the loss of his and Sammy's child.

His luck changed the next day. The skies had cleared, the snow-removal equipment was out, and the highway was opened to those vehicles with chains or snow tires. He was equipped and eager to move on.

The highway was covered with dangerous icy patches, but he was able to progress to Salt Lake City before the fatigue of winter-weather driving forced him to stop for the night. If he could make Las Vegas the next night, he was sure he could reach Phoenix on Christmas Eve. Surely she would be receptive to his overtures on Christmas Eve.

The farther south he drove, the better he found the road conditions, and he reached Las Vegas early in the evening on December twenty-three. He was confident he would be in Phoenix the next night. She would be in his arms.

He slept like a lifeless stone and awoke hungry and anxious to leave. He walked to a nearby casino for an advertised inexpensive breakfast and wasted a few dollars in a quarter slot machine.

As he returned to his truck, he noticed the vehicle had a peculiar slant to its left side. On closer inspection he discovered that both left tires had been slashed and someone had written the word Cowboy on the left rear fender with a spray can of black paint. When he turned the ignition key, his hopes of a quick exit evaporated. He lifted the hood. The vandals had not only slashed his tires, but had also destroyed all the wiring under the hood as well.

The truck was towed to a garage where two mechanics

with Christmas cheer on their minds and breaths agreed to reassemble the loose parts, repair the damage and replace the slashed tires. David spent the next several hours wandering from casino to casino, losing a few more dollars, winning a few quarters and watching the sky grow darker in the southwest.

The rains came at midafternoon and were extremely heavy. What else could possibly go wrong, he wondered. Then, as he signed the charge slip for the tires and repair, he heard a news bulletin on the radio. A portion of the highway north of Boulder City had collapsed because of the heavy rains, resulting in an accident involving a tanker transporting toxic chemicals. The truck had overturned, spilling its contents, and all traffic had been halted by the state highway department.

His hopes disappeared as he listened to the closing remarks from the broadcaster. The highway was expected to reopen sometime Christmas morning.

THE FIRST THING David noticed as he stopped in front of her house was the absence of automobiles. Only her green sedan was in the driveway. Where were her relatives' cars? Surely they were all inside having their Gardner-Roberts family gathering she had told him about. He carefully moved his truck into her driveway close to her car, turned off the ignition and listened for voices. Perhaps from the patio? The weather was in the low seventies, perfect for an outdoor activity.

He had expected a wreath on the door. Where was all the Christmas spirit at this house? He pressed the doorbell, holding the button. He cursed softly as he heard footsteps slowly approach the door.

The door was opened by a sad and disheveled-looking Samantha McCormack, whose expression quickly changed to surprise when she saw him. She ran a hand through her curly hair, trying to bring order out of its disarray, and brushed nervously at her robe. Her hand moved up to cover her pale lips, devoid of even a hint of lipstick.

"Sammy?" he asked. He extended a hand to her, a heavy frown adding years to his fatigued features.

"Oh, David!" she cried in dismay, and slammed the door in his face.

CHAPTER EIGHTEEN

SAMMY SAGGED against the closed door. The power of his presence outside filtered through the heavy wood and swirled around her, choking the breath out of her. She heard him knock again, but she felt faint from the rapid pounding of her heart. She tried to turn the doorknob, but her hand trembled and her fingers were too weak to function. She heard his receding footsteps and then the slamming of a truck door.

He was leaving her again. She had to reach him! She clutched the heavy brass doorknob with both hands, turned it in spite of its resistance and pulled the door open.

"David!" she screamed. She heard him kill the engine as she ran to the truck. She clutched the handle and shook it hysterically. "Please, David, don't leave me again," she sobbed.

"Let go, Sam," he called. "Let go of the door handle."

She knew he still wanted to leave without her. She dropped her hands and stepped back, leaning against her own green sedan. She closed her eyes and waited, listening for the engine to start up, the blue truck to roll out of her driveway, taking the man in it out of her life forever.

Steel hands gripped her shoulders, and a deep velvet voice said, "I couldn't get out of the truck until you let go of the door, my love." Arms embraced her in warmth, and she surrendered to the heat of his mouth. She gasped for breath as he smothered her face with kisses. Her confidence soared when he murmured, "I love you, Sam."

She never wanted to leave his arms again, but she pulled back a little when she realized he was laughing softly. "What's so funny?" she asked.

He grinned down at her, still holding her in his arms. He looked around her and whispered, "Do you think the neighbors are peeking? Still a prude, Sam?"

She pulled away self-consciously, but he refused to release her.

"I'll wave to them," he said, then kissed her warmly again. "May I come in?" he asked.

"Of course...I didn't expect you. I must look awful," she said, brushing at her hair again.

"You look lovely," he assured her, and turned her toward the house. "Where's your family?"

"No one would come," she replied, a hint of disappointment in her voice.

They entered the house, and as he closed the door, he turned the dead bolt. "No one?"

"No one!" she repeated, her shoulders rigid. Her chin quivered slightly.

"Where are they?" he persisted.

"They each thought the others would be here, and they each decided to spend the holiday with their other families." She turned to him defiantly, but her composure started to crumble.

"Perhaps it's time you joined your other family, too," he suggested.

"My other. . .?" She looked at him, her emotions in confusion.

"Me, Sammy, me!" She tensed and his patience broke. He grabbed her shoulders and shook her.

Her eyes widened in fear. She tried to escape and kicked at his shin, but he stepped aside and laughed. His laughter angered her, and she ran into the kitchen. "Get out, I don't want to see you. You don't really love me, and you don't need me. No one does. I hate you all," she cried as she disappeared into the darker hallway.

He charged after her and caught her as she attempted to close the door of her bedroom. He shoved the door open and grabbed her upper arm. She tried to twist away, and he tightened his hold. He'd all but forgotten her eager response when he'd left the truck and erased her fears that he would leave her again. Anger and rejection seemed to boil just below the surface of their emotions, and he fought to recall his vow of patience when he'd first decided to go after her and bring her back to be his wife again.

Now as he stared down at her pain-filled blue eyes, his anger left him completely. He whispered hoarsely, "Why are we doing this to each other? I came here to love you, not to hurt you. Oh, my darling. . .my sweet Sammy. . .my summer love. . .let me love you forever." His fingers moved to her soft throat, cupping her chin with his thumbs. He brought her face up to his and murmured words of love as his mouth joined hers. The trembling in her body eased as resistance left her, and she began to respond to his kiss.

Suddenly she broke away from him, but as she turned, she stumbled and fell across the bed. He reached for her, catching her ankle as she rolled to the far side. He pulled her slowly to him, and when she reached the middle, he dropped down beside her.

"Sammy, stop," he exclaimed.

She lay panting, her eyes riveted to his face. Her hands began to slide along his ribs and around him. She felt the powerful muscles of his back flex, and her anger and doubt warmed to passion. Still, she shook her head. "David, you should hate me. I ran away from you. I embarrassed you by fighting with your friend. I sided with Sarah over something that I know you were right about. I returned to Phoenix and made an absolute shambles of my life. How could you possibly still love me?"

He studied her face, read the sadness written in her eyes and smiled slightly. "But I do. Now quit fighting me. Love me, my little softie. Love me and I'll love you...like we did before...in the pool...and under the stars. I want to bury myself in you and drown in your softness and know that you'll always be near me." Gently he kissed her face, exploring each eyelid, working his way leisurely down her cheeks, moving to probe the recesses of her mouth.

His warm lips caressed her ear, and he whispered, "Love me, Sammy, love me."

She returned his kisses with impassioned but incoherent murmurings as she tugged at his shirt.

They came together with slow deliberate movements meant to satisfy, and the barriers crumbled and dissolved at last.

SAMMY AWOKE FRIGHTENED in the predawn darkness, then relaxed in the pleasurable feeling of David's familiar warmth pressed against her.

He was molded to her body as though heaven had designed their shapes. She smiled as she remembered his whispering the phrase to her during the night.

She turned her mind loose and allowed it to wander over her loss of employment, the significant changes looming ahead of her as she joined him in a new climate, far away from everything she'd ever known, but always her thoughts returned to David and the love she felt for him. Even during the lonely period without him, her love for him had grown deeper until it permeated her entire body and soul—a love that mixed pain with joy, ecstasy and explosive passion with simple contentment just knowing he was near.

She turned in his sleeping embrace and admired his face in the breaking light of a new day. He had come to get her. He had always been her friend. Less than six months ago he had become her lover. Was she now ready to accept him as her husband?

He had been willing to do his part in their marriage, but she had been the skeptic. My husband...the words moved through her mind...my husband...she thought again of the marriage vows exchanged in D.A.'s small apartment so far away. "To love and to cherish"; she did. "In sickness and in health"; he had certainly been devoted during her illness. "For richer or for poorer"; her job and her house were her financial umbilical cords to security that she had been unwilling to cut. He had been ready to make his home her home, but she had refused his offer.

She thought of her joblessness. Perhaps she had a new career ahead. David's wife...she liked that sound; she would be his partner...for life.

He was rousing from the deep sleep of an exhausted traveler and looked at her from under one half-opened brown-lashed eyelid. She could see him watching her as she whispered softly, "My husband."

His other eye opened, and he seemed to look at her in disbelief. She felt ashamed. She had hurt him and failed to trust him in their brief months together. "My husband," she repeated, overwhelmed with feeling. "David, I love you so very, very much. Thank God you came to get me."

"My wife," he murmured. "Let's go home...really home...to stay!"

THEY CELEBRATED CHRISTMAS a day late, after hurriedly spending a few hours buying two special gifts.

Sammy gave David a gold pocket watch similar to one she had seen him admire when they had shopped in Missoula on their first day together in Montana. On the face of the front case she had his name engraved. On the back, in small lettering, was the cryptic message: "I was wrong. It was right after all. Love, Samantha."

The jeweler had expressed skepticism at the message and charged an outrageous fee for the fast service.

"I'll wait. The price is no object. Please hurry." She had kept smiling as she watched the nervous, irritated jeweler complete the inscription.

David's gift to her was a fine gold chain with a charm in the shape of an infinity figure eight suspended from the center. Two stones were set in the lower loop of the symbol. One was a soft blue sapphire, the other a green peridot stone. As he fastened the cool gold chain around her neck, she fingered the circles, touching the stones.

"It's beautiful, but how did you find a necklace with blue and green stones in it?" she asked.

He laughed. "It had a diamond and a ruby, but I told the jeweler the settings were wrong and insisted they be changed to the proper stones. It cost me a small fortune, but it's worth it. You see, my love, infinity is the only symbol that can apply to us now."

They left Phoenix early the next day and spent the first night in Sante Fe, the second in Colorado Springs and the third in Cheyenne. After lunch in Casper Sammy fell fast asleep against David's shoulder.

As she awoke and looked around, she asked, "Where are we?"

"Somewhere between Casper and Sheridan. I think the next town is Buffalo. We'll stop for a while."

"Are we really going to be there tomorrow?"

"We'll spend tonight in Sheridan," David smiled. "I could drive faster, but I want you all to myself for just a little longer. I'll call Uncle Jeff from our motel and check on the weather. We should be at his place for lunch."

She studied his profile in admiration. "You're clever," Sammy declared.

"True," he agreed.

She turned to look out the rear window of the blue cab but found it covered with a moist film. Raising herself onto her knees she stretched, finally coming into contact with the cloudy glass. She brushed a small viewing hole on the moisture-covered window with her fingertips and smiled as she spied her green sedan being towed behind the truck.

As she turned back to the front of the cab, a large black-and-white tomcat mewed, and she smiled again. Duke was in a traveling cage on the floor by her feet. She slipped her fingers through slats of the cage and stroked his soft fur. He began to purr.

"You're thoughtful," she said.

"Sometimes." He smiled.

"You're clever and thoughtful, and I love you."

"Good," he replied, then returned his concentration to the icy road.

Sammy was pleased to see that some of the weariness he had displayed the day of his arrival had gradually been replaced by vigor and lightheartedness. The care lines in his face had smoothed, and a smile often tugged at the corners of his mouth, even while he focused his attention on the silver ribbon of road ahead.

"What if you hadn't come for me?" she asked.

"But I did."

"I was so miserable." She frowned. "You called that night."

"Yes, but I was still angry."

"But you came anyway?"

"Yes." He paused. "Why were you home that day when I called? You should have been working or Christmas shopping. I was too angry to care then, but you sounded sleepy. Why were you in bed at 5:00 in the afternoon?"

"That was the day I was fired." She laughed.

"That pleased you?"

"It didn't then, but it does now. I think I owe a certain person at Mastiff a debt of gratitude. He did me a big favor. Losing my job forced me to realize that I... well, I've always been determined, almost obsessed, with paying my own way. I decided at the time of my divorce that I could count on only one person for survival...*me*! Jake never made a child-support payment, and I was too proud to beg. That habit became so ingrained in me that it prevented me from accepting certain financial gifts from you."

"I don't understand."

"My medical bills, my clothes. It even bothered me at first to ask you for grocery money. See how bad I was?"

"But that's what husbands are supposed to do, honey."

"Well, I had one who didn't, and maybe it warped my attitude. Losing my job at Mastiff really knocked the financial blocks from under me, but it freed me at the same time. I spent four days alone, wallowing in self-pity. Then you came. Maybe I have talents and skills that can be used with you. After all, my background is finance and computers. Do ranchers use computers?" she asked with a laugh.

"Several of my friends have microcomputers in their ranch offices."

"You're kidding!"

"No, not at all. We're not quite as primitive as you big-city folks might think." He spent the next half hour telling funny stories about the computers at Anaconda and his experiences with the new color-graphics terminal in his own office at Butte. "I get to plot air pollution in living color. I'll have to take you to the office and show you around. Just don't get too interested. Oh, Sam, just one more month, and I'm through. I can hardly believe all my plans are falling into place. Especially you. You really gave me a scare.''

AS THEY DROVE through the gate to the Jeff McCormack ranch, Sammy remarked on the difference between this country and southwestern Montana, where they lived. ''Where are the mountains?''

''We're on the edge of the Great Plains here,'' David explained. ''The land is almost arid...with droughts wiping out the farmers some years.'' He glanced at her. ''Does this mean you miss our home?''

''I think so. I'm glad we've kissed and made up, but is the making up so enjoyable because the parting was so painful? I don't think I could stand another separation from you, David. Maybe we can just do the making-up part from now on?'' She was pleased to see a grin spreading across his face. As she noticed the small lines scattered across his features, she tried to imagine their life on the ranch when they would be in their sixties, and she laughed aloud.

He looked at her, raised an eyebrow and asked, ''What's so funny?''

''I was just wondering what we'd look like in twenty years. Can you imagine?''

''You just might get a chance to look into the future,'' he said.

''What do you mean?''

''Just wait until you meet my uncle. Unless he's changed a lot, you'll see.'' He turned the truck into a large circular drive through a grassy yard.

"Oh!" Sammy exclaimed. She had been so engrossed in watching him that she had failed to notice their arrival at the main living compound of the large cattle-and-wheat ranch. She looked ahead and suddenly she understood what David had meant.

He whispered near her ear, "People used to say I looked more like him than his own sons did."

Standing on the porch of the old family homestead was an image of David McCormack projected thirty years into the future. It had to be Uncle Jeff. The family resemblance was striking.

He could have modeled for a Charles Russell sculpture. He was tall and heavy but hard rather than fat. His battered felt cowboy hat was sweat stained from years of roundups and wheat harvests. His face was lined from wind and age and tanned from his seventy-three summers on the edge of the plains. He had the McCormack head of thick hair, but it was snow white. His face was smooth shaven and his chin every bit as stubborn as his nephew's. His eyes—ah, his eyes were the same rust-flecked tamarisk green as David's.

His gray brows furrowed as he squinted to see the occupants of the truck. Rummaging through a shirt pocket, he withdrew a pair of glasses and adjusted them to his eyes. A smile brightened his weathered face.

His faded plaid wool shirt stretched taut across his midsection. He had just enough of an old-age spread to hide the silver belt buckle that reappeared to glisten in the sun as he moved down the stairs. His well-worn Levi's seemed to be permanently bowed from encasing legs that had spent so many years draped over the back of a horse. His boots were scuffed and worn and run down at the heels.

He looked as though he was an integral part of his environment. As he moved to the truck, David climbed down and met him a few feet from the driver's door. It was a collision of arms as the two men embraced.

Sammy couldn't hear the voices but saw David gesture to her as they turned their attention to the cab. The door opened, and he helped her to the ground. He placed a hand firmly on each shoulder and guided her in front of him, forcing her to face his uncle directly.

"Sammy, I want you to meet my favorite uncle, Jefferson B. McCormack, patriarch of the Montana McCormack clan. Uncle Jeff, this is my wife, Sammy."

She could hear the joy in his voice and was sure his face would split if he didn't ease the strain of the grin she sensed. She felt him kiss the top of her head as he pushed her gently forward to greet this special relative, but she was frozen in uncertainty as a flashing image of her first meeting with Russ crossed her thoughts.

The old man took the initiative and said, "Howdy, little lady. You're as purdy as my nephew said you were. Welcome." Then, to her surprise, he embraced her.

It was like being hugged by a large Scottish bear. Ah, the hugs of the McCormacks. She found them irresistible. He had the charming McCormack smile, and she knew she was in love again. As he released her and stepped back, she was certain everything would be all right, so she smiled at him in return and reached up on her tiptoes and gave him a kiss on his cheek.

He was surprised and pleased and smiled broadly.

"It's a little chilly out here. Let's go in and meet the rest of the family."

David floated with high spirits across the yard and up the steps, his arm around her shoulders, and she had to run to keep pace with his long loose strides.

LUNCH WAS FINISHED, the dishes cleared, and Uncle Jeff's sons returned with their families to their respective homes in the compound. David and Sammy were ushered into the den for after-dinner coffee. Uncle Jeff assisted his wife, Helen, as she maneuvered her wheelchair through the wide doorway. They had been married fifty-one years. For the last three, she had been confined to the chair because of arthritis. A hip replacement was scheduled for the spring, and they were both optimistic about the outcome.

Uncle Jeff's granddaughter served the coffee and brownies, then excused herself. David knew the time had come for reminiscing. As much as he loved his uncle, he always felt apprehensive when memories of his childhood surfaced. Time should have healed the old injuries, but it hadn't.

He tuned in on the conversation and heard his uncle talking.

"You know, he was so quiet when he first came to live with us. I think he was bitter and felt abandoned. I gave him a gentle gelding shortly after he arrived, and my sons taught him how to take care of the horse and tack. Now those were the days. My sons and Dave rode their horses to school. They rode five miles each way to a small country school that had three classrooms and two or three grades in each room. Remember, Dave?"

"Sure. The largest class I was in contained fifteen kids, and that was the seventh and eighth grades combined."

"There were times when I worried about you, Dave, but momma here said I should leave you alone to work out your problems." He reached over and patted the wrinkled hand of his white-haired wife. "I remember once you disappeared for the whole weekend. It was March and a snowstorm hit. I was really concerned that time, but late Sunday you came trudging home, wet and cold and hungry, but you had survived. You'd stayed in the east line shack, remember?"

David laughed. "Do I! I was so green that when it started to snow Friday night, I was afraid the horse would freeze, so I pushed and shoved and pulled until I got him inside the shack with me and kept him there until Sunday. That was a very confused animal, and did that shack smell by Sunday afternoon! I learned to solve a lot of problems that weekend," he said. He frowned. "I decided not to waste my time being mad at my mother. I partly blamed her for my father's death when I was five, but I—"

"Dave, what do you mean, when you were five? You were eleven when your dad died."

"No, sir, I was five. It was before I lived with my stepfather, Jim Caldwell."

"No, Dave, it was the year before you came to live with us."

Sammy interrupted the two arguing men. "Now wait a moment. How could you disagree on a thing as important as when David's father died?"

"I don't rightly know," Uncle Jeff replied, "but it

was the year before Dave came to live with us. Isn't that right, momma?'' He turned to his wife for confirmation.

"That's correct, dear,'' Helen McCormack assured her husband. She looked at David. "Why would you think he died when you were five?''

"I remember my mother coming home one day and saying that we were moving. I asked her where my dad was, and she said he was gone and would never be back. Then several weeks later I was crying for him, and she said, 'Shut up, your dad is dead, now just shut up. I don't want to ever talk about it again.' I kept crying, and she got mad and made me give her my belt, and she hit me with it. The prong took a chunk of flesh out of my side, and I still have the scar, so I remember.'' He looked in pain.

"Uncle Jeff, when my sweet bitch of a mother told me that my dad had left and would never come back, she said it was my fault. I was five years old and loved my father dearly. I remember him as a tall dark-haired man who told me cowboy stories and taught me Scottish folk songs that he said his father had taught him. That's really all I can. . . remember. . . all!

"When she shouted at me that he had died, she said that he had died because of me. I must have spent the next several years trying to figure out what I had done to kill him. I accepted the responsibility for his death but still didn't know why or how. And *she* refused to talk about it.

"Just after my sixth birthday, Jim Caldwell began living with us. I remember she told me to call him dad, and I refused. She insisted and I still refused. She whipped

me with my belt again...she did a lot of that...but I
never did call my stepfather dad. I was a little stubborn.''

Uncle Jeff reached over and laid his hand on David's
knee. "Son, you're in for a shock, and I'm just sorry I
didn't realize long before this that you didn't know.
Your father, my brother, died when you were eleven.
That I know. I used to try to show you pictures of him,
and you always left the room. Is that why you wouldn't
look at them, because you thought you were...? Oh,
good Lord!'' he exclaimed as David nodded in agreement.

"He remarried about a year after your mother left
him,'' Uncle Jeff said. "That's right—she left him! He
was brokenhearted, Dave. He loved you very much.
She'd met some damn fruit picker who promised her
heaven knows what. Your father came back here to take
care of some ranch business, and when he returned to
Hungry Horse, the house was empty and you two were
gone. She served him with divorce papers through the
courts, but when he tried to find you, she had already
moved on again. That's how he happened to be in California. He had followed her there, looking for you.

"Goodness, Dave, I can't believe that you never
knew. Your mother did. That damn crazy woman. I
told her all about him when she called me about your
coming to live with us. She really wanted to send you to
your father, but when I told her about his death, she
didn't even care. She just immediately asked if you
could stay with us, and I said of course.''

David stared at the flames in the fireplace, thinking of
his mother. The pains in his stomach were intense, and

his head began to throb. He sat staring at the hypnotic flames, trying to maintain his self-control.

"David, are you all right?"

He turned as he felt a gentle touch on his arm and looked up into Sammy's soft blue eyes.

He stared at her for several seconds. "Sammy, my mother would remind me sometimes of what I'd done to my father. That morning we left Phoenix, she said she'd tell the police about me if I caused her any more problems. I'd asked her if I could stay with your family, and she'd threatened me with the police. Now do you understand what she was like to live with? It was all a big lie...all those years. It was just a big evil lie."

"David, I'm so sorry. I didn't realize how bad it was. I was a child and didn't know adults could be so cruel. Oh, David, we could have been together!" She stared at him as images of what their shared lives could have meant flashed before them. A squeeze of his firm hand brought her back to the room.

She turned to his uncle. "Uncle Jeff, can you tell us more about David's father—fill in some of the missing years and show us some pictures, perhaps?" she asked.

Jeff McCormack did his best to recall the events of thirty years past and told them of his brother's trauma at losing his wife and only child, his search for his son, a remarriage in southern California and then the telephone call telling Jeff of his brother's death in an industrial accident. He couldn't recall where he had worked, but only that he had been crushed by some heavy equipment and had died instantly.

"Dave, I can't remember where he's buried, or if he had any more children. I just can't remember. I haven't heard from his widow for more than twenty years. She may be dead herself.'' He looked to his wife for confirmation.

Uncle Jeff nodded in sympathy as David turned again to stare into the flames. "I'm glad we got you away from that crazy woman, Dave. You'll always be like a son to us, won't he, Helen?"

Helen McCormack nodded her agreement.

"Don't forget that, Dave," said Uncle Jeff. "We love you like a son."

David sat quietly staring into the fireplace. He tried to recall the name of the man who had written him a letter after he'd placed that newspaper ad. His name had been McCormack, and he had suggested that they might be relatives. "Uncle Jeff, what did you say his wife's name was?"

"Why, Helen Ellison. We laughed about both loving and marrying women named Helen." Again he patted his wife's knee.

"David, are you all right?" Sammy asked, concerned at his ashen hue.

"Don't you understand, Sam? All my life I've wanted to really belong to a family, my own flesh and blood family. I know we all have impossible dreams, but I always wanted mine to come true. Even though I was invited into your family, my uncle's and even the Russells', it was never what I wanted. To really belong and have brothers and sisters to play with and to reminisce with at holidays. Sammy, even at my age I feel left out when families like the Russells begin to tell those special stories about their families.

"I remember that letter from a man named McCormack. I'm quite sure his first name was Ellison. I think his middle initial was W. My father's middle name was Wallace—*W* for Wallace, Sam! He could be my half brother! And I didn't even answer him. I was so engrossed with your letters that I forgot all about his.''

"I can find the letters when we get home," Sammy assured him. "I remember placing all the responses to your ad in a safe place when I sorted out that collection of books and magazines. I just know I can find the Mc-Cormack letter. We'll write as soon as we get home. Now let's just enjoy the few days we have here, because I think these wonderful people are still your family. I know they love you—not as much as I do, but almost.'' She smiled and they all laughed. The tension broke, and a festive mood returned as the group turned their attention to the thick photo albums spread before them on the oak coffee table.

CHAPTER NINETEEN

DAVID MCCORMACK'S FINAL MONTH OF WORK at Anaconda passed quickly. Sammy attended a farewell dinner in his honor and met some of his co-workers. Meeting his fellow employees reminded her of Mastiff and her antagonist, Wes Franklin. She wondered who his next female target would be. All in the past. Her future surrounded her here in a new land, and she was beginning to feel at home. Even the cold didn't frighten her as it had before. The warmth of David's presence had made a protective cocoon against the dangers of the primitive land.

His year-end royalty check was larger than ever. When it arrived in February, his first suggestion had been to save it, but she remembered the magazine called *Simmental Shield*, and knowing of his long-sustained interest in purebred cattle, she suggested he invest some of it in livestock. After all, at Julie's nudging she was contemplating a joint venture in the chicken business with Mary Russell for a 4-H club project, so why couldn't he have his fancy cows?

He agreed with her, and in late February they traveled to Great Falls, where they purchased two young full-blooded, polled Simmental heifers, guaranteed to be safe in calf, with due dates in the spring. David raved about their good breeding, telling her they had both been serviced by artificial insemination from Galant Chief of the famous Galant genetic line. The bull's name meant nothing to Sammy, but she was pleased that when the young caramel-and-white-colored heifers were unloaded at the ranch, she was able to tell them from the darker red-and-white-faced Herefords.

"After all, they do look quite a bit alike," she said. "Don't they?"

He laughed. "Considering the price we paid for them, I should hope you could identify our investment."

In spite of the wintery weather in March, Sammy joined David in moving all the cows heavy with calf into the pasture near the cow barn. She enjoyed riding Melody and helping David with the work. Her confidence soared when he complimented her for being a quick learner. He seldom lost patience as he taught her such skills as how to herd the cattle without startling them.

In the latter part of March they spent many nights out with the young heifers who were dropping their first calves. Sammy was surprised to learn that the animals often had no maternal instinct at all and would abandon their newborn calves. The experienced older cows were fine left alone, but the first-timers were moved either near or into the cow barn, where Sammy often had to bottle-feed the newborn calf. Once the new mother acknowledged her calf and permitted it to suckle naturally, David moved the pair out to make room for the next heifer. The long hours were exhausting when several cows were calving at once.

When quiet periods came, they sat on a stack of hay

bales and shared their coffee, talked about their plans for the future and kissed occasionally. It was a good time, and she treasured the intimate moments.

An April Fools' Day snowstorm left the countryside white and beautiful and reminded Sammy that her tiny vegetable and flower seedlings would have to remain in their hothouse flats for a few more weeks. Gardening in the Rockies was proving to be quite different from the lowland deserts of Arizona.

D.A. came for the weekend in late April, his first visit since Sammy's return to the ranch. He had taken Julie and Mary Russell into town and promised to return in time for dinner.

Sammy mixed a meatloaf and reminisced about the good period since her return. Life was perfect, peaceful, slow-paced except for calving, and her love for David was mushrooming now that she felt secure in the knowledge that he'd be by her side in the years ahead.

She looked up from her reverie as David entered the kitchen. He laughed as he came to the sink and kissed her.

"What's so funny?" she asked.

"I was thinking how Mary Russell has changed into a very pretty teenager and then tried to imagine what you were like at her age. Tell me," he said, nuzzling her neck and kissing her sensitive skin.

Sammy thought back over the years. "Well, for one thing, I didn't think I'd ever be able to fill a bra, and I knew my hips were much too large, and I thought...."

David's hand slipped under her sweater as he whispered something in her ear. She turned in his embrace and looked up into his face. "Are you listening to me?" she asked.

"A little. . . you tear me up when you don't wear a bra." His hands moved to her breasts. His thumbs worked soft circles around the sensitive tips, and they peaked as she leaned into his body.

She slid her arms up around his neck and brought his head down to hers. His hand moved under her sweater to caress her bare back, then he crushed her to him, taking her breath away with a kiss of passion.

A groan came from him as she felt his arousal when his long hard body pressed into hers. Her mouth opened to allow his exploration.

"David," she moaned, and then suddenly she froze. D.A. was standing at the kitchen door.

"I. . . forgot something in the car," D.A. said and whirled back out the door.

When he returned, David was seated at the table, and Sammy was placing the dinner plates. D.A. apologized for walking in on them unannounced. "I've got to remember to knock. I really am sorry," he kept repeating.

"It's okay, D.A. It's your house, too." Sammy patted his hand as he joined them for dinner. "Did Julie and Mary get home all right?" she asked.

"Sure did. Mary's getting sort of cute, isn't she? Give her another five or six years, and she'll be a real beauty. Those big brown eyes of hers are going to really hook some man some day. Speaking of real beauties, guess who called me on the phone last week? Sarah!"

Sammy gasped, then asked hesitantly, "What did she want?"

"Just to talk. She called from San Francisco. She said to tell you two hello."

"Just like that?" David asked.

"You misjudge her, dad," D.A. replied. "She's glad you're back together. Really...I've talked to her more than once."

David and Sammy exchanged glances and both wondered what had transpired between their two children.

"She's working as a cocktail waitress," D.A. continued. "She's left Paul and is sharing an apartment with another waitress. She said to tell you she's fine and has plenty of money. In case you're wondering how she knew where to find me, I gave her my phone number in Missoula that weekend I first met her, just in case she needed help sometime. She's not as bad as you two think. She's just a little mixed up. She's young and has some growing up to do, but...I rather like her."

Sammy shook her head in disagreement. "I hope you think twice before becoming too friendly with her. She's my daughter, but she's trouble, D.A., bad trouble. She would only bring you grief. I'm not saying not to be friendly, just don't get too involved. She's beautiful, but sometimes I just don't think she has a heart for others...even when she was young. She'll use you and hurt you and discard you...she's...." Her voice cracked, and she stopped talking as her eyes filled with tears of anguish.

David touched her hand. "Sam, it's over. That's in the past. D.A. has enough sense to handle himself with women. Let's leave such matters to him. He'll knock on our door in the future, and we'll leave his love life to him. Okay?''

She gamely smiled at both of them. ''Yes, I'll try.''

THE MONTH OF MAY brought activities almost to a standstill, which puzzled Sammy after the dizzying activity of calving.

''Consider it the calm between storms, Sam. Next month the branding is done, then we move the stock to higher summer pastures, and I want to build another solar generator, and I've been working in the meadow east of here all month. Some of us still have work to do,'' he teased her, chuckling over her novice's knowledge of the constant demands requiring his attention outside. ''Honey, there's a stockgrowers' meeting tonight in town,'' he said. ''They're discussing some new legislation regarding oil exploration I've told you about and a water-rights filing rule that has some old-time ranchers uptight. I really must go.'' David glanced at her. ''Do you want to come?''

They had been having coffee in the living room after supper. Sammy rose and stretched. A small area of her stomach was visible through the opening between her sweater and jeans as she finished the stretching motion, and she didn't see his hand ease toward her. She covered her yawn and suddenly felt his finger poking her belly.

''Ouch! Stop that,'' she cried as she playfully slapped at his hand.

''Don't you tell me to stop, woman,'' he replied as he grabbed her hand, pulled her down onto his lap and slipped his arm around her waist. One hand moved up beneath her top, but he frowned as he felt her bra and complained, "You're cheating, love."

"Sometimes I need protection from dirty old men like you who are always trying to feel my body," she answered, smiling, and reached up to kiss him lightly.

"Do you want to come?" he asked again.

"I always do with you." She smiled provocatively and moved suggestively on his lap, then ducked her head as a blush began to spread over her face.

"Why, you dirty old woman," he laughed as he caught her double meaning. "Don't you know that too much of a good thing is bad for your health?" He held her chin in his hand, enjoying her embarrassment.

"Are you sure? What will it do to me?" she asked, her curiosity getting the best of her.

"It'll make you crazy."

"How?" Her blue eyes were wide as she studied his face.

"It'll make you crazy for more." He laughed and brought her down against him and began kissing her in earnest.

Breathlessly she broke away and sighed. She laid her head against his chest, then raised her face to nuzzle his throat and kiss his neck.

Her lips inched up his neck to his ear.

"Stop that," he said, trying halfheartedly to move away from her warm breath. "I really should get ready to go." But as he looked at her, his eyes darkened and he whispered, "Sammy! I love you." His mouth brushed her lips as he whispered more words.

"Make love to me before you go," she murmured softly, and her hands tugged at his shirt front.

He watched her face as she unsnapped his rust-and-gold plaid shirt, then unbuckled his belt and tried to loosen his Levi's. Her pupils were large and the blue of her irises disappeared behind the midnight black.

She moved off his lap and began to shed her clothing, watching him as she slowly undressed. He finished stripping as she moved to give him room on the sofa. He sat beside her and his hand slid up her leg, tarried to stroke her prominent hipbone and came to rest at her waist. Her desert tan had faded, changing her skin to the color of rich cream. The soft lamplight threw shadows on her curves, highlighting the peaks and causing the valleys to disappear into the darkness as he leisurely admired her.

Her hands explored him. One investigated his chest and discovered that his nipple could respond to her touch. The other caressed his abdomen and the light touches of her fingertips ruined his self-control.

"I've never made love to you on the sofa," he said, his voice hoarse with anticipation. "I think it's about time I did." He eased his free hand between her thighs, feeling the smooth skin, and felt her press against his hand as a soft moan escaped from her throat. The boldness of her action heightened his desire for her.

Their bodies meshed as two finely tuned instruments, and they both knew what rapture would engulf them; a crescendo of feeling that soon left them forever merged in body and spirit.

They were covered with a moist sweat of love, and he pulled the afghan over their bodies. He moved her to the crook of his arm and held her tightly against him on the long sofa.

He listened as her breathing softened. Taking a deep

breath, he hesitated, then asked, "Sammy...do you have any regrets about moving here and living with me?"

"Oh, no, darling, none at all. I'm just so glad that you had the determination to come for me. I shudder to think what might have happened to us if you hadn't. I love you very much, David. I can't imagine living without you." She sighed, and as she finished her declaration of love, she kissed his chest.

They lay quietly, listening to the sounds of the spring night coming through the partially opened glass storm door, thinking private thoughts.

"I really must go, honey, and if I lie here much longer, I'll be asleep for sure," he said and began to move away.

She watched him dress, but as he looked at her questioningly, she answered, "I'll stay and catch up on our letter writing."

She wrapped herself in the afghan and ran to the bedroom, reappeared in her pink print smock, and went with him to the door. "Stay awake," she said as she kissed him goodbye.

"I love you," he called as he turned and waved from the truck.

She smiled as he shouted to the dog, Two, and invited him to accompany him on the trip to town. She remained at the door as he drove down the dark lane to the gravel road and watched until the red taillights disappeared into the black void of the moonless night.

She was soon engrossed in the backlog of letter writing. She enjoyed the correspondence responsibilities she had volunteered to assume when she learned of his distaste for them.

"Telephone's easier," he had commented.

"But a little extravagant," she had reminded him.

"Then you do it," he had replied—rather stubbornly, she had thought.

After a few hours, she closed the interior wood door, slipped into her warmer blue robe and lay down on the sofa to await his return. She looked at the clock. It was just past nine. He wouldn't be home for a few more hours. His handsome face was in her thoughts as she drifted to sleep.

SUDDENLY SAMMY WAS WIDE AWAKE. The house was still. She clutched her robe tightly around her waist and, after glancing at the small clock, ran to the kitchen to confirm the time on the large electric clock on the wall. It also read 2:00 A.M.

Had he come in and gone to bed without her? "David?" There was no answer. She rushed to the door and threw it open. The cold May night air brought her senses to a sharp awareness. "David?" she called again, and walked out into the yard. The truck was still gone.

She jumped as one of the dogs licked her hand, and she remembered that David had taken Two with him. One began to whine softly. She stroked the dog's soft back and said, "It's okay, One. They'll be home soon."

Her confidence evaporated as her imagination took over, and she began to think of all the reasons for his absence. Perhaps he had had mechanical trouble. She should return to the house in case he called. Perhaps he was just visiting some of his ranching friends and had lost track of the time...but that wasn't at all like David. Maybe he was having a drink with his friends, but he seldom drank, and besides, the bars were closed. Maybe he'd had an accident. Fear struck her numb, and she pushed the idea from her mind.

She remembered that he had said Russ would be at the meeting. She hadn't seen Russ since her return but knew David had resumed their friendship. Julie came to visit her often and had recently talked her into becoming involved in community activities.

Sammy had felt the time was still not right for a confrontation, but now she had to talk to Russ. She dialed the Russell phone number, and on the sixth ring a sleepy-sounding Ed Russell growled into the receiver, "Who the hell is it calling at this hour?"

Sammy shook with intimidation at his tone. She quickly hung the receiver back in its cradle and stood trembling, feeling utterly helpless.

She ran to the bedroom and changed into a pair of jeans, a flannel shirt, walking shoes and a warm jacket. She grabbed her car keys and ran down the steps to her green sedan. She would hunt for him herself. If she didn't see him between the ranch and town, she would call Russ again.

She called to One. The dog jumped onto the front seat, and Sammy started her search. She drove the route she assumed David had taken to the stockgrowers' meeting. She saw nothing out of the ordinary as she turned onto the road into town. She passed the Russell ranch entrance and drove on toward the soft lights of the town in the distance. She tried to study both sides of the road. Her eyes played tricks, and she saw objects that weren't there at all. One whined softly. Sammy felt confident she would find David somewhere along the road soon.

She was at the southern outskirts of town, and still she saw no sign of him. She drove to the organization's regular meeting place. All the cars and trucks were gone. She drove north on Montana Street. The bars and saloons were quiet. Her heart sank as she traveled the return route to the ranch.

She entered the kitchen with a pounding heart and ran to the phone. As she dialed the Russell number, she glanced at the clock: 3:00 A.M. The phone was answered by Julie Russell.

"Oh, Julie, this is Sammy. David hasn't returned from town, and I'm frightened. Can you wake Russ and ask him when David left the meeting? I hate to disturb you, but I'm so worried."

There was silence as she waited and mentally counted the time needed to get a response from, in all probability, a very grouchy Russ.

"Sammy?"

"Yes, Julie."

"Sammy, Russ said that he, that is Russ, left first— that David had been appointed chairman of a special committee to go to Helena and talk with some legislators and was still holding a meeting with the other men when Russ decided to come home. Russ got home about 11:00. Do you want us to come and look for him?"

"No, not yet. Thanks anyway, Julie. You're a real friend. I think I'll drive the route once more. He must be having trouble and can't get to a phone. I'm sorry to have bothered you so late. Good night." She quickly hung up the phone.

She returned to the car and began the trip to town once again. This time she drove more slowly, observing the shoulder for any sign of an accident that might have been cleared away. She drove to the meeting place again, then drove through some of the residential streets where she knew he had friends, hoping to spot his truck.

She even drove past the reputed local prostitute, Nelda Brockmeyer, whom Julie had told her about, then felt ashamed that she could have thought such a thing of David. She smiled slightly as she observed that tonight's customer owned a red Camaro.

She began the slow return trip home, her pulse racing as the car traveled through the darkness. There was only one stretch of the winding road where a vehicle could go off and be out of sight. A steep dropoff down to an old road led to an abandoned mining town called Reverse. The town had received its name in the 1870s when the miners' luck kept reversing from good to bad to good. David had told her that the name had stuck even when the luck stayed bad and the town had died.

The turnoff was almost halfway between the Russell ranch and their own. She drove very slowly once she'd passed the Russell entrance. As she steered around the curve in the road just past the turnoff to the old mining town, she saw something moving ahead, far down the road. She turned on her brights and again saw a staggering motion ahead. A wild animal? There were a few coyotes in the area. When she drew closer she recognized David's dog, Two, limping along the edge of the road, heading for the ranch. She accelerated until she was alongside the animal, then stopped the car and called to him.

She gasped as she got a clear view of the dog in the bright glare of the headlights. His thick fur was matted with dried blood. A gash still oozed a trickle of blood and fluid down his face, causing his eye to blink continuously. He came to her, whining in pain.

"Oh, Two, where's David?" She stood up and looked around in the darkness. She remembered the flashlight in the glove compartment. She ran to the car, fumbled with the compartment latch, finally got it open and grabbed the flashlight.

She ran to the side of the embankment and shone the light into the darkness, but the beam was absorbed by the night and she started to cry.

She scolded herself for losing control. This was no time for hysteria. Methodically she shone the light first in one direction, then in the other, studying the end of the light rays intensely, until finally she saw an object off in the distance. It was about one hundred yards back toward the junction. She helped the injured dog into the car and backed the vehicle down the road, jumped out again and shone the light down the embankment.

Her heart stopped as she recognized his truck. It was overturned and wedged between a stubby pine tree and a huge boulder. She screamed his name as she scrambled down the rocky embankment. She was sobbing as she reached the truck. She crawled around to the front window of the cab and shone the light into the compartment.

"Oh, my God," she cried. His face was covered with blood. She saw a small hole knocked in the window glass. He must have hit his head as he careened down the cliff bank, she thought. She couldn't tell if he was alive or dead. As she tried to keep control of her panicky thoughts, she noticed that the rear window of the cab had popped out. Perhaps she could get to him through the opening.

She scrambled around the cab, then stopped. Stupid, try the door! She shook it, but it was stuck. No, it was locked. David was always cautioning her to keep the doors locked when she drove at night. Maybe she could unlock the door if she could just squeeze through the small opening in the back where the window had popped out. She crawled around the truck and flattened herself against the dirt and underbrush, trying to reach his motionless body.

She could just fit through the inverted V made by the overturned truck cab and bed. She pushed her head through the small opening and with great fear she touched him. He moved slightly. She heard a low moan.

"David?" she cried, "Oh, David!"

He tried to turn his head to her but stopped, and a pain-filled groan escaped from his bloody lips. His six-foot length was twisted in the inverted cab. She tried to straighten his legs, but there was no room. If she could just get the door open. . . . She tried to wipe some of the sticky blood from his eyes and nose with her fingers, but her hand shook so badly that it was wasted effort.

"David," she whispered again and his mouth moved, but she couldn't understand his sounds. She reached for the door-locking button and pulled. It moved. She tried the handle, but the door was jammed. She unrolled the window and carefully moved his long legs through the opening. He groaned, but responded to the more comfortable position. She tried to open the driver's side of the cab and encountered the same jammed situation.

Again she tried the window, but this one wouldn't budge.

She returned her attention to his face, and as she shifted her shoulders past his torso, she accidentally pressed against his chest. He screamed in pain and she recoiled in horror. She carefully opened his jacket and his shirt. A massive bruise covered several of his ribs, and the area was extremely swollen. His breathing became shallow and labored, and she returned to his face to make sure that his breathing passage was unobstructed.

She took the corner of her shirt and used it as a wiping cloth to cleanse his nose and mouth, and then she laid her lips against his still mouth in a soft kiss. She moved to his ear and whispered, "David, can you hear me?"

She studied his face, and when his mouth began to move she placed her ear against it and heard him say, "Hi, love."

She returned to his ear and said, "David, I must get help," and again his mouth moved.

This time she heard the single word, "Russ."

"Yes, I'll get Russ. Oh, David, don't leave me...I love you. I'll be back."

She scooted backward out the inverted opening and ran up the rocky embankment, sliding down and skinning her hands and knees, losing precious time. She tried to suppress the sobs, but the tears blurred her vision as she again attempted to climb the cliff, clinging to bushes, roots and tufts of grass. She reached for a branch that turned into a dead bush, and dirt flew into her face.

Her tears helped wash out some of the dust particles, and her vision cleared. She tried again and this time succeeded in reaching the road above. She was closer to their own ranch than to the Russell place, so she climbed back into the car, pressed the accelerator to the floorboard, then raced down the dark winding road. She steered into the ranch yard and slammed on the brakes, stopping near the kitchen door.

The door took forever to open, and she finally raised her foot in exasperation and kicked it, splintering the wood doorjamb. She rushed to the phone, and as the ringing repeated itself at the other end of the line, she glanced at the clock. It was 4:30.

Russ answered the phone on the third ring, and this time he was expectant. "Did you find him?" he demanded before she could say a word.

"Yes!" she cried. "He's badly hurt. The truck's overturned and the doors are stuck. Please call an ambulance. He may have a back injury. Come as fast as you can—he asked for you."

She started to hang up when she heard him ask, "Sammy, where is he?"

"Oh, my God! I'm sorry, Russ. He's down the embankment about a half mile from the turnoff to Reverse. Take the old road, and you'll be able to reach him better. I'll be there."

She slammed the phone in place and ran out the broken door. Within minutes she was back at the scene of the accident and scrambled down to the truck. As she approached the cab, she saw that he had extended his arm out the opening where the window had popped. She tried to rejoin him, but the area seemed tighter this time.

She sat beside the cab and held his hand, felt his fingers move and was reassured that he was alive. She called to him, "Help is coming, David. . . Russ is coming. . . hold on, darling," but she wasn't sure if he could hear her words. His fingers occasionally moved as she clutched his large hand, and she prayed for his life. Where was Russ? What was taking so long?

Suddenly she felt his hand relax, and as she stared down, his fingers began to uncurl.

She clung to his lifeless hand and laid her head against the overturned blue cab, sobbing her grief and sorrow.

"No, no, no," she cried as she continued to stare at his hand.

Fifteen minutes later Russ and Julie Russell found her clutching his motionless hand, and they had to pry her fingers away from him in order to remove him from the truck.

CHAPTER TWENTY

THE REVOLVING LIGHTS of the emergency vehicles had turned the breaking dawn into a brilliant kaleidoscope as the amber of the wrecker, the blue and red of the sheriff's car, and the red of the ambulance mixed with the bright flood of the rescue lights.

Julie led Sammy away from the activity and held her in her arms. Julie looked up as Dr. Morrison joined them.

"How is she?" he asked.

"She's over her hysteria. I think she's in shock. She fought us and wouldn't let us get near him at first. It took Russ quite a while to just get her to release his hand. She's convinced he's dead."

"She's almost correct, I'm afraid."

"I've tried to tell her what's going on, but she doesn't understand what I say to her. She just keeps repeating that he's dead and shaking. Can you help?"

"I think so. Let me finish with David."

Julie looked fearfully at Dr. Morrison. "What's wrong with him?"

"He's broken several ribs, and his sternum may be cracked. I need X rays to confirm. He can hardly breathe. One of his lungs is collapsed, I'm sure, and he's bleeding internally. There's always hope, but it's not good. We can't give up. Julie, keep holding her. I'll be right back.''

Julie watched as the doctor returned to the bloody, motionless body of her friend and neighbor. A tube was inserted into his nostril and an intravenous unit attached to his arm. A thick compress had been applied to his forehead, but his face had the least of his injuries, Dr. Morrison had said. The emergency crew carefully lifted his body into the back of the ambulance, and as David disappeared from view, Sammy screamed and fainted.

Dr. Morrison returned to the two women. He looked at Sammy's limp body, then called to one of the emergency volunteers and asked him to carry the unconscious woman to his car.

''Russ will ride with David,'' he told Julie. ''You and Sammy can ride with me. She'll be awake by the time we arrive. I'll need her at the hospital.''

He turned and called to the ambulance driver and his attendant, ''Okay, guys, head to Barrett Memorial and hurry, for God's sake! I'll meet you there. It's a matter of life and death this time.''

The movement of the car helped to revive Sammy, but when she saw the whirling red lights of the ambulance just ahead and turned to look at the gray-haired physician driving the car, she knew everything was wrong, so wrong. The convulsive shaking began again as she turned to him.

''He's...?''

''Alive.''

''No, he's....''

''Yes, Sammy, he's alive. He's critically injured, but

he's alive. Remember that, Sammy—he's alive. You found him in time. It's going to be rough, but he's alive.'' Dr. Morrison repeated the words through clenched jaws. He reached over and patted her hands, trying to still their wringing motions, and repeated, ''He's alive.''

DAVID WANTED A DEEP BREATH OF AIR, but when he tried to inhale, the pain was excruciating. He was being forced to breathe.... Didn't they know how much it hurt? He tried to move away from the hands that prodded him, but a wave of unbearable pain swept through his body. His head was splitting when he tried to think. Why didn't they take the knife out of his side and leave him alone? Stop trying, it's not worth the pain...pain...pain.... Slowly everything slipped into blackness, and the agonizing pain went away.

SOMETHING COVERED HIS FACE, and cool oxygen drifted into his bronchial tubes. He was a tree being given a drink of cool water after a long drought. With just a little concentration, he felt the relief filtering through his body. All the pain seemed to be on the side where the knife had lodged. How did the knife get there? Had he been in a fight? He couldn't remember going into any of the saloons in town. In an involuntary reaction, he gulped a full breath of air. The pain paralyzed him, and he couldn't even scream. The knife twisted into a burning torch and the flames engulfed him, then the black void mercifully re turned.

SOMEONE WAS HOLDING HIS LEFT HAND, but when he tried to see the person, the splitting pain returned to his brain. The knife was still in his right side, and he tried to tell them to remove it, but he wasn't sure if he had spoken the words or just thought them. He tried again and this time he heard his own detached voice.

"Take it out...."

A woman's face with soft blue eyes appeared, and a frightened voice asked, "What, David?"

"The knife...it hurts...."

The woman with blue eyes moved closer to him. He thought he knew her, but the effort it took to think of her name brought back the pain. Such a soft shade of blue, he thought, as he felt a prick on his right arm.

He wanted to see the blue-eyed lady again, and he forced his heavy lids open. She was closer than before, and he felt her hands hold his face. The burning abrasions felt cooler when she touched him. She drew closer and gently kissed his parched lips. The soft blue eyes were inches from his, and he saw her smile slightly, but then he saw that her eyes were red as well as blue and she was....

Her two blue eyes changed into four, the overhead lights rotated in circles and he felt the pain float away. He drifted over green pine trees on a cloud of soft blue cotton and into the sky...it was the same shade as the eyes of the woman. The blue darkened as though a storm was brewing...he'd better hurry home...Sammy would be worried...the sky turned to black and he knew he couldn't make it home...he just couldn't make it...she'd understand.

"HE KEEPS TALKING ABOUT A KNIFE. What does he mean?" Sammy turned first to Julie, then to Russ, expecting an answer. They were both silent as they sat in the hospital's intensive care unit waiting room.

"Where is he now? What are they doing to him? Where's Dr. Morrison?" She bombarded them with questions they couldn't answer.

"They'll have to shave some of his hair in order to sew up his forehead. He won't like that...he's a little vain about his hair...did you know his hair was red when he was a boy? Not carrot red, but rusty-bark reddish...you didn't know him when he was a boy, did you...?" Her voice faded away as grief overshadowed the memories.

"He's going to...die, isn't he? That's why no one will come tell me what's happening. He's going to die." She didn't wait for them to agree with her conclusion; she knew it was true.

"He'll be upset...he starts the spring roundup in a few weeks. He's planning to build another solar generator for the west range. He's going to Bozeman next week to buy the materials...he...he said he loved me...just before he drove away last night...." Her voice faltered.

She turned to Julie and began again. "We've known each other for less than four years, Julie, and three of those were as kids. That's not long enough. Julie, you and Russ have had so many years together...David and I have had just a few months...it's not fair! We keep having terrible separations." She grabbed Julie's hands. "Julie," she pleaded, "why can't we just have some quiet time together. Is that too much to ask?"

Before her friend could respond, Dr. Morrison entered the room and pulled a chair up close.

"Sammy, listen carefully now. I'll start from his head and go down to his feet." He smiled slightly and added, "He's managed to damage it all. He has a concussion, but no skull fracture. His forehead will require stitches, probably about a dozen. His memory will be faulty for a few days, but it'll come back. His facial cuts and bruises are minor, and we've been able to remove the glass slivers without difficulty.

"Apparently he hit the floor-mounted gearshift knob very hard as the truck rolled. He must have really slammed into it, because it broke four ribs, and one of them has punctured the middle lobe of his right lung."

He stopped and stared at Sammy. "That must be what he thinks is a knife in his side. He has had a great deal of internal bleeding into his chest cavity. He has a great deal of blood in his stomach, but I've been treating him for an ulcer, and I can't tell if it's from that or the internal injuries. Our greatest concern now is to treat the collapsed lung and remove the bone fragments and fluid from his chest cavity and lung. This means surgery, and although I'd like to see it done in a larger hospital, he can't be moved and he can't wait. If the damage is too severe, it means removing the lobe. He can get by on what's left; he just won't be able to run any marathons. I've done this kind of surgery before, and I feel confident that with Dr. Peters as my assistant we can handle it. This is a great little hospital.

"Sammy, he won't be very handsome for a while. When you see him afterward, he'll be full of drainage tubes. Don't be alarmed. He can't do without them."

Sammy's face grew progressively paler as his description of the necessary surgery unfolded.

"Are you okay?" he asked. She nodded silently, and he reached out to her and gave her a fatherly embrace. "David's being prepared for surgery right now. Do you want to see him?"

"Of course," she whispered, and began to rise.

"Wait. There's a few more injuries. I realize that this is almost anticlimactic, but somehow he also managed to break his big toe and three of the five metatarsal bones in his right foot." He smiled. "We had to cut his boot off because of the swelling. Sorry. He liked those boots."

Dr. Morrison stood, then sat down again. "Sammy, this operation will take several hours. I don't want you to be alarmed at the length of time that you won't see your husband or me." He stood again and motioned for her to follow. He led her down a sterile-looking corridor, and as she looked ahead she saw David's body strapped to a gurney that was being rolled through the double doors of the operating room.

"Wait, nurse," Dr. Morrison called. "This is Mrs. McCormack. She needs a few moments with her husband." He guided the nurse into the scrub room.

David lay silent, pale and naked, with only a white flannel sheet covering his body. The hospital staff had removed most of the dried blood from his face and neck, but the cuts and bruises were swollen, and his handsome features were hidden from her searching eyes. She spoke his name several times, but he gave no response. She leaned close and whispered unheard words in his ear and touched his lips with her fingers.

"Please, David...stay with me...please," she murmured. She held his hand for a few moments as time stopped for her. Then she turned, nodded to Dr. Morrison and walked back to the visitors' room where Julie and Ed Russell were waiting.

Russ was on the sofa and Sammy joined him. She turned to him in desperation and implored, "What if he doesn't make it, Russ? I just can't go on without him. I know you may still hate me, but I...I love him so much!" She clutched frantically at his shirt front.

Russ was in his own private agony. "Oh, Sammy," he declared to her, "I love him, too. He's my friend; he's like a brother. He'll make it, I promise." He put his thick arms around her and drew her against his chest, consoling her.

Julie Russell watched them and nodded her understanding.

DAVID MCCORMACK'S HEAD THROBBED when he turned it, the tube running down his nostril drove him crazy, and his mouth was dry and sore. His right arm was strapped to the bed, and he visually traced a tube from the needle inserted in his vein to an inverted bottle suspended from a hook near his head. He had several tubes taped to his side and had the peculiar feeling that they were installed inside his body. The idea was frightening. He tried to cope with the embarrassment of a urinary catheter. He had discovered it when a wise-cracking nurse had teased him during a few moments of consciousness as she changed the collection bag. He thought it was yesterday, but he wasn't sure. Thank goodness he had been unconscious when it had been inserted, and he shuddered at the embarrassing thought of having it removed.

His right foot had a heavy weight that he finally decided was a plaster cast. His chest was encased in tape and bandages and a brace to keep him immobile, but at least he could breathe without having the knife twist in his side.

As he explored his left side he found another tube. It was carrying blood from a plastic bag by his head to the needle in his arm, but his arm wasn't strapped down and he savored the freedom of being able to move it. His left leg was the only undamaged part of his aching anatomy.

He heard the door swing as someone entered, but it hurt to try to see who it was.

"Why, Mr. McCormack! Welcome back to the world of the living. For a few days we thought we were going to lose you. How do you feel?" As the owner of the voice moved to his left side, he saw a tall robust-looking woman wearing a white pantsuit and a big smile. Before he could attempt to reply, she stuck a thermometer in his mouth and reached for his pulse, counted silently, then read a blood pressure device that seemed permanently attached to his upper arm. She finished her small chores, then stopped and peered at his face.

She smiled, patted his bearded cheek, and said, "What sexy green eyes you have, now that we can see them. Bea Lambert is right. I must be sure and tell her that she's right. I'll go tell Dr. Morrison that you finally decided to rejoin us. See you later." She waved a friendly salute and left the room.

How had he arrived here? Where was Sammy? The last thing he remembered was a sharp pain tearing his stomach to shreds. How long ago was that? He could remember brief periods of time, but they were filled with intense pain.

Dr. Robert Morrison rushed through the door with a smile spreading across his dignified features. "How are you, David? How do you feel?"

"Terrible. Can you take this damn tube out of my nose?"

"Do you think his complaining means that he's getting better, doctor?" the sturdy nurse commented.

"Probably so, Mrs. Mason. Isn't it good to hear? Let's make him happy. Help me remove the tube."

Within minutes the nose tube was gone as well as the IV containing the blood replacement.

"How about this other thing?" David asked, pointing to the bag suspended from his bedside.

Dr. Morrison laughed and said, "Patience, my friend, patience. In a few days. I think the other IV can come out later today, though. Are you hungry? How about some food through your mouth today? It won't be steak, of course. We'll start with some broth."

"I have some blank spaces," David said. "Do you have time to help me fill them in?"

"I'll be glad to, just as soon as I finish my rounds. I'll be back in about an hour. You'll be having a visitor shortly. You do remember that you have a wife?"

"Sammy...of course...how is she?" he asked with a smile.

"She's fine. Exhausted, but now that you're better, I'm sure she'll be better, too. She's a lovely woman, David. You're a lucky man."

"Where is she? How long has it been? What happened?"

"Easy, now. She's been staying with my wife and me. The accident occurred almost a week ago. I'll tell you more later."

Dr. Morrison left with the nurse. David lay in the bed, exhausted from the short exertion, wondering what had happened during the missing week. He remembered blue eyes and gentle hands.

He drifted to sleep; restful sleep; satin smooth, black velvet sleep.

When he awoke, a lamp spread soft light over the features of a sleeping woman curled in a chair next to his bed. It was dark outside, and he wondered what had happened to the day?

Sammy's head was close enough that he could reach her cheek. In her sleep, she reached up to brush away the object that had touched her. Her eyes flew open when she realized *he* had touched her. She grabbed his hand and squeezed it. She stood by the side of the bed but found it a barrier, so she eased herself onto the mattress, holding tightly to his hand.

He stared at her and knew his voice would fail him. Her eyes filled with tears and her chin began to quiver. She bit her lip, trying to control herself, but the tears in her eyes overflowed and ran silently down her face. He freed his left hand and brushed some of the tears away, but they continued to fall in a steady stream.

He motioned for her to lie beside him. There was just enough room for her body to fit next to his, and she slipped around the bed's safety railing. She moved into his offered embrace, and his uninjured left arm held her. He closed his eyes.

He awoke once during the night and was aware that someone had covered them both with a warm blanket.

She was gone when he awoke. Had he dreamed that she had been with him during the night? Morning sun streamed through the window. He heard voices outside the door and turned to see who would enter.

It was a procession. Sammy entered and came to stand at his left side. She smiled and kissed him lightly on his lips. Dr. Morrison was second and stood at the foot of the bed, nodding and smiling his approval at his patient's improvement. Next came the sturdy-looking tall nurse who kept sticking things in his mouth. An attractive woman in her thirties wearing a physician's coat joined Dr. Morrison at the foot of the bed. This must be the famous Dr. Peters, whose medical reputation had been discussed and admired by Julie and Sammy one afternoon over coffee at the McCormack ranch.

Last to enter was a small woman in a white uniform carrying a tray full of impressive-looking instruments and rolls of tape and gauze. The smiling entourage surrounded his bed, and he realized that this was no social call.

Dr. Morrison took charge of the meeting and began to give instructions. "Sammy, you may stay because some of the treatments must be continued after he goes home."

Dr. Morrison smiled at the younger woman and said, "Dr. Peters, since you installed the catheter, would you like to do the honors?"

"Oh, God, no!" David groaned and looked pleadingly toward his friend and physician. Everyone moved at once. Sammy came to his side again and held his hand and talked, but he couldn't concentrate on her words.

The bed linens were removed and he discovered he didn't even have the protection of a modest thigh-length hospital gown to cover his nakedness. The sturdy nurse began to take his temperature just as he heard Dr. Peters speak, and he frowned at her.

"Mr. McCormack, you must know that you're not the first man I've seen naked, and you're certainly not the first male I've catheterized, and I'm sure you won't be the last." She smiled at him and said, "Now, that wasn't so bad, was it? It's out. You can finish blushing now." She covered him then turned away for a moment.

"Thanks," he mumbled, shielding his eyes with his forearm. The room became quiet. He looked at the group suspiciously then asked, "What's next?"

"The remaining IV. You reneged on eating yesterday, so I left it in. We'll try for breakfast this morning. It's time for the sutures to be removed from your forehead, too."

David touched his head gingerly and exclaimed, "I didn't know I hurt my head...you shaved my hair?" He looked at Sammy questioningly.

"Just a little, dear. You're still handsome. What's gone from your head is now on your face," she reminded him and smiled.

He looked at himself in the mirror after the procedures were completed. "With the stitch marks, these two black eyes, and all these scabs and scrapes, I look like Frankenstein."

"I think that's enough before breakfast," Dr. Morrison said. "We'll come back in about an hour and tend to your side."

DAVID WAS DEFINITELY RIGHT-HANDED, but each time he tried to move his right arm, pain engulfed his body. He was a helpless invalid, and it didn't set well. Using his left hand, he tried to move a shaky fork full of soft scrambled eggs from the plate to his mouth. He missed the target each time he tried with the uncooperative muscles. He was furious with himself and grumbled when Sammy insisted on helping him.

"David, it's only temporary," she assured him as she scooped the scattered pieces of eggs from his nightshirt, which had been draped across his chest and tied around his neck.

His strength was gone, and he lay back on the pillow, feeling completely exhausted. He accepted three bites, then refused the next. He motioned her to stop and closed his eyes.

She cleared the tray away and rejoined him, sitting near him on the edge of the bed. "David, please look at me," she pleaded. His eyes remained closed.

"David, I almost lost you twice the first day after the surgery. You just stopped breathing, and they had to resuscitate you. It wasn't until the third day that Dr. Morrison held any hope for your survival. Do you think I care if you can't get some stupid eggs to your mouth?

"For four days you were on a life-support system that breathed for you and kept your heart beating when you stopped trying. There was no fight in you. It wasn't until the fifth day that you even opened your eyes, and yesterday was the first day you spoke an intelligent statement. Oh, my darling, you were so close to dying, and I was so frightened!'' She reached up to touch his face and brushed the soft beard.

David opened his eyes, and she saw the moisture in them. Their rusty greenness shone like the peridot jewel in her treasured Christmas necklace.

''David, when you made love to me that last night, and I said I didn't think I could live without you, I didn't know that I'd be tested so quickly. When I awoke that night and you were missing, I hunted for you for two hours before I found you, but I didn't stop until I did.''

She smiled. ''Do you know what you said to me when I did find you? You were covered with blood and you said, 'Hi, love.' You were dying and still you called me love. I don't care if it takes you months to get well. Didn't our marriage vows say in sickness and in health? Well, now you're the sick one, and I have good health. That means I'm going to take care of you. Is it so hard for you to accept my help when you need it?''

David took a deep breath and winced in pain. ''You've had part of your right lung removed,'' she continued. ''Dr. Morrison says you'll have to learn to breathe a little differently. You'll be given some exercises on a respirator here at the hospital before you go home. Then we'll continue them at the ranch. You'll need my help for that, too. He says you'll be as good as new within six months.''

''Six months?'' he groaned.

''That's just for breathing fully,'' she smiled. ''Other activities can be resumed sooner...in moderation...

when you feel up to it. I missed you very, very much, darling. I'm glad you're back with me to stay."

He studied her as she outlined his recuperation schedule. He moved his hand up her arm and rested it near her neck. "I'm sorry, Sam. I just need time to catch up and adjust to what's happened." He looked at the meal tray. "I've decided I'm hungry after all. Can you help me...for a while?"

CHAPTER TWENTY-ONE

"YOU MUST BE THE WORST PATIENT in the whole world," Sammy declared in exasperation.

"And you're the prettiest nurse any sick man could ask for," he teased.

"Oh, how can I stay angry at you when you say things like that."

"Then don't." He smiled.

"But Dr. Morrison says you must do the exercises exactly the prescribed number of times each day. You quit too soon."

"I'm bored. I wish I could take Bay out for a ride to the foothills. Do you want to go see the wild flowers? I'll bet they're all in bloom."

She put her fists firmly on her hips and challenged the idea silently as she struggled to maintain a firm frown. "David!"

"Okay, okay, maybe next week. I'll make up the exercises tomorrow." To get her mind off the therapy, he said, "Hey, look what I can do." He eased himself out of the bed, hobbled a few steps on his waking cast, and stopped at the dresser, where he carefully poured himself a glass of water from the pitcher, using his right hand. "Now watch." He grasped the glass and slowly lifted it to his mouth, took a long drink, then returned it to the dresser with only a slight tremor as he set it down. He beamed. "I've been practicing."

"I think the best way for you to strengthen your right arm is to start giving yourself baths from now on. No more nurse Samantha's special treatment for the poor helpless patient," she suggested.

"How about one last time? You can't just cut me off cold turkey from the most enjoyable part of my care," he complained as he returned to the bed. "I'd have withdrawal pangs."

He was panting from the short exertion, and Sammy's heart lurched as she watched him grimace slightly. He'd been a surprisingly cooperative patient in spite of his usual self-sufficient and independent nature, and Sammy once again acknowledged how close she had come to losing him forever.

She brought the bath supplies to the nightstand and went to fill the basin with warm water.

"Ouch, that's a little hot, isn't it?" he complained as she started to lather his chest.

"You need to be sterilized. You probably have cooties growing in there. Feel them crawl?" She tickled his chest, tugging playfully at the fine curly hairs. She stopped and asked, "Does it still hurt when you laugh?"

"Just a little." He rolled onto his stomach, groaning twice as he adjusted his body. She quickly washed him, then massaged his shoulders and back, noticing the weight loss as she worked his muscles. She leaned down and kissed the firm skin and whispered in his ear, "I love you."

His head rested on his folded arms, and as she finished the back rub, he said, "I must be getting well. I was thinking how much I miss making love to you."

She leaned down and kissed his cheek, admiring his handsome profile. Its strength was softened by the gray in his hair, which had increased considerably since she had become reacquainted with him. At times her love for him brought a physical pain to her chest. She caressed his back in order to give herself time to regain control of her emotions, then said, "I'll help you get dressed." She helped him slip into pajamas and a robe, then waited while he ran a comb through his hair.

"When is Russ coming?" he asked.

"In about a half hour. Take your time."

"What happened between you two? I'm glad you're friends, but I don't understand the change."

She stared at him for several seconds, then said quietly, "Let's just say we discovered a common interest."

David was lounging on the sofa when Paul and Ed Russell came to report on the spring roundup. The head count of yearlings was very encouraging, with minimum losses during the winter. The new calves had benefited from the mild weather in April and May. The commercial Hereford herds had increased substantially over the past two years. One of the Simmentals had a healthy, sturdy bull calf, and the other was due any day. David was hoping for a heifer.

In spite of his years on the ranch, David felt like a novice now that he was devoting his full effort to making the ranch pay. It had been his hobby for ten years, but now it was his vocation. Time would tell if he could make it profitable.

Sammy had taken over the ranch's financial books and, over David's mild objections, used her accounting knowledge to set up what she described as a decent set of books so they could keep more accurate records of the gains and losses. He had always just put the money in and paid it out, he'd told her.

"Trust me, dear," she assured him. "When you're well, I'll explain how the books are set up, and you'll know just where you make a profit and where you may have problems. Especially now that we've the start of a purebred Simmental herd, it's going to be important for tax purposes as well as American Simmental Association records."

"Honey, you catch on fast," he said with pride. "You sound like a ranch manager. And you thought you couldn't learn? I think you're a pro already." He laughed. "Now that you and Russ have decided to become working partners, perhaps you can keep his records, too."

"Hardly. I don't have time, but I can show Julie the changes I've made. There's always room for improvement," she said with confidence. "Someday I'm going to have all your little cows on an inventory file in your very own personal computer. You can play video games in your spare time, and I'll do your bookkeeping. Doesn't that sound like fun?"

SEVEN WEEKS HAD PASSED since the accident, including the three weeks David had spent in the hospital in town. Sammy stayed one week in town with the Morrisons, then two lonely weeks at the ranch before she'd brought him home to recuperate. She had been sleeping in D.A.'s room since David's return. Each night was a restless period of tossing and turning, waiting for him to call. Just when she would finally fall asleep, his moans would awaken her, and she would rush to his side fearing a relapse, thinking his side had ripped open, his headaches had returned—all sorts of imaginary catastrophes. Usually she'd find him still asleep, unaware of her checking on his condition.

Sometimes she had nightmares of finding him in the overturned truck. She didn't tell him of the nightly difficulties. He had enough to be concerned about without her minor problems.

She looked at the clock. It was almost midnight. Sleep refused to come to her in D.A.'s bed. Perhaps if she was very careful, she could slip into bed beside him and get a decent night's sleep. She had been getting increasingly irritable and had lost weight, and both were from lack of sleep.

She slipped out of bed and moved down the hallway. When she opened the door quietly and looked in, he was lying on his back, sleeping like a baby.

A full moon was shining through the window across the bed, as though a Phoenix streetlight had been installed in the Montana sky to light her way to him. She followed its path and eased under the covers.

He murmured something in his sleep, slipping his strong left arm around her, and she had no choice but to snuggle next to him.

SHE FELT THE HEAT, and like a moth drawn to a fire she had to get closer, closer. The fire was in his truck. The flames were blue and amber, and she saw his face through the intense heat. He would burn to death if she didn't get him out. She tried to open the door, but it was stuck. She pulled and pulled, and still it refused to give way. The rescue people grabbed her and pulled her away from the burning truck. She knew he would die if she didn't get him out. They jerked her back, and she cried, "No, no, no!" She fell back moaning, "No...no...no, he'll burn to death." Then she heard him call to her, and she opened her eyes.

"Sammy, wake up. It's all right, honey." He held her hand to prevent her from thrashing at him in her confusion. The fire was his body, and he was warm and alive and safe with her.

She turned in his arms and began to kiss his face and smother his neck and chest with caresses.

She cried softly and he comforted her, drawing her closer to him. As she tried to suppress the rasping sobs, he said, "I think I have a problem, and it's all your fault, my sweet Sammy."

She understood. A feeling of exultation swept over her as she moved, knowing that they had been apart much too long. She ran her hand down his chest and across his belly. She paused, then her fingers fanned out to confirm his desire. He gave her room, and she heard him groan softly.

"Oh, Sam, that feels good...."

"Yes," she murmured, her mouth gliding over his warm hard body. "Yes, yes," she whispered, because she had needs, too. She nipped his skin and thrilled as it quivered beneath her lips.

"I want you, David. I need you." Her warm moist

mouth found his again. Her small tongue darted past his teeth and claimed him with a boldness that shook them both.

Suddenly his hand shot down and stopped the motions of hers. "Enough," he murmured. "I'll take over now." He tried to pull her up and turn her over, but fell back. "I can't," he groaned in disappointment.

"I can." Carefully she moved astride him, sitting up to avoid his injured side, and gloried in their union.

His hands slid under her gown, but the gown hindered his exploration. "Take it off."

She complied, bringing the long gown up and over her head and flinging it from her. Her body seemed to glisten in the moonlight as she said, "Touch me, David." His hands caressed her breasts, his thumbs quickly bringing her nipples to a rigid peak.

"Move easy," he instructed her, "like that... easy...that doesn't hurt at all...easy...that's what I need. Oh, Sammy!" She felt the shuddering tremors begin for him, and they seemed to go on and on and merge into her own. He pulled her toward him and she collapsed against him, luxuriating in the splendor of the endless moment.

As she lay spent in his arms, he stroked her bare back, down to the flare of her hips, up to her waist and shoulders, enjoying the satin smoothness of her skin.

"You know, love," he said, "I realize this isn't everything in a marriage, but it sure adds to the contentment factor, doesn't it?"

"Mmmm," she replied, pleased that this time she had made love to him.

THE NEXT MORNING her confidence was shaken. David came hobbling into the kitchen as she poured two cups of coffee. When she turned, she discovered him standing nearby frowning down at her.

He caught her chin and turned her face up to his. "You look awful," he said.

His words stung, and she tried to withdraw.

"You have dark circles under your eyes, and you've lost a lot of weight. Has taking care of me done this to you?"

"I haven't been sleeping very well," she admitted. "But now things are better."

She smiled and looked up at his gaunt face, accentuated by the reddish brown beard he had kept since the accident. His leanness was unnatural for his size and bone structure. "You're not so fat yourself, David."

"My foot cast comes off today," he said. "Sammy, when you drive me into town to Dr. Morrison's office, why don't you go shopping...a new dress...get your hair fixed." He frowned as he looked at the top of her curly head.

Sammy touched her hair and asked, "Do I look that bad?"

"No, no," he assured her, "but in a few days, I'd like to take you out on the town. I've already talked to Dr. Morrison, and he thinks it would be good recovery therapy for both of us. He says we've both become too serious. There's a new supper club in Bozeman that he's told me about...dinner...floor show...and dancing after the show. If you'll drive...do you think you'd like to be my date?''

She looked at her husband. "It would be fun, wouldn't it? Do you think you're really up to it?"

"I'm willing to give it a try."

The following Saturday evening his admiring glances thrilled her as she dressed. "How do I look?" she asked.

"You look ravishing; absolutely beautiful, my love," David said. He fastened the hook at the back of her filmy coral organza bodice. The muted color accented her creamy shoulders. He placed a warm kiss against her nape as she finished adjusting the thin straps. She twirled around and the gauzy layers of the skirt reminded him of the veils on a belly dancer he had seen once in a San Francisco nightclub. He watched in fascination as she made a final adjustment to her sheer pantyhose, then completed her outfit with high-heeled sandals of the same soft orange color.

"How did you find shoes to match the dress?" he asked.

"That's my secret." She turned to him. "My feet will probably kill me later tonight. Do you know how long it's been since I've been in a pair of heels? It's been boots and tennies for months."

She assisted him with his tie, a pin-striped rust-and-beige pattern. The rust matched his trousers. She complimented him on the jacket. It was a barleycorn weave in beige, a pure virgin wool Harris tweed—imported from Scotland, he assured her, smiling.

"I picked it up in San Francisco on a business trip

one time," he said. "I like to think maybe a relative raised the sheep that donated the wool."

She gave his cream silk shirt a final pat. "You're so conservative, David. Someday I'm going to buy you a Brooks Brothers shirt to complete your wardrobe." She smiled, nodding her approval of his attire.

"I'm that bad, eh?" he chuckled. She began to frown, and he asked, "What's wrong? I thought you approved?"

"You look quite handsome, but you're too thin. I should fatten you up a bit. I'd better have a talk with Julie Russell, and she can tell me how it's done. You're beginning to look like Honest Abe with that beard." She gave his tie clip a final adjustment, then slipped her arms up around his neck. "Ole Abe didn't have green eyes, did he? Remember that tall nurse, Mrs. Mason, at the hospital?" she asked, lightly laughing.

He nodded, and she continued. "Mrs. Mason and Bea Lambert both think you have the sexiest green eyes of any man in the county. She told me so. They're right. You have the sexiest eyes of any man I know, and they're all mine."

His eyes sparkled as he smiled his pleasure, and she pulled his head down.

He inhaled her scent and whispered, "You smell like wild flowers in a mountain meadow in the springtime."

"You're a romantic, aren't you?" she asked.

"Only with you, sweetheart, only with you."

WHEN DAVID AND SAMMY MCCORMACK entered the Bozeman nightclub, they were bombarded with sounds and colors and smells. The food was delicious: steak and lobster, baked potatoes smothered in sour cream and butter, fresh warm miniature loaves of bread. They capped the meal with the most expensive dessert on the menu—flambéed oranges with strawberries.

The floor show received mixed reviews. The singer was superb, with a voice that was throaty, suggestive and brilliant in its range—a performer definitely on the way up. The stand-up comedian was a different story, relying on off-color jokes to keep his audience's attention.

The music began. They listened as the band played disco, rock and country swing music. After a break, the music changed to slower dance numbers, the strobes were replaced with a soft blue revolving sphere, and David reached for Sammy's hand. For the first time since they had met, they danced.

"I'm not a good dancer," she apologized as she stepped on his toes.

"Just out of practice. We should do this more often," he said as he pulled her closer. He was graceful and skilled, and she felt clumsy as she again collided with his feet.

"Relax," he murmured. "You're too tense. This isn't a competition. It's just me dancing with the woman I love." He brushed a kiss against her forehead. The music softened, the lights dimmed, and the mood of the room changed to one of romance. As she began to feel more confident she relaxed into his movements, and they began to move as a team. The band played a long medley of slow romantic numbers, and they continued dancing.

She heard him hum the melody every once in a while.

He lowered his head and whispered, "Your feet, m'lady?"

"I haven't even noticed them. Your foot, m'lord?"

"Fine. I wouldn't admit it hurt, even if it was killing me...which it isn't," he replied, drawing her just a little closer.

The hours flew by as they danced the evening away. She suspected he had overdone the exertion and was relieved to see that he dozed off as they traveled home.

As the miles slipped past, Sammy thought of her children. Her granddaughter was eight months old, and Lawrence and Eve were already expecting another child. Lawrence had called to inform her of the anticipated addition to his growing family and inquired about buying the family home, which they had rented from her when she had returned to Montana with David.

He had made inquiries into home financing, and with his recent promotion at the bank and a substantial salary increase he had qualified, he proudly informed her. He would see that she received a fair profit on the transaction. He had already had a new appraisal done on the house.

"You could probably use the money up there, right?"

The offer was so tempting that she had accepted. Selling her house was Sammy's final break with Phoenix, though she still had family there.

Her son David had been accepted into a graduate program in anthropology at the University of New Mexico in Albuquerque, which placed him closer to his fiancée's family. John was happy and enjoying his naval enlistment. Sammy tried not to think about Sarah, who was still in San Francisco. Apparently D.A. was staying in touch with her daughter.

She sighed. Her family had indeed grown up and ventured down very divergent paths. Reaching across, she patted the hand of the sleeping man beside her. Her own future was now irrevocably entwined with his, and she was happy.

CHAPTER TWENTY-TWO

"LET'S GO FISHING," David said.

"Sounds great. Let's really make a day of it," Sammy suggested. "Do you know where there are any good trout streams?"

"Are you kidding? We have one of the greatest trout streams right here at our back door. The Beaverhead has the reputation of being the best trout river in the entire state."

"Well, excuse me, but I didn't know we had a river at our back door," she chided him.

"Okay, okay, so it's a little to the west. I stand corrected. Actually our Blacktail empties into the Beaverhead just past town. It's better fishing from a float boat, though. Too many willows to snag your line.... Let's make that a later trip. We'll go up the Blacktail. I didn't know you liked to fish."

"I've done my share. When I was a kid, I went catfishing on the canal banks of Phoenix. And Jake, bless his macho soul, taught me the right way to catch trout. I have no gear. Do you have extra?"

"Sure," he said. "D.A. leaves his here. You can use it." He looked at her and nodded. "You know, Sam, I like you. You really have become my friend again. Friends and lovers. It sounds like a song, doesn't it?"

As he searched for the scattered fishing equipment, he said, "Let's leave early in the morning, fish, then take a drive. I need to check out the cabin; you know, the line shack where we...." He stopped and looked at her. "I'm sorry, I didn't think. Will it upset you if we stop there? I need to take a quick inventory of supplies and then stock it for this next winter. Since Paul Russell will be working for us part-time, he may have to use it if he gets caught in a snowstorm. Oh, God, I'm sorry, Sam...I keep saying the wrong things." He stood in dismay, running his fingers through his graying rusty hair. Finally he looked at her and pleaded, "Help me, Sam."

"It's all right, David," she tried to assure him. "If I haven't accepted what happened there by now, then I must really have a.... I haven't thought about that for...." But as her mind returned to the experience of almost a year earlier she felt herself losing control, and the cold fear and pain of the memories shook her. She looked at him, her eyes tear filled, and said softly, "I guess I still have a problem."

Apprehension over the scheduled visit to the cabin cast a pall over the morning of fishing.

"Are you sure you'll be all right?" David asked, as they approached the line shack in the new truck.

"I have to face it sometime. I'll be...okay. Just bear with me, please."

As they stepped from the truck, he handed her a notebook and a felt pen and said, "We won't stay long, Sam. It'll go faster if I call out what we have, and you make the list. Then we'll go back to the house and figure out what we need. I can come back here by myself and bring in the supplies."

He hurried ahead to unlatch the cabin door. His long legs covered the ground quickly, and she had to run to keep up with him.

She felt like a puppy tagging along behind its master as they moved from room to room. He called out the items, and she recorded them in the notebook.

"Damn," he growled when he discovered that weevils had contaminated the flour and cornmeal. "Damn it again," he barked, then laughed. Squirrels had somehow entered the storeroom and made themselves at home by shredding parts of several rolls of toilet paper and using it to make a comfortable nest. "I hate to disturb all their hard work," he said. "However...." He swooped the confetti into a trash bag.

They moved through the living room, checked out the bedroom, then headed for the small bathroom, where he thought they would find some extra cleaning supplies. She was right on his heels as he opened the door.

Suddenly he stopped, threw his arm out to block her way, and commanded, "Don't come in!"

The alarming sound of his voice frightened her, and shoving his arm aside, she forced her way into the small room. There in a pile on the floor were her clothes from the terrifying week. She immediately recognized the beautiful white fleece robe that he had purchased for her. Her gaze fastened on the numerous stains, now brown with age.

"Oh, my God," she exclaimed, dropping the notebook and pen. They clattered and bounced and came to rest near the clothing. She covered her mouth with her hands, trying to suppress the scream she could feel moving up her throat. She fought his hands and stared at the denim skirt she had been wearing when she had fainted. It was the last event she could recall with any clarity. All the horrible memories came tumbling down on her, each inflicting its own sharp wound as it ricocheted through her brain.

"It's really true, isn't it?" she cried, turning to him, tears streaming down her face. "Do you know that sometimes I try to convince myself that it didn't happen at all?"

He took a firm grip on her upper arm and forced her to leave the room, closing the door behind him. He leaned against the wall next to the door and pulled her to him.

She buried her face in his broad chest and sank into the shelter of his arms.

Her body trembled against him, and he held her until the shaking stopped.

She pulled slightly away from him and looked up into his face. "David, do you know what my problem has been? At my age, I didn't want a baby, but at the same time I did want your baby. I couldn't have it both ways, could I?"

"Sammy, I know what you mean. I really do. I didn't want to start a family again, but I wanted to have a child that would be part of you and part of me—proof of our love. Yes, we both wanted the impossible." He continued to hold her, massaging her shoulders gently.

She wept against his shirt, "Oh, David, why? Why couldn't we have found each other sooner...why?"

He had asked himself the same searching question so many times and knew there was no answer.

"Sammy, I think we need to finish the...the death...do what people normally do when someone dies. I think we need to bury the clothes, Sam. End the unpleasantness, bury the hurt. Do you understand what I mean?''

Reluctantly she agreed.

Together they placed the soiled clothing in a trash bag and went out of the cabin to an area behind the old building. David dug a small hole, deep enough to ensure that any coyotes or bears in the area wouldn't attempt digging. The task was completed, and as they stood together looking down at the low mound of fresh damp dirt, Sammy said, "Amen."

They walked away from the cabin, into the forest and soon came to a small glen. David stopped, turned to her, and lifted her chin.

"For the longest time, Sammy, I thought you'd blame me for getting you pregnant, because it was my carelessness in Phoenix and my overzealous desire for you that did it."

"You gave me a precious gift," Sammy replied.

"I thought you blamed me for taking you roughly that afternoon when I got carried away in my lovemaking. . . and hurt you."

"You loved me, that's all, and showed it."

He began to look a little embarrassed. "I thought you'd blame me for getting us marooned in that damn blizzard."

"You saved me!" She took his hand. "You don't have a monopoly on guilt feelings, my darling. I thought you would think me a loose and easy woman that first weekend when I gave in to you so quickly."

"You shared yourself, your emotions, your warmth," he replied.

"I thought my inability to carry your child to term was a sign of my own failure as a woman."

"It was beyond your control, my love."

"I thought you would resent me for being unable to produce another child. I knew how much you'd wanted more children."

"You aren't a prize breeder cow, sweetheart. You're my wife."

"But I'm incomplete...and always will be!" Her blue eyes searched his face for understanding.

David wrapped his arms around her snugly. "Of course, you are," he said softly, "and so am I. Maybe that's what we've been trying to tell each other. I don't think there's any such thing as complete. We'll both keep changing and changing. Part of us never changes because we're born that way, but part of each of us must change in order to survive. Sammy, there's nothing either of us can do about the lost years of our lives. We can only live for the future now. We're both survivors, Sam. I want to survive with you because I love you. Do you understand, my sweet butterfly? Don't ever fly away from me again."

"I won't," she said, as he sealed their convenant with his kiss, warm, strong, yet tender.

EPILOGUE

SAMMY MCCORMACK looked out the window and saw her husband returning to the house, the big bay gelding prancing high through the new-fallen snow, the dogs One and Two bounding at its heels. It would definitely be a white Christmas. Her first. Six inches of snow had fallen during the night.

David had promised her a freshly cut Christmas tree from their own forest and was just returning with it tied securely to the back of the packhorse behind the bay.

She opened the kitchen door to let him in and the stinging cold shocked her senses. The thermometer by the door read one degree. He stomped his boots and shook the powdery snow from the tree's branches while she remained by the door and shivered.

He entered the warm room and kissed her with his icy lips, and she shivered again.

"I must take the horses to the stable," he said. "Damn these glasses. They only bother me when I come in from the cold."

"I think they make you look distinguished," she assured him. The glasses were the only remaining after-effect of the accident.

Dr. Morrison had suggested that he see an ophthalmologist. "It's probably from the concussion. It may clear up in time."

"Are you sure it's not just age?" David had asked with a heavy frown.

The doctor had only smiled.

The glasses were aviator-style and rimless. She smiled as she said, "They make you look like your son. Now, if you'd just get a curly perm...."

He shot her a look of disgust, then smiled. Her cooking had enabled him to regain weight, and he had shaved the beard. He looked like the familiar stranger she had first seen so many months before at the Phoenix airport.

"Want to help me with the horses?" he asked. "Then I'll set up the tree for you."

He buttoned the sheepherder's jacket snugly up to her chin and helped her with the gloves, knit cap and snow boots, then rushed her out the door.

They finished the chores in the stable. She stood aside as he secured the double doors, and suddenly she felt overwhelmed by his presence.

To think that she had actually been reunited with such a dear friend from her childhood, known him again for more than a year and a half and celebrated a wedding anniversary just two months earlier. She'd been blessed with the eternal love of a special man.

He came to her side, but before he could move toward the warm ranch house, she turned to him. "David, sometimes I still wonder, how do you love me so?"

He pulled her to him and lowered his mouth to hers in a searing yet haunting caress. As he reluctantly lifted his head, he spoke to her in the hushed white surroundings of the mountain valley.

"'How do I love thee? Let me count the ways.'" And he began.

About the Author

Until Forever, Sally Garrett's first Superromance, played a very special role in the author's life. At a writers' workshop several years ago Sally was asked to jot down her "blue-sky fantasies"—things she'd like to do if money, time and family responsibilities were removed as restrictions. She listed 1) write a novel 2) move to Montana and 3) remarry. All seemed impossibilities at the time. She did start a novel, though. Like her heroine in *Until Forever*, Sally was born and raised in Phoenix, Arizona, but she has always felt drawn to the Northern Rockies, so she chose a ranch in Montana as the home for her hero. After writing the first draft she decided to make a trip to the mountain state to verify her research. She spent three weeks there, fell in love with the rugged countryside and knew she had to return: "It was almost as though someone was calling me home." On her second trip she met and fell in love with her own real-life "David McCormack." After they married, Sally, like her heroine, moved to Montana, where she is now working on her next novel, a sequel to *Until Forever*.